Roses for a Diva

RICK BLECHTA

DUNDURN
TORONTO

Editor: Jennifer McKnight
Design: Courtney Horner
Printer: Webcom

Library and Archives Canada Cataloguing in Publication

Blechta, Rick, author
         Roses for a diva / Rick Blechta.

Issued in print and electronic formats.
ISBN 978-1-4597-2191-3

         I. Title.

PS8553.L3969R68 2014   C813'.54   C2014-901017-6
                                                                              C2014-901018-4

1   2   3   4   5   18   17   16   15   14

    Canada

We acknowledge the support of the **Canada Council for the Arts** and the **Ontario Arts Council** for our publishing program. We also acknowledge the financial support of the **Government of Canada** through the **Canada Book Fund** and **Livres Canada Books**, and the **Government of Ontario** through the **Ontario Book Publishing Tax Credit** and the **Ontario Media Development Corporation**.

Care has been taken to trace the ownership of copyright material used in this book. The author and the publisher welcome any information enabling them to rectify any references or credits in subsequent editions.

J. Kirk Howard, President

The publisher is not responsible for websites or their content unless they are owned by the publisher.

Printed and bound in Canada.

Cover design by Jesse Hooper.
Cover photo by André Leduc.

VISIT US AT
Dundurn.com
@dundurnpress
Facebook.com/dundurnpress
Pinterest.com/dundurnpress

Dundurn
3 Church Street, Suite 500
Toronto, Ontario, Canada
M5E 1M2

This book is dedicated to
Jackson Reno Blechta
by his very proud grandfather.

You may not be able to read this for a few years,
but it will be waiting for you when you're old enough.

Pursuit

Prelude

I had to admit, Leonardo Tallevi, general manager of the Canadian Opera Company, had the touch when it came to getting the press out in force. Maybe it was the Italian charm (his accent was always thicker at these events), maybe it was the fantastic finger food and open bar, or maybe there actually *was* this kind of interest in today's announcement. Whatever it was, the lobby of the Four Seasons Centre, Toronto's opera house, looked pretty darn full.

I'd never seen Lenny in anything other than a suit, and all of them were gorgeous. I knew nothing of his personal life, and couldn't think of anyone who did, but to those who had contact with him he seemed married to his job. Even the recent profile and interview in *Opera Canada* focused only on his rise from humble beginnings in Italy. The COC had certainly scored a coup when they'd lured him away from La Fenice, Venice's legendary opera house.

He had not disappointed. Tallevi had the golden touch when it came to big opera productions, and the world premiere of the first grand opera by wunderkind composer Andrew McCutcheon was the biggest of the big. Not even completed yet, there was already considerable buzz around the work. It had been rumoured that The Met in New York and La Scala in Milan were very interested. Hometown boy McCutcheon had been successfully wooed by the Tallevi charm. This was the big time in the opera world, and Toronto was making a bold play to enter it.

The head of the COC finally stepped to the podium on a small stage that had been set up at one end of the lobby. Behind him, covered by a curtain, was a large banner headed by the new opera's name. Below it was my current promotional head shot — in which I actually look pretty good. Next to it was a brooding portrait of McCutcheon, who actually was movie-star handsome. As Tallevi held up his hands for silence, cameras flashed and the TV guys rolled tape. Showtime.

"Ladies and gentlemen, and members of the press," (the usual laughter), "thank you all for joining us this afternoon. The COC is extraordinarily pleased to announce that we have been chosen to premiere the first opera written by world-renowned Canadian composer Andrew McCutcheon."

Here the curtain was whisked dramatically upward and I actually heard gasps.

"In two years, our main spring production will be *The Passage of Time*. It is the first world premiere the company has hosted in many years, and certainly our most important. We are honoured Maestro McCutcheon has chosen us to stage his masterwork. He will also be conducting." This was news to me. "In a work where the opera's soprano is so much the centre of the plot, it is only right that Canada's reigning spinto soprano, Marta Hendriks, will be creating this role. I cannot think of anyone better suited to the part."

Eventually, McCutcheon and I were called to the podium where we spoke. I knew the composer wasn't convinced about me being completely right for the part, and I wasn't convinced about having to work closely with him. He was reported to have a volcanic temper to go along with a very high opinion of himself. There was no doubt he was exceptionally talented. I'd really enjoyed his two symphonies, numerous chamber pieces, and song cycles. But grand opera? A lot of great composers had found their Waterloo there.

The opera orchestra had recorded the finished overture, and it was played for the audience. Like all McCutcheon's compositions, it was surprisingly accessible. My husband Tony likened him to the current crop of movie soundtrack composers: well-orchestrated, lots of brass and percussion, and while the harmonies and melodies were definitely cutting-edge, they were melodic in their own way. Everyone in the lobby seemed to be listening very closely.

When it was my turn to speak, I ramped up the charm and told everyone how honoured I was to be cast and how much I was looking forward to actually creating what would most certainly be an iconic role for years to come. That might have been laying it on a bit thick, but McCutcheon had always delivered the goods on his commissions. Imagine a composer of contemporary music who actually had attained rock-star status.

The opening scene was finished, and McCutcheon, being from a wealthy family, had paid to have it recorded. The previous week I'd worked with him on it and found it was not difficult to sing over the instrumentation. Clearly, he was looking for sonority in his scoring, not volume, although with a fourteen-piece brass section he could get that in spades when he required it. I came away deeply impressed with the quality of composition, but ambivalent about the composer. It was hard to tell if he was just extremely awkward socially, or deliberately being offensive when he spoke to me.

The last person to be called to the stage was the production's patron, Peter Grant. Famous for his largesse in the Canadian opera world, his investment firm had been part-sponsors for a few other productions over the years. His late wife, Rosa Latini, generally got one of the soprano roles — not that she didn't deserve them. She had been an excellent singer, but possessed a regrettably small voice. With her dead for several years now, I guessed Peter had felt left out of the game, so he'd agreed to pay the lion's share of the production costs for the new opera — and with all the whizz-bang electronics and multimedia called for, that meant a hefty price tag for the honour.

I liked Peter. Tall, still young-looking at sixty-six, and reputed to be a wickedly good tennis player, he wore wealth and importance easily. A self-made man in the investment industry, he nonetheless fitted in comfortably with the old-money crowd who were well-represented at the gathering.

Earlier, I'd chatted with him briefly.

"Marta! How good to see you, my dear. Lovely as ever."

I leaned forward for a kiss on each cheek, the old smoothy. "Peter, still as handsome as ever."

"I am so pleased you will be in our production. As a matter of fact, I insisted you be considered. Happily, they agreed at once."

"As did I."

"What do you think of the boy wonder? I understand you sang for him last week."

"He's, ah, very interesting. The music is absolutely fascinating."

"So you think we may have a tiger by the tail? I must admit my own tastes run to Verdi and Puccini. When Lenny approached me, I did take a good bit of convincing. That is, until I heard the music. Absolutely stunning. Andy may be the next great opera composer. And we're all in on the ground floor."

"Yes, we are."

"So what do you think of your part?"

"I've only seen a bit of it, but I'm really looking forward to working on it. And I get to sing in English." I leaned forward. "I have never sung in English in my entire professional life."

"Amazing."

A young man was standing behind Peter, who suddenly seemed to remember he was there.

"This is my son, Alan. Alan, this is Marta Hendriks."

"I know, Dad. I've been standing here listening to you talk."

Alan was in his late twenties or early thirties and looked very much like his father. I shook hands, we exchanged a few pleasantries, and he was off, following a waitress carrying a tray of champagne.

Peter watched him go. "He didn't want to come. Since his mother died he hasn't wanted to be around opera very much."

"Understandable. We lost a very fine talent when Rosa passed away. You must miss her greatly."

Peter nodded. "It was a great shock to us all."

It had never made the news, but the scuttlebutt was she committed suicide. Officially it was "died after a brief illness," an oft-used press phrase to cover a multitude of tragedies.

We passed over the awkwardness quickly, chatted about my upcoming season, and soon parted.

Tony sidled up. "What did Grant have to say?"

"Well, dear husband, I think I owe it to him that I'm at this little shindig today. He as much as said he insisted I get the role of Naomi. I was wondering why they didn't get one of the *really* big names to do it. I'm a pretty big fish in our little Canadian pond, but hardly one of the stellar name sopranos. You would have thought they'd go for the brass ring by bringing in a heavy hitter, given McCutcheon's status."

Tony leaned forward and kissed my forehead. "You always underrate yourself, my dear Marta. You're going to be absolutely amazing in this role. And watch, it will be a stepping stone for even bigger and better things."

"I'd hate to be forced to wait nearly two years for bigger and better things."

Chapter One

"It's all rather romantic, Marta." My friend Lainey panted out her words in time with her trotting feet.

"Maybe at first," I answered, equally out of breath.

"I sure would like to have someone sending me roses now and then. That would be absolutely lovely."

Below us at the busy intersection of Wellington and York, Toronto businesspeople hustled themselves through the January cold to yet another day in some hermetically sealed cube farm and a job many of them probably tolerated at best. I was fortunate enough to be doing *exactly* what I wanted: literally singing for my supper. But that lucky life as an operatic soprano came with its own set of obstacles and problems — like the small one I was facing now. Somewhere along the way, I'd picked up a mysterious and rather persistent fan.

I heaved a large sigh, not easy to do when you're running faster than you should on a treadmill. Ah, the wages of sin — and the temptation of Viennese food, especially those pastries. I'd put on four pounds during the six weeks I spent there before travelling to Rome and all those lovely plates of pasta. Visiting the gym was definitely needed.

Then, two days before my flight home for a too-brief five-day break, I'd received an email from my old school chum Elaine Martin, who was head of the performance department at our alma mater, McGill University's Schulich School of Music. She'd landed this plum job because she was dedicated, smart, and most of all, capable. She also had horrible luck with men, but that was another story, and maybe why she thought getting roses under any circumstance was a worthwhile thing.

I'd read her email with slumping shoulders:

> Marta! I'm coming in from Montreal on school business for a few days next week. Tony said you'll be ducking back from Rome about the same time. This is just great! I really hope we can spend some time together. It's been too long and I have lots to tell you!

What I said under my breath after reading that was definitely not ladylike.

Part of me wanted to spend time with my old friend. I still owed her because of something that had happened a few years earlier, but I needed to relax and Tony deserved my undivided attention. We'd had so little time together the past few months.

Tony's grandmother sealed my fate when she'd invited us to dinner on my first evening home, something not to be missed on any account. Nonna Lusardi, besides being an unstoppable force of nature, is also a cook of inspired genius, assuming you enjoy Italian food — and who doesn't? Since I'd been going on and on about her meals to Lainey, it wouldn't have been particularly nice not to invite her along, too.

So I'd struck a deal with myself: spend Monday with Lainey, then focus my attention on Tony before I had to return to Rome on Saturday. Since she was staying at the Royal York, we'd agreed to meet at my nearby gym, then have a bit of lunch, maybe do a little shopping, and a whole lot of gossip before we went up to Little Italy for dinner.

Feet back on solid ground after twenty minutes of treadmill torture, we both spent a moment wiping our sweaty heads with towels.

"Okay now, tell me all," Lainey said. "When did this thing with the roses begin? And how many bouquets have you received? I want to know all about your little mystery."

"It's not that big a deal. Some joker likes to send me anonymous bouquets — very beautiful anonymous bouquets, actually — but he's probably just shy or something and doesn't want to approach me."

"How many other people do you know who have had this happen?"

"Well, none."

"There! That's what makes it mysterious." She threw her towel at me. "Tell Lainey all, dear."

I sighed, sorry I'd brought the whole thing up.

⌒

The first time it happened was eighteen months earlier while I was singing the role of Amelia Grimaldi in a terrific production of *Simon Boccanegra* in Philadelphia. Of course, there are always flowers on opening night, especially if you've had a full-page interview two days before in the *Philadelphia Inquirer*. That had put a bit of extra pressure on me to give a superb performance, but oddly, I'd been able to stay relaxed. My mentor, the late Gerhard Fosch, had constantly pounded it into my hard little skull that relaxation is the essential key to any great performance.

Since it was my first appearance with the company and only the second time I'd sung the role, the artistic director had presented me with a lovely bouquet before I went out for my final curtain call, another one had been sent by my manager in New York, and small bouquets were tossed from the audience, but that was it. Since I'm not the kind of opera fan-favourite who gets showered with flowers, I was quite tickled with what I'd received.

After the long performance, I was ready to get out of my costume, ditch the wig, and go out for a small supper with a few cast members. Imagine my surprise when I found a third large bouquet in my dressing room. On the counter in front of the makeup mirror lay two dozen of the most exquisite, blood red, long-stemmed roses I had ever seen. The air fairly shimmered with their heavenly fragrance, something that's not usual. They were cradled on pink tissue paper and loosely wrapped around them was a wide ribbon of the most delicate ivory lace.

The makeup lights blazed down on this artistic presentation, and I paused in the doorway, breath completely taken away. Never had I received a bouquet like this.

The arrival of my dresser snapped me out of my reverie.

She, too, stopped in the doorway. "Lordy! Would you look at that!"

"Who put this here?"

"No idea. I was in one of the other dressing rooms gossiping. Is there a card?"

I found it underneath. Like everything else, it was exceptional: an expensive envelope enclosing a note card, the words written by a fountain pen in a beautifully fluid hand.

"What does it say?" Suzanne asked, peeking around my shoulder.

I passed the card to her.

"'Roses for a diva'? Who would write something like that and then not sign it?"

"It might be my husband." Taking the note back from Suzanne, I looked at it again, turning it over to see if there was something else. "Though this certainly isn't Tony's handwriting."

Suzanne laughed delightedly. "You've got a secret admirer!"

Lainey had her head tilted to the side when I finished speaking. "How many times has this happened?"

"I don't remember," I lied.

"Really? I sure would."

"You're making too much out of it."

"Maybe, but I love a good mystery, and you have to admit this is mysterious."

I shrugged and changed the subject. "What do you want to do now? Work out on the machines? Visit the sauna? A massage?"

My friend looked around. "This place sure has a ton of machines."

"That's why Tony likes it. Being a gadget freak extends to his physical activity. Me? I think I preferred my old club."

"Why didn't you stay on there?"

I shrugged. "My old one was women only. I get to see Tony little enough. We might as well exercise together."

Lainey's eyes took in the weight training room and the mostly shirtless young men trying to outdo each other physically, while appearing uninterested in what the guy at the next machine was doing.

"Lots of eye candy here," she grinned.

I shrugged again. "I've got what I want — at home."

"Well, I don't. Why don't we use a few of the machines now that we're thoroughly warmed up?"

Clad in spandex, it was crystal clear to all that she still had an amazing figure. I hated her, but the guys present obviously didn't.

I'm seldom the most beautiful woman in the room. In profiles done over the years, the most common description of me referred to my "strong features." At least I'm tall and I have nice skin and thick brown hair, which I unfortunately have to keep short for performing.

So as I watched from the sidelines, Lainey was never without at least one stud muffin helping her understand how to use a machine that I was certain she knew better than they did.

"Do you need somebody to spot for you?" a male voice asked from behind me.

I was sitting in the decidedly low-tech area on one of those benches for doing presses, thinking mostly about whether I should continue or treat myself to a massage.

"I'm not sure what I want to do."

"You might as well do something while you wait for your friend."

Deciding to be virtuous, I laid back. "Well, okay, if it's not too much trouble."

The weights on the bar over my head looked about right, so I stuck my arms ups and got a firm grip on the bar. It was obvious at once that the weight might be a bit too much, but my stubbornness rose up.

I began lifting and dropping the bar slowly and smoothly. Normally I do ten reps, followed after a short rest by twenty, and then another ten.

At ten, I placed the bar back on its hooks and lay there for a minute or two, sweating as I watched Lainey teasing the boys on the other side of the room. The first club I joined was coed and that quickly drove me to a females-only club. It's no fun getting hit on every time you showed your face in the door. Being less lithe, I'd never attracted the crowd Lainey could, but it seemed as if every visit one male or another would latch on to me, hoping to get lucky.

Taking the bar down, I began the next set. I knew I was in trouble around number twelve, but stupidly I kept on. At fifteen, I began wobbling a bit.

It happened at eighteen. I managed to get my arms extended, but unevenly, and then my left started to give out. From where it was, the bar would have crashed down right across my neck or face, neither a very good option. At the last second, the man I hadn't really bothered to look at reached down and plucked the bar out of my hands.

"Thanks," I gasped, sitting up. "I can't believe how fast that happened."

"That's why there's a rule about always having a spotter. I've heard of people doing bench presses having some spectacular accidents." He smiled. "One should always be aware of the dangers that surround us. Things can bite back."

"That's a pretty grim outlook on life."

He shrugged. "It pays off in the long run."

Getting to my feet, I said thanks again.

My saviour was in his late thirties and relatively handsome, with a fit body and large mustache that was beginning to go grey. Looking at him reminded me that we were probably close in age. Colouring was now a permanent part of getting my hair done.

"You seem tired," he said, stating the obvious.

"Residual jet lag."

"Where were you?"

"Rome."

Lainey was finally crossing the room.

"Looks as if you had a bit of trouble over here," she observed wryly.

"Nothing we couldn't handle," the man answered for me.

She looked at me curiously. "Ready to hit the showers and get something to eat? I'm starving."

"We're going to leave now," I said unnecessarily to the man. "Thanks again for your help."

He laughed. "You've said that three times now. It was nothing."

Towels around our necks, Lainey and I headed for the women's change room.

"You know that guy?" she asked.

"Never seen him before in my life."

"Lucky for you he was around."

⌒

Lainey and I wound up indulging in massages, my treat. By the time we walked out of the building straight into a frigid wind whistling down the canyon of buildings along Wellington, it was closer to lunch than breakfast, so I was correspondingly more hungry than usual. That's precisely the situation in which I'll overeat.

I needed someone around to poke me in the ribs if I yielded to temptation, not to mention that control would go right out the window that evening at Nonna Lusardi's. *Nobody* can resist her cooking.

"We're not that far from the Eaton Centre," I said as we walked east. "Why don't I call Tony and see if he can grab an early lunch with us?"

Even though he'd gotten considerably more serious about singing since our marriage, my husband still worked nearly full time at a computer store in Toronto's big downtown mall. I would have been constantly exhausted keeping up a schedule like his, but Tony thrived on it. The big problem to my mind was that he could seldom come on the road with me. Other than the occasional luxury of a long weekend run out to wherever I might be, we were often separated for weeks. Neither of us liked the situation, but there you are. Sometimes it felt like such a struggle to make it all work.

There's a restaurant Tony and I frequent just inside the doors of the Eaton Centre near Trinity Church. It was the first place we ever had a quiet talk together, so it was special to us, and more often than not when we met for an impromptu lunch or after-work drink, we gravitated to it.

Since Lainey and I gawked at more than a few shop windows along the way, Tony was waiting by the time we got to our usual booth. As always, he was banging out text messages on what I called his "superphone." I had one, as well, but I could barely make heads or tails of it past a few basic functions. I needed a twelve-year-old to show me the fancy stuff. Tony lacked the necessary patience with his Luddite wife.

"Hi there, lover boy." I pecked him on the forehead before sliding in next to him.

As Lainey sat down across from us, he looked up and smiled, sliding his beloved gadget into the inner pocket of his sport jacket.

"Glad to see you're willing to give us your full attention," I remarked.

"Marta, don't start with that again. You made your point perfectly clear last time."

I put my hand on his, sorry I'd given him that unnecessary dig, especially in front of someone else. I hate it when I'm talking to someone on the phone and I can hear them tapping away on their computer in the background, their attention divided. It makes me feel like a second-class citizen. It's even worse when they do it right in front of you, as Tony had on numerous occasions before I finally said something.

As we looked over our menus, he asked, "So did you do anything besides the gym this morning?"

"With all Lainey's flirting, it's lucky we even got out of there," I responded, giving my friend a playful dig.

"There happened to be a lot of good-looking 'talent' there. I was just behaving like any other red-blooded girl. Besides, you're a fine one to talk."

"About what?"

"I'm not the one with a secret admirer."

Now it was Tony's turn. "What's she talking about?

"You know, those roses that keep showing up."

He nodded. "Ah, right. It's the talk of every backstage on the continent."

If there's one thing about Tony, he can give as good as he gets. *Return point scored*, I thought sourly.

Lainey said, "He's exaggerating, of course, isn't he?"

"No, I'm not. Old big mouth here," Tony answered, nodding at me, "made the mistake of telling Natalia Petrov. She's the biggest gossip in opera."

I shook my head. "I'm sure no one cares."

"Somebody asked me about it at a rehearsal last week," Tony answered.

Our server came by and took our orders.

As soon as she was out of earshot, Lainey leaned forward. "Tell me everything, you two. I'm sure I didn't get the whole story from Marta this morning."

"Did she tell you how many she's gotten?" Tony asked.

Lainey shook her head. "She said she didn't remember."

Tony raised his eyebrows.

I answered, "All right. One for every role I've taken on since that first bouquet in Philly."

"You mean all over the world?"

"I got the most recent one in Rome last Saturday night."

"Same kind of roses and message?"

I nodded. "This guy must buy his gifts in bulk."

"So you're sure they're from a male?"

"The handwriting certainly *seems* to be male."

"I'm sure it's male," Tony added.

Lainey frowned. "Why?"

He flashed the smile that melts my heart every single time. "Marta's a beautiful woman. How could he not take a fancy to her?"

She picked up her fork, pointing it at him in mock menace. "You have something to do with this, don't you? Come on! Confess."

I pulled her fork down. "He's sworn up and down he knows nothing about it — and I believe him. To be honest, though, the whole thing is getting a bit creepy."

"How so?" Lainey asked.

"Nobody ever sees the bouquets delivered."

"Really?"

"After getting the fourth one, I asked someone backstage to keep an eye on my dressing room door. Unfortunately, it seems my secret admirer somehow knew that, and the bouquet was left in the tenor's dressing room. With my name on the envelope this time, he just assumed it had been left in the wrong dressing room and delivered it to me himself."

"Big blowhard tried to make out like it was his gift for Marta," Tony added. "Damn tenors."

We all laughed heartily. My husband is one of that breed himself.

"I've sort of had enough of it," I admitted.

Lainey shook her head. "Why? You're getting these lovely bouquets from someone who obviously travels a lot and loves opera. He's got money and he's a big fan. What's wrong with that?"

"Why doesn't he step forward, then? It's like he's toying with me."

"You're saying you think the guy is obsessed with you?"

"Yeah. Sort of, I guess. And that last bouquet, the one I got in Rome …"

Tony shifted in his seat. "Marta, it's nothing."

"Tony thinks I'm being silly."

"About what?" Lainey asked.

"The blossom on one of the roses was nearly torn off."

"An accident when it was being delivered?"

Tony nodded. "That's what I told her."

"You didn't see it. It looked to me as if it was done on purpose, like someone pushed with their thumb and nearly snapped the blossom off the stem."

"Marta's attaching too much significance to it," Tony said, leaning across the table and speaking in a low voice, "because she feels she didn't sing very well that night."

"I was tired. I'd been away from home for nearly three months."

"And you were out late the night before at a party," he teased, "and not accompanied by your husband, I might add."

We all laughed again like a bunch of fools and my unease scattered like the cast after the final curtain of a production.

Our food was delivered at that point, and the chatter around the table segued naturally into what was happening back in Montreal, at McGill, and in Lainey's life — her love life, as it turned out. I should have guessed that's why she was so hot to come for a visit. She finally had a new guy.

For January in Toronto, there wasn't all that much snow. If I hadn't been feeling so rundown, I would have gone along with Lainey's suggestion that we walk back to my condo, which is across from St. Lawrence Market on Front Street. After the lunch we'd had, a brisk twenty-minute walk would have burned off some of the calories, a real consideration since we would be dining with Nonna Lusardi in a few hours.

Lainey possesses a cab whistle to die for. I swear I've seen her nail a cab in under a minute in the pouring rain on a Montreal street, in the middle of rush hour, *on a Friday.* Mere mortals couldn't have stopped one of those cabs — even by throwing themselves in front of it.

Needless to say, that early afternoon she had two cabs hovering within ten seconds of putting her fingers up to her lips. We piled into the back seat of one in great spirits.

"I'm thinking I might lie down for an hour before Tony gets home from work," I told her. "I'm still a bit whacked from the past several weeks, and the delay on my flight home didn't help."

Lainey patted my hand. "You've always got a good book or two sitting around. Or I could watch TV. Just make sure you don't sleep all afternoon. We've hardly begun to catch up."

"Yes, and we should do it when Tony isn't around. Did you notice his eyes rolling up in his head when we were talking about all those McGill people he's never met?"

"He was a real trooper," she said with a laugh.

We were still giggling like schoolgirls when the cab decanted us in front of my building. Sam, the building's doorman, rushed out from behind his desk to open the door. He always does that no matter how many times I've ask him not to. It can get pretty awkward since not every tenant in the building receives that treatment.

"And how are you today, Madame Hendriks?" he asked. "You must have gone out before I came on duty this morning."

"I was out the door well before nine. Were any packages delivered for me? I'm expecting some music."

"Not a sign of anything for you. If it arrives, do you wish me to bring it up, lickety-split?"

I sighed. Samatar really was incorrigible. A refugee from Somalia, he'd spent the last eight years learning English and moving from one crummy job to another until he landed on our doorstep. He's a wiry little guy who takes his job *very* seriously, ministering to all the tenants as if we are family. Because he considers me a "celebrity," I get the star treatment.

"If it arrives, just make sure my husband gets it when he comes home from work. That would be really helpful."

"That is all right then. Mr. Tony will be getting the package if it is delivered. You can be sure of that!"

"I know, Sam. Thank you so much as always," I said over my shoulder as the elevator arrived down at the lobby.

Waiting for a workman to get off, I watched Sam return to his seat behind the large wooden unit to the right of the front door. When no one was in the lobby and nothing required his attention, he always sat, back straight, eyes forward, hands folded in front of him. There was monitoring of the many security cameras to do, but he never seemed to be paying any attention to the screens. I often wondered what was going on in his mind as he sat there so patiently.

Walking down the hallway to my door four floors up, Lainey was chattering away about how much she was looking forward to dinner.

"Everything will be homemade," I told her as I unlocked the door. "Tony asked his nonna to make her incredible rabbit and wild mushroom ravioli for the pasta course, and wait until you taste —"

Lainey was paying no attention and crashed into my back as I stopped short, my hand still gripping the door handle.

My condo's front door opens into the dining area. Beyond that is part of the L-shaped living room. On the right-hand wall that separates the dining room from the rest of the living room I have a long walnut buffet for dishes and such. Above it, running the full length, I'd had a series of short glass shelves installed on the wall to display some very special gifts I've received over the years, most of them fragile and very dear to me. When the lights above the shelves are on, it makes quite a spectacular backdrop to a meal, if I do say so myself.

In pride of place on one of the middle shelves had stood my most amazing piece, a large Murano glass vase of blues and greens with threads of gold: delicate, ornate, and utterly breathtaking. I'd always been too frightened to use it for flowers and held my breath every time somebody picked it up for a closer look.

At that moment it lay on top of the buffet and all over the floor, shattered into hundreds of glittering chunks, completely and forever destroyed.

Chapter Two

Tony's voice drifted around the corner from the dining room. "It looks as if the shelf above your vase just gave way. I always said that damned soapstone bear was too heavy to put on a glass shelf, no matter how thick."

I had a blazing headache. Both Lainey and my husband were trying their best to cheer me up (other than that last rather unhelpful comment), but I just couldn't snap out of it. They didn't know what that glass vase meant to me.

Lainey came into the living room with yet another cup of tea, setting it down on the table by my elbow.

I smiled despite the ache in my head and my heart. Anytime anything is wrong, Lainey whips out tea, convinced it's the only panacea for making everything better.

It wouldn't work this time, and with Tony now home, I didn't want to talk about why I was so upset over some broken glass, no matter how beautiful and brightly coloured.

⌒

It had been nearly fourteen years earlier that I was lounging comfortably on a balcony overlooking one of Rome's busier streets.

"Marta? Marta! Where are you?" Gerhard bellowed from the doorway of our rented flat.

"Out here," I answered, putting down my book with a sigh. "It's the first nice day in so long. I just wanted to enjoy the breeze and warm sunshine."

We'd been in Rome for nearly two months as my mentor prepared a new production of Rossini's *Semiramide* for the Rome Opera. Taking on too much as always, he had designed the sets — and practically built them himself if one took his complaining seriously — *and* had a big hand in the costume design, as well as, of course, the stage direction. Now he was in the middle of rehearsals and generally came home in a foul mood.

"Come in here please. I want to show you something."

"Can't it wait? I'm so comfortable."

Irritation was clear in his answer. "Marta, please come in here now."

It sounded as if his meeting that morning with the opera's management had not gone well. Construction of the sets and costumes was over-budget and still not complete, and with the premiere barely two weeks away, the pressure was on everyone, but mostly on Gerhard. Once, in a moment of anger, when I'd called him an overbearing control freak, he'd looked at me blankly, as if asking, "Who? Me?" It was one of the frustrating anomalies about him, but there was no denying he was a genius at anything to do with opera or singing. I was learning so much from him that putting up with his foibles seemed a small price to pay.

I got off the chaise with one last sigh and walked into the rather dark living room. Gerhard was at the far end, arms behind him, beaming with the guileless expression of a child. He was up to something.

"What?" I asked, coming to a halt.

With a tilt of his head, he indicated I should look down at the marble-topped coffee table to my right just as he flicked on the overhead light via a wall switch behind his back.

The day before he'd had a workman in to change the fixture for something more modern and far brighter than I would have chosen. I'd been told at the time that it was because the room seemed dingy in the evening — even though we were seldom in it after dark.

The subterfuge was laid bare as I followed Gerhard's eyes down to the surface of the table.

Under the hard light of the halogen bulbs stood a glass vase of such exquisite delicacy and beauty that it really did take my breath away.

The vase looked as if by some miracle the deep blues and greens of the Mediterranean had been magically transformed into glass, still kissed by the gold of sparkling sunshine. If a fish had suddenly leapt out of it, I wouldn't have been in the least surprised.

I tore my eyes away from this wonder and looked across the room at Gerhard. Finding my voice, I said, "That is the most gorgeous thing I have ever seen."

"Then it pleases you, *ja?*"

I'm sure my face screwed up in puzzlement, something he never liked, but this time his expression registered satisfaction.

"What do you mean 'it pleases me'? Surely you can't be suggesting —"

"*Ja, ja,* it is for you. I bought it for you."

Still puzzled by his extreme largesse, I asked, "But why?"

"Surely I do not need a reason to buy you something beautiful, my dear."

"But this … It must have cost a fortune."

His face darkened. "Why cannot you just accept my gift without asking these questions? You do not like it?"

I walked across the room with all the dignity of movement that Gerhard had pounded into me, took his face in my hands, and gently kissed each cheek, punctuating each with a whispered, "Then thank you … *thank you* … *and* thank you!" The final kiss was on his mouth — and it was definitely *con brio*.

Lately Gerhard had become rather distant and cold, and I knew from past mistresses — from whom he never seemed to become completely estranged — that placing distance between himself and his current lover was always the precursor to severing relations. That had been very worrying — I felt I still had so much I could learn from him.

Did I ever love Gerhard enough to want to stay with him always? I still cannot say, even so many years later. When he had chosen me — and an unlikely choice everyone had thought it was, too — then whisked me off to places I'd always dreamed of visiting, it was like finishing school and graduate school rolled into one. He'd taken an unsophisticated Ottawa percussionist with a nice voice and turned her into a (semi) polished opera singer. Of course, we'd become lovers and he'd taught me much there, as well: how to give pleasure and how to take it in equal measure.

There was no denying the man could be infuriating. He might berate you in the harshest terms and five minutes later claim to have done no such thing. At first I thought it was artifice or embarrassment, but I came to realize that Gerhard lived completely in the moment, much like a child. Infuriating, but brilliant, and I wanted to learn all I could from him. In those days, I was on this roller coaster ride and I wanted to just keep going round and round, gaining huge amounts of knowledge. Deep down, I knew I'd be flung off at some point, but I was determined to hang on as long as I could.

We sat on the sofa to observe Gerhard's lavish present more closely and I snuggled against him. If this was to be a parting gift, it was one to be cherished for a lifetime.

As we watched, Gerhard began undoing the knot holding my robe together. I turned my head so he could kiss me.

We made passionate love right there. Surprisingly, considering his recent horrible moods, Gerhard was very gentle and took his time. I don't think it had ever been better for me.

Afterwards, laying in each other's arms, we continued staring at my present.

"It is, without a doubt, the most beautiful thing I have ever seen," I sighed. "What made you buy it?"

"You."

"I should have stated that a bit better. I meant, why did you buy it for me now?"

He was silent for awhile and I scarcely dared to breathe, figuring I knew what was most likely coming.

"You," he repeated.

⌒

Tony knelt on the floor next to me and smoothed my hair back. "Feeling any better, love?"

I nodded my head carefully. "A bit."

"Perhaps we can find out who made the vase and they could do up another one for you."

How do you tell your husband that your most precious possession was the gift of a previous lover, as well your fondest remembrance of him? Even if Tony came up with an exact duplicate of my shattered vase, it could never be the same.

I decided that lying around was not accomplishing anything and that I'd just wasted a good part of the afternoon mooning around over something that couldn't be made better. Even though Lainey didn't even hint in that direction, I could tell she was disappointed we hadn't caught up on our lives since we'd last been together.

"I'm going to take a shower and get dressed. We'll have to be on our way before too long."

Lainey and Tony simultaneously said, "And your headache?"

"Still there," I said over my shoulder. "I'll take a couple more aspirin. Could someone have a glass of wine ready for me?"

Tony left for the kitchen. "I'll bring it in to you."

⌣⌐

By the time we got to Tony's nonna's house near St. Clair and Dufferin, I was feeling more myself. I wanted this to be a wonderful evening for Lainey, so I pushed my blues into the background and gave Nonna Lusardi my biggest hug as we entered her simple house.

As usual, opera was on her stereo, a recording of *Francesca da Rimini*, a very un-Italian-sounding work because of its almost Wagnerian orchestration. Tony's grandmother's tastes were wide-ranging.

Conversation around the table that evening was confined to English for Lainey's sake. The only Italian she was familiar with was musical terms and food names.

And what food it was.

I had long been convinced there wasn't a better Italian chef this side of the Atlantic, and that evening brought no change to my assessment. Every mouthful was a revelation. It was comical to see Lainey's eyes roll up nearly every time she took a bite. After a sampling of homemade antipasto and salumi while we all got acquainted in the living room, there were bowls of wild mushroom consommé, followed by my favourite ravioli with rabbit, more mushrooms, and herbs. Then came *vitello al limone*, with a ragout of fall vegetables, and her feathery-light gnocchi. Dessert was simple: cheese and fruit, but the cheeses were lovely and the fruit at perfect ripeness, definitely bought *per oggi*.

The shock of the afternoon's disaster at the condo had drifted to the horizon when Tony brought it crashing back by telling Nonna Lusardi what had happened.

Once more in the living room — all the plastic covers removed for honoured guests — I was seated in a chair next to her. Taking my hands, she said in Italian, "You poor dear! I have marvelled at that vase every time I've seen it. Such a tragedy for you, such a tragedy."

Having once told her the vase's provenance, and by the way she looked at me, I wondered how much of the "back-story" she'd guessed. I blushed and quickly turned away. I don't think Tony noticed because of his side conversation with Lainey.

"Where do you perform next?" Nonna Lusardi asked.

"I have to be back in Rome on Monday. We're in the middle of a run of *Tosca*, but there was that gala broadcast of *Il Trovatore*. It's part of a series of Verdi operas being performed in the opera houses where each was premiered. It's an interesting idea. I'm doing *La Traviata* in Venice later this month as the wrap-up to the series. It's being broadcast throughout Europe."

"So many *Traviatas* for you!"

I shrugged. "It seems to have become my party piece, hasn't it? I'm excited they chose me for the role, considering all the outstanding Violettas running around these days."

"Who is to be your Alfredo?"

"Ettore Lagorio."

Nonna's expression was carefully unreadable, but I knew what she was thinking. With the whole Lusardi family opera mad and with many singers among their number, she was well-connected to all the current backstage gossip.

Lagorio was a talent of the first water, and at thirty-two, just coming into his vocal prime. Problem was, he supposedly knew it, and correspondingly threw his weight around.

"Our conductor is a tough old German bastard. Ebler won't let him get away with anything."

"The butting of heads is never a good thing in a production," was Nonna's answer.

"One works with the hand one is dealt. There are a lot of tenors with Lagorio's attitude."

"Don't think I didn't hear that," Tony said, also in Italian. "Sopranos can be just as difficult and they always seem to get their way, too."

Lainey looked puzzled, so I translated for her, but into French which Tony didn't understand.

She threw up her hands, saying, "Singers! You are *all* a pain in the neck."

To keep the conversation from getting any more fractured, we all switched back to English and discussed innocuous topics like the latest political crisis in Ottawa, world debt, and global warming. Easy stuff.

As we took our leave a short time later, I bent down to hug Nonna and she whispered in my ear, "I am so sorry about your precious vase."

I kissed her cheek, but couldn't say a word.

⌒

The next morning, Tony had already left for work when I levered myself out of bed. During the night I'd had a very vivid dream about Gerhard, and while I couldn't remember much of it, the emotional wash left behind was positive. I took it as meaning that I shouldn't mourn over something so fleeting as a glass vase.

With a mug of coffee in my hand, I stood looking south out of the living room window at a tiny sliver of Lake Ontario still visible between the St. Lawrence Market and the new condo tower behind it.

I couldn't decide what to do with my day off. They came so few and far between, it seemed stupid to waste even a moment. To keep my voice fresh and supple, I'd need to do at least some vocalizing a few times this week, but I was determined to do no more than necessary, even though I had the premiere of *The Passage of Time* staring me in the face not much more than a month off. My brain and body told me a bit of distance from singing would be a good thing at the moment. I'd been going full-tilt since the previous fall.

On my way to the kitchen for more coffee and maybe a slice or two of toast, I stopped in the dining room to look at the cleaned up disaster from the day before. Three of the shelves were gone, there was a huge dent on the top of the buffet where the soapstone bear had bounced off. I'd also lost a number of small knick-knacks, all very nice to be sure, but none nearly as precious to me as the vase. Tony and Lainey wanted me to file an insurance claim, but I didn't see the point. Money was not the point. I wanted my vase.

I went over to examine the shelves. The original installation had been a pro job and the guy who'd custom made the series of short shelves had sworn up and down that the thick tempered glass and supports would hold weight up to one hundred pounds each. I picked up the dancing bear. He seemed to be around twenty pounds. Why the heck had the shelf underneath him given way after all this time?

In the far corner of the room was a box holding the wreckage of the accident. I found a dark tablecloth and spread it over the dining room table to protect the surface, then began removing chunks of the shelves out of the box.

Fifteen minutes later, the table was half-covered with litter. I couldn't bear to have the dining room lights on because the brightest one showed the spot where Gerhard's vase had stood, so I'd brought a floor lamp in from the living room. Its glare made the glass look stark and the edges dangerously sharp.

Most of the chunks were fairly large and it wasn't difficult to begin fitting them together. By the end of a second cup of coffee, I had the remains of the shelves pretty well laid out.

One of the smaller pieces had something strange about it. A circular chunk of glass about the size of a quarter was missing from it. I hadn't been able to find the piece that would have fit into it. It must have shattered.

To me it looked as if the glass had been struck with something hard, maybe a hammer. I got up and walked over to my bear — now missing a leg — and picked him up. Strange as it sounded, had somebody slammed one corner into the shelf to break it? If only he could tell me.

When I'd seen the wreckage, the very first thing that flashed through my mind had been the torn blossom on the most recent bouquet of roses I'd received. I knew it was silly, but somehow I'd gotten the feeling the two things were connected.

I shivered as if someone had just run an ice cube up the middle of my back.

⁓

Since Tony had planned his work week so we could get the maximum time together, he was home shortly after noon. Our plan was to drive out to the country, enjoy a nice lunch somewhere, maybe walk a bit. We'd both been looking forward to it.

He found me at the table still puzzling over the chunks of the broken shelves.

Picking up one of the larger sections, he said, "Glass is funny stuff. It can look perfectly normal but have a fatal flaw."

I held up the suspect piece, the one with part of a round chunk missing. "What do you think of this?"

Tony examined it closely. "Looks as if it hit something on the way down."

"I think it looks as if it was deliberately struck by something."

"What are you talking about? Who would hit it? I didn't. You didn't. Then who?"

Taking a deep breath, I told Tony what I'd been thinking. When I finished, he shook his head.

"Marta, dearest, that's just crazy. Some guy sends you bouquets and now he's breaking into our condo and smashing things? That's a huge leap to make. What do you base it on?"

"A feeling. Just a feeling."

"Because one of the roses was damaged in the most recent bouquet?"

"Well … yes."

Tony came behind me and put his arms on my shoulders. "Marta, you've had a tough few months. You're overreacting. The shelf just gave way. That's the start and finish of it."

"No, Tony. I want to know for sure why the accident happened."

"For the insurance?"

"No. For my peace of mind. If someone actually got into our apartment yesterday, wouldn't you want to know?"

"Of course. But no one did."

I got up from the table and faced him. "Well, *I'm* not sure!"

"Oh, so you *want* to be freaked out. Is that it?"

"What are you talking about?"

"Marta, the shelf gave way. Drop it. The road you're headed down leads right to paranoia."

"Now you think I'm just being paranoid?"

Tony took a deep breath, but didn't speak.

"Well, dear husband," I said furiously, "you can just damn well go to hell!"

With that, I turned on my heel, went into our bedroom, and slammed the door, locking it for good measure. Maybe Tony was right, but I certainly wasn't going to admit it.

Even so, there was a frisson of certainty every time I thought about that last bouquet.

Chapter Three

After twice trying to get me to unlock the door, Tony said one or two more unfortunate things before stomping out of the apartment. It wasn't as if we'd never had a fight before. Fact was, Tony and I were both hotheads. But we also did really love each other. Sooner rather than later, one of us would hold out the olive branch and all would be forgiven.

He'd probably been right giving me the gears. My hardheadedness has got me into trouble, once to the point of nearly ending my life — Tony's too.

What I needed was another perspective.

So I called up Lili Doubek, good friend, vocal coach, and therapist, all rolled into one imposing person —

despite her short stature. I'd promised to get in touch as soon as I'd arrived back and here it was already Wednesday. When I got her on the phone, her voice sounded a tad frosty.

"And you are all right, Marta?"

"It took me over twenty-four hours to begin feeling like myself again, but other than that, yeah, I'm well. And you?"

"Too many vocal coachings. At my age, I begin to tire."

Lili was barely sixty-four and normally fit as an ox, so I was immediately concerned.

"You sound as if you have a cold."

"Sniffles only. Maybe some time off is what I need."

"Would you head over to Czecho?"

"My sister is wanting me to visit. 'We are not getting any younger, you know, Lili,' she says to me. Perhaps she is right."

"Would you like some company today? How's your schedule?"

"For a coaching or just a visit?" she asked, not sounding enthusiastic.

"No coaching. I just want to spend some time with my friend."

"I showed my last singer to the door five minutes ago. The other two have cancelled."

"I can grab a cab and be there in half an hour. Would that be okay?"

Lili's house was north and east of our condo in the heart of Cabbagetown, a neighbourhood known for its poor Irish immigrants (hence the cabbages) in the late 1800s. Beginning in the late seventies, it had been "discovered" and was now Yuppie Central, as they'd come in renovating everything in sight. Still, it's a charming part of the city and feels like a real neighbourhood because they haven't torn down the old Victorian houses, as so often happens.

Reflecting the woman herself, Lili's house was different from those surrounding it. Up and down the street, the houses had been sand-blasted to the original orangey-red brick. Lili had hers painted a light bluish-grey. The windows were left in their original single-pane glass, no skylights, no mod cons for her. The place was right out of *Better Homes and Gardens* — a 1950s issue.

Inside it was very old country, in this case Czech, a place she'd physically left behind quite easily, but one that had never relinquished its grip on her heart. Every room was filled with Czech memorabilia and knick-knacks. I once made a little play on words about her penchant for "Czech tchotchkes." Lili's tart response led me to never make light of her foible again. In every other facet of her life, my friend was thoroughly up-to-date. She owned the latest electronic gadgets, and unlike me, could use them with aplomb. I'd never pointed it out to Tony but her nimble thumbs could punch out text messages far faster than his.

It took her longer than usual to answer the door and I soon found out why. Being on crutches tends to slow one down.

"What on earth happened?" I asked, as the opening door revealed the cast on her left leg.

"I had a bit of a fall."

"More than a bit, I'd say. Why didn't you tell me?"

Lili shrugged. "I don't like people to fuss over me."

"But it's okay for you to fuss over others? Lili you take the cake."

She moved back a bit unsteadily as I headed to the coat tree in the corner of her small foyer. She did allow me to help her into the living room.

Lili is a coffee-holic, so I brewed a carafe. Having ducked across to the St. Lawrence Market before hailing a cab, I also loaded a small plate with cookies and brought everything to the living room.

"You always make coffee too strong," she said after a delicate sip.

"Nonsense. The last time you told me that, I watched you make it. This is exactly the same. Why are you being so contrary?"

"Because I don't enjoy being incapacitated." I held the plate of cookies for her, and she smiled for the first time. "Thank you for bringing my favourites."

"Would you like the hassock for your leg?"

"That would be nice."

Once I was again seated in the opposite chair, I asked, "So what happened?"

"I was waiting for a streetcar on Gerrard Street. It felt like someone pushed me. I'm lucky I didn't go under it. Trying to keep my balance, I spun and my ankle collapsed under me. The pain was terrible."

"Did you see who did it?"

"No. There were about a dozen of us waiting and it wouldn't have been that noticeable. Whoever it was pushed me hard behind my knees and I tumbled over. People did stop to help, of course, but I was in so much pain, I didn't think about it until later at the hospital."

"That really sucks."

Lili took another bite of her cookie. "I suppose it was someone trying to push their way to the front and not paying attention."

"Could it have been deliberate?"

Lili looked at me sharply. "What makes you say that?"

"I … ah … really don't know. Just the mood I'm in, I guess."

Lili nodded and I could almost see the wheels beginning to spin in her head.

We silently ate a few cookies. The last thing I wanted was my friend to think I had a selfish motive for visiting.

We talked about my time in Vienna, a city with which she was very familiar. I told her all the backstage gossip. She asked where I was off to next (which she well knew). It was obvious we were both talking around the elephant in the room, the elephant of my own stupid making.

Finally, taking the last sip from her second cup, she put it down, folded her hands in her lap, and stared at me. Lili possesses a very piercing gaze. Coupled with her rather prominent nose, it always makes me feel like she's a hawk staring at a particularly appealing mouse dinner.

"Why don't you just tell me about it, my dear?"

"Tell you what?"

"Whatever it is that is bothering you. I know you too well, Marta, too well."

I knew better than to prevaricate. Lili wouldn't back off until she'd weaseled it out of me. I respected her skills as a therapist too much to lie. An amazing vocal coach she was, but though she would have disagreed violently, she was an even better psychologist. We singers gained what the mental health profession had lost when she packed in her practice and immigrated to Canada to follow her musical dream.

When my life imploded after the death of my first husband, Lili had stepped away from the piano to use her other skills and help me pick up the shattered pieces of my psyche. Barging right into my condo, she'd told me sternly I was a mess and she was prepared to help. The fact that I was now enjoying an even more successful career was completely due to her skill in gluing my life back together. I owed her a lot — and here I was asking for more.

"It's about those mysterious bouquets."

"Did you receive another?"

"One in Vienna, and one in Rome after the performance on Saturday evening." I stopped for a deep breath. "But that one was different."

"In what way?"

So I told her about the damage to one rose. Actually, I told her all about how I'd been trying to catch the person who was leaving these presents — and how spectacularly unsuccessful I'd been.

I finished my story with a question. "Do you think the broken blossom means something? Is this person trying to communicate with me?"

The hawk stare continued. "Why do you think that?"

"Tony thinks I'm imagining things."

"That does not answer my question."

I'd started this but wasn't sure if I wanted to continue.

"My vase, the Murano glass one, I came home yesterday to find it shattered. One of the glass shelves had given way."

"That is such a shame! I have always admired it greatly." Lili wagged her finger at me. "But what else are you not saying?"

"I ... well ... I think it was broken deliberately, that someone had been in our apartment."

Silence for several seconds as Lili digested my statement. She moved to take the last cookie, but then stopped and sat back.

"Why do you think this?"

I got to my feet and looked out her front window, watching scattered flakes of snow skittering down the street in the wind. The cold radiating through the glass made me shiver.

Without turning around I told her, "Just a feeling."

"You have no proof that this is so? 'Just a feeling?'"

"A piece of the broken shelf has an odd marking, as if it was hit by something."

"Have you shown this to someone who knows about glass?"

"No. I just discovered it this morning." I turned and looked at her. "Tony and I had a fight about it. He says I'm being silly."

"Do you have any other reason for thinking your apartment was broken into and your property vandalized?"

"For some reason I immediately thought of that broken rose."

"Why do you think that came into your mind?"

"Because the whole situation is beginning to creep me out!"

"Marta, will you please sit down again? I do not like talking to your back."

"Sure. Sorry."

Now we both stared at Lili's quite beautiful porcelain coffee pot, but I doubt if either of us was seeing it. She patiently waited me out.

"Lili, do you think I'm being 'ridiculous?' That's the word Tony used."

"It is not what I think, my dear. It is what *you* think that matters. You have to live with the way you feel."

"Tony does, too."

"Of course, but your Tony is a good man. He understands you."

"Then why did he make me feel so stupid this morning?"

Lili smiled. "Well, perhaps he doesn't understand you so well all the time. He is a man. You are a woman," she added with a shrug, as if that explained everything.

"I guess I want your opinion on what I should do. Do you think my concern is silly?"

Her smile faded. "First, do you think it is possible that someone could have entered your apartment and you would not have known?"

"We don't have alarms or video cameras, if that's what you mean. Our front door has a very good lock, but that's about it."

"Does it show any signs of being tampered with?"

"I haven't checked."

"I would suggest you do so. It will ease your mind if you know."

"Or creep me out worse than ever."

"You would rather not know for certain?"

I didn't really have to think about my answer. "Yes. I would like to know."

"Then I suggest you look at it."

"What if it doesn't show anything, but the lock was picked anyway?"

"Have an expert look at it. You also need an expert to look at this piece of glass shelf you told me about."

"I really needed these days off to decompress. Right now it feels as if the top of my head is going to blow off."

"Marta, you need to take steps to resolve this."

"Then you think I might be correct?"

Lili sighed and shook her head. "When are you going to understand that it is not what I think or your husband thinks, it is what *you* think?"

The phone on the side table rang and I brought it over to Lili. While she spoke to the person calling, I stewed over my problem.

My ears zoomed right in on the phone conversation when I heard Lili say, "She is here now…. Yes, she is…. I will tell her."

As I put the phone back on the hook for her, I said, "That was Tony."

"Yes. He returned to the apartment and found you not home. He was concerned."

"Why? He seemed in an awful hurry to leave this morning."

"Marta, please. That is not constructive. Your husband was concerned in case what you think is true."

"Oh, now he's decided he believes me?"

"He is coming over now. He would like us to talk this out together."

More coffee was waiting when Tony pulled up in the Corvette, his pride and joy. I was watching as he got out of the car more slowly than usual. He looked tired.

We sat and made awkward pleasantries for a few minutes until I felt like screaming. I'd finally decided that I wanted to know. I wanted to find out what was really going on. The thought of being in Rome, on my own, with the possibility that someone was stalking me would be unbearable, and it was possibly very dangerous.

Tony finally took the lead in our conversation. "Lili, you said that Marta has filled you in about what's going on."

Her head moved up and down once. "That is correct."

"If someone *is* stalking her, what should we do?"

"Actually," I interjected, "would you consider this giver of bouquets a stalker?"

"Your questions are intertwined," Lili answered after considering for a long moment. "Yes, Marta, this is stalking most certainly. The fact that this person is trying to remain hidden is very odd in itself. People with this fixation usually want to be known to the object of so consuming an interest. That you have tried without success to discover this person's identity is ... troubling."

"And the break-in?" I asked.

Tony folded his arms. "If there was one."

Lili turned to him and he got the benefit of the hawk treatment. "Tony, my friend, perhaps something happened in your apartment, perhaps not. It will not hurt to find out for certain."

His answer was a shrug, but I knew his earlier concern about my whereabouts was a good indication that he was at least willing to entertain that I might be correct.

Lili finally took the last cookie and chewed it thoughtfully. "All right. You have both asked for my opinion and thoughts about this, so I will give them to you. I do consider that Marta is being stalked." She turned to me. "Did you keep any of the notes that were left?"

"Yes. Two or three of them at least. I'll have to check at home."

"Good. We should have the handwriting analyzed. You told me you think this person is male. An expert should be able to tell us conclusively.

"Second, I am concerned that this person is following you all over the world. If you received these bouquets only when you performed in Toronto, I would have a smaller concern."

"Yes," Tony said. "Someone has spent big bucks to do this."

"The fact that these bouquets are presented in such an elaborate manner indicates an obsessive nature, and that makes me even more uneasy. I did not know that you had received so many bouquets, Marta. You should have told me." She paused. "Now you have received a damaged bouquet when all of the previous ones have been so perfect. Our stalker is telling you something, but what?"

I shivered. "That he was going to punish me for a poor performance?"

Lili looked at me sharply. "Tell me all."

"The night before the final performance, several of the cast members were invited to a party at a very fancy apartment owned by some Italian nobleman. It was a lovely evening. There was even a small combo and dancing and champagne. I stayed late and enjoyed a bit too much bubbly.

"Next morning I was feeling pretty rough. I laid low most of the day but still didn't feel good. My performance that evening was uneven. In the last act, just after Cavaradossi is shot, I dropped a line or two. Only someone who knew the opera thoroughly would have noticed my made-up lyrics. It was just a little slip and it's not as if I never make any mistakes."

Tony leaned over and took my hand. "You're reading too much into this because you didn't sing your best."

Lili put up her hands. "I cannot agree. There is a careful ritual involved in these gifts. It was no accident the bouquet was damaged. The fact that communication was at last attempted is illuminating."

Tony and I both asked, "Why?"

"First you must understand the pathology of the stalker. Their nature evolves over time. The obsession almost always becomes stronger, more overwhelming to them."

"Are we talking *serial killers* here?" I blurted out.

Lili answered quickly, "No, no. Please do not think this! Serial killers — I detest that term — are something completely different."

"Do you think he's trying to get closer to me?"

"I believe this person has already been close to you."

I nodded. "Getting backstage is so difficult nowadays. It used to be someone just standing by the stage door. Now they buzz you in. IDs are checked."

"Maybe he or she is paying someone to get these bouquets to you," Tony said.

Lili frowned. "It is impossible to know, and that is what we need to work on: finding answers to these questions."

"Do you think Marta is in any danger?"

We waited too long for our friend's answer.

"Perhaps."

Chapter Four

The way Shannon O'Brien dropped onto the chair behind her desk was a good indication of the way she felt.

She'd been vaguely unhappy for weeks now. Occasionally over the years, especially when her marriage was crashing down around her, she'd suffered through bouts of depression, but this was different, and all the more infuriating for its elusiveness.

While she had much to be grateful for — her daughter Rachel was doing well at graduate school (drama), her son Robbie was in his senior year in high school and a star athlete, and she had a solid relationship with a good man — Shannon felt uneasy. There was a "greyness" to life — or so it seemed to her.

The worst effect of this was how distractible she'd become. That was *not* a good thing for a private investigator, someone running a business that required clear thinking and a steady hand at the tiller. It wasn't as critical as it would have been if she was still a cop where disaster was never more than a brain fart away. Today, for instance, she'd been an hour late for work and for no better reason than she'd just been unable to get herself in gear.

Shannon sighed for the third or fourth time as she looked over the day's agenda on her computer, yet another thing she'd neglected to do at home that morning.

"Get a grip," she mumbled, scanning the information on the screen.

It looked as if it would be a day for reading reports from the four operatives who worked for her. There was only one appointment, an early afternoon interview with an operative looking for work: Dan Hudson, a surveillance expert with a résumé as long as her arm.

She desperately needed someone with Hudson's skill set. Lately, businesses, even small ones, were having prospective employees seriously vetted for any skeletons they might have in their closets. It wasn't just for security clearances anymore, either. Weirdness in an employee's personal life more and more often rebounded onto their employers, as well. Increasingly, smart businesses wanted at least some idea of what their employees got up to after hours and on social media.

Based on what she was seeing in Hudson's four-page résumé, Shannon would be a fool not to take him, but she'd been in the game long enough to know that nothing could replace double-checking everything. "Take nothing at face value" had always been her motto. Every single time she'd strayed from that path, investigations had turned to shit. People had gotten angry or hurt — or worse.

"Have you finished checking those phone numbers for me, Karen?" she called out.

"Just finishing them up," her secretary replied from the outer office. "I'm firing an email to you now."

Shannon's mail program pinged a moment later. Picking up the résumé, she turned to the computer. An hour and a quarter later, she'd cross-checked every single reference given. Some of the people weren't available, some had spoken to her, and some made it clear they wouldn't. All to be expected when one dealt with government organizations, especially ones that dealt in secrets — theirs and other people's.

With the wall clock across the room approaching twelve, Shannon got up and retrieved some coffee from the pot in the outer office, shutting the door before returning to her desk. If she got a favourable feel from Daniel James Hudson, she would hire him, but she didn't want to appear too eager. Let him cool his heels with Karen for a few minutes.

Shannon heard him arrive precisely at twelve. Good. At five after, she buzzed Karen and asked her to send him in. She stood to shake his hand, making sure her grip was suitably strong. "I'm Shannon O'Brien."

"Dan Hudson. Pleased to meet you."

From the merest flick of his eyes, she knew she'd surprised him. Good. Her goal was to find out how cocky he was. O'Brien Investigates didn't hire employees who thought too much of themselves.

They sat, Shannon resting her clasped hands on the desk, Hudson leaning back in his seat, but not lounging, another telltale sign of someone with possibly too much ego. While chatting a bit before getting down to the nitty-gritty of the interview, she sized up this possible employee.

There was something appealingly "boyish" about Dan Hudson. He certainly had the demeanor of a fully mature forty-four year old. Using her cop's eye, she already had his height pegged at six-four, and while she wouldn't call him husky, he was well put-together and obviously took care of himself. He had short-cropped, light-brown hair and a fairly nondescript face, good for someone whose work went more smoothly the less they were noticed. But there was something arresting about his brown eyes. Shannon got the feeling they didn't miss much. She was certain he was doing as much "sizing up" from his side of the desk as she was.

Finally sitting back in her seat, she said, "Your résumé is quite impressive. You've worked for some heavy hitters: CSIS, the RCMP, and you were with Special Forces for seven years. Is there anything else I should know?"

"I don't know what you mean."

"Is there anyone you worked for that you didn't list in the résumé? I don't want to be blindsided by something you neglected to tell me. When one runs with the crowd you have, there are often things left unsaid."

"I worked with the FBI on a few things, all done through the RCMP when I was with them."

"Nothing else? No other foreign organizations that prefer to remain anonymous?"

Hudson caught Shannon's gaze and held it. "None."

She let the moment last a second or two longer, keeping her face just as expressionless as his.

He dropped out of the staring contest first. "Why are you asking me this?"

"Because I can't figure out why you want to work for a small company like mine. Your references have all said great things about you. You've been playing in the fast lane, doing a fair bit of travelling, too. Why give that up?"

"Because after nearly twenty years, I'm tired of having no fixed address. I've spent maybe two months all told in my apartment in Ottawa during the past year and a half. I have no close friends and I never visit anyone other than the few relatives I still have. To cut to the chase, I'm tired. It's time I put down some roots."

Shannon had heard something similar from a friend she contacted at RCMP headquarters — and not one of the people on Hudson's list of references.

They spent a few minutes discussing what she was looking for, the expected hours, and how much she was willing to pay.

"Why don't we try this out for a few months, see if we both like the fit?"

For the first time, Hudson smiled, and it was a good one. "Sure. It sounds as if you can make use of my skills. I won't have to travel much and I've heard good things about the way you do business. There are a lot of sleazeball outfits in this game, and you're not one of them."

They shook hands. There would be the usual contract to sign, outlining what he was expected to do, but Shannon felt good about taking him on. He could certainly do anything she'd need in the way of surveillance detection and that sort of thing. The time he'd spent with Special Forces at the beginning of his career meant he'd be able to handle himself if a situation got sticky. Dan Hudson could be a strong addition to her group of operatives.

"How long will it take you to get settled in town?"

"I never even got my stuff completely unpacked in Ottawa and I moved into my current place three years ago." He grinned. "How pathetic is that? Anyway, I could start as soon as you need me. I've already got a place, and my stuff arrived from Ottawa last week, so I'm good to go."

"Well, I have to get the word out that we're going into the employee-vetting game in a big way. I have only one job of that sort going on at the moment, and I've already assigned someone to it."

"Then I'll wait to hear from you."

"I don't think it will be long."

After he left, Shannon spent a few minutes thumbing through Hudson's résumé again. It wouldn't be hard for him to find work with the skill set he had. Why was he willing to work for one of the small players in town? She felt sure he could name his price with any of her larger competitors.

Chapter Five

"So what do you want to do tonight?"
Tony asked as soon as we'd gotten into
his Vette. "We haven't had much time alone and you
only have a few more days."

I was looking out the window, preoccupied by what
we'd been discussing. It was all completely unnerving,
to say the least. Someone was following me around,
possibly breaking into our apartment, and who knew
what else? Rather than being comforted by calm words
from a wise woman, Lili had succeeded in freaking me
out even more.

Tony gave me a few moments before asking again
what I wanted to do.

"I'd like to have you make me something nice for dinner, you know, like we used to do when we first met."

He grinned. "That was because we wanted to have a bed handy so we could just fall right into it."

I put my hand over his as it rested on the gear shift. "I'm just glad you're with me, right here, right now. Let's go home."

Parking in the underground garage, I couldn't prevent myself from looking around for someone sitting in a darkened car or echoing footsteps approaching from the opposite end of the cavern-like room beneath our building. Until the elevator doors finally closed behind us, I didn't even realize I'd been holding my breath.

Everything in our apartment appeared exactly as it had when I'd left. Was it my imagination, though, or was there an almost imperceptible change, as if a guest three weeks earlier had worn perfume and the ghost of it still lingered in the air?

I sat in the kitchen with Tony as he prepared *spaghetti all' amatriciana*, a pasta dish I particularly adore.

Almost as soon as my derrière was planted on one of the stools opposite our island stove top, he had a glass of white wine placed in my hand. An eagle eye was on it, too, because every time it got halfway down, he'd be there refilling it.

"Are you trying to get me tipsy?" I teased.

His answer was not the expected smart aleck kind. "I'm trying to get you to relax. You're like a coiled spring, Marta. If I touch you, I'm almost afraid you'll fly apart in million directions. You were supposed to be taking it easy."

"Well, it seems someone else had other ideas."

"Do you think maybe we're taking this all too seriously?"

I immediately noticed the use of the word "we're" and wondered if he honestly felt that way, or was just trying to be more gentle in his criticism.

I took another sip of wine, as grateful for its alcohol as much as its flavour.

I caught his eye before he looked down at the onion he was about to slice. "Let's say I'm wrong about what's going on, that this is all about some fan who's got a weird sense of humour and more money than God to send me very expensive bouquets. Maybe this is all a big giggle to him."

"If it is a him."

"Let's just say it is, okay?"

"Sorry."

"If what I just said is the case, eventually he'll step out of the shadows to present one in person, and that will be the end of it. But what if this isn't so simple? What if this guy has some serious problems?" I shook my head. "Look, I don't want to go off the deep end on this, but I also don't want to leave myself wide open because we didn't take a possible threat seriously."

Tony began slicing the onion thinly. "Then we have to find that out."

I nodded and took another sip of wine. Tony's hand reached for the bottle, but I put my hand on top of the glass.

"Question is: how do we go about doing that?"

As Tony cooked up the sauce and boiled the pasta, we talked all around my problem and how to go about solving it.

Cops? Why would they be interested? There was nothing much to go on at this point, other than mysterious flower deliveries. Besides, as Tony pointed out, which cops? So far I'd gotten ten bouquets in ten different cities spread over seven countries on three continents. It would be a jurisdictional nightmare.

We opened a bottle of seriously good Chianti for the pasta, but didn't pay it the attention it deserved — nor the pasta, either.

Gesturing across the table with his fork, Tony said, "Your problem sounds like a job for Mike Hammer."

"Who?"

"Sherlock Holmes then. We need a private detective. Someone who's not a cop, but knows about these things. You really should read more crime fiction."

"No thanks. The possibility of the real thing is quite enough for my imagination. Tony, you don't know what it's like being by yourself all the time in other cities."

"You're constantly around people."

"There are a lot of times when I'm out on the street alone. I can't stay cooped up in a hotel room or rented apartment for weeks on end, and I can't always go out with a crowd of people. What do you think it would be like to be constantly looking over my shoulder for trouble? I did that downstairs in the parking garage earlier."

"I did, too," he admitted. "You don't just need a detective, Marta. You also need a bodyguard, someone who'll look over your shoulder for you — and for me."

"Where do we find somebody like that?"

Tony nodded to himself. "I think I know just where to begin."

We made wonderful love later that evening, slow and gentle and heavy on the passion. Afterwards, as we lay next to each other, breathless from our exertions, Tony's hand snaked into mine.

"Marta, I don't ever want anything to happen to you — not if I can prevent it. I couldn't live with myself if I failed you so badly."

"Do you honestly believe what I've been telling you, or are you just trying to cover your options?" I asked, turning on my side to look at him.

"It makes no difference what I believe. I don't want you to even have to *think* about something that might be going on. You're all that matters. I want you to feel safe."

His hand made a move toward my right breast. I grabbed his wrist.

"Do you believe me?"

He took a deep breath before his answer. "Yes."

"Honest and true?"

"Yes."

"Cross your heart and hope to die?"

"*Yes!*"

I let go of his wrist. "That's all right then."

Tony was as good as his word. Next morning, by the time I got out of the shower, the coffee was ready and he was on the phone.

After filling my favourite mug — "Opera is when

a guy gets stabbed in the back, and instead of bleeding, he sings" is what it says on the side — I went into the living room and sat at the opposite end of the sofa from my ever-loving husband, feeling much more at ease than I had twelve hours earlier.

"Yeah, yeah. I think I know where that is.... Sure. I wrote it down.... Yes, I'll tell them that you recommended them.... Okay, and thanks. I knew you'd have a name."

"Who were speaking to?" I asked as Tony put down the phone.

"My cousin, Mario."

"The one who's been in and out of prison a couple of times, the one nobody ever talks about?"

He grinned. "Hey, you want something like a private eye, call up someone who knows about the windy side of the law. Besides Mario says he had nuttin' to do with that holdup. He was framed!"

"And you believe him?"

"Um, no." He held up a scrap of paper. "But he did have the name of a private detective. Thinks they might be good for a bodyguard, too, or can connect you with someone."

"Who is it?"

"An operation called O'Brien Investigates."

"And how does Mario know about them?"

"The lady who owns the company, Shannon O'Brien, was the cop who busted him."

"That makes me feel *so* much better."

I let Tony make the appointment. For some reason, I suddenly felt shy about the whole thing. I mean, it's one thing to say to friends that you think you're being stalked, and it's another thing to say it to a perfect stranger, especially one who's an ex-cop.

⁓

Ten thirty found us racing up the Don Valley Parkway and onto the 404 for our appointment with the private eye. She had an office in one of those business complexes that have sprouted up all over the suburbs surrounding Toronto. O'Brien Investigates was off Woodbine near Unionville, and because of the usual miserable Toronto traffic we barely made it on time.

As we walked toward the glass door with the company's name on it, I had to admit I was more nervous than I'd been the last time I had to audition for an opera gig, ten long years ago.

I wasn't impressed by the state of the outer office. While it was clean, the carpet had seen its best years. The office furniture wasn't much better.

Tony looked at me, obviously thinking the same thing: a low-rent operation.

The receptionist didn't do anything to allay our uneasiness. Her red hair, piled on top of her head, came right out of a bottle. I had no idea how someone with nails that long could expect to type on a computer keyboard, but unless it was all gibberish, her speed and dexterity were impressive. She kept typing even after we'd reached her desk.

"We have an appointment," Tony said. "Eleven o'clock with Ms. O'Brien."

Finally she looked up. At least she didn't have gum in her mouth. "Right. The opera singer."

"How did you know that?" I asked.

"Shannon had me research you on the Internet after your call this morning." She looked over at Tony and I couldn't miss the gleam of interest in her eye. "And you must be Tony. We spoke on the phone."

Tony stuck out his hand to shake, but the redhead handed him a clipboard with a pen on a string attached to it.

"Shannon will be with you in a few minutes. Could you fill this out while you wait, please?"

Without waiting for an answer, she turned back to her computer and began typing furiously again.

We went over to some plastic seats that looked as if they'd come right out of an interview room at a police station. Taking the clipboard, I filled out the usual information about who I was and where I lived. There was a spot at the bottom of the page "For Office Use Only" that had blank lines for listing financial information. It suddenly dawned on me that this was going to cost money — probably a lot of money.

I'd barely had time to put down the date and my signature when the door to the inner office opened.

The woman standing there was as tall as I am. Pulled back in a ponytail, her blond hair didn't come out of a bottle. You couldn't have called her skinny, more like wiry. For some reason I immediately thought of her taking on some bad guy twice her size and coming out on top. Being an ex-cop, perhaps that's the way she'd been taught to present herself. I certainly wouldn't have wanted to meet her in a dark alley.

Her hand shot out. "I'm Shannon O'Brien."

"Marta Hendriks. And this is my husband Tony Lusardi."

"Pleased to meet you both," she answered as we all shook hands.

I noticed her eyes quickly flick downwards at Tony's and my matching wedding bands.

We went into her small, windowless office. To break the blankness of the walls, there was a series of large photos of a rock band in concert, not something I would have expected to see in a private detective's inner sanctum. They were expertly done, capturing the energy of the show and its music.

"Can I offer you some coffee? Tea? Mineral water?"

"Nothing for me, thanks," I replied.

She motioned toward two seats in front of her desk, and as Tony and I sat, she moved behind the desk in one beautifully facile movement. I was instantly envious. I've always had to think out nearly every move I make, especially when I'm onstage. Sometimes stage movement gets in my way so much my singing suffers. It used to be far worse, but even after many years, it's still a more of a consideration than it should be. It used to make Gerhard so angry.

"No, no, *no*! Marta, you *cannot* broadcast your every movement to the audience! What you do, this stage business, must seem natural, unforced — and with you it does not. I watch you and I always see the little wheels turning in your head." He made gyrations with his index fingers on either side of his head. "Always we see that you are play acting only. If you are Lucia, then you must make us *believe* that you are Lucia. Same with Tosca, Violetta. Same with —" Gerhard's arms flew up in the air in a motion of extreme frustration. "Same with all of them!"

That was the closest Gerhard ever brought me to complete despair.

"Ms. Hendriks?" Shannon O'Brien's voice broke through my unintentional reverie.

I noticed another quick flick of her eyes, this time toward Tony.

"You'll have to excuse my wife," he said. "Her situation has her somewhat … distracted."

She made a welcoming gesture across the desk.

"Please, start your story from the beginning. Tell it at your own speed."

I realized some conversation had gone on while I had zoned out.

"I, ah …" My thoughts were hopelessly jumbled.

They both looked at me encouragingly.

"I've already told Ms. O'Brien a bit about the bouquets," Tony offered helpfully.

I grew more embarrassed. I had been really far away this time.

O'Brien gave me time to collect myself by taking a sip from a mug of coffee she had at her elbow.

"I believe someone is stalking me," I said in a rush and then stopped, unsure what to say next.

"When and where did this stalking begin?" O'Brien asked as she picked up a pen. "Take your time and tell me everything you can remember about what's happened to you."

"May I have some water, please?"

While she filled a glass from a carafe that had been on top of a low bookcase behind her, I gathered my scattered wits. Once I'd taken two large sips, I felt more ready to begin.

"I am an opera singer," I began, but she held up her hand.

"I'm sorry to interrupt you so soon, but you need to know that I always research my clients before they arrive on my doorstep. I am well aware of who you are and what you do for a living. Consider that I already know everything about you that can be found on the Internet. It will save time."

"Do you know anything about opera?"

"Not a thing, to my shame, but I do know something of backstage life. Now, please continue."

It took over an hour to get through the interview even though I was getting more polished at relating my tale of woe.

It was soon evident this detective was a highly skilled interviewer. She drew out of me many details that I didn't even realize I knew.

By the end, we all had a much clearer picture of just what had been happening to me.

Spread across her desk were all the notes from the stalker that I had, five of the ten. Tony and I waited a few minutes while she examined each closely with a magnifying glass, causing us to smile over her head.

"Have you ever dealt with a situation like this before?" I asked when she'd sat up again.

"Once, when I was still a member of the police force, but it certainly wasn't *this* involved. Someone has gone to a lot of trouble."

"And a lot of expense," Tony added unnecessarily.

"So what do you think?" I asked. "What should I do?"

She looked closely at me for a moment before speaking. That last question had come out a lot more emotionally than I wished.

"Okay. I know a fair bit about handwriting analysis, and I'm nearly certain your 'admirer' is male. There are a number of indicators that point to this and not a female imitating a male's handwriting. He is intelligent, driven, and very meticulous. He is a creature of habit. He also thinks a lot of himself, probably that he's smarter than those around him. Of course some of these observations stem from what he's done rather than just his handwriting." She indicated the cards spread across her desk. "Which is the most recent one?"

I looked through them for a moment. "This."

Again the long observation and comparison with other examples.

"You may have noticed these are all written using a fountain pen. They're sensitive writing instruments and reveal a lot more. The nib of the pen flexes depending on pressure. If you write faster or more, shall we say, emotionally, it shows up. This most recent one definitely shows more stress."

"Do you think it's because he's angry with me?"

"Hard to say. For that you need to speak to a forensic psychologist. Based on my knowledge and experience, I can say that he was either rushed, excited-slash-angry, or both. Certainly *something* was different about his state of mind."

Now came the big question. "Should I be worried?"

She took a deep breath. "Perhaps. I would need to know a lot more than I do now to give you an unequivocal answer."

Tony leaned forward. "We want to hire you. My wife is going out on the road again and I'm concerned."

"My current engagement is in Rome," I added. "I must be back for a Monday performance. Then I go to Venice before returning home again."

"What do you want to hire me to do?" Shannon O'Brien asked. "We can certainly try to find out the identity of this person for you."

I looked over at Tony. His expression clearly told me, *Your choice, dear.*

I took a deep breath, keeping my eyes where they were. "Yes," I answered. "Maybe if we find out who this person is, he'll give up and go back under the rock he crawled out from."

"Would you be willing to take this to court if he doesn't?"

"What do you mean?"

"It might take a restraining order to get someone like this to back off. The reason I ask is that it would affect the way we would go about doing our investigation."

That set me back on my heels. Stupidly, I hadn't thought about court, even though cases like mine often wound up there. I was still aware the "damaged goods" label wasn't very far in my past and that debacle in Paris two years ago was still reverberating through my professional life.

"You think it could come to that?"

Shannon O'Brien shrugged. "You need to be prepared for the possibility."

Tony, true to form, asked the next most important question. "What are we looking at cost wise for your services?"

That took five minutes of explanations about retainers, reporting, blah, blah, blah. Tony has a better head than I for this sort of thing. I just caught the really relevant things like "five thousand dollar retainer," small stuff like that. The numbers being bandied about were pretty hair-raising.

As my pen floated across the bottom of some forms, I thought about the end-game here. What was I *really* after?

Chapter Six

Our personal detective service certainly
wasted no time getting on the job.

Tony and I arrived home and received a call
shortly after, asking if we'd be there at four. O'Brien
had already dug up a glass expert who would take a
look at the remains of the suspect shelf and give us his
opinion. She also wanted to bring over an additional
person.

"Our surveillance expert, very experienced. I want
him to do a complete sweep of your condo."

"What's he going to tell us?"

"Depends on what he finds. In fact, for your sake, I
hope he doesn't find anything."

I couldn't avoid looking around the living room, wondering whether someone had burrowed his way this far into our privacy. It felt as if my life was coming apart. Taking a deep breath, I willed my heart to slow down. It didn't work.

Shannon was right. I hoped to God she didn't find anything.

Perhaps in an effort to distract me, Tony asked what I would like to do for dinner.

"What about taking Lili out?"

"Great idea. Phone her up."

Uncharacteristically, she answered on the second ring. Generally one had to leave messages, which she would answer between coachings. I questioned that.

"I cancelled a few days of work because I'm feeling so tired."

I asked, "Is your leg bothering you?"

"Not particularly. My arms are aching from these *zatracený* crutches."

My concern deepened. Lili didn't shift to Czech when she knew the other person didn't understand it.

"We'd like to take you out to dinner tonight, dear."

"I don't think I would be very good company."

"It would do you good to get out of the house. When was the last time you were outside?"

She ignored my question. "I appreciate your offer, but no. I would rather stay home."

"Then we'll bring dinner over."

"No. I am not fit for company."

"Nonsense!"

The discussion went back and forth for several

minutes and I grew more concerned. This was very unlike Lili.

Eventually, I wore her down. I couldn't get her to tell me what she wanted to eat, but that was typical of her. The only place the woman ever dithered was over a menu.

Tony and I kicked ideas around for awhile and came up with a great solution: order from a Czech restaurant we'd heard of in the extreme east end of the city. We could pick up the food and reheat it at Lili's. Tony was on it in a moment. We'd order all Lili's favourites. It would cost us, but what the heck. Czech food is in short supply in T.O.

Not knowing how long the detective crew would need to be in our apartment, Tony decided he would make the run out to Scarborough for the food and I'd man the home front. If they weren't finished by the time we had to leave for Lili's, then they'd just have to come back later.

⌒

Shannon O'Brien arrived promptly at four with her two specialists. The glass guy was a little old man from Holland whose English was nearly incomprehensible even though he'd lived in Canada for half his life. From what I gathered, he'd been born into the glass trade and Shannon assured me that what he didn't know about the stuff wasn't worth knowing. He was sloppily dressed and the green sweater he wore was decidedly threadbare.

"Where did you find him?" I whispered as he shuffled over to the shelf remains still spread out on the dining room table.

"He came highly recommended by someone I know in the Ontario Provincial Police forensics unit. They use Hans whenever they have a question about glass."

The white-haired man's sole tools consisted of a large magnifying glass, calipers, and a steel ruler. I had to supply a desk lamp so he could see what he was doing. He quickly shooed us away so he could work undisturbed.

The surveillance expert, on the other hand, brought in two of those flight-case things, the size of large suitcases and very pro-looking.

"Dan Hudson, and I'm pleased to meet you."

Removing his ski jacket, Hudson quickly flipped open the equipment cases. They had compartments in the lids and bases and each was filled with gadgets and cables, all neatly labelled and impressive as hell.

"What's all this for?" I asked.

Shannon motioned for silence by holding her index finger to her lips, then crooked her finger for me to follow her out to the hallway.

"We don't know if your apartment has bugs," she told me in a low voice, "but let's make the assumption it does. It's safer to talk out here. We don't want your stalker to know that we may be onto him."

"I see. Are you confident your expert will find anything that's there?"

"Oh yes. He used to work for the government."

"He's a spy?"

Shannon looked as if she wished she hadn't told me. "I suppose you could say that."

"Cool."

She looked at me oddly, then said, "We'll go back in, but watch what you say. Just remember that someone could be listening. Okay?"

I sat on the sofa in the living room, trying to stay out of the way, and watched in fascination as Dan and Shannon went over the apartment. From the dining room I could hear Hans, our glass expert, mumbling to himself. I found it all highly amusing. The whole thing was completely out of the realm of my experience.

It was clear Hudson was in charge, but Shannon knew her way around this stuff as well.

Dan had given his boss a small black box with a strap that she slung over her shoulder. Connected to it was a cord with an antenna at the end that she held in her right hand and headphones she slipped over her ears.

She began pacing around the condo moving the antenna slowly back and forth as if searching for buried treasure — or looking for land mines. Her eyes were glued to the control panel at one end of the black box and her face held a look of extreme concentration. Twice in the living room she stopped, retraced her steps, and came back, after which she pulled a small notebook out of the back pocket of her jeans and scribbled a line or two.

In the meantime, Dan was crawling around the floor in a quite undignified manner, moving furniture (even flipping chairs over), peering at the baseboards, sweeping his hands in wide arcs over the broadloom. He spent the most time examining the large bookcase and stereo unit that filled one end of the living room.

When they moved to the bedrooms, I followed, but it was more of the same and I was losing interest. There were no eureka moments to prove I was correct in my assumption that this creep stalking me had invaded our living space. I only stayed in case they had any questions. It's tough watching someone go through your undies, even if they do it gently and dispassionately.

Tony arrived back shortly after six in a great mood from his mercy trip to the Czech restaurant. Over the time we'd known each other, he'd become as fond of Lili as I.

I'd introduced them early on in our relationship. Lili had taken Tony under her vocal coaching wing, at first undoubtedly for my sake, but as he began improving by leaps and bounds, more for the pleasure of working with a talented singer. Now she saw him far more than I did.

"What's up with the sleuths?" he asked as he flopped down next to me on the sofa.

"You saw Hans on your way in, I assume."

"Little old guy in the dining room, examining small chunks of glass as if they were the Holy Grail?"

"That's him. Shannon and her other expert are in the second bedroom."

"Have they told you anything?"

"Not a word, but they've consulted in whispers several times. It's all a little unnerving to tell you the truth."

When Tony started to ask a question about bugs, I put my hand over his mouth and my lips to his ear. "Shannon told me not to talk about anything that touches on this. Assume we're being listened to."

Tony nodded. "We've got to leave for Lili's soon. I've left the food in the car."

"I'll ask them how much longer they'll be."

Again, Shannon took me out into the hall to talk.

"We're almost done, but Dan wants to come back tomorrow."

"Have you found anything?"

She took a deep breath. "Yes."

"Oh Christ …"

Shannon looked at me searchingly. "I want to be clear with you. It's now a matter of how much, not if."

"Can you tell me anything?"

Shannon considered for a moment. "I'd rather not. My two experts will give me full reports and then I'll discuss it with you."

"Was the glass shelf broken on purpose?"

She hesitated for a moment, then nodded. "Hans wants to talk to another colleague, but it's his opinion that it was deliberately broken." She patted my shoulder. "I will call tomorrow and tell you what we have so far."

At that point Dan stuck his head out the apartment door.

"Could I borrow your cell phone and laptop for the night? I want to check them for creepy-crawlies. Your husband's too, if I may."

"I'll have to ask Tony, but sure, you can have my stuff."

"Great. I'm just packing up now."

He disappeared inside again.

I stood there for a moment, trying to wrap my brain around Shannon's news when Tony stuck his head out.

"What are you doing out here?"

"Talking, because we can't inside."

Tony grasped the full meaning immediately. "Oh."

"Shannon's surveillance expert wants to check our cells and laptops. I told him he could take mine, but I didn't want to speak for you."

"I'd rather get someone at work to check mine. If you'll excuse me, ladies."

As Tony went in, I looked at Shannon. "What the hell should we do?"

"Carry on as if nothing has happened."

"How can I do that knowing someone is listening to me?"

"You must. We want to catch this guy. The less he suspects, the better. Opera singers are actors as well as musicians, aren't they? Just act."

I didn't have the heart to tell Shannon the acting part was the facet of my craft that I struggled with the most.

⌒

Our evening with Lili was just the tonic I needed after the disturbing events of the day. Tony did his very best to cheer us up, being in turn solicitous and funny. The food, even reheated, was excellent, and by the time we got to dessert, vanilla crescent cookies called *vanilkove rohlicky*, I swear Lili was near swooning.

"Where did you get these? They are as good as my grandmother could make!"

"I have my ways, dear Lili," Tony answered, pouring her a second cup of coffee, "but I'm sworn to secrecy. Don't worry, there are at least two pounds more in your kitchen."

Naturally, after such a fine meal, we were all in the mood for a little music.

We took our coffee, slivovitz, plus more cookies and repaired to the "piano room."

It stretched across the back of Lili's house and she'd rebuilt the outer wall, making it basically all glass with large windows on either side of French doors that opened into her walled back garden. Even though the scenery was winter-desolate, it still looked lovely with the big beech tree in a back corner and the shrubs illuminated by discrete lights.

Since Tony and I hadn't sung in a few days, we needed a pretty thorough warm-up. We'd done duo warm-ups a couple of times in the past, and being in such good humour, we did our best to undermine each other's effort — all in good fun, mind you.

Tony possesses a fine, if light, tenor, while my voice is decidedly heavier and much more powerful. He'd never be suitable for *verismo* roles, much to his disappointment, since he loved Puccini more than anything. On the other hand, I had been leaning in that direction more and more over the past few seasons because it suited my maturing voice and I had the vocal octane to produce the amount of volume required. Whenever I sang with Tony, I had to be mindful of not swamping him.

We ran through a number of favourite bel canto arias from operas by Bellini, Donizetti, and Rossini. There were a few duets that we had sung at parties, and once those had been done, we just sang solo arias with each joining the other whether the role was for male or female. There were some spectacular crashes that dissolved into laughter and I was thoroughly enjoying singing with my husband, something we didn't do often enough, I realized wistfully.

Lili provided her usual scintillating support at the piano, bailing us out when we needed it and spurring us on when the slogging got a little tough. After nearly ninety minutes, we were all toasted.

When Tony left the room in search of the bottle of slivovitz, I sat next to Lili on the piano bench. Finally, she seemed happy and relaxed.

"It has been a wonderful evening, my dear," she told me. "Thank you so much."

I hugged her with my right arm. "We'd do anything for you, you know that. All you have to do is ask."

"Would you like to sing for me tomorrow? I detected some things I am not happy about. You need a little re-adjustment, Marta. Those bad habits are creeping in again."

Lili was probably correct. She knew my voice better than I did, of course. It's the curse of being a singer. We open our mouths and have no real idea what it's sounding like. In my case, when I'm in my best voice, it doesn't sound particularly good in my head. That's why singers depend so much on vocal coaches or *répétiteurs*. Without their ears, we'd be lost.

"Tony is sounding pretty good."

"Your Tony continually surprises me. I am encouraged that he's been offered the role of Almaviva in *Barber of Seville* for Opera York. Has he told you?"

"Told her what?" Tony asked as he returned.

"How come you didn't tell me you might be singing Almaviva?" I asked.

"Because I'm not sure I'm ready."

Lili scowled. "I wouldn't say you are ready if you were not."

"Why are you two ganging up on me?"

I stood and hugged him. "Tony, you're usually a very decisive person. Go for it. What's the worst that can happen?"

"How about I make a complete and utter fool of myself?"

"Have faith in your talent."

It wasn't until we were getting in the car that the weight of the world came crashing down on me again. We'd decided on the way over to Lili's that we wouldn't say anything to her until we got Shannon's report. All evening we had studiously avoided all mention of what we'd found out about our condo. There had been whole handfuls of minutes where I'd forgotten about it completely.

"Penny for your thoughts," Tony said as the car's engine thrummed to life.

"You know what I'm thinking."

"Let's get a hotel room for the night."

"Can we?"

"I'll admit it will look a little odd showing up with no luggage …"

"That's not what I meant!"

Tony smiled. "I know. I'm just teasing you."

"I'm not in the mood to be teased. I just can't face going home knowing that someone could be listening to everything we say."

"It could be worse than that. That guy Dan told me there might be cameras."

I felt like clamping my hands over my ears. My imagination couldn't grasp something that horrible.

"That settles it. We are *not* going home tonight. I'd rather sleep in the car."

"He could have the car bugged too."

"Stop it!"

Next morning, we met with Shannon at her office.

The glass expert wasn't present but Dan Hudson was. Both he and Shannon looked serious. This time we sat around a table in the opposite corner of her office from the desk. I asked for coffee and could have used a shot of brandy in it.

"So what did you find out?" Tony asked.

Shannon's eyes dropped to the sheaf of papers in front of her and Dan pulled out a laptop. They looked at each other for a moment then Shannon looked across the table at me.

"It was as you suspected. Someone has been in your apartment at least twice, likely many more times. Hans reports that the glass shelf was deliberately broken by someone using either a point peen hammer or a tack hammer. They both have heads that can provide a hefty wallop to a small area. The top shelf was struck once at a point where it was most likely to break easily. That circular hole you found was indeed where the hammer struck. The weight of the soapstone bear statue did the rest of the damage."

Into the silence, Hudson added, "And we found surveillance equipment."

I asked, "So how did he get in? We have a good lock on the condo door and there is twenty-four-hour security in the building."

Dan answered. "You'd be surprised how easy it is to get into most buildings if you know what you're doing. As for your apartment, it does have a good lock, but anyone with enough skill can get in without much trouble. I managed to pick it in about forty seconds."

Tony and I looked at each other.

Hudson continued, "We can get you a pick-proof electronic lock and it will allow us to monitor whenever your door is opened. Coupled with a hidden surveillance camera of our own, if someone does break into your condo again, we'll know and have video."

I sat up a bit straighter. "So you're saying you were in our building last night?"

"Yes."

"But the video cameras they have …"

"A bit of a disguise, enter from the parking level — very pickable lock there, by the way — go up to your floor, pick the lock on your front door, and bingo, I was in."

"You were in our apartment?"

"While you were out for dinner. I have the video if you'd like to see it."

"Video?"

"Sure. I'm recording you right now."

"*What?*"

Dan took a pen out of his shirt pocket and handed it to me. "Don't drop it, please. It cost me about a thousand bucks."

It looked like a normal pen. I clicked its top and out popped the pen tip.

"I suppose it writes, too?"

"Beautifully. See that dot near the top?"

It was slightly larger than the head of a pin. Tony leaned over to look at it.

"That's the camera," Dan told us. "If you'd like, I could also put on a pair of glasses and record video *and* audio."

Tony took the pen. "So someone could walk right up to Marta and record her and she'd never know it?"

Both Shannon and Dan nodded. I shivered.

Jesus, I thought, *I've probably had this creep right next to me. Perhaps I've even spoken to him.* It gave me the willies.

"What about the surveillance in the apartment?" I asked.

Shannon took over. "There were two bugs in the living room. One is in the frame of the painting over your sofa."

"It was a pretty basic one, audio only," Dan interrupted, "but well done."

Shannon continued. "It was broadcasting to a receiver that someone added to the amplifier of your stereo. There was another mic in the bookcase, as well."

I felt sick. "What about cameras?"

"Here our man was slightly more sneaky. He used the old camera in the smoke detector dodge."

Tony asked, "The smoke detector in the living room?"

Dan nodded.

"What about the detector in the bedroom?" I asked, not sure I wanted to hear the answer. "There too?"

Dan nodded again. "I'm really sorry about that."

My stomach heaved. This *pervert* had been watching the most intimate part of our lives. It was sick. It was disgusting.

It was beyond imagining.

Chapter Seven

Tony took my hand and squeezed it. "We want all that *shit* out of our apartment — today."

Shannon looked at Dan yet again.

"I understand your feelings about this," she began, "but you want to have the best shot at catching this man, don't you?"

Now Tony and I looked at each other.

"What do you mean?"

Shannon nodded at Dan, who began to speak.

"You must be pretty confused at the moment. Frankly, we are, too. This is uncharted territory for me. Any security breaches I've dealt with in the past had no emotional component. They've been straight situations of surveillance or detection of surveillance. Unless this guy is planning on blackmailing you because of something you've done —"

I couldn't hold back. "There is nothing Tony or I have ever done that we need to be ashamed of!"

"I understand," he answered, soothingly, "but if there's anything we need to know in that regard, tell us now."

"There's nothing."

"Please understand we needed to ask," Shannon said. "I know you must be feeling, well, soiled by what we've told you. I can imagine how I'd feel if somebody was watching what goes on in my bedroom."

"You've got that right!"

"Look," Tony said, "we're talking at cross-purposes here. Let's cut to the chase. Why did you suggest that we need to consider not removing the stuff you've found?"

Dan spoke. "The setup we found in your condo is sophisticated. Someone had access to devices that aren't commonly available — certainly not commercially. He either knows a hell of a lot about modern surveillance or had the help of someone who does."

"Meaning?"

"Well, when I found the devices I expected them to be connected to some sort of tape recorder or hard drive where the information would be stored for later retrieval. That's simple stuff, commonly available."

"But you didn't."

Dan nodded. "No. The feeds from the cameras and microphones, which were separate, by the way, were all broadcasting short range. That meant I'd have to look elsewhere in the building for storage devices — a bit of a complication."

A cold finger traced a line down my spine. "You mean the guy lives in our building?"

"We don't think that's likely. My guess was the storage devices were nearby where our perpetrator could get at them easily."

Tony said, "Meaning you believe he has access to the building. That's why you broke in last night. It was an experiment."

"Exactly. Now I have some pretty sophisticated equipment of my own; anti-snooping devices. I knew how strong the broadcast signals were, so I knew how far away the receivers could be. I struck gold the first place I looked."

"Where?"

"The roof."

"So you've got the recorders."

"Not exactly."

"Explain."

"The signal was being bounced to another location. There's an antenna disguised as a satellite dish, but it broadcasts the feeds from your apartment, rather than receiving television signals. It's with five others that are on the roof of your building. The average technician would just see a bunch of dishes and assume that one had been knocked out of alignment since it's not pointing at any satellites."

"What Dan is saying," Shannon interjected when she saw the confusion on my face, "is that the signals are being broadcast to a secondary location. That's where the storage is, and if we're lucky, maybe even the guy we're all so eager to find."

Tony asked, "Can you follow the signal?"

Dan nodded. "But it's tricky. The signal is boosted a lot by the electronics at the dish, so it can travel quite a distance. However, it also has to be line-of-sight, and fortunately your building isn't a tall one."

The penny finally dropped. "So you want us to agree to leave everything in place or this creep might know we're onto him and disappear."

"There's a good chance he already knows. I should have been more careful yesterday and come in looking like an exterminator."

"An exterminator?"

Dan grinned. "It's a great dodge that I've used lots of times." Then the grin vanished. "I'm sorry about not assuming the setup might be as sophisticated as it turned out to be. Anyway, it's my recommendation that we proceed on the basis of what I've outlined. This afternoon, I'll go back to the roof and take some measurements. I should be able to get a pretty good idea what building that satellite dish is focused on."

"And then we'll check it out," Shannon added. "Who knows? We might get lucky."

Dan pulled a soft briefcase off the floor and took out my mobile phone and laptop.

"Both bugged?" I asked.

He sighed. "I'm afraid so."

"Okay. My laptop I can understand. I leave that at home and he's obviously had access to the condo, but my mobile? That's never out of my sight."

"It's not difficult to bug a mobile, if you have the software and knowledge. The other thing I should tell you is that as long as your phone was turned on, even if you weren't using it for a call, it acted like a microphone and he could listen to every word you said in its vicinity."

Even Tony opened his eyes at that one.

Dan went on to explain how the software program he found buried in my phone's innards basically allowed it to be used as a remote mic.

"And you removed the spyware?" Tony asked.

"Yes. But you need to be vigilant. Even though I put in a program that should help keep your cell bug-free, he can still get at you."

"How?" I asked.

"By finding and removing my protection program. Be very careful to never leave your phone lying around."

"And my computer?"

"All clean, and I've got pretty bombproof software for that. If he adds anything to your computer, it will let us know immediately. By the way, the password for the new software is 'diva.' I'd suggest changing it to something long and complicated and not a real word."

"Thanks for doing this."

Dan smiled, something he did a lot, I was finding. "It's what you're paying us for." He turned his gaze to Tony. "Have you had your equipment checked out yet?"

Tony replied, "I haven't had a chance."

"Do it soon. We need to know how widespread this clown's network is."

"I understand."

Shannon said, "You should know that it's illegal to bug a phone without permission. We could go to the police on this one."

"Would they be able to find the guy?"

Dan shook his head. "Not if I couldn't, and believe me, that's the first thing I tried. The cops' tech guy wouldn't stand a chance. Your stalker is too good."

"If nothing is going to come of it, there's no sense going to the police, then. I don't need that hassle or the risk of it getting out to the media. I've had enough bad press over my personal life."

Shannon nodded. "Then I'm assuming it's okay with you for us to proceed with the course of action Dan has outlined?"

I nodded. We didn't have anything to lose.

⌒

"What should I do?" I tried not making it sound as close to hysterical as I was.

We'd driven directly to Lili's after leaving O'Brien Investigates. The farther the distance, the more upset I'd gotten. And listening to Tony repeating it all to our friend didn't make me feel one iota better.

"I don't even want to go home. I can't believe I let them talk me into leaving all that bugging crap in place."

Tony squeezed my hand. "They know what they're doing, Marta. Try to let it go."

"I can't! When they've checked out where those signals are being sent, I want that stuff out of our condo immediately."

"You could, of course, stay here with me," Lili finally responded. "How many more days before you leave again, my dear?"

"I leave on an evening flight the day after tomorrow."

"Stay here, then. It would not be good to depart for Rome with your head all in a jumble."

"I'm afraid it's going to be that way anyhow. What a frigging mess!"

"Perhaps they will discover the identity of this person before you leave."

I glared at her. "This person is a ghost. He's in and out of my dressing rooms and the condo as if he's made of smoke." I shook my head. "No way they're going to find him that easily. I just know it."

She took a deep breath. "Then I would like you to consider having someone with you at all times."

"That's easy enough around here. Tony's taken the rest week off. But what about Rome and Venice?"

Tony said, "Then I'll go."

"Tony, you can't," I protested. "You're going to take that role you've been offered. I won't let you throw that away."

But I felt as if I'd been thrown a lifeline. The thought of being alone in Rome with this stalker able to stand right next to me without me even being aware of it was giving me the willies. I would be alone far too often. How could I feel safe?

Lili looked at me. "Could I suggest a bodyguard?"

I said, "And how much will that cost?"

She looked wryly at both of us side by side on her sofa: I tended to be more careful with money than Tony, who would spend it on a whim. She answered me. "How much is your peace of mind worth, Marta?"

Stated that way, I couldn't really argue.

"Okay, so we hire a bodyguard. Would they stay with me at night? What's to stop this guy from breaking into my apartment then?"

"Do you think we should be concerned about something like that, Lili?" Tony asked.

She considered for a long moment. "This person seems to have gone to very great trouble and has taken a great risk to do what he has done. That troubles me. But don't you now have enough evidence to take this to the authorities? Surely this kind of spying is very illegal."

"Of course it is, but Marta…. Well, she's reluctant."

Again I got the laser treatment from Lili's eyes. "Maybe it is time to be less reluctant."

"Who do I go to? I have evidence in Toronto, sure. But what about Rome? Then I go to Venice. It would be a jurisdictional nightmare. This whole thing is a nightmare!"

We talked back and forth for several more minutes before deciding to ask Shannon O'Brien what she thought.

Lili had more coachings to do, so we took our leave to go out for a late lunch and make a decision about where to sleep. There was *no way* I was going to spend a night in the condo with those bugs still in place.

Shannon wasn't available when we called, but her secretary said she would pass on our request that she get back to us at her earliest opportunity. I hoped she was out following up where those signals were being broadcast to. That would at least be a step forward in tracking down this bastard.

Probably with a thought at distraction, Tony took me to our favourite restaurant in Woodbridge, the place we'd gone on our first date. Actually, it was our *only* date, really, since we'd fallen in love very quickly. He'd phoned ahead while I hadn't been paying attention, and Gio, the chef and owner, had prepared dishes, all off-menu, that I'd particularly enjoyed on previous visits. Everyone made a big fuss over me and Tony passed it off as if he'd nothing to do with it. Over dessert, Gio took a break from prepping for the dinner hour to sit with us and enjoy a grappa and espresso. We talked about food, opera, everything but my current problems, and for that I was very grateful.

Tony had just started the car when my mobile played its energetic opening theme from *Carmen*.

"Marta? It's Shannon. We need to talk."

Chapter Eight

Dan Hudson waited after the office door had firmly clicked shut behind the opera singer and her husband, and then several additional seconds passed before he spoke.

"Please don't take this as criticism, but why didn't you level with those two?"

Shannon thought for a moment about pretending she didn't know what he was getting at, but decided that wouldn't really serve any purpose.

"Did you notice her eyes?" Shannon held her fingers about an inch apart. "I think our opera singer was that close to losing it. I don't think the truth would have helped her at the moment."

"I thought it might be something like that. But aren't you worried about crawling so far out on that limb?"

"Meaning?"

"This situation could get rapidly out of hand if I'm reading it correctly." He shrugged. "But you have more experience in these things than I do."

"This guy's good. Too good. If I didn't know better, I'd say he's been a spook at some point."

Hudson shook his head. "Not with all the globe-trotting he's done to hand out those posies. The job doesn't work that way. The folks running you want to know where you are all the time." He smiled. "It's nearly impossible to take a leak without them knowing."

"So do you think that makes him dangerous?"

Hudson sighed heavily. "Why does someone go to all the expense and trouble if they don't mean to do something about it? I mean, if I had the hots for someone that bad, I'd send them a bouquet or two and then show up with the third one to profess my love. All this cat and mouse bullshit is sick. Why go to such lengths to stay hidden? What's his game?"

"In my experience, people can do the most jaw-dropping things for little logical reason, especially if they're unstable. Perhaps he's shy, or perhaps he just wants to *really* set the hook before he steps out of the shadows."

"But if he knows as much about her as it seems, surely he knows she's in a happy relationship."

"People with this sort of fetish often don't believe the evidence in front of their eyes."

"But what do *you* think, um, boss?"

Shannon rolled her eyes. "Oh please. Call me Shannon."

"Whatever you say. So what do you think, *Shannon?*"

She was grateful for a bit of banter to give her time to pull her thoughts together. The situation was a hard one to get a handle on. What she needed to do was find someone who'd dealt with a similar situation and pick their brain.

Shannon got to her feet. "I wouldn't want to be in her shoes."

⁓

Hudson's voice crackled over the walkie-talkie. "Where are you?"

"Just going up Church Street. You're on the roof?"

"In position. And it's pretty obvious where this satellite dish is pointed."

"That huge condo tower at the corner of Church and Adelaide?"

"Got it in one, boss … ah, Shannon."

"It was the logical choice based on what you'd told me. The entrance to the building is off Lombard. I'm almost there."

"Good. I'll get out my tools and I should have the exact place pinpointed in a few minutes. What's your plan?"

"Wait to hear from you. Find out which unit it is and then see if I can find out who's up there."

"You're just going to walk in and ask?"

"I've got an angle I can work."

Shannon sounded a lot more confident than she felt. To be truthful, Hudson had credentials out the wazoo, and she felt she needed to appear every bit as good as he. He'd more than likely thoroughly vetted her, as well as her business, before applying for the job. It was a matter of pride to her that he not think he'd made a mistake. Today, it was important to come home a winner. Just how to do that was more up to chance than she would have liked.

If she found just a security guard at the desk, she might be able to bulldoze him. If there was a building manager around, it would get a lot more tricky.

She had a bit of luck and nipped into a vacant parking space on Lombard just as someone pulled out. Over at the entrance to the building with the la-di-da name of "Spire," someone had parked a tradesman's van. It blocked her view into the lobby.

"I'm heading for the building entrance now," she said into the walkie-talkie. "I need to know the floor and window."

"Okay. If it's one of those buildings without a thirteenth floor, then you're looking at thirty-three, third unit in from the west end of the building. At least I think it's the third unit. It's hard to tell from this angle."

"Give me the window. That might help."

"It's the ... eighth window. There's a pretty bad glare from the glass, so I can't see anything inside."

"Okay, Dan. I'm going to sign off. Using a walkie-talkie as I come through the door isn't going to help. I'll call back as soon as I'm out again. Stay in position. Okay?"

"You got it. Except make it snappy. It's damn cold up here."

"That'll keep people off the roof and asking you questions," Shannon answered, then slipped the walkie-talkie into her purse as she entered the building.

True to the design ethic currently in vogue, the lobby was elegant but sterile due to lots of stone and very little decoration or colour. The grey granite security desk was off to one side, a young female guard dressed in business attire behind it. As an attempt at putting a more welcoming look on the place, it didn't really work.

Walking up to the desk, Shannon's brain was going a mile a minute. If she didn't get the information now, things would become more complicated and take time she didn't have. But having a female behind the desk might work in her favour. Her name tag said "N. Richmond."

"Excuse me, Ms. Richmond," she said to the guard. "I'm hoping that you can help me with something."

At least Richmond didn't roll her eyes, but the rest of her face told the story: she already thought the lady in front of her was going to prove to be a pain in the ass.

"What can I do for you?"

"Do you have a thirteenth floor in this building?"

"Ma'am?"

"Does this building have a thirteenth floor or does it go from twelve to fourteen?"

"Why would you want to know something like that?"

Shannon reached into her purse and pulled out her private investigator ID, flipping it open and slapping it onto the polished granite. "I'm interested in someone who lives in an apartment on either the thirty-second or thirty-third floor of this building."

The guard took her ID and examined it. "You're just a PI. Why should I tell you anything?"

Shannon leaned over the desk to be closer to her face. "Because I have a client who is being spied on by someone in this building. I came over to give whoever it is a warning, everything nice and friendly. If you don't want to play ball, then I'll advise my client to take this to the cops, file a formal complaint."

"So?"

"I'll also go to a contact I have at the *Toronto Star* who will be very interested in how high-rise condominiums are giving more opportunities to peeping toms in our city. She'll have no compunctions about naming a building where this is happening." As the guard's brow furrowed, Shannon pressed her point. "I have two photos of this person standing at a telescope on his balcony, and it's obvious he ain't looking at the stars. I also have some of the photos he mailed to my client of her prancing around her apartment in the buff."

"I don't think that's information I can just hand out."

Shannon flashed her best smile. "Now come on, can't you help out a fellow working girl? I'm trying to do my job, and you're trying to do yours, and this guy is a complete scuzzbucket. Would you want someone like that looking at you and drooling? I sure wouldn't. All I need to know is the name of the person who's in the third apartment in from the west end of this building, south side, thirty-third floor — assuming the floor numbering in this building is consecutive and you don't have a thirteenth floor."

For a moment, Shannon thought the guard was going to pick up the phone and talk to someone higher up the food chain. If her hands weren't already in plain sight, she would have crossed her fingers.

The guard made an effort to stall as two young, good-looking men exited one of the building's elevators and crossed the lobby. "Good afternoon, Mr. Blair, Mr. Gluch. I hope you're having a good day."

The bearded one smiled, but that was all the response she got as they left.

Shannon said, "Nice place to work if you get to look at that all day."

The guard sighed. "I might as well not be here for all the attention the tenants pay me — except when they want something."

"May I have what I need, please? I'm not asking that much."

She stifled a triumphant smile as the security guard pulled her computer's keyboard a bit closer. "Thirty-third floor, you say, fourth unit in from the west?"

"No. *Third* unit or eighth window, whichever unit that is. My surveillance photos show this clown was in front of the eighth window with his telescope."

The guard tapped away at the keys for a few seconds, frowned, and then tapped some more. "That's funny." More tapping of keys.

Shannon decided to rest on her forearms, but couldn't see the computer monitor any better. *Just a bit longer and I may just get what I want,* she thought. She knew that an interruption now would probably queer the deal. "What have you got?" she asked.

"According to what I'm seeing here, although someone owns it, the unit has never been occupied.

It's on our watch list to make sure there's no monkey business, but the last time someone checked it —"

"When was that?" Shannon asked.

"About a month ago — and the place was empty." The guard looked up. "You're certain you gave me the correct unit?"

"Positive."

"Well, there shouldn't have been anyone there."

"Could we go up and take a look?"

"I don't know…."

Shannon stood up. "Well, my client is going to want me to check further. The building's manager is going to want that unit checked out. Why not do it now? See if there's someone there who shouldn't be." The guard continued staring at the screen, clearly undecided. "C'mon. Let's go up."

"I shouldn't leave the desk."

"It will only take five minutes, tops."

And that's how Shannon found herself ascending in a high-speed elevator, feeling pretty good about her powers of persuasion.

They walked down the hall of the thirty-third floor. Once there, Shannon knocked on the door. Nothing happened. Shannon knocked again. No answer.

"Just open the door and we can peek inside. If someone is squatting, we'll be able to tell pretty quickly. The cops can take it from there. And don't worry. I used to be a cop myself."

The guard, with a tight expression, stuck the key in the lock and pressed down the door handle.

The place was empty. When the guard said, "See?

No one is here," Shannon just pushed past and walked into what would be the living room. A thin coat of dust covered the floor, but over toward the window was a mark where something had been placed. A box maybe?

"You shouldn't be in there!" the guard said from the doorway. "Please come out."

Since there wasn't much more for Shannon to see, she turned and walked back, but faintly in the dust on the floor, she could see that someone else had also recently done the same.

The bird had flown.

As she left the building Shannon took out her cell phone and dialed her client, knowing that so far the performance of O'Brien Investigates had been less than stellar.

⌒

After a hastily convened and very uncomfortable meeting with their client in her SUV parked on Front Street, Shannon and Dan spent the next four hours clearing the bugs from Marta and Tony's condo. The satellite dish was also removed from the roof.

Neither was in a very talkative mood since each knew they'd blown a golden opportunity.

Going over the apartment again in minute detail, they found three cameras, one of which hadn't been spotted in their previous sweep. It was in the bathroom's exhaust fan. Shannon suggested they keep this knowledge to themselves since the client was already upset enough.

They installed one thing: a high-end miniature camera attached to a motion detector watching over the condo's front door. Anyone entering would be recorded. The next morning a locksmith would be installing a door lock with a special magnetic laser-cut key that was guaranteed to be unpickable. The cost was pretty eye-popping, but Marta hadn't even blinked before writing out the cheque.

When she and her husband had returned just after nine thirty, Marta seemed a little tight, speaking loudly and gesticulating as she thanked Dan and Shannon for their hard work. Shannon couldn't blame her. This whole situation was a getting more concerning the deeper they delved into it.

Marta was sitting on the sofa with Tony. "My husband and I, and a good friend we told what's happening, well, we all think I need to hire a bodyguard. I'm going to be in Rome and Venice for the next few weeks and Tony can't come with me."

Tony patted her hand fondly. "We all want Marta to be safe. Now that we know how serious the situation is, we would feel better if she had someone accompanying her. Can you suggest how we should go about that?"

Dan looked at Shannon. They'd been discussing just that thing a few minutes before the clients had returned home.

Shannon had an answer ready. "I agree that it's a good idea. Based on all we've found so far, we have to believe this guy definitely poses a danger. It's obvious he knew exactly what we were up to, not that we made it difficult for him. I seriously underestimated what we were up against, and for that I'm profoundly sorry." She shook her head. "It's real embarrassing. I'd hoped we'd do better for you."

Tony spoke up. "Do you think you'll be able to find out who owns that condo in the other building?"

"We'll try, but it will take time and my guess is that it may ultimately prove futile. The one thing we all should take away from what we've learned so far is that our adversary is determined, well-equipped, and smart. So getting back to what we're ultimately talking about, yes, it would be wise to have a full-time bodyguard — until we run this joker down."

"Can you find someone for us?" Marta asked.

"I have an excellent operative, a woman who's worked for me for the past few years. Jackie Goode is a real bulldog and smart. Only problem is, she's out on the west coast at the moment, working for a colleague, and I don't think I can pull her off that assignment."

"No one else?"

"Not who's female. I can ask around, though. I should be able to find someone."

"I leave in two days."

Hudson finally spoke up. "Shannon, could we speak in the other room?"

To raised eyebrows from the husband and wife, they left the room.

In the spare room, once he'd closed the door, Hudson said, "I'd like to take this on."

"I thought you'd gotten sick of travelling and wanted to stay put for awhile."

"This has me *really* bugged. This guy has made fools of us … of me."

"Dan, I appreciate the way you feel. He's made me look pretty dumb around an important client, but we can't afford to let things get personal. You know that."

"True, but something tells me you need someone who can level the playing field a bit. I have training that probably all of your people lack, and I have access to equipment that I think is going to be needed. I've worked in Italy a few times. I have connections."

Shannon considered it for a moment. "I don't think you're wrong, but having you stay in such close proximity to his wife may be a hard sell to the husband."

Hudson smiled mischievously. "I promise I'll be a well-behaved employee. Opera singers aren't my type."

"Let's be serious. I don't want to screw this up any further." She pursed her lips. "Okay. I agree you would be the best person for the job, taking everything into consideration, but I don't want to walk back in and say that. I'd like to take a little more time and not rush into it. We also have to talk money here, too. Anyway, if I *do* decide to move in this direction and the client agrees, could you be ready to depart with her?"

Hudson answered, his expression deadly serious, "Yes. And I will do my utmost to protect this woman. You can count on me."

Chapter Nine

I simply could not stay in our condo.

Once we had that fancy new lock on the door I *might* feel differently, but knowing someone had watched Tony's and my most intimate moments left me feeling violated and horribly depressed. Certainly I would not have been able to sleep there that night, super-lock or no, waking at the slightest noise. It was an easy decision, and I distinctly got the feeling Tony was relieved about it.

Even though Lili had generously offered us the use of her guest room, Tony and I felt we would be better off on our own.

With a quick call to the Royal York, we secured a room. I looked forward to putting this whole sordid mess out of my mind while enjoying the company of my husband. We could visit the art gallery, maybe catch a couple of movies or see a play. I didn't really care. I just wanted something to occupy my mind.

⌒

Late the next morning, we spoke to Shannon. The ownership of the condo where the signals from the bugs had been bounced to had been traced to a numbered company in Hong Kong, and would most likely prove to be a dead end. She was still considering who to send with me to Italy. My thought was that I didn't care as long as they could do what was necessary to protect me. I detest every kind of firearm, but someone guarding me with a nice big gun was sounding more attractive by the hour.

"I would feel a lot better if I knew we had this all settled," I told her.

"Would you two be okay if Dan did the honours?"

"Certainly, but can you spare him?"

"He's already volunteered for the job."

"Is there time to get him a ticket? Where will he stay? The apartment I have rented has only one bedroom."

"Give me the phone number of the person you're renting from. We'll take care of the logistics. Don't worry about anything."

Tony and I spent a lovely Friday just bumming around the city. The evening saw us watching a brainless shoot-em-up action movie followed by a nightcap in our hotel's atmospheric Library Bar.

After a long morning sog in bed, we got up around noon and decided to go back to the condo so I could get ready for my return to Rome. I needed to be at the airport by four o'clock.

All was clear at our place, but I made Tony check the video record to make sure.

It felt like coming home after a very long trip.

"How long will it take you to pack?" Tony asked as he dropped our two overnight bags at the door.

"Probably an hour, maybe a bit more. I need to wash a few things since that didn't get done earlier."

"I need to go over to the Market before it closes to get some food for next week. Is there anything I can pick up for you?"

"Not really," I answered distractedly since I was already focused on the task at hand. "No, wait. Could you get a bottle of maple syrup from that guy who's out front of the North Market? I told my landlord in Rome I would bring him some."

"I shouldn't be gone more than about twenty minutes, thirty max. Will you be all right?"

I gave him a peck on the cheek. "I'll be fine, but I will put the security chain on. Just ring when you get back."

The place was now clear of all that electronic crap, but I could nonetheless feel the ghost of that other presence. It crossed my mind that once we got things straightened out, I'd probably want to move. I loved my condo, and Tony had fit into life there just fine, but now it felt, I don't know, ruined for me, like I didn't belong there anymore. That thought filled me with sadness, but also anger. What had I done to deserve this?

I had our small washing machine chugging away and the other clothes I'd be taking spread out on the bed when the doorbell rang.

"Coming!" I called out as I walked to the door.

Normally, I just throw open the door, but this time I looked through the peephole. Tony was indeed standing there, grocery bags dangling from his hands, but he was looking down, a strange expression on his face.

Not suspecting anything, I took off the chain and unlocked the door. Tony's stricken eyes came up to meet mine.

"Oh, Marta…."

I looked down and felt the bile rise in my throat as panic gripped me.

There on the doorstep were two red long-stemmed roses. Both of them had their blossoms nearly broken off. It looked as if one of them had also been stepped on.

✎

As the big airplane began its rapid ascent out of Toronto, I could feel the pounding in my heart begin to ease. Thank the Lord for Tony because I'd completely lost it after finding those flowers right in front of our apartment door.

The room had been spinning as Tony pulled out a dining room chair and got me to sit with my head down.

Kneeling next to me, he kept saying over and over, "Marta, it will be all right." He sounded as frightened as I felt.

Getting out to the airport and onto the plane had all been a bit of a blur. Tony packed my clothes and bundled me into the car. At the check-in, he told them

I wasn't feeling well. An airline rep got me through security in record time and into the VIP lounge where I had a stiff drink. I couldn't stop shaking.

When I entered the plane, I found I was now in the first class cabin. Whether Tony was responsible for this or the airline, I was grateful since I find sleeping on airplanes difficult, even in business class. As the rest of the plane boarded, I asked for a sleeping mask and managed to nod off, only waking up when an attendant came by to remind me to buckle up.

This latest reminder of just how closely this bastard was keeping tabs on me had me more frightened than I've ever been. Even though I tried to put it out of my mind, I couldn't help thinking that this monster must have been following us to be able to respond so quickly after Tony and I returned to the condo. The fact that I'd been alone when he left his awful roses made it clear just how vulnerable I was.

Tony must have spoken to Shannon after he dropped me at the airport, because on my arrival at Leonardo da Vinci airport in Rome, there was an airline representative at the gate who escorted me to the VIP lounge to wait for Dan's arrival on a later flight. Even though it meant I would have to hang around for several hours, I wasn't about to complain. The last thing I wanted was to be alone — anywhere.

For once, two flights in one day landed right on time. I breathed a sigh of relief when my cell phone chirped and I heard Dan's voice, telling me he was just waiting for his luggage at the baggage carousel.

"Everything okay?" he asked.

"Um, yes. Sure. Just fine."

"It might take me a bit of time to get through customs and immigration, because I packed a few extra electronic toys just before the flight. Considering what happened, I wanted them with me now rather than waiting for them to be shipped in tomorrow as I'd originally planned. I know customs will be asking questions, so hang tight. I'll be there as soon as possible."

"What else is going on? I called Tony as soon as I landed, but he couldn't tell me much."

"Shannon contacted the police and she's bringing them up to speed."

I sat up straight. "They're not going to blab something to the press, are they?"

Dan's tone was calming. "No, no. She stressed to them that this must all be as discreet as possible. Don't worry. Shannon still has excellent connections within the Toronto police."

"And Tony? He's okay? I was thinking on the flight over that he could become a target."

"Your friend Ms. Doubek —"

"Lili.

"All right, Lili, then. She doesn't think that's much of a problem, but it is something to keep in mind. I promise to pass it on to Shannon if it will ease your mind. The luggage carousel just started up. I'll be with you as soon as I can."

I waited another forty minutes before Dan showed up.

"All set?" he asked.

Getting to my feet, I stretched my back carefully. It was a mass of kinks. "Let's go."

Dan had obviously been through da Vinci airport before because he got us to the taxi rank by a shorter route than the one I'd used the previous month. As we threaded our way through the crowds the airport always seems to have, he gave me a complete update on how things stood at the moment.

"I only had a bit of a hassle at customs. Most of the equipment I brought either wasn't a problem for them, cameras and the like, or it looks like something else."

"Sounds like I'm in a spy novel."

He flashed that big, sort of goofy smile. "Relax. I'm a professional. It's not as if I haven't done something like this before."

Since it was midday, traffic into Rome wasn't too horrible, and we seemed to have gotten a competent driver who didn't risk his life and ours more than once a minute.

Italian drivers make me nervous. Multiply that by a factor of ten for Roman drivers — and cabbies are the worst of all. Normally, I shut my eyes and pray whenever I'm in a taxi in the Eternal City.

It was a lovely January day, bright sun with a bit of warmth — unlike what I'd left behind in Toronto where a blizzard was imminent. The change in weather and location had my spirits on the ascent.

The apartment I'd rented was on a small side street, Via Flavia, a brisk fifteen-minute walk from the opera house. On days when it wasn't raining (January is notoriously wet in Rome) or too cold (by Roman standards), I'd enjoyed stretching my legs by walking to work.

"I don't know if you'll be doing that much, unless I'm with you," Dan said after letting me rattle on about Rome for about ten minutes.

That brought me back down to earth with an almighty thud.

"Aren't you going to be with me all the time?"

I said it partly in jest, but also keenly aware once more that we had no idea what my stalker had in mind for his next move. None of us were under the illusion he might think things were getting too hot for him and back off. Those two roses at my door the previous day certainly made that clear.

He'd be back, of that I was certain. He may well have been right behind me as I'd boarded the plane. Until someone could put a name or at least a face to this bastard, I would not feel safe.

The closer we got to our destination, the chattier our driver became. It was obvious Dan spoke little or no Italian, so a lively three-way conversation began with me in the middle providing translation.

Seemed as if the Italians were up in arms again about how their government was handling the current economic situation. Food prices were going up. Gasoline was going up. The cost of vino was going up! It was all a national disgrace. There was talk of a general strike. In other words, life was going on as it generally does in Italy.

Dan's amusement seemed to rise as our driver's volume increased. I just hoped the labour troubles wouldn't disrupt the remaining performances of *Tosca*. It was already disorienting enough to be doing this split run due to that special broadcast performance of *Trovatore* over the past weekend.

But I couldn't get too mad because I'd be doing one of those the following week from La Fenice in Venice. I would sing Violetta once again in *La Traviata* in the same house where the opera had been premiered in 1853. The part being glossed over was that the opera was a failure its inaugural run. Hopefully the performance I would be involved in would be anything but.

The really odd thing was that I'd been chosen for the principal role in the first place. There was no lack of good Violettas in Europe at the moment. My manager thought it was because they wanted some "local representation" for North American audiences. Tony thought it was because I still had the whiff of scandal clinging to me after being involved in that restaurant bombing in Paris. Heaven knows, the Europeans love a good scandal.

Whatever the reason, I wasn't complaining. The broadcast audience would be huge, worldwide — and huge is always good.

To me, Rome has always seemed more alive than any other city I've visited. If New York is the city that never sleeps, Rome is the city that never stops. In fact, it never seems to even slow down.

Drivers (as ably demonstrated by our cabby) are absolutely fearless, even those on scooters — of which there are uncounted thousands, racing down streets at terrifying speeds — and are made of sterner stuff than I or else completely insane, likely both.

"How well do you know the city?" I asked Dan during a lull in our driver's monologue.

"Not very. I've only been here a handful of times and never for long. You?"

"This is my second gig here. I passed through with my folks on a summer vacation when I was sixteen. I also lived here for nearly four months with my mentor while he was involved in premiering his new production of *Semiramide*."

"Do you like it?"

"Very much."

"Big history buff?"

"Certainly there's that. The Romans and the history of the Catholic church are on practically every street corner. You can never forget you're in one of the oldest cities in the world."

"And one of the greatest!" our driver said, simultaneously proving he spoke English quite well and had been listening closely to what we'd been saying.

By that point we were navigating our way along Via Flavia, the narrow side street behind Via XX Settembre.

My rented apartment was on the fourth storey of a building that had a small hotel on the first three floors. Reached by a rather rickety elevator squeezed into the middle of the stairwell long after the construction of the building, Dan had to pack his two bags on top of each other in order to fit everything in.

"Must be a wonderful ride when someone's reeking of garlic," Dan commented as the elevator door slid shut behind us.

The elevator let out its usual groans as it ascended and I sent out a silent prayer for it to get all the way to the top without mishap. Normally I use the stairs because I didn't trust the contraption. It seemed to be out of service a couple of times every week.

I'd forgotten to tell Dan that the door behind him was the way out, so it took some juggling of suitcases for him to be able to open it, allowing us to extract ourselves.

"Which place is yours?" he asked.

"It's the door on the right just ahead there."

We wrestled our bags up two more steps. Actually, I wrestled and Dan lifted his two up as if they didn't weigh a thing.

"Nice place," Dan said as he set his bags down once I'd opened the door.

It was a very nice apartment, airy, surprisingly spacious, and very Italian. Marco, the owner, had it decorated using the exquisite taste that many in this beautiful country seem to possess right from the cradle. He rented to a lot of singers performing at the opera house because he had the good business sense to also equip it with a serviceable piano.

"What's my place like?"

"I only stuck my head in the door once when it was open, but it seemed nice."

Surprisingly, the one-room apartment across the hall was available for the duration of our stay. I had the suspicion my landlord had done a bit of string-pulling to make it work for me. Occasionally it helps to be a somebody, I guess.

By the time I got back from moving my suitcase to the bedroom, Dan had the heavier of his two bags open and was removing a couple of small boxes. He went over to the dining area to open them on the table.

First out was a small gadget, the shape and size of an MP3 player. In its centre was a bright red button.

"Panic button. For any reason, you press it, and I'll be in this apartment in a flash." He continued taking things out. "We'll have an alarm for the front door. Don't worry, if anyone opens it, there will be a ding-dong sound like the sort of thing you hear in a shop. We'll also set up this video camera to keep watch when you're out."

"Aren't you going to monitor the windows, too?"

I'd meant it as a joke, but Dan took me seriously. "Good point. Someone agile might be able to get in from the roof. I'll have something shipped over."

I needed a bit of a pick-me-up after the long flight, so I made a couple of double espressos for us while Dan went about his business.

Marco bustled in a bit later. Dan's digs were pretty basic, but clean and tidy. He also had a small rooftop terrazza. Too bad it was January.

I treated Dan to dinner since there was nothing to eat in either apartment and no urge from either of us to get supplies at one of the small shops nearby. There was a good restaurant across the street where we could have eaten outside had the weather been more hospitable. It served terrific pasta, and I indulged that night as a treat after the long flight.

Over dinner we discussed how things would work. We'd already decided with Shannon that Dan would pose as a ghost writer working with me on my autobiography, making it easier for him to hang around without too many questions being asked. I'd already arranged for him to have tickets for the two performances I still had to do.

Knowing that I had big, strong Dan around to keep watch for any low-flying stalkers, I was feeling more relaxed than I had in days.

"Have you ever been to the opera?" I asked.

Dan stopped with a forkful of spaghetti halfway to his mouth. "Actually, no."

"Do you know what opera I'm performing in?"

He nodded, and once he'd swallowed, answered, "Now that I looked it up. It's *Tosca*."

"Know what it's about?"

He grinned sheepishly. "Didn't get that far."

It wasn't surprising. A big macho guy like Dan Hudson probably did sports through high school and university. Heck, I really didn't pay much heed to the opera world until I began singing seriously, and that was not until I was well into university. Even though I now found the subject of opera endlessly fascinating, there was a time where it skimmed right by me, barely registering on my radar.

I'm a firm believer in people knowing an opera's plot and characters beforehand, otherwise they're often unclear as to what's going on and why. So I spent the rest of the meal telling Dan about Floria Tosca and the two men who desired her: Mario Cavaradossi and the detestable Baron Scarpia. The fact that the action is set in real places still existing in Rome and that he'd even visited one of them (the Castel Sant'Angelo) seemed to capture Dan's attention. If he was bored by my chatter, he hid it well.

"And what about this new opera you're doing when you get back to Toronto?" he asked. "The article I read says it's about a woman who died alone in an apartment and her body wasn't found for nearly three years. That doesn't sound particularly romantic or exciting."

"On the surface, it's not, but the composer and librettist have made it interesting, almost engrossing, by giving this woman's back story, starting when she is twelve. Basically, Naomi is a gentle spirit, incredibly naive and trusting, who doesn't 'get it' when those around her take advantage, and in many ways, terrorize her. As the abuse mounts up she withdraws more and more until in middle age she's living alone in a subsidized apartment. The final act is where she's slowly dying, more or less from neglect — her own and others — and fills her days with hallucinations of her 'torturers,' as she calls them."

"But she dies and no one finds her for three years? That's ridiculous."

I shrugged. "Actually, that part of the story is true. It happened in England as few years ago."

"You're kidding."

"I wish I were, but it is true. The music and libretto of *The Passage of Time* are very powerful and I think it's going to be a compelling production. I only wish I could spend more time learning my part. With this mess in my current life, that's more difficult than ever. I'm hoping to be able to put in some hours on it this week."

"I think I'd like to get a ticket for it."

"Better get one soon. All the press and the rock star status of Andrew McCutcheon, the composer, is making a ticket the hot item in the opera world."

Even though I was exhausted, I wanted to go upstairs to exercise my vocal chords a bit, even if it meant singing into a towel so I wouldn't disturb my neighbours at that late hour (a trick I'd learned from a friend whose husband calls it a "singer mute"). I'd barely sung while I was in Toronto, and the role of Tosca is no walk in the park.

I didn't vocalize all that long, more because it's no fun to sing into a towel (difficult too). I just needed to get things a bit loose and warmed up for the next morning when it would be back to work for me.

Before hitting the sack shortly after eight, having been up for close to thirty-one hours by that point, I gave Tony a good night call. Nothing was up in T.O. and he hadn't heard from Shannon since we'd last spoken.

He wished me pleasant dreams and to keep safe. I told him that with Dan on the job, I'd be fine.

As I was drifting off, I realized that probably wasn't the smartest way to put it.

Chapter Ten

There was a meeting and walk-through rehearsal at the opera house the next morning, more to get everyone back into the head space needed for the performance the next evening than to actually work on anything. I felt pretty certain Davide, our assistant director, a fussy little man who obviously thought a lot of himself, would want to give us notes from the previous performance a week earlier — the one where I hadn't sung well.

While I was certainly eager to get back to doing what I enjoy best, the feeling was tempered by the knowledge that I'd have to be around Arturo De Vicenzo, who was singing the role of Scarpia. If

Tosca disliked the wretched Baron in the opera, this soprano disliked the baritone handling the role in our production nearly as much. We'd already had two run-ins, but that was nothing out of the ordinary for him. He'd been unpleasant to nearly everyone in the cast and crew by then. The director of the chorus wasn't speaking to him anymore, the conductor had a scowl on his face anytime De Vicenzo was singing, and I was having a hard time not cringing in the second act whenever he had to touch me. Since Tosca the character is supposed to feel this way, I'd actually received a glowing mention about my acting during this critical scene in a review from Rome's biggest paper, pretty amusing if you knew the situation — which the rest of the cast did.

Problem was, De Vicenzo was a damned fine Scarpia — even if he didn't have to act very much to handle the role. He was also a letch of the first order, and more than a few times I'd grabbed his hands to stop them from roaming a little too freely. I didn't think he'd actually grope me in the middle of a performance or rehearsal, not with everyone watching, but he certainly had pushed the boundaries. And I did not like him getting up close and personal behind me.

We'd be working with a just piano that morning, but Tomasso Giorgi, our wonderful conductor, was present, and as expected we received copious notes from Davide. He still didn't like the way I leaped from the battlements of Castel Sant'Angelo in the dying moments of the opera. In explaining things to him, my Italian vocab was stretched to the limit.

"Look, if I just fling myself the way you want, I'll probably kill myself for real. Tosca isn't trying out for a spot on the Olympic diving team."

The little maggot just snorted. "It must seem real! The way you do it does not seem real to me."

De Vicenzo looked up from his smartphone where he'd been annoyingly tapping out texts nearly the entire time, pointedly ignoring what was going on. "It might give the audience more for their money, especially after the way you sang in the last performance."

With a sneer, De Vicenzo put a thumb to his mouth and tilted his head back in the universal sign for drinking. It was a completely outrageous thing to do. Everyone on or near the stage stopped moving. I was absolutely speechless with fury. If he hadn't been on the other side of the very large stage, I would have marched right over and given his face a resounding slap. Hell, I *should* have slapped him even if it meant walking across all of Rome!

But knowledge that what he said was partially accurate kept me rooted to the floor. True, I hadn't been at my vocal best because of that damned late party the night before, and I had to wing a couple of lines because of an inexcusable mental lapse and not being able to see the prompter without being incredibly obvious, but De Vicenzo's remark was certainly uncalled for — nor was it politic.

Giorgi went over, pulled the baritone offstage, and it wasn't long before they were shouting at each other.

Javier Ramírez, the tenor singing Tosca's lover Cavaradossi, eased in next to me. "He can be such an ass," he said in English. "De Vicenzo *always* goes after cast members who get better reviews. He is an extremely jealous man. I would watch yourself, my dear."

The rehearsal pretty well collapsed after that. De Vicenzo marched out of the opera house in high dudgeon. When the general manager rushed onstage to find out what the hell was going on, Giorgi only looked partly contrite as he filled in the boss, giving me a sly wink when the GM wasn't looking.

Since the weather was rather nice, I'd walked over from the apartment, keeping a brisk pace as Dan followed discreetly about ten feet behind, close enough to be able to instantly help if there was a problem, but far enough to make it seem we were not together. With the rehearsal closed, I'd left him outside the stage door. He said he'd hang around nearby until we were done. Since festivities at the theatre were most definitely over for the day, I could get an early start with my practice session at the studio of the vocal coach I was working with during my stay, something that went back to my days with Gerhard. A phone call fixed that up. Since Giovanni was well on in years, he didn't coach much anymore.

Dan was the next call. "Rehearsal got knocked into a cocked hat. I'm done."

"Have anything to do with the guy who stormed out the stage door fifteen minutes ago?"

"Did he have a brown fedora jammed on his head and an overcoat over his shoulders?"

"That's the one. What happened? His expression could have curdled milk at fifty paces."

I laughed at Dan's description. "I'll tell you about it while we're travelling to my coach's apartment."

"Do we have time for a bite? I'm starving."

"You can eat during my coaching if you want. I can't eat right before I sing."

"Perhaps I can grab a little something on the way, then."

"There are shops on the north side of the Piazza della Repubblica. You can pick up something there before we get on the Metro and cross the Tiber to Trastevere, where Giuseppe Grimaldi lives."

⁓

It was my first opportunity to introduce Dan as my ghost writer, and Peppe wanted to ask him all kinds of questions about getting published since, of course, he'd produced a manuscript of his life's story. Doesn't everybody these days?

Dan did his best to deflect since he knew absolutely nothing about book publishing, and I did my best to move Peppe along to the piano so we could get started.

Because Peppe specialized in contemporary opera, we'd been working on *The Passage of Time*. So we started with that. I'd gotten really good insight into how some of the trickier passages worked with the orchestra, so I now knew where I could hold back and where I needed to sing at top volume, really important information to help me pace myself.

But with a week away from performing and almost no chance to practise in Toronto, I wanted to shake the rust off *Tosca* and get my voice honed to razor sharpness for the following evening. After that crack from De Vicenzo, I *had* to be nothing less than perfect. Javier told me the remaining performances were all sellouts — mostly on the strength of the reviews complimenting what I had done. He was such a generous man and I wished he could pass some of that generosity on to De Vicenzo, whom, incidentally, the reviewer had remarked sang with "his usual competence."

Still upset by the confrontation, Peppe asked me what the problem was. So I told him. He was suitably scandalized, more because he likes me a lot and our relationship goes back so far. He made it clear that he thought De Vicenzo a first class shit, while equally praising his musicality and vocal prowess, which made me smile at his correctness. With Dan sitting there, I was more forthcoming about the way I felt since we were speaking Italian throughout the coaching. Even though my bodyguard and I were becoming friends, you never knew when someone's going to speak out of turn.

Through the warm-ups, which we took slow and easy, and into the first arias I sang, I was holding back until my voice felt supple and comfortable. As expected, Peppe, with his encyclopedic knowledge of Italian opera, had very enlightening comments about some details in the way I was singing various passages.

"You are giving too much too early, Marta!" he said after I finished "*Non la sospiri*" from act 1. "Hold back. Less at the beginning means that more at the end will have greater effect! Dole out the emotion with a very small hand."

Toward the end of the session, we moved to *Traviata* since I wanted to warm up a few key arias and feel like I was truly ready to hit the stage in Venice the following week.

I finished with "*Vissi d'arte*" from *Tosca*, singing full voice and finally feeling whole again after my trying week in Toronto. It is one of my favourite arias in the repertoire, rich with emotion, and for many, it really is the high point of this fantastic opera. Peppe followed me beautifully on the piano, making it easy to add as much expression as I desired.

On the way back to our digs, Dan had a pensive look on his face.

"Penny for your thoughts?" I asked.

"You certainly can sing loud," he responded after a moment.

"It takes a lot to fill an opera house with sound, especially when there's a big orchestra with good parts to play. I've been blessed with a big voice." I grinned at him. "Hope I didn't hurt your ears."

"No, no, it was fine. Honest. It just sort of overwhelmed me, that's all. I've never heard an opera singer up close and personal before. What were you singing about? It sounded so beautiful and so sad."

"That last aria was from *Tosca*. It's called '*Vissi d'arte*' and Tosca just agreed to give herself to the wicked Baron Scarpia in exchange for her lover's life. The words tell how she's given all of her life to her art — she's a singer, you know — and honoured God with her prayers. Lived a good life. Now she feels abandoned and alone and is asking why God is treating her this way. It's heartbreaking, really, when you think about it. The entire opera is completely tragic. Everyone dies by the end. I love performing in it."

Dan was silent then for another long span, before he answered. "I think I may be getting it."

I liked the streets around Via Flavia because it felt like a neighbourhood, as if I was actually living there and not just visiting. All the shopkeepers greeted me loudly whenever I came in (partially a by-product of who I was). There was a fruttivendolo who always steered me to his best vegetables and perfectly ripe fruits, another shop where I could buy fantastic meat, cheese, and pasta, an artisanal gelateria that I tried to forget existed, great restaurants, and a café I adored. All were within a five-minute walk of my apartment.

I dragged Dan into several shops so I could restock my larder and stock his, although he said he wasn't much of a cook. Of course, I let myself be tempted by a few bottles of wine the shopkeepers just *had* to show me. We were pretty burdened with bags as we continued down the street to our building.

I told Dan I'd make him a dinner in repayment for his pack animal duties.

While I was busy in the kitchen putting things away and making a meal of soup, salad, and a bit of cheese with bread, he was in the living room checking the small surveillance camera he'd secreted in a bookcase opposite the apartment's entrance.

Feeling eyes on me, I turned to find him leaning against the kitchen doorway.

"All clear?" I asked.

"Yup. Nothing to show for our time away."

"Maybe your finding his stuff in Toronto spooked the guy."

"Oh, he's still around. You can bet on that."

"Thanks for reassuring me," I responded unhappily.

"Marta … may I call you Marta?"

"Please do."

"If there's anything I've learned over the years, it's to plan for the worst and hope for the best."

"Sounds like words to live by."

He nodded. "In this case, yes."

I spent a quiet rest of that day marshalling my resources for the performance the following evening. Tony called (lunchtime for him) with nothing much to report except for missing me extraordinarily.

"Shannon is working with the police, trying to trace the owner of the apartment where those signals were being broadcast to. I had to file an official complaint with the police. She's of the mind that your stalker may be local, and that, oddly, will make it harder to track him down. They're probably going to have to bring the RCMP in because the situation is international. Interpol, too."

"Do you think that's wise? The more people who know about this, the more likely word will slip out."

"I don't think we have any choice. Lili agrees with me. I have stressed and Shannon has stressed to the cops that we *really* want to keep this out of the public eye."

"I don't know if I'm a particular favourite with the Mounties after what happened in Paris."

"They'll get over it." Then the conversation switched to more mundane topics. "How did rehearsal go?"

"Not well. Arturo De Vicenzo pretty well accused me of ruining the last performance before the break by drinking."

"*What?*"

"Well, that's sort of the way it came out."

Tony laughed. "You didn't deck him did you?"

"I certainly felt like it. Giorgi jumped to my defense and De Vicenzo stomped out. End of rehearsal."

"Sounds exciting."

"More excitement is just what I *don't* need at the moment."

"I don't get it. Why do they continue to hire this guy if he's so obnoxious?"

"Because he does Scarpia like no one else. He's utterly diabolical and very believable."

"Typecasting?"

"Oh, Tony, love, you do make me laugh."

"Just forget about him. Three more performances then you're out of there, and hopefully you'll never have to work with him again."

"One can hope."

I'd had a glass of wine with dinner so I curled up with a novel I'd picked up in the airport back in Canada to enjoy a second. Dan knocked on the door about nine, saying he was bored, and checked once again that all his gadgets were operational. We even tested how fast he could get to the apartment if the alarm went off. Even from his bed, he could manage it in under ten seconds. I told him to make sure he had his pajama bottoms on.

"Why would you think I sleep naked?"

"I thought all spies do."

"Only in the movies."

"So you don't?"

"Modesty prevents me saying."

At the apartment door, I told him I was hitting the hay early so I'd be well-rested for the next evening. "I don't plan on getting up before ten. Hopefully you won't hear from me until then."

And I was as good as my word.

$$\sim$$

It's easy to get caught up in the backstage excitement of an opera house on the night of a performance. Everybody is racing around making sure all is ready when the maestro raises his arms to begin the performance. I make every effort to keep myself aloof from that because I don't need backstage distractions keeping me from focusing on my job. With a full house, I wanted to be at my very best. A day later, De Vicenzo's words still stung.

In act 1, I tried really hard to forget the fact that I would have to be touched by De Vicenzo. When the director had blocked the part where Scarpia tricks Tosca into believing that her lover, Cavaradossi, has been meeting another woman, he specified for De Vicenzo to touch my hand as he approached me from behind.

When the time came that night, instead of touching my hand lightly, in a gesture to get my attention, De Vicenzo grabbed my wrist roughly and squeezed very hard. To say the least, I was shocked and just froze. Nobody from the audience would have noticed what was happening, but Giorgi from the pit sure did. He jumped to my rescue, mouthing the words for me, a good thing because I'd completely lost the thread of what I was supposed to sing next.

It was a childish attempt to make me screw up and it would have worked if my magnificent conductor hadn't noticed. In my surprise, I'd once again completely forgotten to look at the prompter.

My next entrance was a bit ragged and I spun out of De Vicenzo's grasp, rubbing my wrist, which I was sure would be bruised. From that point on, I kept my distance, looking daggers at the baritone who returned a smirk when he got the chance.

To say I was pissed off would have put it mildly. As soon as I was offstage, I ran to the safety of my dressing room, hoping to regroup in time for the critical second act. The hugely ominous chords from the brass that end the first act sounded to me in my state of upset like the earth opening up to reveal hell.

Lauretta Santarossa, my dresser, was suitably shocked when I told her what had happened, having already spoken to me about what had occurred at rehearsal the day before.

"What are you going to do, *signora?*"

I caught myself frowning into the mirror in front of me. "I am going to *massively* enjoy plunging that knife into him in the next act, real or not."

About five minutes before the curtain, Giorgi knocked on my door. Sticking his head in, he said, "Marta, I will make that swine pay for what he did. Leave it to me. He has caused trouble which I will make him regret!"

I hugged him. "Tomasso, let's not make this any worse. I can take care of myself."

He shook his head violently. "No, no! He has crossed the line. *No one* does that when I am in command!"

To make this a truly operatic moment, he should have cried out, "*Vendetta di Giorgi!*"

As I waited stage left to make my entry, I fought a losing battle with the butterflies in my stomach. Here my voice was feeling really excellent, I had a full house to share it with, but I had to deal with De Vicenzo's idiocy. I made a silent prayer to get through this and turn the adversity into a strength, though I had no idea how that could be pulled off. At least I would have no trouble conveying to the audience that I was completely and totally repelled by the man attempting to claim my body. My skin crawled at the thought of his hands touching me.

We both chewed up the scenery that night. I had to give it to De Vicenzo. He was absolutely brilliant in conveying the lecherous and cruel Scarpia. I expected the audience to hiss whenever he opened his mouth. He had a magnificent voice and acting chops I could only dream about. Why did he have to be such a miserable bastard?

For my part, I didn't have to act at all. The result was I could give one hundred percent of my attention to singing, and since De Vicenzo had my back up, sing I did, pouring everything I had into my performance, especially in the exquisite "*Vissi d'arte.*" The bravas at the end of it were simply deafening. I acknowledged them with a tiny smile and nod of my head. Giorgi in the pit was beaming.

In the climax of the scene, when Tosca agrees to give herself to Scarpia to save Cavaradossi, De Vicenzo again surprised me by wrenching my right arm behind me and pulling hard. A spasm of pain shot through my shoulder, certainly visible on my face, but I kept my head. To get back at him, I tromped down hard on his instep with the heel of my shoe and felt him stiffen satisfactorily. It must have been pretty painful, but ever in control, he sang right through it as if nothing had happened.

Moments later, when I had to stab him, I might have slammed the stage knife into De Vicenzo perhaps a *little* hard, and the words *"Questo è il bacio di Tosca!"* (This is Tosca's kiss!) had probably never been sung with greater conviction. De Vicenzo, unlike the way he usually went about dying, fell like a stone. A few people in the audience actually applauded.

With the stage finally mine alone, I sang my heart out, at one with what my character was feeling — and believe me that wasn't hard.

The "bravas" as the curtain came down were absolutely deafening. De Vicenzo's expression was worth a couple of photos as he got to his feet.

⌐

With De Vicenzo out of the picture for the third act, I could relax and I felt, as I took my curtain calls at the very end, that I had never sung Tosca better. I got six solo curtain calls from the enthusiastic house and Ramírez planted himself firmly between me and De Vicenzo for each curtain call of the three principals, something for which I was quite grateful. How I'd get through the final performance was anyone's guess.

I met Dan at the stage door. So far, no one had questioned his presence, not that I'd advertised it, but I'd done my best to head off any gossip by telling people our cover story about him being a ghost writer for my book which was due out "shortly." I didn't want people to see us together and wonder what was going on. Backstage gossip can kill you, and Rome is full of paparazzi. He always walked a few paces behind me when we were out on the street.

It was chilly that night, so I had the security guard at the stage door get a cab and Dan just hopped in when everyone's back was turned.

I was ravenous, but also exhausted after the events of the evening, so I invited Dan back to the apartment where we made up a plate of cheese, sausage, bread, and some really decent apples. He supplied a bottle of red wine he'd picked up that morning.

Dan had been completely unaware of the personal drama onstage, but that was probably due to him seeing his first opera. I filled him in at length. Tony called and I also told him. He sounded as if he was going to hop on the first plane to come over and personally punch De Vicenzo in his big fat nose. After we talked, he asked me to pass him over to Dan. They had a short conversation before the phone was passed back to me again so Tony and I could say our good nights.

Dan left quickly after and I enjoyed a second glass of wine as I continued decompressing from the evening's festivities.

Something would have to be done about Arturo De Vicenzo before the next performance in two nights' time or we would come to blows. It just wasn't right to cheat the public by trying to mess up a performance. Tonight, though, I'd been as guilty as he. Perhaps I could speak to the company's general manager and we could sort out this whole mess in the quiet of his office. I felt certain we could make De Vicenzo see reason. He was only harming himself, after all.

⌒

I was woken up at the ungodly hour of six the next morning by the overly cheery sounds of the overture to *Carmen* coming from my cell phone. Cracking open one eye, I noted the time and cursed as I groped for the source of the racket.

"Hello?"

"Marta? It's Javier. Have you heard the horrible news?" That woke me up. "A friend just called. It's all over the television and Internet. De Vicenzo apparently fell down some stairs last night and broke his neck. He's dead!"

I just about dropped the phone. I have no idea what I said to Javier after that, but the call ended shortly after. What was there to say? I immediately thought of pushing the panic button, but decided to knock on Dan's door to wake him up more gently.

Slipping my robe over my shoulders, I padded across the living room and opened the apartment door. There on the mat lay a perfect blood red, long-stemmed rose.

I pushed the panic button as I fell to my knees.

Chapter Eleven

I have this illusion of myself as a strong person, able to handle whatever life throws at me, bounce back, and be even better than ever. It's all a fabrication.

It's certainly not intentional. It's not a matter of trying to exert mind over matter, talking myself into things that aren't true so the force of believing in something so much will *make* it true. People who are really ill try this sort of thing — and apparently it can work if they just believe strongly enough. That's not what I'm talking about.

When I was a kid, I decided I wanted to be the best goddamn rock and roll drummer ever. I took lessons, and practised my ass off, and you know what happened? This black kid moved into our school, and he had nowhere near the chops I did. I could play rudiment rings around him any day of the week.

But then he sat down behind the kit with his limited chops and just blew me out of the water. There was a feel in the way he played I instinctively knew I would never have — even if I tried for the rest of my life. He was loose, he was funky, and I found my traitorous foot tapping even as I was choking back bitter tears.

So I switched gears and decided to make myself a percussionist. If you think that's just an extension of being a drummer, you're very mistaken. It's worlds different, and there were times I felt like I was right back at square one. Again I worked my ass off and I became good, really good. I was a shoe-in for the Ottawa Youth Orchestra and all-city band every year. People were calling me up to play in their pit orchestras. I was seventeen and I was making money playing. Because I was the best high school percussionist in the city, I thought I had the world by the tail.

But I was sorely mistaken.

I was over the moon when McGill gave little ole me a scholarship to study there. I felt as if I had it made. Then I heard the other students who were my direct competition. Even as I kept going with my studies, still trying my hardest, I saw myself falling farther and farther behind them. Where it was easy for them, it was hard for me. Each battle won was a battle hard fought, too hard fought.

I didn't know it then, but my subconscious was already looking for a way out. I knew I wanted nothing else than to be a musician — but doing what? It was too late to start again on another instrument. There's a common belief that if you haven't become really good on an instrument by the time you're eighteen, the boat has sailed without you and there's almost always no catching up.

All except for one instrument: the human voice. In many ways it's a good thing not to get too serious about singing until you're well beyond puberty. Your vocal chords just aren't tough enough. I'd sung in choirs all my life, but only as a fun thing. I'd never looked at it as a potential career, even though everyone told me I had a nice voice.

In the spring of my third year at McGill, luck in the form of a flu epidemic changed the course of my life. The head of the faculty's opera department was watching the chorus of his fast-approaching production dwindling to a handful of croaking, half-dead zombies.

My audition for this abrupt change of direction to my life consisted of a meeting in a hallway of the school as I hurried to an ear-training class.

"Do you sing?" this man whom I'd seen around the school asked me. He didn't look particularly friendly.

"Do I what?"

He pursed his lips and looked as if he thought I was a moron. "I need voices for the chorus of our production of *Der Freischütz*. We're performing it in two weeks. *Do you sing?*"

For some reason that defies any explanation by me to this day, I answered, "Well, yes, a little. I sang in choirs when I was younger."

Then he smiled. "Room 204, five o'clock today. Tryouts. Be there."

Seven of us showed up and all were taken. I only remember one thing from my first rehearsal the following Saturday morning. "Tall girl in the back row… Yes, you! You are singing too loudly! Try to blend in, if you please."

I've had trouble blending in ever since.

That extreme left turn because of a chance hallway meeting, paid big dividends. Things began happening, good things. Heaven knows I wasn't an overnight sensation. It was a long, hard slog and continues to be. Long ago I faced the fact that I'm not a person for whom music comes easily and naturally. I still have to work hard every day, wrestling every little thing to the ground. I've thrived because I'm bloody-minded and won't give up. I do have ability, but it's not easily accessible. It's as if God put it all there — only forty feet below ground where I had to dig to access it.

But I've become successful now. The school of hard knocks paid off. I guess you *might* say I'm an overnight sensation at the age of forty. I've survived the death of a husband, then the discovery that not only wasn't he dead, but he wasn't anything close to the person I thought he was. I was naive. I was stupid. I never asked questions. That naïveté almost got me killed.

Going through all that, however, made me stronger. I had conquered bad things when I could have easily crumbled.

Or so I thought.

Now, a flower on the doorstep of an apartment in Rome had brought my house of cards crashing down, shocking me into complete immobility. Staring at the TV or screen on my laptop, waiting for the latest update about De Vicenzo, my inner dialogue continued like a broken record: *I was weak. I was weak. I was weak.*

⌒

Dan made coffee for me that morning. Not being used to the coffee press, it was too weak, but I drank it gratefully. All I could think about was the fact that my problem with this interloper in my life had caused the death of another. Yes, I'd really detested De Vicenzo and hoped I would never have to even set eyes on him again, let alone sing with him, once we finished our production — but he didn't deserve to die.

Dan, of course, tried hard to talk me out of feeling that way. "We don't even know if this wasn't anything more than an accident. This probably has nothing to do with your problem."

"What about the rose on my doorstep? Explain that away, please."

"It could mean anything. He could just be telling you he's around, that despite our being on to his cameras and recordings, he can still get as close to you as he wants."

"I want to go to the police. Tell them what's going on."

"For the love of Christ, Marta, don't do that. Not yet, at least. Wait. Be patient."

"But somebody died!"

"Wait," he said, almost pleading, "please. You'll look like a fool if De Vicenzo's death has nothing to do with you and you're blabbing about some joker who's stalking you. Believe me, you don't want to go down that road."

Pleading was so out of character for him. It got my attention.

"Okay … for the moment."

While waiting until one o'clock, when I could decently call Tony who'd had his first rehearsal the previous night, I finally got my lazy butt in gear and did some vocalizing. I fully expected to be singing the next evening. It always all boils down to dollars and cents and it was a sell-out.

To say my heart wasn't in singing that day was not entirely accurate. I knew some warming up needed to be done, even if I didn't want to do it. As the hands on my watch slowly dragged around to the time I could call home, I occupied myself in doing a vocal exercise, checking the news, doing another, wandering around the apartment. Stir and repeat until frantic.

Dan had moved to the kitchen where I could hear him talking softly on his cell phone or tapping away on his laptop. I supposed he was trying to get information, communicating with his boss, maybe calling in some favours. But it mustn't have been going very well, judging by his frequent loud sighs. I knew the situation was bugging him. That's why he'd signed on to be my escort on this trip. Now this — and right under our noses, too. I tried to put that all out of my head and concentrate on the business of keeping my voice in prime shape for performing. It didn't work and I did my vocalizing basically by rote — not a good thing. Singing must always be done with one's brain actively engaged. That day my brain and body were in two different places and never met. Thank the Lord Lili wasn't there to hear.

At one o'clock on the nose, I picked up my mobile and dialed home. I was going to be cool. I was going to be together. I was going to tell it like it was.

Tony answered groggily on the third ring.

And I began to cry.

Chapter Twelve

Tony returned the phone's handset to its cradle and lay back on the bed, looking at the ceiling. Would this never end? Something needed to be done, but what? So far they'd had no luck with anything. Chasing this Will o' the Wisp was the most infuriating thing he'd ever experienced. The man was a bloody ghost.

And now this.

Glancing at the clock he saw it was only seven twenty, too early to call either Lili or Shannon O'Brien.

By eight, Tony felt slightly more human. He'd taken a shower, shaved, and downed a double espresso. After fifteen minutes spent drumming his fingers on the kitchen table as his mind raced uselessly, he felt he could decently call Lili. She would certainly be up since her first coaching of the day began at nine. Christ! Who could sing at that ungodly hour?

"Good morning, Lili. How is your leg today?"

"You did not call me this early to inquire about the well being of my leg. What has happened?"

Since Tony only had a bare-bones story, it didn't take long to put Lili in the picture.

"So what do you think?" he finally asked as Lili remained silent.

"I do not like this. But just as you and that other man feel, this may all be a storm in a teapot."

He didn't bother correcting her word choice. Also, for some reason known only to her, Lili always referred to Hudson as "that man," although Tony couldn't imagine why she'd taken a dislike to him. Sure, he was a bit uneasy his wife was in Rome with the bodyguard/ security expert presumably around her twenty-four hours a day, but Shannon had assured him Dan Hudson was a professional.

"What don't you like?" he prompted.

"This stalker is continuing to change and evolve in his relationship to Marta. It is clearly becoming more active and intense. I have been consulting experts I know in this field and the case is following the classic arc. Even if he did not murder the opera singer, he is clearly keeping close to her. The rose proves that."

"And if this madman *has* killed?"

He could hear Lili take a deep breath before she answered. "Marta could be in real danger."

"Do you think he might become violent toward her?"

"We cannot be certain, and it would be a marked contrast to his behaviour so far. I don't believe that would happen, unless —"

Tony's interruption was swift. "Unless he has actually killed De Vincenzo. Oh God…."

He knew his place was in Rome, protecting his wife. Why had he not insisted on accompanying her?

"My dear Tony, you always look at the dark side of every situation."

"And we keep underestimating this guy's resolve and abilities! You've said it yourself: Marta could be in danger."

"Take a deep breath and look at this without emotion. You have told me that there is no proof he has done violence. We must remain calm."

"Easy for you to say," he mumbled.

But loudly enough for his wife's closest confidante to hear. "No. It is not easy for me to say. I am becoming quite worried. But we really do not know anything yet. Is that man still with Marta in Rome?"

"Of course, and he's going to stick to her like glue from here on in."

"And she will call you when she knows something about the death of the baritone?"

"I've asked her to do that. Look, I've got to get off to work, but can I call you later?"

"I am coaching all morning until noon, then there is a two-hour break, with three more coachings after that. I will answer any call from you, though."

As he clicked off, Tony reflected on the fact that Lili must really be worried. It was strictly against policy to let any phone calls disturb a coaching. Why did she always have to appear as the calm in the centre of the storm? The Italian in him didn't allow anything to get in the way of a good emotional outburst, he reflected as he gathered up his jacket, stuffing his mobile into its pocket.

To blow off some excess energy, he'd walk to work at the Eaton Centre, but on the way he would make good use of his time by trying to get in touch with their private detective. He desperately wanted her viewpoint. More than anything he was hoping Shannon would be able to convince him not to just jump on the next plane departing for Rome.

The rehearsal had gone very well the previous evening.

Chapter Thirteen

I had a job to do and I had to keep focused on that. The show would most definitely go on. The GM of the Rome Opera had made that clear in his first appearance in front of the media. "While we are still sorrow-filled our colleague will not be with us except in spirit, there is a tradition of continuance in our business. It is our duty to see that done."

I looked over my shoulder to where Dan stood in the doorway to the living room. "No, actually it's more about making sure the receipts from that performance are safely in the hands of the opera company."

He grinned. "And are all singers such a cynical lot?"

"No, realists. Opera is very, very expensive. We all understand that. I don't think you'll find anyone backstage tomorrow who doesn't believe the most important thing is to do the scheduled performance."

Not long afterwards, I got another phone call from Javier telling me we'd be joined by Edoardo Furci who had just finished a run of *Rigoletto* at The Met the previous evening. He'd be severely jet-lagged, but was game to help out. I'd never worked with him, but knew him by reputation. A very nice man, I hoped he could ramp up the menace for Scarpia. After all, he was following a newly-minted tragic legend and De Vicenzo's personality had made him *very* good in the role.

"See?" I said to Dan. "Didn't take long for someone to step into the breach. It will be a good career move for Furci — and he knows it. Lots of publicity."

"You *are* a cynical lot."

My return smile was grudging. "This business is a lot tougher than you can imagine, and careers have been made simply by subbing in for someone. That's not the case here. Furci is well-established, but not so much that all the publicity he's going to get wouldn't help with future bookings."

That afternoon I had scheduled another vocal coaching, mostly to again trot over parts of *Traviata* for the following week's gig in Venice. Distracted as I was, I knew it wouldn't be worth the bother to make the cross-town journey. It meant disappointing Peppe, but I felt he'd understand, considering the circumstances.

Anyway, I did need to stretch things out, so I used the first part of the afternoon to do some work on my own, accompanied by rudimentary thumping on the apartment's piano to help me keep the pitch. I'd taken two years of cursory lessons when I first started singing, but I have little affinity for the piano and knew it. I sound like a drummer playing piano. Nuff said!

Dan made himself scarce, whether to avoid distracting me or because he didn't want me disturbing him, I didn't know. So far he hadn't said much about what he thought of opera in general or my singing in particular — other than to say the day before that my volume had startled him.

When I called Peppe to cancel our session, I asked if he'd heard any further details of what had happened early that morning.

"One of my other sopranos had sung with the man a few times, and knows his daughter well. She said De Vicenzo had been out for a meal with friends that had ended very late. Later, the friends dropped him off near his apartment. He wanted to walk a bit to clear his head after too much wine. There is a long flight of stone steps that leads down to his street. He must have stumbled and fallen."

"And nobody saw what happened?"

"Someone down the street heard a shout, then saw De Vicenzo's body come to rest at the bottom of the stairs. There was nothing to be done. His neck was broken."

"So no one else actually saw him fall?"

"Why do you ask this?"

"No reason," I answered hastily. "Just curious, I guess."

"It was nearly three in the morning, Marta. Even in Roma the back streets are generally deserted at that time."

I thanked Peppe for all his help during my stay, but got off the phone rather quickly. I didn't like the idea that the baritone shouted out as he fell. What had happened on those stairs?

Crossing the hall, I knocked on Dan's door to tell him what Peppe had told me.

"Let yourself in," he called out.

He was on his cell, but also typing furiously on his laptop.

I knew better than to disturb him, so I just asked when he'd be free.

At least a half-hour, he mouthed, so I pantomimed knocking on my door, after which he nodded.

Back in my place, I realized we had nothing for dinner but some pasta and a few veggies. If I waited for Dan, had my talk with him, and then we went shopping, the stores would be closed. I didn't want to eat out.

Via Flavia always has a lot of traffic, vehicle as well as foot, so I felt it would be safe to nip out for a few items since I had to travel barely a block.

I grabbed my purse, coat, and a warm hat and made for the elevator — but not before leaving a note for Dan.

It felt good to be out in the fresh air again. The sun had long disappeared behind the buildings, but the temperature remained quite nice as I hurried west. I knew Dan wouldn't be happy I'd gone out by myself, but we needed to eat.

My friend at the fruttivendolo managed to talk me into buying more salad fixings than I needed. As an opera lover, he'd heard the tragic news and asked me all kinds of questions, but I didn't tell him much.

At the salumeria, I waited a bit to buy a small chunk of parmigiano and a piece of their wonderful guanciale. To go with it, I chose a nice bottle of Orvieto and a small box of Baci for dessert.

My arrival back at the apartment with my booty couldn't have been more than twenty minutes after my departure. Nothing had happened. Great. Taking the groceries out to the kitchen, I was humming "*Amami, Alfredo, amami quant'io t'amo*" from *Traviata*.

Next week was going to be a lot of work, but also a lot of fun. I'd never graced the stage at La Fenice before, and it would feel good to add it to my list of great opera houses where I've sung. A bonus was that Venice is also one of my favourite cities.

I stuck my hand in the second bag. My involuntary recoil took me nearly the length of the room.

I didn't have to look inside to know what I'd just touched: a long-stemmed rose.

Chapter Fourteen

As he got the video link up and running, Tony was reflecting that this was all getting to be a bit too much.

At the other end, Hudson moved his laptop around to show him and Marta pressed side by side at a table. From the way she sounded on the phone when she'd first called, she looked to be more composed than he expected. Then the laptop moved a bit more and he could see a glass of wine near her right hand.

"We have more people here than will fit in front of the screen," he told them in Rome, "so how do you want to work this?"

Hudson answered, "Why doesn't everyone at your end say something to make sure we can hear all of you?"

Shannon spoke first. "Here, Dan."

Lili then said, "And I am here, as well."

"Everything cool?" Tony finished.

"Reading you four-by-four."

Lili tapped Tony's elbow. He leaned toward her.

"What does that man mean?" she asked quietly.

"It means he can hear us just fine."

"Then why doesn't he just say that?"

Dan said, "It's obvious our adversary is still keeping close to us, murder or no murder. Shannon thinks he might have a confederate working for him, but I'm not sure. Somebody like him would want to be pulling the strings himself."

Lili nodded and leaned toward the laptop. "I agree."

Shannon had nominated herself to run the meeting. "Dan, can you bring us up to date on what's happening over there?"

"I've made contact with the Rome police via a friend, all under the radar, of course."

"What's the status of the De Vicenzo investigation?"

"Ongoing and active."

"What does this mean?" Lili asked.

"It means there are questions about De Vicenzo's death."

Shannon's decision was swift. "I think we have to bring the Rome police fully into this. Dan, you're the one on the ground over there. What's a likely scenario as to how this happened?"

"Marta had trouble with De Vicenzo during the performance last night. I've never even seen an opera before so I didn't notice anything. But you can bet if our friend was in the audience, he wouldn't have missed what was going on. It wasn't until later when Marta told me exactly what had been happening that I realized how outrageous it had all been. If De Vicenzo hadn't died, opera people all over Rome would have been talking about it today."

"Is that accurate, Marta?"

Tony noticed his wife push over a bit to be more in the centre of the screen. "It was pretty bad. I was tempted to paste the old bastard one. It never occurred to me at the time what our tussle must have looked like to the audience."

Shannon turned to Lili. "Do you think what happened could have pushed our enemy over the edge?"

Again Lili didn't hesitate. "Yes."

Tony felt a shiver rocket up his spine. He wondered if anyone else had a similar reaction.

Returning her gaze to the screen, Shannon said, "Okay, Dan, your call. You know how I feel. You're there, we're not. You have some idea of what the police are thinking. Should bringing them in be handled from here through the Toronto police, or should you make the contact and then we work backwards from there?"

Marta leaned in again, "I guess it *is* time to bring the police in, but I'm concerned about what happens after that. Obviously, I'm going to have to speak to them, probably for a long time — and I have a performance tomorrow. First thing Friday morning, I have to be on the train to Venice. Are they going to make me stay here? That gig at La Fenice is very important."

Shannon thought that over. Having been a police detective, she knew how these things generally worked. "Okay. Here's what we should do. As soon as we sign off, I will get on the blower to the Toronto police and speak to my contact there, bring him into the picture. It would be best to have this start through official channels. Interpol will probably need to be involved as well. I don't know where this will go, but I will make it clear that you wish to cooperate fully but also have commitments.

"I will have Dan take the lead as much as he can, act as a buffer, but they will want to speak to you — assuming they don't blow us off, which could also happen. You are in Italy, after all. My question is this, Marta: if we can swing it, would you rather speak with them before your performance, or after?"

Tony knew what the answer would be.

His wife didn't hesitate. "Definitely after. As soon as that curtain comes down, I'll talk. Not before. It would be far too distracting."

"Anyone have anything else to add?"

Lili spoke up. "I wish to caution Marta about being alone at any time. You stood right next to this man today and did not know it. You cannot be too careful. Mister Hudson, please do not leave Marta alone for any reason." Then she added the most surprising thing. "And you watch out most carefully for yourself. Today's events prove that you are in danger as well, unless I am very wrong."

On that happy note, the video link-up ended, Shannon made a phone call, and quickly left.

Once they were seated again in her parlor, Tony asked Lili, "You are very worried, aren't you?"

She nodded. "Yes. I do not like the ease with which this man can get so close to Marta. We must all redouble our efforts to discover his identity before it is too late."

Detective Leslie Dobbin looked at Shannon blankly. She could read his anger by the turned down corners of his mouth.

He had every reason to be sore. She had not been completely frank with him — and they were former colleagues supposedly working together on this. Old friends, especially if they were cops, didn't do that to one another.

She had quickly realized that doing this over the phone would not have been a good idea, so she'd driven to headquarters after making sure Dobbin was still there.

The older detective always reminded her more of a kindly school teacher than a tough cop. Perhaps that was the secret of his long and successful career: no one saw him coming until it was too late.

Now she'd (quite rightly) ticked him off and that wasn't good, because she still needed a favour — a big one.

"I'm sorry, Les, it was wrong of me. I was just trying to shield my client, at her request."

He wasn't going to make it easy. "You know better than that, Shan."

"I know and I'll keep saying I'm sorry until you're satisfied, if it will help. When people are paying for the work you do on their behalf, you've got to respect their wishes as much as you can. I agitated to be allowed to tell you everything that was going on, but she was completely against it."

"But you made this fellow out to be no more than a high-tech peeping tom, not someone who's been following a woman all over hell's half-acre, harassing her for nearly two years. Now you waltz in here and tell me you want to come clean — only after you suspect this guy might have murdered someone on the other side of the planet? Shannon O'Brien, I expected better from you."

From experience, she knew Dobbin would go on until he felt satisfied he'd verbally beaten her up enough, then would move on. She only had to wait him out.

When he was ready to get back to work, he brought in one of the squad's youngsters to take notes. While the boss had been yelling, she'd used the time to organize exactly how to tell her story. Regardless of how Marta might feel, it would include all details, nothing left out.

It only took thirty minutes and included the notes left with the flowers that Marta had given Shannon. She knew forensics wouldn't get any new information out of them, but it would mollify Dobbin even more. And this case needed his help badly.

"So you want me to contact the police in Rome, is that it?"

Smart man. He'd seen it in an instant.

"Yes. We need them to take this seriously. If I send my man Hudson to see them, or worse yet, my client, they could well be ignored, if I know the Italian police."

"Worked with them before, have you?"

"No. My dad did, a couple of times. They don't think much of foreign cops — especially us freelancers."

"I'm going to have to go upstairs on this, you know. We're talking extra expense here and they now watch every nickel and dime like it was their own money. Makes things tougher…"

She tried hard to put on a sympathetic expression. "I can believe it."

"Also probably Interpol needs to be brought in since this is cross-jurisdictional." Dobbin ran a hand over his balding head and sighed. "The paperwork is going to be a nightmare." Finally he got to the heart of the matter, and the potential sticking point. "How certain are you that the man you're after might have killed this singer?"

"Well, if you mean do we have any hard evidence, we don't. But he did leave another rose right on her doorstep —"

"Or had someone else do it." Dobbin rested his arms on his desk and leaned closer to her. "Let me get this straight. You don't know who this person is, you don't know where he — or she — may live, you aren't even sure if he or she is doing this directly or through an agent. What exactly *do* you know for sure, past the bugging of the apartment for which you at least have evidence? Shannon, you used to be a top-notch investigator. You know what they're going to say upstairs. You've got to give me something solid."

Shannon blew out a lungful of air. "Les, I know it's not a lot to go on. You haven't met Marta, but you've met Tony. They're reasonable, intelligent people. These things have happened to them. They're paying me a lot of money to help them. She's got one of my people over there with her now. He is experienced and he believes it is possible this stalker has killed someone. Do you really want me to come in here sometime soon and say, 'You should have listened to me?' I think we have someone here who's about to leave the reservation, if he hasn't already.

"This person is smart, well-funded, and seems to be enjoying his little game of cat and mouse an awful lot. Today he even managed to slip a rose into this woman's shopping bag for Christ's sake, and she was only out for a brief time. He's there, he's active, and I definitely feel he's ramping up to something. I don't know what his endgame is, but I don't think it will stop with one murder. Will you help?"

Dobbin turned to his note-taking assistant. "Go downstairs and get us some coffee, will you? You still drink it black, Shannon?"

After the door clicked shut, Dobbin leaned forward again. "All right, Shannon. I'm going to put my faith in you. You absolutely believe everything you've said to me? Because if you don't, you'd better tell me now."

She nodded once.

"Okay. When Mike gets back, you're going to help us write this up. They're going to want documentation up the yin-yang and I want your name to be front and centre on all of it."

⟲

When she started her car two hours later, Shannon was mentally exhausted, but more significantly, apprehensive.

What if she was wrong about all of this?

Chapter Fifteen

Dan camped out on my apartment's sofa that night, and I slept the better for it.

We made our breakfast early the next morning on cheese, toasted bread, and the remaining fruit I'd bought the previous day. I like to eat sparingly but frequently before I perform so I remain feeling light and my diaphragm "bouncy" while also not feeling hungry.

Outwardly I may have appeared calm, but inside I was a complete wreck. The police wanted to see me right after the performance was over — something I'd have to try to forget about until the curtain fell (good luck on that).

Dan took their call as per instructions from Shannon. Tony had already informed me late the night before what might be in the works. I felt like clamping my hands over my ears while Dan spoke.

A few hours later I received a surprise second call: Lili. The surprise was not her phoning. It was the fact that she wished speak to Dan, not me.

The call was brief and consisted at his end of a series of answers like "Ah-ha," "yes, of course," "I understand," and one "I agree with you completely."

He hung up and I was sort of miffed that Lili hadn't wanted to speak to me. When I asked what she'd said, his answer was slightly evasive, telling me she just wanted to let him know what we might expect from our adversary now that the police were directly involved.

"And what sort of things are those?" I asked sweetly.

"Technical stuff mostly. Basically she said I should stay close, that there could be a good chance to stop him because he might be getting nervous now."

"Do you believe that?"

For a moment, I thought he might lie to me. "No, my guess is he was already well aware that with Shannon and me on the scene, the cops wouldn't be far behind. Hasn't seemed to cramp his style a bit, has it?"

I looked at him closely for a moment, then decided with the stress of a performance in a few hours, it would do no good to think about anything beyond the job at hand. Other things would just take care of themselves in time.

I've gotten good at shutting out the world on performance days. One has to. We performers are expected to be perfect. The real opera enthusiasts know their favourites as well as anyone, and are instantly aware if anything slips. Every musician appearing that night (and despite the jokes I used to make when I was a percussionist, I'm including singers in that list) would be trying their damnedest to not make a single mistake — or shall I say not make a single noticeable mistake.

I would also be a horrible liar if I said that I wasn't aware *he* would certainly be in the audience that night.

A walk-through with our new Scarpia had been scheduled for eleven and my plan, enthusiastically taken up by Dan, was to remain at the opera house all day, warming up with one of the house répétiteurs mid-afternoon, followed by a quick cat nap on the day bed in my dressing room, a light meal, makeup and wardrobe, and by then it would be show time.

Post performance would be show*down* time: my visit to the cops.

Edoardo Furci was a slender man with a natty beard, charming manner, and ready smile. He took direction gracefully, was enthusiastic, engaged, deferred to Javier or me at all times, and even made Giorgi grin, something not easy to do on a performance day when he was always tense and brittle. In short, Furci as a person was everything that De Vicenzo was not.

Things were definitely weird backstage, hardly a big surprise. It really was disgusting to see many of the same people who'd been cursing our ex-baritone as recently as Tuesday evening now openly weeping over his death.

The devil in me wondered what they'd say if I told them I was indirectly the cause of it.

By one o'clock when rehearsal broke, I felt confident we wouldn't embarrass ourselves, and if Furci's voice was as good as advertised, we might even be special. I doubted he could bring the menacing weight that De Vicenzo naturally possessed, but he was also aware that the spotlight would be on him. Being a veteran of the opera wars, you could be certain he would bring his A-game.

Javier, Furci, and Giorgi were going out to lunch, and even though I longed to join them, I thought it best to keep my distance. With the excuse I simply *had* to spend some time with my ghost writer, I begged off. At this point, having him keep his distance was definitely off the job description. We both knew the danger. No sense encouraging another late-night stumble on a stairway. While the rehearsal had been on and I'd been safely surrounded, Dan had gone out for food.

We went back to my dressing room where he'd laid out the food. There were two selections of pasta, crusty bread, salad, and even a split of wine.

"I thought this early in the day, you might be able to indulge a little."

Gratefully accepting a glass, I chattered on about the rehearsal, not noticing in the slightest that my guardian angel was rather distracted.

⌒

That evening, I was already in the wings when Giorgi raised his arms and the orchestra began. Sweet Javier came up behind me with big hug as he moved forward to wait for his cue. Furci, still in his dressing room, probably struggling with an almighty case of nerves, poor man, was the only cast member not yet on hand.

One thing I had noticed from the moment I entered the building that morning had been a nervous energy. The whole place buzzed like a hive, everyone on their toes. We were the big story in Rome that day, probably in most of Italy (take *that* La Scala!), and everyone knew it. Attendance was at the bursting point with the last bit of standing room gone hours before. Apparently, the curious who couldn't get in were even roaming the piazza out front.

One thing about show biz people is that when the spotlight is on, you just can't help but give it your all. Worrisomely, after a short tribute to our fallen comrade by the GM of the opera, the orchestra sounded a little hyper in the overture — or was that Giorgi? Even though their sonic force could obliterate us on stage if they chose to, they knew their business and sounded as if they were on their game. A little circumspection would have made me feel more confident, though.

People tend to pull together in a crisis, and we all hoped for an excellent night. I was out to prove that the success of our production was *not* due to the extreme menace — and to be truthful, artistry — that De Vicenzo brought to his role as one of the most memorable villains in all of opera. Javier as much as said the same to me. Since *Tosca* is very much a three-horse opera, it was in our hands: Edoardo, Javier, and me.

And we pulled it off.

The ovation at the curtain was thunderous. As I looked out at the auditorium when we three came out, hands triumphantly joined above our heads, standing in the very spot the principals had stood at the premier of this opera in this very theatre over a hundred years ago, I felt proud of what we'd accomplished.

Javier and I (by prior arrangement) had playfully pushed Furci in front of us to indicate to the audience we felt the night was his. He had indeed risen to the occasion; his Scarpia had been excellent, although I hadn't enjoyed dispatching him with my knife at the end of act 2 nearly as much as I had his predecessor.

By the time Giorgi ascended from the pit to take his bows, everyone in the theatre was in a rare good mood, knowing they'd all been part of an exceptional night of opera.

As is usual on most closing nights, everyone was heading out to dinner. I begged off by saying I had a 7:55 train to catch. I wonder what they would have said if I'd admitted I had to go to the police station.

Dan had been keeping watch on my dressing room from a discreet spot, but unknown to me he'd also stuck a spy camera in there. Both of us were disappointed a bouquet hadn't appeared and the video sent to his computer showed nothing out of the ordinary. We quizzed my dresser Lauretta, knowing it might have wound up in another dressing room, as had happened before.

"I haven't heard a thing about bouquets, signora."

"I'm in a bit of a rush, Lauretta, so if you could hurry, I would appreciate it a lot."

Dan left and she helped me off with my costume, and donning the light robe I use, we both worked at getting the long wig off and makeup removed.

Almost at the end, there was a knock on the door.

Furci was there and my heart nearly stopped when I saw the long box he was carrying.

Our foe had done it again.

But I was wrong.

This time there was a difference.

"Marta, dear," Furci gushed in effusive Italian. "I am speechless. Thank you so much. I cannot say how grateful I am, not only for your wonderful singing and support this evening, but also for this token."

"The bouquet?" I asked, nearly stuttering in my confusion.

"Of course! I must admit that it is a bit out of the ordinary, but the beauty, the presentation. I have never seen anything like it."

Even Lauretta was gawking a bit because she'd seen me (and my distress) when the exact same bouquet of roses had been found in my dressing room after a previous performance.

"I … I've forgotten what I asked to be written on the card," I said. "What does it say?"

"It is in English," he said, appearing a bit confused because we'd been speaking only Italian all day. "It says, 'Please accept these roses and my best wishes for a superb performance.' It is signed 'Marta,' but this is a man's writing. The florist, perhaps? Still, it is a gesture most kind. *Grazie mille!*" He kissed me on both cheeks.

It felt as if the whole world was going crazy. This was completely unexpected. What did it mean? We were entering uncharted waters. Had things changed as we all feared they might?

Dan returned at that moment and sized things up in an instant. "May I see that, sir?"

He took the box and laid it on the counter in front of the mirror. "My wife asked me to take a photo of this when I told her how lovely it was. She's a nut for flowers." His phone was out and snapping pictures before anyone knew what was happening. "And the card, may I see it, too?" He shot that from a few different angles. "You're happy with what I did, Marta? It is satisfactory?"

The change in Dan's demeanor was astonishing. No one would believe for an instant that he was a spy along on this little joy ride to protect my posterior from evil forces. In fact, they might find it hard to believe he had a wife.

As fast as he bustled in, Hudson was out the door again, then stuck his head back in. "Marta, remember our ride is waiting. Chop, chop!"

Furci got the message, thanked me again, and left. Lauretta looked as if she had a thousand questions, but I just gave her the evil eye and she knew enough not to ask. We got my de-costuming completed in record time.

As I gave her a handsome tip for all her help over the run, she leaned forward and whispered, "Someday you will tell me what this is all about, *si?*"

⌐

I hadn't really formed an idea what it might be like to be interviewed by the Roman police. I've never had anything to do with them, but knew they could be abrasive. None of that was in evidence that evening.

First of all, the car was unmarked and the driver waited patiently while I did more than the usual few autographs at the stage door. Dan faded into the background but I knew he was keeping a close eye on everyone in the crowd, not just to those who approached me with programs and pens. It took close to fifteen minutes to get through them all. It was gratifying, if a little unnerving, knowing my stalker could come right up with his pen held out and I'd never know it.

Eventually Dan bundled me into the car and we roared off, showing a little of the impatience of the driver who'd been sent to fetch me. He screeched his tires impressively at the first corner, and my impression was that, besides being late, we had a long way to go. But the distance was laughably short, a matter of three or four minutes and only because the maze of one-way streets forced us rather out of our way. I could have walked to our appointment in under five minutes. It was rather comical, but it did do one thing: I felt the coiled spring in my stomach relax a little.

Someone on lookout duty at the door hustled us inside, into an elevator, and up to an office on the third floor.

We were shown to two chairs set in front of a large antique desk, the kind up on four legs. As the factotum helped me remove my coat, I looked around. The office was elegantly appointed, with a beautiful carpet, soft colours, lots of photos, and bric-a-brac on a few tables. You would have supposed this to be the office of the manager of a large bank.

The gentleman who came in a moment later was equally impressive: over sixty, tall, and handsome with a long face and large, expressive eyes. He didn't look at all like a cop. If I hadn't known better, I would have supposed him to be an actor, writer, or perhaps a musician. His English was impeccable.

"Thank you for agreeing to meet with me at the end of your long evening, Signora Hendriks. My name is Stefano Pucci and your file has landed on my desk. I understand you wish to aid us in our investigation of the death of Arturo De Vicenzo in the early hours of yesterday morning."

Dan had told me earlier that the best way to talk with these people is to "let them do all the talking." Next to me, he sort of faded into the upholstery of his chair, but I knew he was memorizing everything he saw and heard.

Pucci was very suave. He gave no rank. I had no idea what he did here, but he seemed very much in charge. He asked if I would like an espresso or something else to drink. I didn't think they would serve wine, even in Italian police stations, so I told him sparkling water was fine. I could also have used a sandwich but didn't ask.

After speaking softly into his phone, he opened the file on his desk. "Until we heard from your Toronto police, we had been ready to close this file. De Vicenzo had much to drink after his performance. It is reasonable that he stumbled and fell on those stairs. They are old and uneven, as well as long and steep."

The drinks arrived and the officer who brought them in took a seat behind Pucci then pulled out a pad and pen.

"Now, tell me your story, signora."

I did that with as much clarity and succinctness as my tired brain would allow. The first part took over twenty minutes, and I watched Pucci turn pages on a sheaf of papers resting in the centre of his desk as if following what I was saying. When I got to the parts of my story that had taken place in Rome, his eyes came up, watching me narrowly and asking occasional questions. This took considerably longer. I wished I knew what was going on in his head.

"And, as a matter of fact, something also happened just before we left the theatre tonight," I said at the end.

"And what was that?"

"Another bouquet was delivered. Mr. Hudson," I said, indicating Dan, "and I had discussed during the afternoon whether this man making my life a misery would give me another of his bouquets. He did, but this time it was given to Signor Furci. He brought it to my dressing room and it was undoubtedly the same as the ones I've received, but this time it was made out as if I had given it to my colleague."

"And where is this bouquet now?"

Dan finally spoke up. "With Furci. We couldn't very well ask him to hand it over. However, I did take a number of photos using my cell phone. I would like to offer them to you."

Pucci nodded. "You can send them to me via the Internet?"

Dan smiled. "Simply give me your address." Then he reached into his pocket. "And I managed to palm this."

From the inner pocket of his suit jacket, he pulled out something wrapped in a handkerchief.

It was the card that came with the bouquet. Still resting on the cloth, Dan slid it across the desk.

"Sorry I didn't have an evidence bag at the ready. The bastard really caught us off guard — again."

Pucci studied the card carefully, referring to some scans that were included in the package of information sent from Toronto. "This is the same handwriting as on the other cards you received."

Dan and I both said, "Absolutely."

"Do you know where Furci is staying while in Rome?"

I shook my head. "No idea. He did say something today about needing a good sleep before catching a plane home tomorrow morning. If there's anyone left at the opera house, they may be able to tell you."

The note taker was summoned by the wave of a finger, a few words were whispered, and he hurried out of the room with the note card. I looked at my watch: nearly midnight.

Pucci closed the file, then rubbed the bridge of his nose. "What you have told me is most interesting. If it had been me to have told this story, would you believe that your troubles and the death of De Vicenzo were connected?"

"I don't know what I'd think. I'm an opera singer, not a police official."

"But you are intelligent, are you not? Tell me. What would you think?"

"I would be happy to have this information if I had doubts about the death."

"And so I am. But I did not have doubts until you came in and told me your story. With only what is in this file I received and what you have told me, I would have sent you away — except for two things."

"What?"

"First, the fact that Furci received a bouquet this evening and that it was from you."

"But it wasn't from me!"

Dan shifted in his seat.

Pucci held up his hand. "If the conflict between you and De Vicenzo led to this, ah, madman taking his life, then why give the bouquet to Furci from you? Because of you, Furci got the engagement. Do you understand what I mean?"

My eyes opened wide. "I hadn't seen it like that."

"And the second reason?" Dan asked

"That is something known only to the police."

"But you're going to tell us?"

Pucci hesitated, but only for a moment. "You will not speak of this to anyone. I have your promise on that?"

We both nodded.

"At the restaurant where De Vicenzo had his late dinner with two friends, someone at another table bought them a bottle of very fine grappa and also champagne. Between the three people at that table, they consumed much alcohol — especially Signor De Vicenzo."

I asked, "You're thinking this man was trying to get him drunk?"

Pucci shrugged. "The two friends have also told us that this man said he was American, but they thought his accent wasn't quite right."

Dan and I looked at each other, saying simultaneously, "He's finally made a mistake."

Descent

Chapter Sixteen

The Italian countryside whipped by as I drowsily stared out the train window. I had every right to feel like the floor of a taxicab. Four hours of sleep after singing a three-hour Puccini opera, then enjoying another two hours of intimate chatter in the office of a police inspector will do that to a gal.

It looked cold outside, very un-Italian-like. The temperature had plummeted during the night. The tops of distant hills had a dusting of snow and the sky had the leaden quality that often means more white stuff on the way. It was nice to feel warm and snug as the Eurostar rocketed through the Tuscan countryside. After a stop in Florence, we would hang a right and continue to Bologna then bear right again for our ultimate destination of Venice. I glanced at my watch. It was nearly nine in the morning.

Thankfully, the police had given us a lift back to Via Flavia after my interview. I had any number of things I wanted to ask Dan but he gave me the signal to keep my mouth firmly shut during the ride.

Later he told me, "It's amazing what people will say in the back seat of a car. Sitting in the front seat does not make the driver deaf. And if you really want to know, yes, I have bugged the back seats of cabs when I needed information for projects I was involved with."

Once back in the apartment, Dan did a sweep for any newly placed critters before letting me speak.

My first comment was, "Are you checking for bugs placed by our friend or the police?"

"Certainly for our friend," was his oblique answer.

Whatever. I had been completely forthcoming with the police as Shannon and Dan had instructed, so my conscience was clear.

I settled back in my train seat and shut my eyes, hoping sleep would come. But every time I started to drift off, a new thought would pop up and jolt me back to full waking.

Dan had disappeared as soon as we'd found our seats. I must have finally dozed off because I was startled awake when he jostled my leg as he was sitting down.

Struggling up from the depths, it took me a moment to realize where I was. Outside, we were crossing a high bridge with the Apennines all around us. Obviously we hadn't reached Bologna yet, so I couldn't have been asleep that long, but I had slept right through our stop in Florence.

"I brought you a coffee. Here."

I pulled up one of the little table thingies on the central post placed between our seats and those of the people facing us.

For train fare, it wasn't bad — a double shot of decent espresso, and nice and hot. Of course, Italians never put up with bad coffee the way we North Americans do.

"Where'd you disappear to?" I asked.

Dan had a cappuccino. I indicated he'd given himself a bit of a moustache, which he wiped off with a napkin before answering. "I had this wild idea that our friend might think it exceptionally clever to be on the train with us."

"You believe we'll hear from him again on this trip?"

"I'd be shocked if he just gave up and went home. I'm sure he believes he's untouchable. So, by the way, does your friend, Lili."

"You don't think the police here and in Toronto might have spooked him?"

He stopped mid-sip, looking at me over the rim of his Styrofoam cup. "Do you?"

"I guess not. So, did you see any likely suspects?"

"A few. I took a number of discreet photos, which I've sent back to Shannon to see if they're any help."

The thing that most concerned me was that this all had to be kept hush-hush. There are some singers I know who'd be only too pleased to benefit from the notoriety accruing to them for being part of a murder investigation.

I wasn't one of those. If I thought it would have done any good, I would have met with this bozo, had a nice chat, given him whatever the hell he wanted, and sent him on his way if he promised to just leave me alone.

Leaning closer to Dan, I asked, "So what do you make of what Pucci told us last night?"

"You mean someone plying De Vicenzo with wine and booze was a big mistake? No, in thinking about it, I don't believe that was it. He *had* to have known that either the two dinner companions or people at the restaurant would have mentioned him to the cops and that they might want to check it out."

"So beyond the obvious reason, why did he do it?"

"Either he felt completely secure there would be no blow-back or he's toying with everyone some more. Still, he did have to give up some valuable information in order to do what he did."

I thought for a moment because I didn't see it initially. "Okay. They can get his identity from the credit card he used."

Dan shook his head. "No way. He'd be a fool if he used anything but cash. And he's most definitely not a fool."

"Hmmm … They'll get a description of him from De Vicenzo's friends or the restaurant staff?"

"You can be sure Pucci's men are all over that angle, and we may get lucky, but I doubt it. You've been on the lookout for this person for well over a year now. How has that gone?"

"You mean disguises?"

"Is the Pope Catholic?" Dan put down his empty cup and wiped his mouth again, just to be sure. "Stands to reason, doesn't it? This jerk enjoys toying with people. Of course he'd be into playing a bit of dress-up. This isn't completely about you, Marta. This is a power trip. He's out to make fools of everyone involved. That's where he really gets his rush. It's having power over all of us, but you most of all."

"So what is the valuable information he's given up?"

"First, we can be certain he is male, not that we really had any doubts about that. The other bit of information is more subtle. He's wearing disguises, of that we can be fairly certain. Why would he wear disguises?"

"To keep us from seeing him around all the time."

"Certainly, but I'm betting there's more to it than that. Try this on for size: you might recognize him because you've actually met him someplace before."

"Oh my God…."

Dan excused himself to make another phone call somewhere out of people's hearing. Alone again, my mind was flooded with all kinds of angles and possibilities. It took me well past Bologna to sort through everything that had happened in the past forty-eight hours, based on what Dan had told me. In the end I came back to the very first question I'd had for over a year: why me and what did he want?

∽

I'd been in Venice only twice, the first time to spend a week of R&R with Gerhard and once by myself, for much the same reason. This visit I was there to perform and it was the dead of winter, not that winter here approaches anything like what I grew up with in Ottawa and Montreal. Even Toronto weather is awful by Italian standards, and the rest of Canada makes fun of the way we go on about the weather there.

Both my previous visits had been in June when the weather in the lagoon tends to be about as good as it gets. But even in the warm sunshine and gentle breezes of that time of the year, something has always struck me that Venice is a sad place: breathtaking in its beauty, striking in its individuality, but ultimately aware that someday it will sink from sight beneath the waves. Venice is sailing along in a boat of its own building, every inhabitant bailing for their lives to stave off its inevitable watery grave.

Dan and I stood on the wide concourse in front of Venice's modern train station for a few minutes, just watching the world float by. In front of us was the Grand Canal, the main street of a city built entirely around its relationship with water. It's as busy as any street in Manhattan, London, or Paris, simply vehicles on wheels being replaced by boats of all sizes and shapes.

"So what do you think?" I asked.

"I've seen it many times in photos and movies, but to actually stand here looking at it in person, well, it's pretty damned amazing."

"I think Venice has that effect on everyone. There's no other place like it on the planet."

"So how do we get to where we're going?"

I raised an eyebrow. "I thought that would be your call — seeing how you're my spy and security expert."

He shot right back, "But you've been here before. I'm the new guy in town."

Looking at my small mountain of luggage, I said, "I don't know about you, but I don't feel like struggling with all this on a vaporetto. This calls for a water taxi. Wait here, I'll get one."

Dan looked sort of disappointed at my mention of water taxis. The famous Venetian gondolas are a wonderfully romantic way to get around the city, but since they're now used nearly completely by tourists, they're frightfully expensive. And unless you're ready to make a substantial commitment of time to go with that money, they're no good to travel any distance. I made a mental note to treat him to a gondola ride, preferably at night, before our return to Toronto.

Another reason I wanted to shake a leg was because I'd had so little sleep the previous night. I needed a good lie-down before the six o'clock supper meeting with the cast and crew of the TV production in which I was involved.

The producers had arranged for everyone to stay at the Danieli, one of the more famous hotels in Venice, which was right on the water near Piazza San Marco. But with my current situation, Dan had decided it was more prudent to get rooms as close to the opera house as possible. Fortunately, there's a sweet little hotel right next to La Fenice, so close in fact, it shares the same name.

Our rooms weren't quite ready when we arrived, so we dumped our luggage at the front desk and went in search of food. The desk clerk recommended an osteria just the other side of the small piazza in front of the opera house, and it turned out to be a very good suggestion.

"I'm so hungry I could eat a horse," Dan said after we'd both ordered grilled fish.

"Me, too. I'll never be able to get used to the continental tradition of starting one's day with coffee and some bread-like object, although I will admit I adore a good croissant.

Dan grinned. "Where on earth would you find something like that in Italy?"

"You don't," I replied with mock sadness. "That's one of the reasons Paris is my favourite city."

"Even after what happened to you there? I hate to admit it but that's the first time I heard the name Marta Hendriks."

He was referring to my horrible experience as I searched for a husband who I thought had died in a house fire.

"I know. I'm the person who caused the destruction of a beloved Paris landmark, the death of three people, and, oh yes, I also sing opera. It was a bloody cock-up from the get-go. I'm lucky to be alive myself."

Our appetizers arrived.

"Sounds as if you're pretty bitter."

"You could say that. My motto now is 'be careful what you wish for.'" I stabbed salad with my fork. "Still, I'm getting lots of singing engagements, and since leading sopranos have a limited shelf life, I should be grateful. Take this week's gig. I still have no idea why they hired me. It's not as if there's a lack of great Violettas in Italy, let alone Europe. It was probably a case of 'get that infamous soprano. She'll bring in some extra viewers.'"

Dan raised his wine glass. "Then, to success in Venice!"

I clinked glasses with him. "Wasn't there a famous book with that title?"

He surprised me. "I think you're referring to *Death in Venice*."

We laughed at my little joke, although a better response might have been to shiver.

I looked over his shoulder at nothing. "After Rome, let's hope that doesn't happen."

⌒

The group that had been assembled for this television performance was indeed impressive, echoing the pan-European production. I was the lone North American in the cast. As we sat down to eat at a long table at the Hotel Danieli after the producer (Italian), director (French), and conductor (German) had welcomed us with "a few suitable words," all telling us unnecessarily how huge the potential audience could be.

The person sitting across from me (the broadcast's lighting designer) said, "Let's hope our little show does better than the premiere of this blasted opera here at La Fenice."

We all laughed, but he was right. The original production of *La Traviata* was a major flop, greatly disappointing Verdi — and his backers, I'm sure. The subject matter, as well as the casting, offended the audience, with hisses and jeers greeting the final curtain.

I spent the rest of the evening getting to know everyone. The imported production was the one I had been part of at the Paris Opera two years earlier. Despite my words to Dan that afternoon, it was probably the reason I'd been hired. Since mine was the biggest role in the opera, I was more familiar with what was needed than anyone else and would need only a quick refresher. With the talent of the rest of the cast, I was pretty excited about my involvement. Beamed around the world, this performance would be seen by millions of opera lovers. My manager in New York was over the moon about that.

During the meal, everyone spoke of various productions of *Traviata* we'd been part of. No one was crass enough to mention it, but I could tell from the way people looked at me that everyone was aware of my star-crossed history with this opera.

Costume fittings were scheduled for early the next morning with a blocking run-through in the afternoon, so we all made an early night of it — except for the crew, who stayed at the restaurant to discuss details into the wee hours. They didn't have to worry about their voices after a late night of boozing.

Dan had been somewhere nearby and I phoned him as the party was breaking up. He met me at the front door of the hotel.

Since the evening was reasonably pleasant, it would have been very enjoyable to walk back to Hotel La Fenice. It was Carnevale time and the city was filled with people in costume.

Dan nixed the idea. "A water taxi would be wiser."

"You're probably right," I sighed.

"That's a good girl. Always listen to your security expert. I hear Venice is a dangerous city."

I smiled. "Not since the last doge."

From a musical standpoint, the next seven days went by in a complete blur. Everyone in the cast agreed that the pace made it feel more like repertory theatre where you have to mount a production every two weeks. Fortunately, the crew had their end down to a fine art due to the earlier performances in Naples and Rome. Everyone in the cast had played their roles a number of times, so we felt confident that we'd pull this off well when we went live on Saturday evening.

The cast bonded quickly, and since everyone spoke Italian at least reasonably (and the majority of the crew was Italian), it became our production language.

The lone exception was Tobias Ebler, our conductor. They were using a different conductor for the four productions in the series, each of a different nationality. There was no doubt he was a very competent man with a stick, but he was definitely old school, expecting instant obedience from everyone. His Italian was so minimal that I was surprised he'd been considered. I learned later he had seldom conducted in this country.

During the first piano run-through in the upstairs rehearsal room, he immediately got into it with the chorus.

"*Nein, nein, nein! Sie sind nicht der Mittelpunkt der Vorstellung! Und Sie singen als würden Sie hier sein um Lärm zu machen. Mehr Musik und weniger Geschrei wie ein verletzter Esel, bitte!*"

The poor soul who'd been tasked with translating immediately jumped to his feet, a sad look on his face since his unenviable task was to tell the singers they'd been likened to braying donkeys.

I looked at our Alfredo, the excellent, but turbulent Ettore Lagorio. He shrugged and made a disgusted gesture, which unfortunately Ebler must have caught, because during our first aria together, "*Un dì, felice, eterea,*" he was stopped three times for piddling reasons. None of this boded well. Lagorio was rumoured to think a lot of himself and it was only a matter of time before he'd blast off at Ebler.

Based on what had happened in Rome as a result of my run-in with De Vicenzo, I made sure there was no friction between me and anyone. That had to include Ebler, even though I soon longed to give him a piece of my mind — as did everyone. So whenever he addressed me, I was suitably subservient.

The news from Rome followed hard on my heels. It didn't help that shortly after my arrival in Venice, it was revealed the police in Rome were now investigating De Vicenzo's death as a possible homicide. Mercifully, my name hadn't been mentioned in the reports, but of course everyone asked what I knew. I made the appropriate comments about the tragedy of the situation, but nothing more.

⁓

Outside the safety of the opera house, things were less enjoyable. Dan kept himself discretely away from me, but I knew he was always close, except when I was in rehearsal. During those times, he cautioned me to never be alone. Going back the few steps to the hotel, I could always see him watching from a distance. I began to chafe at what seemed more and more like confinement to quarters since I had to beg off from going out to dinner with members of the cast or spending any social time with them outside the opera house. I used the excuse that I needed to work on memorizing my role for the opera I was premiering in Toronto in less than a month's time — which was to some extent true. With that deadline staring me right in the face, I was terrified I wouldn't know it well enough and spent my evenings working on it.

Sad to say, I sort of took it out on Tony, since he was the only one who understood all I was dealing with. Our nightly phone calls became one long gripe session from *moi*.

"And tonight, they were all going to Piazza San Marco to have dinner and listen to the music, while I'm stuck in this miserable hotel room!"

Even to my own ears I sounded like a whining child, but I couldn't stop myself. Here I was part of this great production and I couldn't take part in the fun bits.

"Have the Roman police been in touch with you at all?" Tony asked.

"Not since the night they questioned me, thank the lord. I don't need that distraction. Have you heard anything?"

"The Toronto cops aren't saying much since De Vicenzo was murdered. Shannon is getting pretty frustrated by the stonewalling."

"Has she gotten any further on who owns that apartment?"

"Toronto cops again. To put it simply, they don't want her in the way. Any sign of our friend?"

"Nothing so far, but Dan has me so separated from everything and everybody, I don't see how this bozo could get near me. Every day he sweeps my room for bugs. It's sort of comical."

There was silence on the phone for a moment. "Where is he now?"

"I suppose he's in his room."

"Which is where?"

"Right next to mine, of course. Why do you ask?"

More silence. "I just don't like the fact this guy's practically living with you."

"Do you honestly think something is going on between Dan and me?"

"Well, you do keep talking about him a lot."

I shook my head in disbelief. "Tony, for God's sake! Don't you trust me? Sure, I like Dan. He's good company, but he has a job to do, and our relationship goes no farther than that."

"Relationship? You have a relationship with him now?"

"Oh, for the love of God, Tony, get a grip. When I go to bed at night, I'm alone. Period!"

My temper got the better of me — as it often does — and I slammed down the phone. It rang almost immediately, but I didn't answer.

Chapter Seventeen

I felt absolutely wretched as I paced in my dressing room waiting for the curtain that Saturday evening. It wasn't just pre-performance jitters.

No, they had done everything humanly possible to get us ready for this live opera broadcast. The dress rehearsal two days previous (to allow our voices to rest) had gone frighteningly well, and yesterday we'd run a *sotto voce* one so the camera angles could be improved a bit more. That went incredibly smoothly, too.

We all should have been calm and reassured. Right?

All it did was make the more superstitious of us feel that we might be courting disaster, using up all our luck before our performances *really* counted.

"Just forget the cameras are there," the director had told us at our final meeting that afternoon. "Perform this opera as you would perform any other."

Next to me, Ettore Lagorio mumbled, "Easy for him to say."

Surprisingly, after all I'd heard, he'd kept his legendary temper in check. I enjoyed the way our voices sounded together and he was a splendid Alfredo. I was sorry we were only doing this one performance.

I put my arm around him. "Relax. You are going to be just great."

"But my entire family will be watching," he'd answered. "That's *real* pressure."

"I'm the same way. My husband's family are all opera crazy. They're watching it on the Internet."

He put his arm around me, squeezing me against him as he landed a big fat kiss on my cheek. I wondered what Tony would say seeing that. Lagorio was very handsome. Then my pursuer flashed across my mind.

Pushing myself to my feet, I scurried to my dressing room, regardless that the director's meeting hadn't completely finished.

Tony and I had patched things up within twenty-four hours. I couldn't understand where he'd ever gotten the idea there was anything between me and Dan. He said there was some talking backstage at the opera. Of course, our craft is exceptionally incestuous. Everyone knows everything and most singers are shameless gossips.

Word had gotten back to Toronto that I had a rather handsome man, supposedly a writer, constantly with me in Rome and also in Venice. Of course, hanky-panky was suspected. Why someone would have been tacky enough to ask Tony about it was beyond me. But there it was, the source of his jealousy.

Then there was my cabin fever. I love nothing more than to stroll around Venice. There are so many surprising little alleys opening onto hidden piazzas. Marvelous shops are tucked away all over the place, many having been in the same family for generations. For entertainment, you can sit in Piazza San Marco and watch the world go by. Later at night, there's Harry's Bar. Dan had kept me from doing any of that, and I really missed it. I understood the reasons, but that didn't make it any easier.

The producers had planned a cast party at the Hotel Danieli after the performance, and I talked Dan into letting me attend. He'd become more and more jumpy since there was no sign of my damn "shadow." Every morning he'd checked my room for bugs and cameras. No roses had shown up on my doorstep. There had been nothing.

"Oh, he's out there, never fear," Dan had told me that morning after breakfast. "Maybe he's keeping his distance because of Rome, but I will be shocked if he doesn't try to leave another bouquet or some other sign."

We didn't think it was a good idea to bring him into the opera house, and security was pretty tight anyway, so under Dan's direction I wired up one of his little cameras and a broadcast device, so he would be able to monitor what was going on in my dressing room. I only turned it off when I was changing.

"Maybe we'll catch a break. I don't see how he can spot where you've put that camera. And if he's watching us — which I'll bet he is — he'll know I haven't been inside so he won't suspect anything."

"I really hope this nightmare ends soon. I wake up at the slightest noise. I can't be anywhere without constantly looking over my shoulder."

Dan put his arm around me. "Relax. We've got everything covered that we can cover. I spoke to Shannon last night and she told me they should shortly have the name of whoever owns that apartment overlooking your building. All we need is a lucky break, some footage here in Venice, or news from Hong Kong about the ownership of that condo, or something else, and we'll have this clown."

"Have you heard anything from Rome?"

"Nothing. Shannon is working to get one of her old friends on the force to give us news. You watch. She'll come through."

I got the feeling Dan was whistling past the graveyard just a bit.

Two hours later, over the backstage intercom, someone said, "*Attenzione, mancano dieci minuti. Per favore vi preparate!*"

I felt my gut tighten. Only ten minutes before we met our fates on the stage of one of the world's most storied opera houses.

Despite everything going on around me, I had to clear my head and replace all the crap with the glorious music of Verdi I was about to sing — in the same theatre where the world had first heard it (even if the place had burned to the ground in the interim). The crew was ready, the auditorium jammed with those lucky people who'd managed to get tickets. We had the best cast I'd ever been part of. All I had to do was be perfect.

Heading for stage right where I'd wait for my cue, I was wondering where the inevitable cock-up would happen and how bad it would be.

⟵⟶

I love the opening act of *Traviata* above all operas. It just sparkles throughout as Verdi and his brilliant librettist Piave draw you into what is actually a rather sordid tale. And that was the composer's problem at the start. Yes, he was Italy's — and arguably, Europe's — greatest opera composer at that time (though Wagnerites would violently disagree), but the subject matter was pretty out there for the society of the day. Courtesans, living in sin, sticking up a middle finger to much of what people thought proper, had certainly been shocking.

There was also the problem that the opera in its original form dragged. Its worst sin, though, had been casting a famous but rather old and very overweight soprano as the consumptive courtesan Violetta. The audience back in 1853 at La Fenice had understandably let Verdi know in no uncertain terms, even though the bad casting wasn't his fault. Critics savaged *Traviata*, and Verdi was saddened and angered by what he saw as everyone's misunderstanding. The opening was a disaster, but the composer recovered, did a bit of pruning, got a more appropriate cast, and a new production was mounted in 1854, but at a different Venetian theatre. This time, the opera was a triumph and is now loved by millions — me among them.

So that night, we didn't have to face a hostile audience, we just had to get everything perfect because we were live on air throughout Europe and eventually around the world. We couldn't stop if someone messed up. Not that you can do that for any live performance, but this was being recorded and any mistakes anyone made would be digitally hung around their necks for all eternity. You can bet everyone involved was *very* aware of that fact.

I heard my cue and breezed out of the wings dressed in a perfectly gorgeous gown, the belle of the ball, the hostess with the most-est, and greeted my party guests with "*Flora, amici, la notte che resta.*" I was off to the races.

I absolutely adored singing with Ettore. He was so musical. We gave each other the space and support we needed, and Ebler had the sense to stay out of our way. My voice that evening made me feel I could do anything, so I reached as far as I dared. Since I was so familiar with the production — unlike the rest of the cast — I could just relax and let it rip. The auditorium gave lovely feedback to our voices, so we didn't feel as if we were singing into the vast unknown. In short, the first act was magical and I enjoyed myself immensely.

Judging by the response of the audience as the curtain came down, they loved it, too. I gave Ettore a huge hug and headed back to my dressing room a happy camper. It was only as I approached it that I remembered what might be waiting there. I took a deep breath, turned the knob, and went in to find ... nothing.

Before the dresser arrived, I pulled my mobile out of my shoulder bag and dialed Dan, who was waiting in his hotel room. "Coast seems to be clear. Did you see anything while I was out?"

"Not a thing," he answered. "So far, so good. How's the performance going?"

"Didn't you hear the bravas in your hotel room?" I teased.

"No. I had a soccer match on," he shot right back. "I'm glad it's going well."

I was back in the wings a good five minutes before time, ready, willing, and able to go. I couldn't wait for Ebler to strike up the band.

The second act is far more intimate, with only two singers on stage most of the time. Violetta is there for most of it, so the weight of the production was firmly on me. The blocking was also a bit more complex, especially in the party scene that closes it. That had been the only place we'd stumbled during our dress rehearsal. Everyone was a bit more tense, so I don't think the performance was our very best. There were no train wrecks, but to me it felt tentative, as if we were all expecting a disaster at any moment.

They had included the dance sequence in this production (scaled way back in the Paris production) so the stage was crammed between the singers, chorus, supers, and over a dozen dancers. I had a chance to catch my breath and look out at the house. Every seat was full, and I was wondering who the lucky sods were, sitting in the royal box in the centre of the first ring.

One of the chorus members sidled up, and noticing where my eyes were fixed, said from the corner of her mouth, "I heard the German chancellor is here, along with the president of Italia."

I was about to ask who else might be there, when I heard my cue coming up. Time for Alfredo to throw money at me, the ultimate insult to what he perceived was my infidelity. It's the dramatic high point of the opera and Ettore did it very well indeed, almost going over the top — almost. Knowing the effect of his acting and singing, I was waiting to hear gasps of shock from the audience, it was that powerful.

The opera gods smiled on us and everything went off without a hitch. Ettore was brilliant, and sadly, I couldn't hear any gasps of horror — which he deserved.

Violetta's exit for the act was to run off stage left, humiliated beyond bearing by Alfredo's harsh words and actions in front of so many people. It is all the more poignant because the audience is well aware of the reason for Violetta doing what she did because of her promise to Alfredo's father. I had just turned to watch the last few minutes of the act when I stepped on something.

It was a single rose. Around it on the floor I counted eleven more, along with a small note.

How I managed to keep from screaming is beyond me.

⌒

Somehow I did the curtain call, but I was pretty wobbly and out of it.

"What is wrong, my dear?" Ettore asked.

I curtseyed to the audience, then answered, "Something happened in the wings. I'll tell you later. I'll be all right. I'm just a little shaken up, that's all."

I prayed that I was telling him the truth.

Back in my dressing room, I had my phone out in record time.

"Dan! He was here! He may be backstage even now."

I told him what had happened.

"I know you're really upset, Marta, but can you do something for me?"

"I can't stop shaking. The bastard! Goddamn him. Doesn't he know what this is doing to me?"

"That's precisely why he's doing it."

"Is he trying to ruin my performance?"

"Probably. Now, take a deep breath. Pull yourself back together. I need you to do something for me."

His even tone and calmness began to have an effect on me. "What?"

"Can you go down to the stage and ask anyone on that side if they saw anything? I need to know. I'm looking at the stage entrance right now, and if anyone comes out in the next few minutes, I'm going to be all over him."

I took a few deep breaths. "I have to get ready for the last act."

"Once that's done, go down to the stage. Can you do that for me?"

"I'm really freaked out, Dan. I don't know …"

"C'mon, Marta. I know you can be a real tiger. You're not going to let this bastard beat you, are you?"

It was just what I needed someone to say to me.

"No. I'll pull myself together. What I could really use is a good belt of something strong."

"I'll buy you two after the performance."

I could feel my breathing slow down. "I'm going to keep the phone line open, Dan, so you can hear everything, and I'm keeping it with me until I walk on that stage."

"Good idea."

"My dresser, Sabrina, is coming in. Can't talk anymore. Just stay with me, okay?"

"I'm here, Marta."

I'm used to acting onstage, *not* in my dressing room, but I put on a pretty good show for the dresser. Just as she was putting the finishing touches on the fall I wore in the last act, there was a knock on the door.

Ettore stuck his head in the door. "Is everything all right, my dear? You were as white as a sheet."

"I, ah, almost fell down. There were a bunch of long-stemmed roses all over the floor backstage."

"Roses? How odd."

The dresser, still fussing with my fall, added, "Yes. They were talking about them just now. Apparently one of the chorus members proposed to another during the first intermission, and she turned him down. They had a raging quarrel in front of everyone and he stormed out. He must have thrown away the bouquet he'd brought. Beautiful pink roses."

"What?" was all I could manage to say.

I hadn't been able to see the colour well in the backstage gloom, and to be frank I didn't even look all that closely. I just saw roses and freaked out. I felt like a complete fool.

"I, ah, need a minute to myself, Sabrina." She took the hint and scurried out. Picking up my mobile, I said to Dan, "Did you hear all that?"

"Loud and clear. Guess it was all a false alarm."

"I'm such a dunce."

"Not at all. You've been under a lot of pressure. I probably would have done the same thing."

"I shouldn't complain, but I'm mentally so far away from what I have to do…. I have to get myself pulled back together."

"Take a few deep breaths and then go out there and knock them dead."

"You sound just like Lili."

"God help me."

Chapter Eighteen

The curtain came down and the audience roared. The stage manager gave me two thumbs up as I got myself off the floor after having expired a couple of minutes earlier.

Ettore was beaming as he took my hand. I latched on to the evening's Germont (Martin Smith from the UK) and we took the first of many curtain calls.

Everyone in the cast was in a jubilant mood as we left the theatre. The producers had supplied water taxis to take us from La Fenice to the Danieli. Dan felt that was safe enough for me. He'd follow discretely behind in his own taxi.

I was sitting in the back of one boat with François

LaPierre, the director, on one side and Ettore Lagorio on the other, with everyone around us chattering about how splendidly it had all gone.

Canalside, Carnevale was in full swing. With the final few days upon Venice, it was party central and we passed many laughing groups fully decked out in the traditional costumes: women as Columbina and men as Bauta, Pantalone, or Volto. We passed someone in a gondola dressed as the *Medico della peste*, the mysterious Plague Doctor, with a long black cloak, tri-corner hat, and the mask with the long beak and pince-nez glasses that always gave me the willies.

Someone commented that we should have worn our costumes. "We would have fit right in."

I wanted to soak in my only night of freedom in Venice, and the weather had cooperated. February can be frightful, with high tides causing flooding throughout the city. The Venetians handle it with aplomb, donning rubber boots and putting out temporary elevated walkways through Piazza San Marco, but it's still messy. The weather had been fine all week, and that night it felt almost warm. High in the sky above us, a full moon rode some scattered clouds.

"It is so nice that you can come out with us this evening, Marta," Ettore said as we passed the bridge over the canal next to the Doge's Palace. "You have hidden yourself away all week."

"It's this damned opera I'm premiering next month. I don't know how I'm ever going to memorize my part. It's long and it's complicated, and fiendishly difficult."

"Are you sure it has nothing to do with the mysterious gentleman who is always somewhere around?"

My heart almost stopped. "What gentleman?"

LaPierre said that some of the cast and crew had seen me having breakfast with him in my hotel. He patted my arm. "Don't worry. We do not make the judgment."

Not wanting to give rumours any oxygen, I told them, "That's Dan. He's a ghost writer who's helping me with my memoirs. He's been with me on this whole trip."

"But why have you not introduced him?"

"He wants me to forget he's there. He says it will give him more perspective on how I live my life. Don't worry, he's a good friend of my husband."

I could tell they weren't really swallowing my story, but it was better than telling them exactly why Dan was with me.

Trying to change the subject, I looked up the canal passing by. Leading from the palace to the building next door was a stone bridge, high up. It had tiny little chinks of windows that seemed out of place.

"That's the Bridge of Sighs, isn't it?" I asked.

"Yes," Ettore answered. "I pity the poor bastards whose last sight of the outside world was through those windows as they were led off to prison."

"That's the building to the right?"

"Yes. Have you ever been in it?"

"No. When I was here with Gerhard Fosch, he wanted me to see it when he was showing me the Doge's Palace. I didn't want to go. Small confined areas like those old cells make me very uncomfortable." I took my two gentlemen's arms. "Perhaps in a previous life, I was a desperate criminal who spent the last months of life in a cell like that."

"You, a desperate criminal? I will not believe it!"

We were laughing again as we went ashore not far from the other side of the bridge and hustled off along the Riva toward the Hotel Danieli.

It was well after two when the party broke up. I was several glasses of champagne to the plus side and feeling just wonderful for the first time in several weeks. *Traviata* had gone off very well, and I'd sung as well as I ever had. The false alarm with the roses backstage had faded from my memory, as had the horrible events in Rome. A good party and champagne will do that for you.

I did have my wits about me enough to call Dan on my mobile as I descended the stairs to the Danieli's famous lobby.

"Where are you?" I asked.

"In the bar. Care to join me? I still owe you a double."

"I've had quite enough, thank you."

"Ready to go, then?"

I walked up behind Dan and took his phone out of his hand. "It seems stupid to talk on this thing when I'm standing right behind you. Some spy! You didn't even notice."

"Of course I knew you were there. I was just trying to get you off balance."

"But what if I'd had a knife?"

He smiled. "I could disarm you in a heartbeat."

I put my arm around his shoulder and gave him a big kiss on his cheek. "I'll just bet you could."

"My, you *have* had a bit to drink."

"Just champagne."

"I've heard that one before," he said with a grin before heaving himself to his feet.

"Have you been drinking?"

"Sparkling water."

But I could tell he'd had at least one drink. I looked at my watch, realizing Dan had been waiting for me for well over two hours.

When I started to apologize, he put his hand over my mouth. "All part of the service. I've been enjoying sitting here watching all the revelers. Some of the costumes are truly amazing."

"It will go on around the clock between now and Tuesday. In the old days, they got up to all kinds of debauchery. Really quite shocking in such a Catholic city."

"The Church's strictness is probably precisely why they got up to some hanky-panky. Let's hit the road. We've got a plane to catch tomorrow."

The Riva was still quite crowded for so late.

"Pretty please, Dan, can we walk back to the hotel? I'm not the slightest bit tired and the walk might sober me up a bit."

Dan was clearly not happy. It took a lot of convincing before he gave in.

"There are tons of people around. Even if our friend decided to stay up this late, he's not going to try anything in a crowd."

Dan decided to humour me, but insisted on walking right next to me and I was fine with that.

The cafés around Piazza San Marco were still going strong, filled with revelers. We stopped in the centre of it, listening to the old standards from competing orchestras echo off the buildings, all very atmospheric. Tonight was Venice at its timeless best. It could have easily been a hundred years ago.

As we got to the far end of the square and passed through a short arcade, I told Dan, "It's too bad we couldn't have gotten away to wander around. It's great fun to just follow the alleys and small piazzas to see where you wind up. Since Venice is all a group of islands, you can't really get lost here. Eventually you'll get to the other side, and then you just hop on one of the vaporetti that circle the city."

"I've definitely seen enough to want to come back. Now I get what everyone goes on about when Venice is mentioned."

"It's best to come back here with somebody. Venice is much better with two."

"I don't have anyone."

"May I ask why that is?"

He shrugged. "Too busy and always on the move. There have been women along the way, but nothing that lasted. Guess I haven't met the right one."

The party people weren't so much in evidence around here, but there were still enough that I felt secure. I continued regaling Dan with things I knew about the city. Since I was a bit wobbly from the champagne I'd consumed, Dan took my arm as we walked. Passing a darkened storefront, I stumbled on an uneven cobble and nearly went down. Nimbly, he swung me around and we wound up face to face.

"Steady there, Marta." He laughed. "You've got enough trouble without twisting your ankle."

His expression was unreadable.

"I'm fine, really. Just wasn't watching where I was stepping."

"Too much champagne and a good performance, I expect."

I looked up into his face. "Thanks for catching me."

"All part of the service. Let's shake a leg. It's getting late."

We walked several minutes longer, finally entering a large square. I turned us left and we walked a bit further.

"Whoops! This is the Grand Canal. We shouldn't be here. We must have taken a wrong turn someplace."

It was the Academia Bridge. Back at the previous piazza, I should have had us turn right rather than left. I was pretty sure La Fenice and our little hotel were in that direction. When we got back to the piazza, the restaurants and cafés were all closing and the crowds were melting away. I felt sure I'd been here before. In the centre of it was a large statue of a large man. He seemed very familiar.

"It's this way," I said with more certainty.

We passed straight through, went down an alley, and then into a smaller piazza that was nearly deserted.

Dan said, "Perhaps we should ask someone."

I giggled. "Was that a male I just heard, suggesting we ask for directions?"

"We have no idea where we are and it's getting late."

There were two people on the other side of the piazza. I called out in Italian, "Hey! Can you help us with some directions?"

They looked back but kept on walking. We were now alone.

"I'm almost certain we should go that way," I said, pointing to a wide alley on our right.

We walked along it, came to one of those arched bridges that are so Venetian, went up and over, and found ourselves in a smaller alley. It was completely empty and lit only by a light at the end.

We hurried along it and came out in a small piazza with four exits. I picked the most likely one and we entered an even smaller alley. It came to an end suddenly at the edge of a canal.

The alcohol had worn off and I was beginning to get nervous.

"We should go back to the Grand Canal," Dan said, putting his arm around me, "catch one of those vaporetto boats and return to San Marco. I'm sure we can find a water taxi there."

Turning around, we walked quickly back up the alley. We'd just about gotten to the end when Dan sort of went "Uhhh," and slumped against me. Taken off balance and by surprise, I couldn't hold him up and he slithered down my body to the cobblestones.

Someone pushed me hard against the opposite wall of the alley, one hand on my stomach and the other holding my chin.

"Do not cry out or I will break your neck," he whispered in Italian. It reminded me of a hissing snake.

He was hunched and wearing a black cloak. As he moved against the light from the square behind us, I saw with horror a tri-corner hat and a long beak where his face should have been. The Plague Doctor. My blood ran cold.

"You should have listened to your friend Hudson and not gone to that party, Marta Hendriks."

"Who are you?" I asked through clenched teeth.

"You know who I am. And you should not be trifling with me. Right now I could kill you. You know that, don't you?"

I managed a nod.

"You think you did well tonight? What if I were to tell your husband that you were walking arm in arm with another man? What if he knew the way you were looking at this man? Eh? What if I told him you were in Hudson's arms? Where would you be then?"

"What do you want from me?"

I realized the man was trembling as much as I was, but whether from nerves or emotion, I couldn't tell.

He stood up taller and moved his face toward my left ear. "I want your voice, your talent, your being. I want all of you. Know that I am always here, in your life, in your dreams. I am your nightmare. You cannot stop me, Marta. I will have you. Know that."

He released me and disappeared as quietly as he'd come. I would have loved to cry out, brought people running who might have grabbed him, unmasked him, so that I would have known who this foul creature was. But I was just too petrified by fear to do anything except sink to the ground.

Next to me, Dan moved his head and moaned.

Thank God he was still alive.

Pulling myself together, I stumbled to the mouth of the alley, took a deep breath, and cried out for help. And believe me, when someone with my vocal capacity cries out, the entire city of Venice should hear it.

Chapter Nineteen

The jangling of the phone by his elbow jolted Tony out of a very sound sleep. The Leafs were still on the TV, down five to two in the dying minutes of the third period, no closer to the Stanley Cup than they'd been since 1967. The last thing he remembered they'd scored two quick goals halfway through the first period. He must have been more zonked than he'd thought.

The phone was now on its third ring. He picked it up. "Hello?"

"Tony. It's me. I was ... I was ..."

"Marta? Where are you?"

"In Venice. Where else would I be?"

He wiped his hand over his face. "Sorry. I dozed off in front of the TV. I'm a bit groggy. What's up?"

It still hadn't sunk in that his wife was near hysteria. He suddenly remembered that tonight was the broadcast. He was supposed to watch it on the Internet. Oh geez. Was he going to catch it now!

"Tony. I saw *him* tonight. He was here. He spoke to me."

Finally he was awake enough to realize something was very wrong.

"You saw him? Where? How? What did he say?"

"It's Dan. The bastard hit him or did something to him. I don't know. I'm at a police station."

Marta was making little sense. She sounded at the breaking point.

"Marta, love, take a deep breath. Start at the beginning. Tell me what's happened."

It took a number of minutes to get the full story out of her in any intelligible form. To say the least, he was horrified as to how close it had been to something *really* bad happening.

"And you say Dan's in the hospital?"

"When people finally came to my shouting, he was still unconscious. When the police arrived, they separated us. I only know that an ambulance boat came and took him away. They brought me to a police station and they've been questioning me ever since. I don't know where Dan is or what's happening to him!"

Tony wished he'd listened to his heart and gone along with Marta. He'd thought Dan had everything in hand, but obviously that was a very false hope.

"Are you okay? Were you hurt?"

"No. He just spoke to me. Threatened me, really. I was sure he was going to kill me. Oh my God, it was so horrible."

"And you're at a police station right now?"

"Yes."

"Stay there. He can't get at you when you're with them."

"Believe me, I am not going anywhere. Oh Christ, I wish you were here, Tony!"

"So do I. Can you put one of the officers on the line?"

He could hear a muffled conversation, then a brisk voice asked in Italian, "Who is this?"

"I am the husband of Marta Hendriks. I'm in Toronto. Can you tell me what's going on?"

The inspector was puzzled about exactly what had happened. Tony told him quickly about the murder in Rome.

"Contact Chief Inspector Stefano Pucci, or whatever his rank is," he told the Venetian cop. "He knows far more about this than I do. But you must promise me that my wife will not be left alone. The person stalking her is very determined and very clever."

"I can assure we will look after Signora Hendriks."

"And what about the person accompanying her? Where is he and is he all right?"

"Signore Hudson. He is at the hospital being examined."

"Can you find out how seriously he's hurt?"

"I will do my best. You have to understand that it is very late at night here."

"I understand. My wife is coming home this morning. Her flight leaves in," he glanced at his watch, "five hours. I don't think she should go back to her hotel, do you?"

Tony could again hear a muffled conversation and then Marta came back on the line.

"Tony? They say I can't go back to the hotel to pick up my luggage."

"No, dear. Stay there until it's time to go to the airport. Can you see if they will personally take you there?"

More muffled talking.

"They'll do that. The inspector you first talked with is speaking with the Roman police right now."

"What about Dan?"

"Wait…. He just walked into the office. Oh God! His head's all wrapped in bandages."

Tony waited impatiently as more conversation happened.

Dan came on the line. "Tony? This sure is a bloody mess. I'd like to apologize for screwing up so —"

"No apology necessary. Just get Marta out of there and back to Toronto safely. That's all I ask."

"I'll do my best, although I'm feeling a little out of it at the moment. I got slugged pretty hard."

"What happened?"

"No idea. One moment I was talking to Marta and the next I was flat on my back with a Carabinieri shining his bloody flashlight in my eyes. All I know is I've got a huge lump on my head and the doctors say I have a mild concussion. They wanted to keep me in the hospital overnight, but I checked myself out and came here searching for Marta."

Dan was in agreement that it was best for Marta to leave directly from the police station. He'd try to get the Venetian Carabinieri to go with him to the hotel for the luggage. Failing that, he'd go by himself. He assured Tony that Marta would not leave the police station until it was time for her flight.

After the conversation ended with Tony telling Marta that he loved her and couldn't wait to see her, he sat for several minutes trying to digest what had happened. It must have been horrible for poor Marta, but at least nothing worse had happened. Again, they'd seriously misjudged her stalker.

The next call was one that had to be made, regardless of the hour.

"Shannon? Tony…. Yes, I'm well aware what time it is. I just spoke to Marta and Dan in Venice…. You're not going to like what I have to tell you."

Chapter Twenty

Dan walked back into the first-class lounge at Venice's Aeroporto Marco Polo, looking like some sort of foreign potentate with that huge bandage swathed around his head.

He sat down gingerly next to me, pulling something from a plastic bag. I could tell his injury was really bothering him.

"Here. You're going to use these on the flight."

It was one of those sleeping blindfolds and ear plugs that airport stores sell.

"Is this so I can't see and hear trouble coming?" I asked lightly — but I wasn't really joking.

"No. I want you to sleep if you can. You didn't get a

wink last night."

"How about you? You should probably be in a hospital bed right now."

"The reason this whole mess happened was because I didn't do my job very well. That hurts my professional pride a lot. I'm going to be sitting in the aisle seat, and I'll be keeping my eyes open. Besides, the doctor told me I shouldn't sleep for twenty-four hours."

I took the blindfold and slid it into my shoulder bag.

Dan was right. Sleep would be good for me. Only problem was, every time I closed my eyes, I would stare into the blackness and hear the terrifying raspy whisper of my enemy, telling me horrible things. Perhaps it would fade in time, but right now it was too near and too raw.

When we'd arrived at the airport (via police escort), I discovered that Tony had changed my reservations to first class. Dan's, too. Check-in was a breeze. Heaven only knew where our baggage went, but I really didn't care at that point. Dan had disappeared with one of the cops during more questioning, returning only just before we departed the police station. He had my laptop and partially filled shoulder bag. I guessed he'd been removing all the surveillance equipment in my room. The fact that he allowed one of the cops to accompany him was telling. Dan, at his usual, wouldn't have done that. He definitely looked the worst for wear.

When it came time to board, I was escorted right onto the plane while everyone else was waiting in line. Wearing my large sunglasses and a black beret, they must have thought I was a *someone*. The way I was feeling at the moment, locking myself into one of the washrooms sounded like the best idea.

"I have a favour to ask," Dan said as we got seated, "but if you don't want to do it, I'll understand."

"You want me to look at people as they come on the plane, don't you?"

He smiled. "Got it in one. Can you do that?"

I nodded.

"Good. Now here's what we're going to do. You told me our friend's accent when he spoke to you could have been Canadian or American."

"Yes. His Italian was good, but it had an accent that I'd say was North American — like mine."

"Look at every male getting on this plane. If you see someone you think reminds you of your adversary — and I want you to think of him that way, because that's what he is — what I want you to do is squeeze my hand. I have my pen camera in my pocket, and I'll take a photograph. After that, you're off duty and I want you to get some sleep."

"This seems like kind of a long shot."

"It is, but we could get lucky."

"The only other thing I can say for sure is that he's maybe three inches taller than me. When he whispered into my ear, I don't think he was standing on tiptoes. He could be young or old, bald, blond, or dark-haired. I could shake his hand and not even know it was him."

"Answer this without thinking: slender or overweight?"

"Slender. Oh! How come I didn't realize I knew that?"

"There's probably more that you know, but we'll have to dig it out of your subconscious. Shannon has spoken to your friend Lili. Maybe we'll try hypnosis when we get back to Toronto."

As the plane boarded, I did my very best. Only four men fit our rather generous description.

"He's probably not stupid enough to be on this plane," I said as the last two passengers, a grandma-type and a small boy, passed by.

"But that tells us something in itself," Dan said.

"I don't follow."

"I doubt if he would board a plane in this day and age with a disguise on. He'd need to have a second set of papers for one thing and he'd have to be certain no one could tell he had on a disguise. Seems like a high level of risk just to make a point, doesn't it? I don't think he'd bother."

We looked at each other for a moment, then said simultaneously, "Oh yes, he would."

Neither of us felt inclined to laugh, though.

⁓

I buried my face in Tony's shoulder so no one could see I was crying. Behind me was a skycap with a trolley full of our luggage. Off to my right, Dan stood talking with Shannon, who'd also come to meet the plane.

"I've never been so glad to be home," I sniffled into Tony's coat.

By way of answering, he just squeezed me tighter.

Shannon had brought her SUV and we all piled into that: them in the front, Tony and me in the back.

"How do you feel, love?" he asked.

"Rotten. Dan bought me a sleeping mask and ear plugs. I spent most of the flight in that sort of grey zone between sleep and waking. What good I'm going be at rehearsal tomorrow is anyone's guess."

"Shannon and I have talked a lot over the past few hours about what to do. Things have gotten beyond serious now. We have some ideas, but I think it's best to hear what Lili has to say before we make any decisions. Do you feel up to visiting her? She's cleared her afternoon."

"I suppose so, although what I need most is to sleep for at least twelve hours."

Shannon was negotiating traffic on the 427, one of the big highways encircling Toronto. As usual, traffic was miserable. The sky looked as if we might get a major dump of snow.

As we took the ramp to the eastbound Gardiner Expressway, Shannon asked, "So where to? Your place or Lili's?"

"Take us to Lili," I said, feeling calmer now that I was back in my usual surroundings with my husband's comforting arm around me.

We couldn't hear what Shannon and Dan were discussing as we crept along with the other rush hour traffic, but there was a lot of head shaking between the two of them. Neither seemed to like what was being talked about.

I leaned back and continued trying to process exactly what happened to me less than twenty-four hours earlier. Maybe it was the fact that it was Venice — and there really is something decadent and mysterious about this most unique of cities — or maybe it was the terror of finally meeting this person face to face. I could not close my eyes without being right back in that dark alley, shoved against the wall and not knowing if I was going to live or die.

Somehow I had to quickly regain my equilibrium. With the premiere of *The Passage of Time* less than three short weeks away, I was hard up against it. I could not imagine rehearsing the next day. The music was extremely challenging and I barely had control of my part. What was I going to do?

Perhaps sensing the trail of my inner thoughts, Tony pulled me tighter against him as if to say, *Marta, you are not in this alone*. It was infinitely comforting — and I needed that more right now than anything else. From comfort and calm would come focus. In order to premiere this new opera, I needed as much focus as I could get.

⌒

Lili stared across the room at me in that way she has. All she'd asked me was, "How are you feeling, my dear?"

Upon our arrival at her house, she'd asked if she could speak to me alone. We were now in her studio, with Tony, Shannon, and Dan waiting in her sitting room. They had a lot to discuss, I was sure.

When I didn't answer immediately, Lili kept her death stare on me, making it clear we weren't going any further until I spoke.

Why was I so hesitant? Physically, I felt like garbage. I wasn't sure I had it in me to go through with this opera premiere. I was depressed. But mostly, I was still frightened out of my wits.

A minute ticked by, then another while I looked out the windows into her snowy backyard. I looked down at the floor, the ceiling, her piano — but not her.

"I feel …"

Lili leaned forward expectantly.

I began to cry again. She did nothing. It wasn't as if we hadn't been through this before. My friend had supplied countless boxes of tissues as I sniffled my way through therapy sessions when she'd helped me get over the supposed death of my first husband. She thought this was the best way for me to "rediscover my backbone," as she once put it. Eventually, something would click in me and things that were bothering me would bubble to the surface, often in a nearly uncontrollable torrent. Then Lili would help me sort through it all.

Today, I guess she decided there wasn't the time to wait me out.

"I have been listening to the partial recording you gave me of the new opera. It is very interesting, I must say. How do you feel about it?"

"Like I'm about to go headfirst into a meat grinder. I've learned most of the notes, the rhythms, but nothing speaks to me yet. Rehearsals begin tomorrow and I am so woefully at sea with the part."

She nodded. "That is a problem, but I do not think it is insurmountable, knowing you."

"How can you say that?" I asked, shaking my head. "Opera is not built around regurgitating a composer's musical ideas. A performance has to have emotion and subtlety. It has to be done as an adjunct to acting. I have absolutely no idea how to *perform* this role."

That was one thing I'd been thinking about a lot while I'd been under Dan's house arrest in Italy. I would have to create this role — with the director's help, of course — since it was brand new. I should know how to do this sort of thing, but I had psyched myself to near immobility.

"Are you having trouble because the situation in the plot of this opera is so close to what you are experiencing in your own life?"

I'm afraid my jaw hit the floor. I already knew Lili was an extraordinary woman, but with the insight of those few words, she simply took my breath away.

She sat back again and waited while her question pinballed through my brain, setting off lights and sounds all over the place. Her analysis was so simple, and yet so complicated.

At its heart, *The Passage of Time* is about a human soul being gradually cut off from everything that has meaning. This is precisely what was happening to me. My privacy wasn't my own any longer. I now spent a lot of my time looking over my shoulder. I was a captive in my hotel room, my apartment, in the opera house, basically everywhere. Everything that mattered was slowly being taken away from me. Why hadn't I seen the parallels?

Either she was developing psychic powers or I'd said that last thing out loud, because Lili answered, "Because you are too close to it."

"Is it so obvious?"

"To me, yes. To others, I cannot know. Now, before we go to join the others, do you have anything else to tell me?"

"I could confess how stupid I was in Venice. There was no reason to take the risk I did that last night."

"You did it because the performance went so well. I well know the invincibility a great performance can generate. And you *were* great, my dear. The best of that very excellent cast they assembled for the production. I was so pleased for you."

Her praise opened a door and suddenly I was able to tell her what had happened and how I was feeling. I was ashamed, of course, for holding hands with Dan and then almost kissing him. I could blame it on the champagne, of course. Isn't that what they do in opera? The fact that my shadow knew all about it both alarmed and repelled me. After all, this man had no doubt watched Tony and me make love many times. Now this — and all because of my own stupidity. That was no doubt a large part of my emotional funk.

"Marta, you must make a decision right now on only one thing: can you continue with this opera production?"

"That's the problem. Despite what's happening in my personal life, I *have* to go through with this opera. It is the biggest opportunity I've had so far. If I bow out, who can they call in at this late hour? No one knows the part but me and my understudy — and who knows how good she is. Bottom line: I do this, or the show might not go on. That's what's so awful. Right now I just want to run away and hide. What do you think I should do?"

"How can anyone but you make that decision? I can tell you that it will not look good unless you make it clear to everyone what is happening to you. This is not a time when an opera singer can say she is 'indisposed' and get away with it."

I drew myself up, well aware that I was being psychologically kicked in the butt by my friend.

"I'm being a big baby, you mean, and I should get on with it rather than feeling sorry for myself?"

"No! Not at all. I am thinking that this is a very dangerous time for you. As I feared, this stalker is changing, becoming more aggressive, more out of control. He is taking chances. And now he has made contact with you. It is not the time to talk about this, but I must hear *exactly* what he said to you in Venice. I will be frank. These latest developments have me very worried."

⌒

"I am just so pissed off I could scream," I said to Tony as I looked out the window at the headlights of the cars on Richmond Street fourteen storeys below. "I spend my professional life living in places that aren't my own. Finally I'm performing in my own city, and I *still* have to live in a frigging hotel!"

While I had been talking to Lili, it had been decided for me that I needed round the clock protection. Frustratingly, Lili immediately agreed with Tony, Shannon, and Dan. I thought out of all of them she would understand. My husband at least had the grace to look guilty about it. He knew how much I was looking forward to being able to go home after rehearsals or performances. Now, two hours later, I was trapped in yet another hotel room.

"Marta," Shannon had said back at Lili's, "you have to be reasonable. The less available we make you to your stalker, the safer you are."

"It's a done deal," Dan added. "We've already arranged for security guards to be with you at all times."

I threw up my hands. "Oh, won't that look great at the opera house. You think no one is going to notice these guys? What about keeping all this quiet?"

Shannon spoke my doom. "The police in Rome are going to hold a news conference in a few hours. Of course an 'unnamed source' has blabbed to the press some of the details about the investigation of that singer's death. It's gotten out that he was murdered. Now they *have* to say something because the press is all over them."

"I don't have to tell you what the press is like in Italy, do I?" Dan added.

I passed a tired hand over my eyes. "What are they going to say?"

"We have no idea. They haven't told anyone over here what kind of progress they've made on the case."

Shannon said, "I finally had some luck prying something out of the police today, probably because of what's been going down in Rome. If Rome says anything about you, then Toronto will obviously have to respond because you're here right now. What happened in Venice will probably come into play."

I looked around the room at everyone. "So I should prepare for a shit storm."

Tony, who had been sitting next to me on Lili's sofa, took my hand. "That's why we've arranged for you to stay at the Hilton. All you have to do is cross the street and you're at the opera house. Easy-peasy."

"And your security guards?"

"We've booked a two-bedroom suite. You and I will be in one, and they'll use the other. This clown will never be able to get near you, I swear."

I squeezed his hand. "I suppose I would be a complete ingrate if I didn't thank all of you. It's just that … I hate this so much."

"We understand," Shannon said. "We're going to get this bastard. He made his first mistake in Rome."

"Venice, too," Dan added. "Every time he comes into the light, he makes it more possible to unmask him."

I had looked around Lili's living room again. "Is everyone feeling as confident as I am? No? Well, why doesn't *that* surprise me?"

While Tony had gone back to our apartment with Dan to pick up some clothes and other things, Shannon had sat with me in my Hilton prison.

"Marta, we're doing everything we can for you."

"I know that. I'm just tired and cranky. Things will probably look a lot better in the morning."

"We all know it's more than that, so let's not fool ourselves. It's clear we have to take every precaution until this man is caught. Tony and Lili have explained what you need in order to prepare for the opera premiere, and we're going to make it as easy as we can for you to do that. You have to trust us."

Even after Tony had gotten back and we were alone in our bedroom, I was still seething. How dare this man do this to me! Why did he seem to think I was his to play with? What gave him that right?

Tony came up behind me as I continued to stare out the window. "Marta, after this is all over, we'll go off somewhere, just the two of us."

"No security guards?" I asked, but I know he saw my hint of a smile.

"Not a single security guard, I promise."

I pulled him down onto the bed. "Hold me."

Someone knocked on the door. "Just wanted to let you know: room service delivered your food."

I said something very unladylike and wondered if the duties of the burly man in the other room extended to serving our meals.

Chapter Twenty-One

The battle was lost before we even woke up the next morning, not surprising since the police in Rome held their news conference at what was four in the morning in Toronto. The world media had plenty of time overnight to decide this was indeed a major story.

Unfortunately, we didn't hear about any of this. When Tony and I came out of our bedroom shortly before nine, two different behemoths were on duty. They did have the TV on, watching a sports channel. We usually listen to CBC radio in the morning. Because we were in a hotel, we didn't that day. Shannon and Dan, both exhausted, had slept in.

Even my manager, Alex Bennison, whose voicemail I found out later had been bombarded overnight by requests for interviews, had gone into work at the unheard of hour (for him) of eleven.

So we walked unknowingly into the perfect shit storm.

We'd dawdled over breakfast, so I was in a huge hurry to make sure I was at rehearsal on time. I threw all my music, notes, and other things I'd need, and Frick, Frack, Tony, and I piled into the elevator. Rehearsal started at ten and it was already nine thirty-five. Still, all we had to do was go out the front entrance of the hotel, hop in a cab, and drive to the Tanenbaum Centre at Front and Berkeley, a couple of hundred-year-old brick factories the COC had renovated into their rehearsal and workshop areas. It was a matter of *maybe* fifteen minutes, even if the traffic was bad. I'd be there in plenty of time, right?

Wrong. Big wrong. *Huge* wrong.

I believe someone from the front desk called to us as we walked from the elevators to the big revolving door, but I was deep in conversation with Tony about what would happen during the rehearsals, and Frick was discussing the latest basketball results with Frack. In other words, we were not paying any attention at all. We didn't even look outside as we came out of the revolving door.

The media knew better than to trespass on the hotel's car area out front, but their broadcast trucks lined Richmond Street on both sides. An ocean of reporters and cameras, both flash and video, swarmed forward as we exited, blissfully unaware of what was about to happen.

To give them their due, my two bodyguards sized up the situation quickly, got between me and the charging horde, and pushed us back into the hotel lobby.

Shaking like a leaf, I asked, "What the hell is going on?"

Tony was fumbling in his pocket for his mobile. "Something must have happened, maybe in Rome."

While he talked to Shannon, I stood there trying to gather my scattered wits. Frick and Frack were also on their phones, gathering information. One passed me his mobile. It was playing a video of something on CNN. Jeez, this was huge if the U.S. networks were covering it.

Tony touched my arm. "Shannon wants us to go upstairs and wait for her."

"I can't! Rehearsal will start soon. I have to be there."

He looked at the two bodyguards, who both shrugged.

"You actually want to wade through that mess?"

"I have to, Tony."

"Okay…."

While he talked with the two big guys, I tried calling Leonardo Tallevi. His line was busy — hardly surprising in the circumstances. I left a message saying I was stuck in my hotel. "We have no idea how I'm going to get through the media swarm. Please call back. I'm so sorry about this, Lenny!"

The guards insisted on talking to Shannon before they would agree to anything. She wasn't any help, being totally against me leaving the hotel.

Tallevi returned my call to say he was coming personally with a van and two of his largest employees. "Don't worry, my dear. No one will get near you."

In the end, I had eight big men surrounding me as I got into the van. Tallevi, being used to talking to the press (although not in such overwhelming numbers) delegated himself to tell them I wasn't going to say anything. It was all so silly on one level, but let me tell you, I have never felt so intimidated in my life.

"Ready, my dear?" Tallevi asked before we all plunged into the maelstrom.

The camera flashes were blinding, and the racket made by everyone shouting their questions was unbelievable — and indecipherable, which sort of defeated their purpose. Frick and Frack, being the largest and most experienced, formed the front of our flying wedge. I felt reasonably safe in the middle of it, but I had to squint so as not to be blinded by the starbursts of the flashes and put my hands over my ears to shut out the din. A small part of my brain told me I'd look like a blooming idiot on the news, but I really didn't care.

People were banging on the windows, screaming questions as I was pushed into the middle of the back seat, Frick on one side of me and Frack on the other. The burly driver honked his horn loudly and began moving slowly forward. The media had no choice but to move.

As we pulled out of the hotel and turned south on University, reporters were scrambling for their cars and trucks to follow us. It must have been a right merry parade going east through the heart of Toronto's business section on Adelaide. At the Tanenbaum Centre we turned in a driveway on Berkeley that was quickly blocked by more big men and security guards. I was hustled into the Opera Centre via the back door.

Tony told me later Tallevi was masterful in telling the media absolutely nothing. They were all pleading for something, *anything* about what was going on.

"Madame Hendriks will speak when she is ready. Now, if you will forgive us, we have an opera to rehearse. Thank you for your understanding."

Meanwhile, I'd been shown to someone's office where I could only sit, shaking. Somehow I had to pull myself together.

Eventually there was a knock on the door, and Lenny entered with Tony. I could see Frick and Frack standing like atlantes on either side of the door.

"I have spoken to the cast and crew and told them the situation. Tony has explained to me how you feel, but now I must ask you myself. Do you feel prepared to continue?"

I did not hesitate. "Yes. With all my heart, yes."

"Then we are prepared to make this work, too. Your colleagues are, of course, appalled by what has happened, but I have asked them not to speak to you about this. Of course, if you want to say something to them, that is your business. I have also asked them not to speak with the press."

I gave Lenny a kiss on both cheeks, followed by a tight hug. "I cannot thank you enough. Rest assured you will have my best for this production … somehow."

He smiled. "I would expect no less from my favourite soprano."

Behind him, Tony rolled his eyes. *Every* female opera singer was the general manager's favourite at one point or another. Still, I know Lenny spoke with what he would have called sincerity.

Tallevi raised an eyebrow. "So can we begin our little rehearsal, *cara mia?*"

"Little rehearsal" my big toe. They'd been going along without me for a week now with my understudy doing the part. It wasn't ideal, but the best we could come up with when the performance of *Traviata* had come along late in the game. We had a good director (Simon Stone from the UK), a great cast made up of many top Canadians (part of the benefactor's deal), and me creating the lead role — and currently barely able to be coherent. Even with me at my best, everyone knew we were hard against it. This opera was filled with extremely tricky music.

There was another knock on the door. Shannon and Dan both immediately stepped in.

She was still against me doing anything but getting under cover, but Tony and I stood firm: the show had to go on.

"Okay," she sighed, "if that's your wish." She turned to Lenny. "Is it all right if our security guards accompany Marta to the rehearsal? I don't want her left alone for even one second."

"But of course."

Tony stepped in. "I want to be with Marta, too. I know how these rehearsals work. You don't. I can keep them out of the way, Leonardo, but close enough to deal with anything."

Shannon considered for a moment. "Good suggestion. All right. We'll do that."

"Three is too many," Tallevi said. "I have to think of the other artists. Two only."

Shannon blew out some air, clearly trying to keep her temper. "Okay, Tony and one guard at the rehearsal."

It took a couple more minutes to get everything worked out, but eventually I left for the rehearsal hall while Dan and Shannon tried to find out what had been said by the Rome police — or anyone else. It was crucial to know what was going on.

The morning's rehearsal was to run over blocking for the first act. As we walked to it, Tony had his arm around me.

"I know it's stupid to say this, but try to relax and forget about what's going on outside. I will call Alex and find out what he thinks we should do. Leonardo has also said we can rely on his promotional department for help, too. I'll get something set up and we'll have solutions and options for you to consider by the time the rehearsal's finished. Okay?"

"I'll try my very best. I've *got* to. Oh God! What a mess."

In the end, professionalism kicked in and I actually managed to forget about my situation for whole minutes at a time.

The cast was great. I could tell all they wanted to talk about was the carnival outside, but any small talk made around me was strictly about business. I was completely aware, though, that when they were far enough away from me, my troubles were the hot topic of conversation.

Rehearsals had been going on for a week already, so my first day was all about bringing me up to speed. Simon was very clear in what he wanted and helpful whenever I had questions, mostly along the lines of "exactly what am I supposed to be feeling here?"

About an hour into the rehearsal Andrew McCutcheon showed up. Tallevi was agitatedly buzzing around our composer, so I knew McCutcheon had probably said something characteristically blunt to the media throng that had followed us from the hotel. Of course he immediately stopped the rehearsal and motioned to me.

Even though I disliked being summoned like some sort of lackey, I went over. Tony rushed over from the sidelines, but hung back at a discreet distance.

"What are you doing to our production?"

"Have you seen the news reports?"

"I have. That is why I'm here." He leveled his piercing blue eyes at me. "You are going to be able to complete your contract, right?"

I returned his gaze steadily. "I will."

"And this media disaster outside won't deter you?"

"It will not."

Lenny interjected, "Marta has assured me the production will premiere as scheduled."

Our conversation was not in a place that gave one iota of privacy and I could see the cast and crew edging forward to catch every word.

"I hope that will be possible. You are involved in a lot of trouble right now. The Roman police —"

"Have *nothing* to do with what is going on here. I am an opera singer under contract to premiere your opera and I will see that through. I have done nothing wrong. This is about something being done to me, and others, and I want everyone to know," and here I turned to look at the cast, "that I am determined to give everything I have on opening night and at subsequent performances of our run." There was a smattering of applause as I turned back to McCutcheon. "Now if you don't mind, maestro, I would like to continue the rehearsal. We have a lot of ground to cover today."

Tallevi deftly peeled McCutcheon off and they walked out of the room. Tony gave me a huge smile and two thumbs up, then disappeared himself.

The rehearsal went on. I forced myself to write copious notes and a diagram for later study, trying to concentrate on crucial details to keep the static in my head at bay.

We broke for lunch around twelve thirty. Tallevi had sandwiches brought in since it was inadvisable to go outside before we actually had to. I wolfed down a rather good ham, cheese, and tomato while on the phone with Alex in New York.

"I'm going to schedule a call with a crisis specialist. I want you to listen to what he has to say. He comes highly recommended."

"Alex, all I want to do is get rid of the media."

"You have to send them on their way happy, then. This situation can be manipulated to your advantage if we play our cards right."

"This is not about business. I would gladly become *more* anonymous if I could only see this creature who's stalking me caught and punished."

He sighed and I knew well what my manager's sighs meant. We talked a bit more and he told me he was drafting a press release. He'd email it to Tony, I could review it, and then he would send it out to the media.

"What time is your rehearsal is over?"

"Four thirty."

"I'll tell the media the release is coming at that time. It will perhaps draw some of them off."

"Thanks, Alex. This is all extremely trying."

"I know it must be. Just remember: listen to the crisis specialist and do what he says."

"I'll try."

"Do more than try. Call me at home later this evening. I want a complete update."

"Will do."

I'd had Alex on speaker phone so Tony, Dan, and Shannon could hear the conversation.

"I'd certainly recommend listening to your manager," Shannon said.

It had to be faced. "So what's the word on the street?" I asked.

Everyone looked at Shannon for a cue.

"The police spokesperson —"

"It was Pucci," Dan interjected.

"This man Pucci said they are certain De Vicenzo was pushed down the stairs, they have a person of interest in mind —"

"We watched an Italian feed and I translated directly," Tony interjected.

Shannon's face had a disgusted expression. "Would you guys *please* let me tell this story? Okay. Pucci had a partial description. De Vicenzo's friends and the restaurant staff say the suspect had facial hair: a full beard and mustache. Dan is certain this was a disguise."

"I think so, too," I said, suddenly flooded by the memory of that beaked mask close to my face. Even in darkness and with that cloak on, I'm pretty sure I would have detected facial hair leaking out from beneath it.

"But we do know he's roughly six feet and slender. He's right-handed. His voice is rather high-pitched and —"

"No, it isn't. I heard him speak. There's no way that whisper came from someone whose voice is light and high-pitched. Those are easy to fake. His voice is deep and guttural. Tony's a tenor. When he speaks, what does he sound like?"

Shannon shrugged. "His voice is pretty low."

"Exactly. Our man was faking it in that restaurant."

"I also have some other news. The Hong Kong police are sending records to the Toronto police. Nothing is official as yet, but a little bird has told me that condo up at Church and Adelaide is owned by a shell company in Hong Kong. The owner of it may well be Canadian. We're getting close. I can feel it."

I blew out a lungful of air. "I sure hope so."

There was a costume fitting at one and I used that time to also warm up. The costume department is accustomed to stuff like that and didn't bat an eye. I had to wear four different costumes. One was pretty form-fitting, and since it was meant to show me in my sexual prime, it was rather daring. Being aware of this early on, I'd worked hard for the past six months getting my weight down and struggling to keep it there. Long gone are the days when audiences will shelve their disbelief and watch an overweight singer pretend she's a nubile young lady. The worst example of that is usually found in the "Dance of the Seven Veils" in *Salome* by Richard Strauss. I'll tell you one thing, even though I'm in pretty good shape, you'd never catch me performing that in front of an audience. Too bad. It's a juicy part for a singer with the octane to do the role.

From two until we ran out of time at four thirty, we were back working with piano on the prologue, as well as act 1 and a bit of 2. The rest of the cast was at the top of their game, having a week's head start on me, but even though I held on to my music as if I was in the middle of the ocean and it was a life preserver, I did better than I expected.

That was especially gratifying since McCutcheon spent the entire day buzzing around as we worked. With a score as complicated as his, this might have been useful if he had stuck to clarifying issues that arose (seeing as how he was also the conductor) and making the odd suggestion. But he had the bad habit of stepping all over everyone. Our tenor in the first act (and Naomi's first lover) was a pretty funny guy who kept making snarky comments about McCutcheon that had us in stitches, albeit discreet ones. Through all of this, I somehow managed to keep my focus.

Reality came crashing in as soon as the rehearsal ended, of course. We went into Tallevi's office so they could give me an update.

Shannon looked frazzled, her hair in a not-very-tidy ponytail. "Well, everyone, it's been a busy day. Here's where we stand." She looked at me. "The police have been doing some digging on the person who had their receiving gear in that vacant condo. They've found another resident on the floor who saw a man come out of the apartment late one night. They rode the elevator down together. This resident has provided a limited description and they're going to put the resident together with an Identi-kit technician and see —"

Tony interrupted. "What's an Identi-kit?"

"Software for assembling a portrait of our suspect based on what the person who saw him remembers. Let's all hope our person has a very good memory."

Since Shannon was stopped, I asked, "And when is this going to take place?"

"Tomorrow, I very much hope. As for Hong Kong, the Toronto police say the information is en route. Why the Chinese can't send a simple email is beyond me."

I asked the question I most needed an answer to. "Are all those reporters still outside?"

The COC promo person nodded her head. "If anything, there are more."

As I looked around the room I saw concern on everyone's face, except lurking under Tallevi's was the hint of excitement. All this attention was huge for his opera company. Our run of shows would not only be a sell-out, but it would probably be scalpers' heaven — and that doesn't happen often for an opera.

"So I guess I'll have to say something."

Shannon nodded. "That would be appropriate."

The PR woman said, "We've worked up a little script between us and someone your manager hired." She handed me a sheet of paper. "If this meets with your approval, I can go out and we'll invite the press into one of our larger rooms where you can make the statement. Is that okay?"

"Sure," I said. "Let's get this over with."

While the press was herded into the room, I looked at the statement they wanted me to read. I don't know what they thought the purpose of it was, but it was incredibly fatuous. The situation came across sounding way more mild than what it actually was. My adversary had invaded my life in the most blatant and heartless manner. It was as if he was trying to cripple me in every possible way. I could not trust my privacy, the people I met. He'd killed someone. He'd assaulted me. I couldn't even live in my own apartment. I was afraid, constantly afraid.

To stop these spiraling inner thoughts, I took a deep breath. Facing the media horde that had been camped out all day and say what needed to be said, I needed to have utter control of myself.

Tallevi stuck his head in the door about fifteen minutes later. "Okay, my dear, are you ready?"

I looked at Tony, sitting quietly next to me. He gave my hand a squeeze then pulled me to my feet. "I will stand just behind you, my darling."

Shannon and Dan had disappeared several minutes earlier.

"Ready as I'll ever be," I said, and tried hard to smile.

Why did it feel like I was walking to my own execution?

Chapter Twenty-Two

"Wow! That news conference sure was an eye opener," Dan Hudson said to his boss as they sat down on stools at the bar at Quinn's Irish Steakhouse, down the street from Marta's hotel. "I spent the last two weeks with her, and I had zero idea Marta had been bottling up that kind of anger."

Shannon sighed heavily. "You've got that right. If our mystery man had popped out of the media crowd, I believe she would have gone out and personally throttled him. I *really* need a drink," she added, signalling the bartender. He came over. "A scotch on the rocks. Make it a double."

Dan said, "Bring me a Guinness. Thanks."

While they waited, Marta's face came up on one of the bar's TV screens. Shannon immediately asked the bartender to turn the sound up.

"I'm here today to address reports that have appeared in the press," Marta began, reading from the prepared script. "I know there are many questions about what you've heard and I would like to give my side of the story in order to quell the rumours and innuendo presently circulating."

She stopped, looked down, looked out at the media throng in front of her, flashes still going off like a lightning storm gone mad, then Marta slowly and deliberately crumpled up the paper.

Shannon took a sip of her drink. "I wonder what was going through her brain."

On the TV, Marta remained silent a few more seconds before she began speaking again. "My life has been invaded by a human being whose capacity for evil is breathtaking. At first, I thought it was lovely, a mysterious admirer, perhaps painfully shy, who would leave me beautiful bouquets of roses. This poor excuse of a man is anything but shy. All the while he was worming his way into the most private parts of my life. Two weeks ago, I discovered nearly every square foot of my apartment here in Toronto was bugged for sound and video. My every footstep has been dogged since. I'm afraid to be alone, constantly looking over my shoulder. He seems to be everywhere — and nowhere.

"A week ago, while I was performing in Rome, I had a minor disagreement with one of the other members of the cast, Arturo De Vicenzo. It was the sort of thing that goes on in productions all the time, all over the world. This monster took it upon himself to wreak his vengeance on Arturo for some warped reason of his own. I had no involvement in what happened other than to have set the tragedy in motion by disagreeing with a colleague.

"In Venice, two days ago, this man attacked a bodyguard I had hired and accosted me, threatening my life and frightening me out of my wits. The police in three cities are working their hardest to find this madman and bring him to justice. I pledge my utmost to help in this effort."

Again Marta paused. The room in the Tanenbaum Centre was silent except for the continued clacking of camera shutters. She took a drink of water. Then slowly her expression hardened. The camera that had shot the clip they were watching must have been right in front of Marta because she looked directly into it.

"I am telling you, the bastard who murdered Arturo by pushing him down a flight of stairs, who tried to frighten me in Venice, who has invaded my life…. you will not win. I don't know what your game is. I have no idea who you are, nor do I care. You will be caught and you will be punished, and when I see you I will spit in your face. I am not afraid of you. I will not run and hide, since this is what you seem to want. My participation in the premiere of this opera, and every other appearance I have booked, is assured. I will be here and you will be rotting in jail — and I hope it's for the rest of your unnatural life!"

With that she turned on her heel and disappeared through the doorway behind her.

Wendy, Tallevi's beleaguered PR person, jumped behind the microphone practically screaming, "No questions! I'm very sorry but at this time Madame Hendriks will not be taking questions!"

Obviously, she'd promised the press precisely that. Pushing a piece of loose hair off her forehead, she took questions, mostly around how the Canadian Opera Company was trying to protect their star. She blustered her way through it admirably, saying nothing really — as good PR people should.

Shannon and Dan looked at each other, still amazed by what they'd already witnessed live less than an hour earlier. They'd been standing at the side of the room. Their purpose had been trying to spot someone who should not have been there, someone who might stand out for some reason. Undercover members of the Toronto police were present as well, attempting to do the same thing. They all knew it was a long shot, but still, it had to be tried.

Shannon swallowed the remainder of her drink and immediately signalled the barkeep for a refill. Normally she wasn't a big drinker, but tonight she needed it.

She'd told Tony and Marta to stay in their suite, but whether Marta would take that advice considering the mood she was in, Shannon couldn't know. As additional insurance, she'd called Lili, given her a heads-up, and asked if she'd come down to talk directly to her friend.

"I was planning to do that anyway. I need to find out much from Marta," the Czech woman had said in her heavily accented English. "What you have just told me makes it even more urgent that I speak with her. I will leave at once."

"We've done all we can for the night, I suppose," Dan told his boss. "Do you think it would be best if I stayed with our guards tonight?"

Shannon laughed. "Dan, even with that fedora on, it's pretty darn obvious you have a honking big bandage on your head, and several times today you've had a rather glazed expression on your face." She patted his arm as her fresh drink appeared. "Go home and rest. Tomorrow will be another day in the meat grinder. Tony put a very interesting bug in my ear, and I think I'm going to follow up on it. And who knows? Perhaps we'll finally get that info from the Hong Kong police to brighten our morning."

Dan smiled for a moment, then his face got serious again. "You do realize what she's done, don't you?"

Shannon nodded. "Yeah. She's called him out. I don't think that was the smartest thing to do."

"And I've got the lump on my head to back that statement up."

Chapter Twenty-Three

After my emotional outburst at the press conference (where had all that fire and brimstone come from?), it hadn't surprised me that Lili wasn't far behind. It had taken her several minutes to convince the desk clerks to even consider calling upstairs to find out if this short, very properly dressed foreign woman was who she told them she was. Her mood was considerably darkened by this encounter, as well as the one at the door to our suite when the two security guards wouldn't let her in.

I responded to their knock on our bedroom door and found Lili with a huge frown on her face sitting on the living room sofa. Her cloth overcoat and hat were still on. Her gloves and a cane were on the coffee table.

"Lili!" I called out. "Why didn't you tell us you were coming?"

A frown etched her tired face as she looked up. "I came right over after speaking with the O'Brien woman. She told me what you have said to the press."

Oh boy, I should have expected something like this.

"It just came out. They gave me a release to read that said nothing. This man is destroying my life! I had to say something."

My friend and confessor shook her head. From the corner of my eye, I saw Tony herding the two burly guards into their room and motion toward ours. No sense sharing the grief that was likely to come. Having an empty room in between seemed a good idea.

Tony and I sat on the bed and gave Lili the chair by the desk. She was moving more comfortably but she still looked drawn and older.

"How's your ankle?" I asked.

"It is still very sore. This new walking boot they gave me is lighter and so it is easier to move around, but I hate feeling like a cripple."

Tony spoke up. "Can we order up anything, Lili? Coffee? Something to eat?"

"No. I came to speak to your wife." She turned and fastened her laser-beam stare on me. "You did something very foolish today, Marta."

"I know that."

"No! He is more dangerous than you think. He crossed a line in Rome. He has killed. I am sure you've heard the saying that 'the first murder is the most difficult.' Well, I believe that may be the case here. Never having examined this man, I cannot say if he is psychotic or merely a sociopath. But without any doubt I can tell you this: he is very, very dangerous."

A knot formed in my stomach. What I'd said at that press conference had come from deep inside me — and it was the truth, the way I *really* felt. I wanted my life back. However, I could see now that what I'd said might not have been the wisest course of action.

"You challenged him, Marta dear. The psychopathology of this type of person demands of him that he must respond. We know he is very resourceful. I am sure he will attack. It is the where and how that we don't know. That is a worry."

Tony said, "I've spent the day doing a lot of thinking. Lili, do you believe we might know this man? I mean, he seems to know everything about Marta and he certainly also knows a lot about me. Would this sort of person hide right out in plain sight? McCutcheon, for example?"

I chimed in. "Dan Hudson and I have discussed the same thing."

Other than some meetings the previous fall to discuss the thrust of the production of *The Passage of Time*, I hadn't had all that much of a chance to be around the opera's composer. We'd shared several emails, as he'd sent me the final version of my part and then a revised final part, followed by another, and another. This wasn't hard to understand in light of the fact that he was an odd duck — brilliant, but definitely odd. During the rehearsal, the bass singing the role of my character's father had joked we'd probably get revisions brought to our dressing rooms as the orchestra was playing the overture. He probably wasn't far off.

But to think this man had been dogging my footsteps for over two years was really pushing it — until I began to listen to what Tony had to say on the subject.

"I looked him up on my phone during the rehearsal. His family is loaded. Grandfather was a cabinet minister, his uncles and father own one of the most successful Bay Street law firms. If he never earned a cent from composing, he could cry himself to sleep on a mattress stuffed with money. He's also not your stay-at-home-locked-in-a-room-writing-music-all-day sort of composer. He's all over the world, always at the high-profile events. He tweets. He uses Facebook. He is totally plugged in. He knows computers, software, and hardware. I'm telling you, he could be our guy."

I was definitely seriously considering Tony's theory, but Lili obviously was having doubts.

"Much too obvious," she practically snorted. "Our adversary enjoys playing his game from the shadows. Marta knows well enough what Andrew McCutcheon looks like. Do you think he could have fooled her over and over backstage in different opera houses?"

"But he could have been disguised and —"

Lili swatted away his argument with her hand. "Oh pish! Your wife is not stupid or unaware."

I had to stick up for Tony. "Lili, to be honest, I *am* unaware. It's dark. There isn't time to even notice backstage crews, much less study their faces during performances — and that's when the flowers are always delivered. And who says he didn't pay someone to plant all those bouquets? Tony's theory is worth looking into."

Our friend backed down, but she didn't look at all like we'd changed her mind.

The rest of the time she was with us, she only asked about my encounter in the Venetian alley. The horrifying event was so implanted in my psyche that I could recite everything verbatim. Lili even took out her pocket recorder to tape the interview.

"So what do you think?" I asked.

Lili shook her head slowly. "I do not like it at all. How much do you know about the psychopathology of serial killers?"

"You're not suggesting we're dealing with one of those?" I asked, genuinely shocked.

"No, not really, but I think the same thing might be at work here. Many serial killers start by attacking people, usually women, and usually ones who fit a certain profile. Every few months, the steam builds up and they must feed the monster inside them. Then that isn't enough. They kill. Their psychosis follows the same arc. As time goes on, the speed of their breakdown increases and they need to kill more often. I am getting the feeling that it is the same with your stalker. He began to attack you by ruining his roses. You are failing him in some way."

"This is all about bad singing?"

"No. He is fixated on you for some reason."

"Lucky me."

"At first his notice was about praise. Now it is about the things you are doing that displease and anger him. It changed when you started to fight back."

Tony said, "You mean bringing in Shannon, going to the police? Stuff like that?"

"Exactly. You displeased him and upset his plans — whatever they may be." Here I got another laser beam glare. "And today you have challenged him openly. Our man is clever, perhaps even a genius, and this makes him very, very dangerous."

"You could be describing Andrew McCutcheon. We have to follow this lead up, even if it does prove to be wrong."

Lili shrugged. "Do what you must. But I have to warn you, my friends, to be exceptionally careful. If I had to predict, I would say his next attack will be more violent. And it might not be directed toward you, Marta, but someone close to you."

"That could include you, Lili!"

"I know."

⌒

Immediately after Lili left, I grabbed the opportunity to take a shower. Tony was going to order burgers and salad from room service.

The hot water felt wonderful as I stood under it, washing away the day's outer (and inner) crud.

Considered only by what had gone on at rehearsal, today would have been an excellent day and a great start to the three weeks of rehearsals between now and the premiere of *The Passage of Time*. For the first time I felt I was getting a handle on creating this role. What I brought to the stage on opening night at the start of our ten-performance run would define the role for everyone following me. It was an exceptional opportunity many singers never get.

The more I worked on McCutcheon's artistic creation, the more impressed I was. Everyone else involved seemed to feel the same. It was something unique and really, really special. Here was a contemporary opera that just might have legs. Already there was buzz in the opera world and several companies were nosing around thinking of renting the COC's production, according to Tallevi. That was significant. Most operas composed in the last fifty years have been "one and done," meaning they didn't get remounted very often.

It was really exciting to be a part of something like this. The intense, three-week rehearsal period where I could immerse myself in the creation of something new was my idea of musical heaven.

Except that some moral degenerate had chosen this particular time to drop his shit-bomb in the middle of my life. If Tony's theory was correct, though, everything with the opera production was in jeopardy. I cursed and fumed as shower water flowed over my head and shoulders. If it turned out McCutcheon had been making my life a living hell, all bets were off. Odd, yes, but a murdering stalker? It was all so depressing, I could scarcely believe it.

From the back of my memory came my mother's

patient voice. "Marta, just realize that you at least have your health." Back in my teens, I used to get absolutely furious when she'd say stuff like that to me. Typical of many kids that age, I thought I knew it all, had everything figured out. In my mind, she was a platitude-spouting fool.

It was Christmas break during my first year at McGill when my dad sat me down in our living room immediately after I arrived home. Without a preamble, he told me that Mom was really ill. In fact, it was cancer and it had been an ongoing battle for nearly a year. The outcome was no longer in doubt.

It felt as if someone had punched me in the stomach. Mom hadn't wanted me to know earlier because she thought I wouldn't head off for school (she was right), and the thought of coming between me and my dreams was something she couldn't bear.

Heart pounding, I went to her bedroom. She was asleep. I sat down on the opposite side of the bed and just stared, trying to come to grips with what I'd just been told. Her face had aged dramatically. I had last seen her at Thanksgiving, barely two months earlier, and she easily looked ten years older.

Maybe a half-hour later, Mom woke up. We stared at each other for at least a minute before she spoke.

"So your father told you?"

I nodded.

"I hope you don't think less of me for not being able to tell you myself."

"No. I understand. But I've been sitting here praying that I wake up from this bad dream." I began to cry and

Mom sat up to hold me. "What are we going to do?"

"Help make my passing easier."

I began to say how I would quit school to be around and take care of her. "You know how hopeless Dad is around the house."

"Having you quit school would make me exceptionally unhappy, dear. Your dad and I will do just fine, and we'll make sure you can come home every weekend if you wish."

"I will!" I told her, and I tried my hardest to carry through on that vow, but sometimes there were concerts or the odd gig that got in the way, and that made me feel dreadfully guilty.

Knowing I was soon going to lose my mother was a harrowing experience, but it forced me to do a lot of growing up. My sister and I also became much closer when she took time off from work to fly east to help out at the very end.

It came far too soon for all of us. I think my mom sort of gave up so her end wouldn't be dragged out. Regardless, the end of my first year at McGill found me without a mother.

Standing in that hotel shower after a very difficult day, hearing my mother's voice in my head gave me strength as well as comfort. The chips would have to fall as they would. All I could do was keep a tight grip on those things I could control. Lili's concern be damned, I was right to call the bastard out.

I hoped.

Tony was on the phone when I came out of the bathroom. Our food had been delivered. While I ate my dinner — not really hungry, but knowing I needed something in my stomach — I listened to him talking to Shannon.

Tony finished the call and sat next to me. "I have to go out for awhile. Shannon and Dan are just down the street and rather than keep you up, I'll go there. Will you be okay?"

"With those two gorillas in the other room? I should think so." I gave Tony a tight smile, the best I could imagine under the circumstances. "Pretty weird day, huh? Do you think I was right, saying what I did at the news conference?"

He shrugged. "Bit late to worry about it. You spoke from the heart, and that's one of the things I love about you. Mind you, I wouldn't want to be your publicist." At the door, he turned and smiled. "Don't wait up. You've got a big day again tomorrow."

"Even if you've managed to get my opera's composer thrown into the hoosegow?"

"If it's any comfort, Shannon thinks that's unlikely."

"And Dan?"

"He says the jury's out. It is a long shot, but we at least have to take a look at McCutcheon, don't you agree?"

"Do whatever you have to. I'll be here when you get back and I wouldn't take it amiss if you give me some cuddles when you come to bed, even if I'm fast asleep."

He flashed that smile I loved. "How will you know if you're fast asleep?"

"Believe me, I'll know. And just before you go, could you see if there's some white wine in the bar fridge in the living room? A glass would go down very nicely."

"You got it, babe."

Getting out the copious blocking notes I'd made that day, I sat down to do some memorizing before I got too sleepy.

Chapter Twenty-Four

Shannon was shaking her head vehemently. "Some of what you're saying makes sense, but the sticking point in my mind is why would Andrew McCutcheon do this? What does he get out of it? If he is the bastard we're after, his big opera project is dead in the water. Why risk that?"

Tony, Shannon, and an increasingly tired-looking Dan were the last patrons of Quinn's that night.

Tony had been busy with his mobile, pulling up as much information from the Internet on Andrew McCutcheon as he could find.

"Shannon," he said for the second time, "obviously, our man has a few screws loose. You can't expect a person like that to make sense. As Lili pointed out to me earlier tonight, he may be reaching a crisis point. You've said the situation seems to be spinning out of his control. Maybe now he's just responding to the situation, rather than controlling it. Maybe he didn't plan for this to happen during the run of his new opera. Regardless, from what we know of this ghost we've been chasing and Andrew McCutcheon, they're both arrogant pricks. Hiding out in plain sight would be just the thing that would appeal to him."

Shannon picked up her still-empty glass, seemingly surprised it had nothing in it. Three doubles was way more than was good for her, and she knew enough not to order a fourth. She looked at her watch. Nearly midnight. She'd better give her boyfriend Michael a call soon if she wanted him to pick her up. Much later and it wouldn't be fair to drag him out.

She sighed. "I guess this is at least worth a shot. So far we've come up with nothing else."

"I agree," Hudson added.

Tony puffed his cheeks, letting the air out slowly. "What about getting the cops to investigate him?"

"Tony, you've got to understand: the McCutcheon family is very powerful," Shannon said. "Not just here in Toronto, but also in Ottawa. His grandfather was a cabinet minister for heaven's sake, his dad runs one of the biggest law firms. Four people in the family are members of the Order of Canada. You don't go running to the cops with even a moderately checked out story on people like this. We're only going to get action from them if we have cold, hard facts linking Andrew McCutcheon directly to Marta's stalker."

"So how do we get those facts?"

"I'll start checking out his itinerary first thing in the morning," Dan said. "I'm still owed a few favours in Ottawa."

Shannon nodded. "And I'll start building a profile of his background."

Tony raised his hand as if he was in school. "What should I do?"

"Your job is to stay close to Marta, strictly line of sight at all times if you can't be standing right next to her. I don't know what our boy might try, but I'll bet your friend Lili is right: he's going to try something. Our hired bruisers can take care of any rough stuff, but you have a good set of eyes and will be able to recognize if something isn't right way quicker than any of us."

"Any word out of Hong Kong yet?"

An ultra disgusted expression appeared on Shannon's face. "Yeah, police got the records late this afternoon, but they're not sharing as of yet."

"Can you find out what they've got anyway?"

She shrugged. "Perhaps. But I'd rather get it without calling in any favours. I have a feeling we're going to be calling in favours a lot before we see an end to this thing."

Dan said, "What we need to do is hit the ground running tomorrow. If we push hard, we can probably find out a fair bit about McCutcheon by day's end. By all accounts he leads a pretty public life. We should also put a tail on him when he's not front and centre at those rehearsals."

"I'll take care of that."

Dan shook his head ruefully. "And here I always thought opera was pretty well the most boring thing on the planet."

∽

Michael Quinn reflected on the drive back to his place after picking up Shannon that he'd only seen her loaded one other time, and that was the night her divorce became final.

"Tough day?" he asked as they drove west on King Street.

"You didn't see the news? It was all over it. The circus came to town outside the opera house's stage door. Then Marta threw a giant effing monkey wrench into a press conference that had been arranged."

"What did she do?"

"Basically, she called out this dude we're chasing."

"Called him out?"

"Yeah. Sort of 'come and get me if you dare.' Look, I understand the pressure she's under. It must really suck to be her right now, but this is going to make matters worse."

"Why?"

"Because if we're reading this guy right, he'll try to do just that."

"So? Don't you have her surrounded by bodyguards, and isn't that new employee Hudson on the job?"

Turning a bit in her seat, Shannon had that look of forbearance Michael never appreciated.

"My dear man, the person we're after is a fucking ghost. At every turn, he's one step ahead of us. Now he's killed someone so we know he's *really* serious. I could surround Marta with a battalion of soldiers and he'd manage to get at her. He's got me that spooked."

"And no leads?"

"Only one so far. Marta's husband thinks we should check out the composer of the opera."

"You mean McCutcheon, that bloke we met at the arts gala two months ago?"

"The very same."

Michael turned the Jag off King into Liberty Village where his loft was located. "Interesting theory. I'd put my money on it."

"Why?"

"He had strange eyes."

Chapter Twenty-Five

First thing the next morning, I looked out the window. Only four media vans. That was four too many, but a lot better than what had greeted us the past two days.

Tony was still asleep, having come home rather late, so I turned on the reading light on my side of the bed, opened my vocal part, and went over the first half of the third act, singing in my mind. This sequence involved a ballet dancer doing an artistic representation of what I was singing, which explained exactly how Naomi's life went off the rails. It would be a tough slog for me (lots of high notes, trills, and volume), but I had dedicated a considerable amount of time learning it with Giuseppe in Rome, mainly because of some late changes by the composer.

The first time I'd heard about the concept of the third act, I had to stifle a roll of my eyes. Interpretive dancing is not my idea of something that belongs in the opera house. Later, I was sent a video clip of a run through of the choreography with piano, and I had to say I was impressed.

Then McCutcheon got in the act. He hadn't been happy with the orchestration, so right in the middle of the orchestra's first rehearsal of it, he threw a hairy fit and withdrew the ballet, then spent a week re-orchestrating it. Of course this played hell with the carefully worked-out schedule. That had required Tallevi to meet with Peter Grant, our main donor for the production, who had to okay the significant added expense of extra rehearsal time with the dancers and the orchestra.

This morning we'd be working on that particular section of the opera and we'd be on the main stage with the orchestra on hand (probably a cost-cutting measure). McCutcheon would be in the pit, so by the end of the rehearsal, I'd have a pretty good idea what he'd be like at the helm.

Needless to say, I was really looking forward to it — particularly so since the media circus seemed to have folded their tents and left town during the night. I was more than happy to be yesterday's news.

"Tony," I said softly as I kissed his cheek. "Wakey, wakey. The sun is up, the birdies are singing, and the press has pretty well gone home."

He opened his eyes and smiled. "You're in a good mood today. What caused it?"

"A better night's sleep than I was expecting, an empty street outside, and just a feeling that today is going to be just fantastic. Now get up, you slugabed! I'm hungry and I've got to be ready to sing in a little over an hour."

Later, we crossed the street and got to the stage door of the Four Seasons Centre with only three mics stuck in my kisser.

I smiled sweetly and said, "No comment. I've got a rehearsal and I'm focused on that."

"You're not worried about this madman stalking you?" a woman reporter asked.

How she could have such perfect hair this early in the morning was beyond me.

"I'm not worried. My security is more than adequate. Bye now!"

The stage door opened and I was safe inside with my husband and the same two bruisers who were on duty the day before. Just let this jerk try to get near me. Then it crossed my mind that I just might be seeing him in five minutes.

"What's up with your theory about McCutcheon?" I whispered to Tony as we made our way to one of the rehearsal rooms so I could warm up.

"Don't worry. It's all in Shannon's hands, and we both know she's a pro."

McCutcheon showed up late, which didn't help things. The opera's official "assistant conductor" was on the podium when he arrived, and that didn't go over well, but what were we to do? Pay for all those musicians to sit around waiting?

A few of the bolder cast members came up to express sympathy for my situation. Everyone would have seen coverage of my press conference, as well as the Rome press conference, so they knew my predicament. I asked them all nicely to drop it because we were there to rehearse.

Even with our petulant composer present, everyone was relaxed and happy. The orchestra was in excellent form, and getting to actually hear instruments instead of the sterile playback of the composing software drove home even further what an incredible job McCutcheon had done.

One of the problems with writing contemporary music is the need most composers feel to do something unique and fresh. What they often come up with is total BS, in my opinion. Things are made difficult for the sake of making them difficult. Dodgy scoring abounds. The effect on an opera audience to this sort of music can be profound. Most opera goers are in love with the past and steeped in its music. They want to leave the theatre with melodies singing in their heads. With most contemporary works, that just won't happen.

McCutcheon, though, had managed it. His musical vocabulary was definitely firmly in the present, but his melodies were oddly tuneful without sounding like "Verdi revisited."

"Movie music," said Granville Barker, who was singing the role of my character's father. "McCutcheon's written bloody movie music."

We were sitting off to the side while the orchestra worked on something, sharing a cup hot broth he'd brought with him.

"I beg to differ, Granville, dear. Yes, some of the orchestration sounds a bit like *Star Wars*, but it's the fact he's backed off from stuffing his opera with harmonies that make your ears bleed that makes his vocal lines so singable. Tell me, when was the last time you sang something contemporary that contained anything like what an audience would call a 'recognizable tune?'"

"And that's precisely why I hate contemporary music!"

"Nonsense. What you hate is bad contemporary music. A lot of it *is* bad, but I believe this opera just might stand the test of time."

I don't think I convinced him, but then Granville has always been an old fuddy-duddy who believes the days of great opera ended when Puccini died in 1923.

It had been several days since I'd been able to sing full voice and it felt great to let it rip that morning. With the brass-heavy orchestration of this act, I did have to air it out in some of the dramatic parts. But our director Simon, Tallevi when he stopped in, and even McCutcheon in the pit were all smiling, so I knew I was doing the job.

What the rehearsal brought into sharp focus, though, was that I needed time on my own to hone my part to razor sharpness, to really live with it. I was too busy concentrating on getting the technical aspects correct to be able to relax and let the music happen. The pressure of creating what could turn out to be an iconic role demanded musical perfection, but it also needed soul and humanity. I wasn't close to being able to do that yet, but with the amount of rehearsal time left, I found myself believing I could make that happen.

Frick and Frack were always around, comforting for me, and they were causing fewer raised eyebrows. Everyone had been told why they were there and my colleagues seemed to be taking it in stride, thank heavens.

Lunch was again sandwiches and water in a dressing room with Tony. If nothing else, the menu options would be excellent for my waistline. I was again beginning to suffer from cabin fever, though.

"So what's up with Shannon's investigation of McCutcheon?"

"It's going fine."

"Fine in what way, dear husband? Is she finding out anything?"

"I haven't spoken to her today."

"Oh, that is such a crock! You keep disappearing and reappearing. Where are you going and what are you doing?"

Tony put his sandwich down and took both my hands. "Marta, dear, you're working today — very hard — and I really don't think you need to worry about anything other than what you're doing. Let Shannon and Dan and me handle things. Believe me, you'll be told if anything comes to light. How about this evening we sit down and I'll give you the day's events complete and unabridged? Or I'll get Shannon to tell you herself. Deal?"

He was right, of course, so I just shut up, finished my sandwich, and then went in search of our conductor to get his opinion on one or two things. Frick and Frack followed me at a discreet distance and Tony disappeared again.

⌒⟋

The afternoon was a rehearsal for just me, at my request, with the director, working on the blocking for the final scene of the opera. This is where my character, desperate and alone, and having told her story as a flashback for the first two acts, basically just gives up. It's a lot more complicated and gripping than that, but that's the plot in a nutshell.

She's living alone in a claustrophobic and very messy apartment. Various characters from earlier in the opera appear and disappear, some communicating with her, others just staring. It was all a bit spooky, but I thought it demonstrated beautifully her disintegrating mental state. I sing from a ring circling the back of the set, but I also appear within the set through video screens. It was all very complicated and technical and I needed to find out how it was meant to work. On paper it was indecipherable.

Anyway, the act was all me, me, me, and I wanted to get really comfortable with the physical actions necessary because I needed to be able to concentrate on the really difficult singing. We had our rehearsal pianist play while we worked so that I could annotate my part with where I needed to be when. It would have been great to work on the main stage, but that wasn't available, so we made do with a different space, unfortunately smaller. But by the time we called it quits just past four, I had a pretty good idea what was needed, and a hell of a lot of memorizing to do before the first full rehearsal of this act in five day's time.

I was in a fantastic mood when we left the opera house. Lo and behold, no media trucks, no microphones, and no cameras.

"Seems like I'm yesterday's news," I said.

Tony laughed. "Disappointed?"

"Hell no! But I'll bet Alex back in New York feels differently. I've been a manager's wet dream the past few days. Poor man."

I hooked my arm into Tony's and we jaywalked across Richmond Street. Frick and Frack were on either side of us, scanning the horizon for signs of trouble. That was us: just a carefree couple out for a stroll with our two bodyguards.

Putting my foot down that evening, I insisted we eat in the hotel's restaurant like civilized human beings. Of course that had to be discussed with Shannon, and she grudgingly agreed, but insisted that the overnight security guard — Emilio, a huge, hulking Italian with whom Tony had hit it off — either sit at our table or one *very* nearby. I wasn't happy about that but could see the point. And of course we had to pay for his dinner. Having someone at the next table drinking espresso and staring at us while we ate would have been too unnerving.

Back in our suite with Emilio camped out in the living room, Tony and I sat in our bedroom, talking about the day's rehearsal. I was about to ask what was up in the investigation of McCutcheon when Tony's mobile went off. He grabbed for it as if it were a life preserver thrown to him as he floated in the middle of the Atlantic Ocean. Clearly, he'd been waiting for something.

"Yeah…? Okay, I can do that.…" As he listened he mouthed "Shannon" in response to my raised eyebrows. "Yes. Dinner was lovely.… He's in the next room.… We're just sitting around chatting. I'll ask."

As he lowered the phone from his ear, I asked, "What's up?"

"Shannon wants me to meet with her and Dan and possibly the police."

"Now?"

He nodded. "It will be a quick meeting. I promise. Shannon wants to know if you'll be okay with just Emilio in the next room."

I made a sour expression. My mood was such that a quiet lovemaking session would have been very welcome.

"Well, if you have to go."

"I'll have news for you when I get back. Okay?"

"I may be asleep by then," I answered, which was probably not true. My time would be spent going over my notes from that day's rehearsal.

Tony got up and kissed my forehead. "I'll be back before you know it. If you need anything, just yell for Emilio."

"Anything?" I smirked to drive home my tease.

Tony rolled his eyes. "You sopranos. You're always so damned horny."

"And lucky for you loser tenors that we are!"

He paused at the door and smiled. "Don't I know it. I'll be back soon, Marta dear. Promise."

The door clicked shut and I could hear talking in the next room. A minute or two later, I went out to the living room to search the bar fridge. A bit more white wine while I worked would go down a treat. Emilio was on the sofa watching TV (basketball) so I tossed him a beer.

"You might as well enjoy yourself," I said.

"I really shouldn't."

"But you will. Don't worry. I won't rat you out to the College of Security and Bodyguards, or whomever it is you guys report to."

He smiled. "Thanks."

"Don't mention it," I said and went back to the bedroom.

I lasted all of about twenty minutes before I felt too tired to keep my eyes open. Figuring I'd take a shower in the morning, I just took off all my clothes and got under the covers. Maybe Tony could rouse me enough when he returned to the room. Until then, I'd sleep.

⌒

I had no idea what time it was when I woke up. Still pitch black, I fought against intense grogginess. It felt as if I'd been asleep for days.

Actually, I wasn't even sure if I was awake. Eyes open or shut, complete and utter darkness surrounded me. I put my hands up in front of my eyes. Nothing. There was a total absence of light.

I reached over to see if Tony was back yet and found the edge of the bed where I expected to find him. That was strange, too. I must have rolled to the other side while I was sleeping.

It wasn't until I reached over to that other side and quickly found another edge that it finally sank in something was horribly wrong. This bed was very narrow. It was not the bed I'd fallen asleep on. Fighting down panic, I thought I was just in the middle of a really weird dream. Considering what I'd been going through, that was not unexpected.

Okay. I'd go with the flow until I woke up. Where was I? Something felt cold on my ankle. I moved my leg.

And that's when I *really* woke up.

A thick metal band was around my ankle. Reaching down, I also found a thick chain attached to it. When I lifted my leg, the chain clanked loudly. Then I explored the bed some more. I was on a rather thin mattress over a metal cot.

"You cannot panic," I said out loud. The sound died almost as soon as it passed my lips. "Keep it together. This is just a bad dream."

I got up and walked gingerly around the cot, afraid to trip over something unseen in the darkness. The chain clanked around in my wake. I quickly discovered that both the chain and the bed were bolted quite securely to the wooden floor. I went out to the limit of the chain and could feel no walls.

It wasn't until I stubbed my toe returning to the cot that I realized this was not a bad dream. It was real. The darkness and the silence around me were complete. If I screamed until I lost my voice, no one would hear me.

It didn't matter where I was. I was a captive.

Of him.

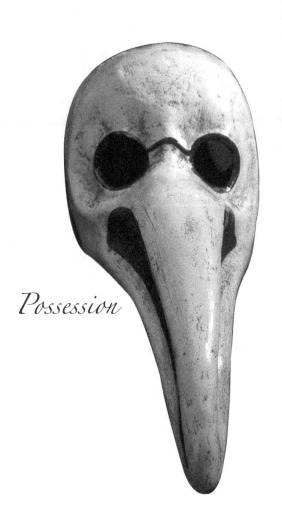

Possession

Chapter Twenty-Six

If ever somebody sounded hysterical, it was Tony when he called Shannon O'Brien that night.

"She's gone! He's got her. Oh my God. Oh my God. He's got her!"

Having been a cop for fifteen years, Shannon had dealt with highly emotional situations. A learned response, she slipped back into it easily.

"Tony, listen to me. You have to calm down."

He babbled on until she repeated the same words for the third time. Then he shut up as suddenly as if someone had removed his batteries.

"Are you at the hotel, Tony?"

"Yes."

"And the bodyguard on duty tonight —"

"Emilio."

"Yes. Where is he?"

"In the living room. Out like light."

"He is breathing, though, right?"

"Yes. But he's unconscious, drugged. I can't rouse him."

"Okay. Here's what we're going to do. I will call the police and hotel security. I'm nearly at my house in Caledon and it will take me close to an hour to get back downtown. I'll get Dan over there, if I can reach him. When the cops arrive, cooperate with them fully. Understand?"

Tony sounded calmer. "Yes. What are we going to do?"

"We're going to find Marta, Tony. Have no doubt about that."

"I'm really worried, Shannon," he almost whispered.

"I'll be there as soon as I can. Stay strong. I've got to make those calls now."

Shannon cursed as she disconnected from the call and immediately speed-dialed the detective unit, explaining quickly and succinctly what had happened.

"Alert Dobbin," she told them. "He's handling this at your end and he'll want to know."

Dan was already in bed. The bandage on his head had been traded for a smaller one, but she knew he was still under the weather.

He quickly told her, "I'm getting dressed now, and I can be down to the Hilton in twenty minutes, max. Do you think I should get in touch with that woman —"

"Lili. Yes. That would be a good idea. I'm sure the police will want to bring in their own psychologist, but

Lili has information and insights they can use. Get her over, if she'll come."

"Will do. Signing off. See you soon. And," he added, "try not to get pulled over for speeding."

"As if!"

⁓

Fifty-five minutes later, Shannon walked into a complete and total disaster. The hotel room was off limits as the crime scene team did their investigation. The hotel had moved everyone to a conference room in the basement. She was expected and let right in.

Dan was sitting with Lili and Tony, who looked incredibly distressed.

Shannon pulled up a chair. "What's the latest?"

Tony looked up. "Your detective friend said he'll be talking to me in a few minutes. What the hell should we do?"

"Did our friend leave anything? A note? One of his damned roses?"

Tony shook his head. "When I returned, Emilio was snoring in front of the TV. I didn't think much about it, except that it was pretty sloppy of him. When I got into our bedroom, Marta wasn't there. I thought she was in the bathroom. It wasn't until I checked and then tried to rouse Emilio that I realized what had happened. That's when I called you."

"Is anything else missing?"

Tony looked more unhappy — if that were possible. "I didn't even think of looking."

Lili still had her coat and gloves on, sitting stiffly upright with her handbag clutched on her legs. "He does not care about us. We are of no concern to him." The group all looked at her. "I am certain there will be no communication from this man. This is about possessing Marta, for whatever ends he has in mind."

Tony said sharply, "You don't think he's harmed her?"

"We cannot be sure, of course, but I take comfort in the fact that he could have, possibly many times now, and has not."

Les Dobbin wandered over. "And you are…?" he asked towering over Lili.

She stood up. "I am Madame Hendriks's vocal coach. But I am also her therapist."

Shannon got up and peeled Dobbin away from the group. She explained exactly who Lili was and why she should be listened to.

"We have our own expert we'll be using."

"I'm telling you, Les, Lili knows her stuff. She also knows Marta — probably better than anyone. She is a good resource to have."

Dobbin shrugged. "You have a point. We have nothing to go on other than she's gone."

"What about the bodyguard?"

"The hotel doctor has brought him around, finally. I was just going to see him. Maybe we'll get lucky."

"May I tag along?"

He shrugged again. "Suit yourself."

"So where are we now?" Tony asked Shannon, Dan, and Lili several hours later.

It was going on four in the morning and Marta's friends all felt and looked pretty rough. Tony had just been asked how he wanted the police to release information about the kidnapping.

"According to what I've heard off the record from someone," Shannon said, "they think our friend got into the room earlier today and replaced everything in the bar fridge with drugged stuff. Both Marta and Emilio had something from it. Emilio says he was watching TV, drank the beer that Marta gave him, and doesn't remember a thing after that, so I think that's a workable theory." She turned to her employee. "Dan, what do you have?"

"As I told you and Tony last night, I followed McCutcheon all yesterday and I'd be willing to swear in court he came nowhere near this hotel."

"Could he have had someone else do his dirty work here?" Tony asked.

Hudson shrugged. "Sure. That's always a possibility."

Lili shook her head. "No. He would desire to do this himself. It is the cat and mouse game he loves. I am certain of it."

Tony stood. "Surely the hotel must have some video?"

"They do," Shannon answered, "but it's been given to the police. They're going to take their time analyzing it if I know procedures."

"But we're wasting time! Who knows what this creature has done to Marta."

Shannon got Tony to sit again. "You're right, of course."

"He will want to play with her," Lili said. "He has her in his power now and he will not waste that opportunity. I am sorry, dear Tony, but the situation is grave."

Tony looked appalled. "You're saying that he might be assaulting her?"

"He could be doing anything, but if you were to ask me to put some money down, I would say that Marta is not in immediate danger for her life. If he wanted to hurt her, he could have done it in the hotel room."

Now Shannon stood. "We're getting off the track. Dobbin wants to know if you want the police to hold a press conference about what's happened, or do we play it close to the vest for a while? Lili?"

She tilted her head to the side, considering. "I do not believe our man will be intimidated by anything we do. Perhaps making the public aware of Marta's abduction would garner useful information. Our man is very clever, but not infallible. As he becomes more volatile, he will be more prone to making mistakes."

"But he will become more unpredictable, won't he?"

"There is always that danger, yes."

"Dan?"

"I spoke to the crime scene team and told them exactly what I found in Marta and Tony's condo. They're going to go over the hotel room with a fine-tooth comb looking for bugs. My guess is they'll find something. This clown *had* to know what was going on in that hotel suite this evening, and that's how he knew he could get away with what he did — and respond so quickly once the coast was clear."

All eyes turned to Tony. He shut his eyes for nearly a minute, head up, breathing deeply.

"News conference," he said. "If we have an opportunity to get information, then we have to go for it. You're sure about what you said, Lili?"

"No one can be certain about these things, but I would be surprised if my guess is the wrong one."

"Then I'll give Dobbin the go-ahead."

The detective hadn't been in the makeshift hotel command centre for the past half-hour, so Tony spoke to a sergeant and was led from the room.

Shannon looked at Dan and Lili. "I sure hope we just gave him the right advice."

⌒

At ten o'clock that morning Detective Sergeant Les Dobbin stood in front of the hastily assembled Toronto media at police headquarters. Tony stood behind him.

"Yesterday evening, sometime after seven thirty, Canadian soprano Marta Hendriks was abducted from her hotel room by a person or persons unknown. We have been on the scene since the abduction was discovered by her husband. We believe it was carried out by the same person who attacked her last weekend in Venice, Italy, and who allegedly also murdered another singer in Rome the week before.

"As well, we have video from the hotel showing the man we believe was responsible loading a very large suitcase into the back of a van. This van was stolen and has been recovered from a residential area in the west end of the city, along with the suitcase. Our forensic specialists are examining both for further clues.

"At this time, we have no further comments, except to ask any members of the public who might have information concerning the whereabouts of Ms. Hendriks to contact us. Now, her husband would like to address you. Tony?"

He stepped to the podium, clearly uncomfortable.

"Marta, if you see this, know that we are working tirelessly to find you and bring you home. And to her abductor: Marta has done *nothing* to deserve this. Please let her go. You have made your point. Please release her, I beg of you. Let my wife come home."

Dobbin stepped back to the podium. "Now, I will take a limited number of questions."

There were nearly forty members of the media present, and of course, they all began shouting at once.

⸺

In his sanctum, the man of the hour watched the pathetic news conference live on the Internet from multiple computer monitors. Leaning back in his chair, completely at his ease, he chuckled throughout the whole thing. The police were really quite pathetic. They would blunder around for weeks and not make any progress. The singer's husband was equally pathetic. He'd looked as if he was about to burst into tears.

No, the man felt quite safe. He could play with Marta as long as he desired and they could do nothing to stop him. Everything was going exactly as planned, although he would rather have grabbed her just before the premiere of the opera. That would have indeed been sweet.

Last night, though, had just been brilliant. In and out of that hotel room in less than three minutes, out of the building in less than seven. Hell! Just wait until they viewed the surveillance tapes. What had actually happened would drive them insane when they found out.

There were only two flies in the ointment. That Czech vocal coach was too smart for her own good and sooner or later she might put two and two together. The blond detective might be a threat too.

The man would have to keep a close eye on them and move fast if their actions warranted it.

Chapter Twenty-Seven

I spent a long time, eyes squeezed closed to keep reality away, certain I would go insane if I opened them. Where had he taken me? My worst fear was that I'd been buried alive, that I would be left alone until I died of thirst or starvation. How much time did I have? How do you keep track of time when you can't see, hear, or even smell anything? My entire existence consisted of a metal cot and the chain binding me to the floor of my prison.

Eventually I dozed off, because the next thing I was aware of was being jolted awake. Had someone or something made a sound? I blinked a few times, making sure my eyes were actually open.

I listened but detected nothing. Perhaps I'd moved in my sleep and the chain had clanked.

Needing to pee, I got off the bed and again searched to the limit of the chain around my ankle without discovering anything that would help me. Then I had a brainstorm and looked underneath the bed. I found something that felt like one of those enamel chamber pots I'd had at my old log home near Ottawa. It was no big deal to squat and shoot since I'd done that many times before when I was too cold or too lazy to descend two floors to the basement where my parents had added a bathroom shortly after buying the place.

Sitting again on the bed, I took stock of things. I'd gone to bed naked, and I was here naked. Since this bastard had already seen me in that state many times through his frigging cameras, it really didn't matter. It would certainly be part of his agenda to humiliate me, and I was damned if I would make that easy for him.

I was also absolutely starving. That probably would have concerned me more, but after finding the chamber pot, I got the feeling he hadn't locked me in here to let me starve to death. Also, if I knew this creep, he'd want to come in with his smug voice and lord it over me.

I thought of poor Tony. He must be going out of his mind with worry. Of course he would blame himself for not being there when I needed him, but I looked on that as a good thing. He was still alive and would move heaven and earth to find me. And he *would* find me.

I lay back down, put my hands behind my head, and thought about my part in the new opera, going over everything I remembered (quite a lot, actually) in an attempt to fill the empty hours that stretched ahead as I waited to be rescued.

Eventually, that got boring so I vocalized a bit — good for my voice *and* it just might attract attention if the room wasn't completely soundproof. It also could bring my captor running, which might not be a good thing.

My voice felt really good and it was a shame to waste it on emptiness, but singing made me feel I really did still exist, regardless of my isolation. They were probably rehearsing the opera right now, with my understudy thinking she could actually be getting her big break. I idly wondered whether she had something to do with this. The opera world could be pretty cutthroat. But I wasn't really serious. Best to keep my dauber up any way I could.

Then I *did* hear a sound. I was sure of it. Straining my ears, I counted out twenty-two seconds before I definitely heard the unmistakable sound of bolts being moved. It came from the blackness directly in front of the bed.

A moment later the light of a thousand suns assaulted my eyes. I gasped and covered them with my hands. A door opened — and he came into the room.

This time my enemy used his regular voice. "You're awake."

It sounded jovial and friendly, as if I was his guest for the weekend.

"Turn off those damned lights! They're killing my eyes."

He chuckled. "In a feisty mood, are we? That's not the wisest course to take with me."

"Turn off your bloody lights!"

"No."

His voice suddenly went calm and dead sounding —
and it scared the crap out of me.

Change of tack. "Why are you doing this to me?" I
asked, with a hint of a whine.

Friendly voice again. "Well, now that *is* a
complicated question, one that deserves an answer. But
not just now. You must be hungry."

I didn't answer.

"Okay Miss High-and-Mighty Opera Singer, what
you have to learn is that when I ask a question, I expect
an immediate answer."

Like the flick of a light switch, his mood had
changed again. If Lili were here, she'd have had a field
day analyzing what was going on. To me, it felt as if I
was standing on shifting sand. This guy seemed majorly
unstable. It would probably be best for my wellbeing to
not antagonize him in any way.

"Well?" he asked.

My inner thoughts had distracted me to the point
I'd forgotten his question. "Well what?"

"*Are you hungry?*" he thundered. "Good God, Marta.
Focus!"

I bit back a tart reply, simply saying, "Yes, I am hungry."

"That's better."

"May I have something to wear?"

"No."

"Please? Just a blanket. I'm cold."

"Really? The temperature in this room is eighty-five
degrees, just the way you say you like it."

A memory of the previous summer floated back. The
AC in our building was out for a few days and Toronto

was under a heat advisory. Tony was feeling the effects and I told him eighty-five degrees was just fine with me. I prefer it hot. Of course this bastard would have heard it, considering the way he'd had our condo wired for sound. I also remembered Tony and I had just finished making love and were covered in sweat.

I felt ill.

"Bastard," I mumbled under my breath.

"*What was that?*"

"Nothing…."

"What did you say, Marta? Tell me!"

I didn't see any reason to lie, and this wasn't the first time a short fuse and a big mouth had got me in trouble. "I called you a bastard."

"And you're going to go hungry for that. Marta, you will learn or you are going to die."

With that he walked to the door and slammed it behind him. I could hear bolts being moved again. Then the lights mercifully went out.

I said a few more unladylike things, not caring that he probably had the room bugged.

The past few minutes had been completely surreal. I'd just had my second conversation with someone I'd still never seen. This time he'd forced me to keep my arm over my eyes since his lights had seemed to be about sixty gazillion watts, all of them focused on the cot. After having spent hours in utter darkness, there was no way I could have seen a thing. Standing outside the ring of lights, he'd been as good as invisible.

Think, Marta, I told myself. *There are things to be learned here. What are they?*

Well, considering the first time we'd been face-to-face in that Venetian alley he'd whispered, it seemed obvious he'd been afraid I'd recognize his voice. Was that a reasonable assumption? And if it was, did it mean now that he didn't care any longer? Maybe he'd just been playing with my head. What did that say about my chances of getting out of this? He had used those lights so I couldn't see him — or had that just been part of his control thing?

I sighed. How I wished I had the knowledge Lili did. Maybe it would be best for my survival to appear like a whipped dog. Still, he was smart enough to probably realize what I was doing if I played him that way.

I certainly needed to play my cards smarter, because having talked about food so much, now I was *really* hungry. Thirsty, too. Maybe there was water under the bed.

So I got up, crawled all around the bed, feeling with my hand. By one of the legs I found a roll of toilet paper. No water. Great.

The only thing I could do now was wait for him to come back. Next time I'd do whatever I needed to get food and water. I squeezed my eyes shut. No. I couldn't do *that*, not for anything.

I'd starve to death first.

Chapter Twenty-Eight

Shannon looked at each of the people sitting in Lili's living room, sizing up their chances of doing any good for Marta.

The diminutive vocal coach was a formidable woman, no doubt. Tony was still beside himself with worry and that didn't bode well. Anyone helping needed to have a cool head under fire, and her gut told her she couldn't rely on him. He had every reason to be in the state he currently was, though, and she had to cut him some slack.

Where the hell was Dan? He should have gotten here by now.

Even though she hadn't known Dan Hudson for long enough to be sure of him, he'd come highly recommended and had proven reliable so far. The real issue was that he seemed to be taking the situation far too personally. In her experience, things could get ugly in a big hurry when that happened.

If it was simply a matter of wounded pride, she could hopefully get him past that. But if it was more, what then? Marta and he seemed to have become pretty chummy while in Italy. Had something transpired between them? That would definitely *not* be good and she'd have to move Dan out. Things were enough of a mess without something like that.

The doorbell rang. Hopefully it was Dan.

Lili got slowly up and limped out of the room, the cast on her leg giving her gait a rolling quality.

Dan came in lugging his two large flight cases of equipment.

"What's with those?"

"Could you help me with something outside?" Dan said by way of answer. Once out on the sidewalk, he told her, "We've been played again by this asshole."

"What do you mean?"

"I just came from your office. He had the phone bugged *and* a live mic right behind your desk."

Shannon felt almost nauseous she was so angry. "Anything else?"

"I wouldn't be surprised. That's why I brought my equipment. We need to check Lili's house. We should probably check your house, your car, Tony's car, any place this bastard might use to get information. Then we have to make certain everything stays clean." Dan pounded his hand on the roof of his car. "Damn it! This guy is like some freaking ghost. I am so pissed right now, I can't stand it."

Shannon sighed. "That makes two of us. Okay. We'll get this done tonight, but we should leave one 'channel' open. Make him think we've missed something. We might find it useful to feed him a bit of misinformation somewhere down the line."

Dan nodded. "Good idea."

"Dan …"

He turned to her. "What?"

"I need to know. Did anything happen between you and Marta while you were in Italy?"

"No. Of course not. Why are you asking?"

"Just a gut feeling, a vibe you two were giving off before she was taken."

"Well, there was something…."

"What?"

"That night in Venice when we were attacked, Marta had enjoyed too much bubbly, so I took her arm to make sure she didn't stumble or fall while we were walking. It wasn't anything much, really, just my arm in hers, walking a bit close together. A little later, she *did* stumble and I had to grab her other arm to keep her from going down. We wound up face to face. She was completely embarrassed. I told her to forget about it and laughed it off. Thinking about it now, though, a person watching might have thought there was, well, something going on between us."

"And was there?"

"What do you mean?"

"Was there any attraction for you?"

"She's a lovely lady. I like her a lot, but relax, I can separate work from pleasure. Besides, she's not really my type — too high strung."

Shannon moved right into Dan's line of vision. "I need to know I can count on you."

"To the bitter end."

"And you swear you're telling me the truth."

His gaze was steady right back into her eyes. "Absolutely."

"I had to ask."

"Understood. Now, let's get to work."

⟳

From his command post, the man watched as one by one, his observation stations winked out over the course of the evening. *Shit!* It was probably that damned spook the O'Brien woman had hired. Time to turn up the heat, let them know he was not to be trifled with.

When he checked a few hours later, there was a big smile on his face. They hadn't thought of all the places to look for bugs. He still had an opportunity to find out what they were up to. O'Brien liked talking to her boyfriend about her cases — and he might get the added pleasure of watching them make love again. She was quite the athletic minx.

He loved technology.

⟳

Tony and Lili decided to go out to dinner at a nearby

restaurant while the two experts went over her house. Both were uneasy about the implications of what Dan had discovered and Tony was beginning to understand the pressure Marta had been under, knowing as he did now that every move they made could well be observed by unfriendly eyes.

"I need to ask you a question, Lili," he said after their order had been taken, "and I need an absolutely honest answer."

"And from me you will get that." She reached across the table and put her hand over his. "I also know what you are asking. Yes, I believe that Marta is in a very bad situation, but I also think she is still alive. This man has no reason to kill her. It is about having power over her. But you also need to know that he may feel the urge to do something to her. I know that is hard to think about, but you have to be prepared for it."

"I know. I've thought about nothing else today. God! I feel so helpless."

"We all do, Tony dear, and that is also part of his game. We have to be strong for Marta and we cannot rest in our quest to find her."

"The police called me just before I arrived at your house. They didn't verbalize it, but I don't think they're having much luck. Apparently, too, the Roman police are not coming up with anything."

"If you want my opinion, I believe it will be up to us to find her."

Tony nodded. "Me, too."

"That is where we must put our energy."

"Well, let's start right now."

Lili smiled across the table. "My sentiments exactly!"

Before they began speaking, both looked around the tiny restaurant. It was Lili's favourite, but their adversary seemed so resourceful, they couldn't be sure he hadn't followed them.

"How many people do you recognize here?" Tony asked.

"Except for that couple in the corner, everyone I have seen before. Luckily, this is a slow evening, or we could not be sure."

Tony rubbed his hands together. "Okay, then to work."

After having found several bugs at Lili's, as well as the two Dan had previously located in the office, two more and a camera were uncovered in Michael's place. There had even been one in Shannon's car. She had to admit, their adversary was very good, very resourceful, as well as wealthy. The gadgets being used didn't come cheap. After checking in with Dobbin, she learned that Marta and Tony's hotel suite had also been bugged.

"He obviously was nearby and knew Marta had minimal protection," he'd confirmed. "The kidnapper knows what he's doing."

Michael naturally put his foot down when Shannon suggested they keep the audio and video bugs in his living room active, but with the way the similar setup in his bedroom had been hidden, she felt it would be convincing they might have missed it. She had her fingers crossed that would be the case. Their string of failures was getting embarrassing. Eventually, she convinced him.

Shortly past eleven, Tony called, insisting on meeting with Shannon and Dan.

"I wonder what those two cooked up at dinner?" she asked Dan as he packed his flight cases.

"Lili said they were going to brainstorm, whatever that means."

"We could certainly use a few good ideas right about now."

Shannon suggested her office since it was now clean of bugs. Hopefully, for once, they were ahead of the bad guy. Regardless, Dan insisted on doing yet another sweep of the inner and outer offices, just to be certain. High-tech surveillance cameras were due to be installed in the morning to make sure there were no more "accidents."

Lili and Tony arrived a few minutes later. They seemed to be almost giddy as Dan let them in.

Shannon was seated behind her desk, looking over business-related emails. At least her computer's firewall had stood up to their adversary's assault.

She swiveled her chair. "So what's up?"

"We have some very good ideas," Lili said, taking the seat in front of the desk.

Tony smiled for the first time all day. "I don't know how the cops will feel about it, though."

Shannon frowned. "What do you mean?"

"The list of suspects we came up with is made up entirely of high rollers, the kind of people I suspect cops don't like to bother."

She leaned back in her chair. "Explain."

"I've sent you an email of our preliminary list. Have you read it?"

"I will now." Shannon turned to her computer, clicked a key or two, read for several seconds, then gave a low whistle. "Quite the list. Why are they on it?"

"Because they all fit the physical profile of our adversary, are all connected to the opera community in some way, and all of them have plenty of money."

"This could take weeks. The kind of information we need is often tough and even impossible to get on this type of citizen."

Tony looked disappointed. "We've arranged them in descending order of likelihood to make it easier."

"Great, but I don't have the manpower to get through this list in the time we realistically have."

"The police do," Lili said calmly.

Shannon looked at Dan, who rolled his eyes. He knew the difficulty of getting the cops onboard with a scheme like this.

"So you think I can convince Dobbin to drop whatever they're doing to jump all over this list of some of the most influential people in Toronto? Tony, with all due respect, this isn't going to fly. You know the difficulty we ran into investigating Andrew McCutcheon? Everyone on this list is just as connected." She shook her head. "And how do you know it's someone who's so obviously connected to opera? What if our man is just another ticket buyer?"

Dan, leaning against the wall to her left, mumbled under his breath. "A goddamned sick ticket buyer."

"Mrs. O'Brien," Lili said, leaning forward, "you are being far too negative. If we all go to the police and speak to them, I am sure they will act."

"You have no idea how these things work."

"Do not they want to find Marta?"

"Of course! But you'd be asking them to stir up a monumental hornet's nest. These people do not like the police — or anyone for that matter — prying into their affairs, and they have the sort of clout that can stop the police dead in their tracks."

Tony said, "I won't accept that there's nothing we can do."

Shannon thought for a moment. "I do have a thought. We don't have anything like the resources available to the police, but we do have some very useful things, nonetheless. Lili, could you make a profile of the man we're after? You know, the sort of thing a police profiler would do?"

Lili nodded once. "Right now? I am rather tired and I would like to think on this."

Shannon looked at her watch and realized it was nearing one in the morning. "Time is of the essence, but we're probably all pretty tired. A bit of sleep might help us all think more effectively. And none of the people Dan and I will need to speak to will be available until morning."

"What do you have in mind?" Tony asked.

Shannon looked over at Dan. "We'll do a preliminary workup of the people on this list, see if there's anyone who warrants a closer look. You and my receptionist Karen can access public records, search the Internet and the like. Dan and I will work our contacts for any inside dope. If we're lucky and get pointed in the right direction, we'll take our information to Dobbin."

"Can't we start now? I don't care what time it is."

"If everyone feels as strung out as I do, we're not going to do good work. You don't want to miss that little clue we need because you can hardly keep your eyes open, do you?"

Tony nodded but looked unhappy.

"Okay, then," Shannon said, getting to her feet. "We'll meet here at nine o'clock sharp."

"I would prefer to work from home," Lili said. "I can fax or email my profile as soon as it is finished."

"Fine with me," Shannon answered, getting up. "Hope everyone sleeps well. Tomorrow you'll need every ounce of concentration you can muster."

Chapter Twenty-Nine

The door opened again, this time without any advance warning.

Once again my enemy used his damned lights. It was useless to try to see through them, so I just covered my eyes with my forearm.

"Push your chamber pot toward me."

"That's sort of hard with all that light in my face."

"Deal with it. If you prefer, you can just leave it where it is and enjoy the stench."

I got up and pulled the pot out from under the cot, gauging where my body was pointed in relation to him. I'd be damned if I'd give him a view all the way to China. When I got to the limit of my chain, I put the pot on the floor.

"Lie down on the cot," he ordered.

"Afraid I might try to strangle you with the chain or beat you to death with my bare hands?"

"Hardly."

"Why are you doing this to me?"

No answer as he backed out of the room. I took heart he was trying to protect his face. If he'd let me see him, it would be clear I was a dead woman walking.

He returned almost immediately. "Do you want food and water?"

I knew better than to challenge him. "Yes," I answered meekly.

I could hear him place some things on the floor, his footsteps moved back toward the door, and the lights switched off. "I'll be back in a short while to collect the dishes. I suggest you be finished by then."

The door was shut, but I didn't hear the sound of bolts being thrown. Did he believe I couldn't do anything against him, or was he waiting to see if I'd try anything? With the thick loop of metal attaching the chain to my ankle, he didn't have anything to worry about.

Crawling on my hands and knees was pretty undignified, but I was too hungry and thirsty to care. When I felt the plate and thermos he'd left, I picked them up and shuffled carefully back to the cot. The food was Chinese takeout. Again it sort of freaked me out that he knew I really liked barbecued pork lo-mein, but then he knew all about my personal life, didn't he? And if I wasn't mistaken, it certainly tasted like it was from my favourite place in the basement of the St. Lawrence Market. The thermos contained hot, unsweetened green tea, something I drank a lot when alone at home. I wolfed down the meal in a thoroughly animalistic fashion since he hadn't supplied utensils.

I'd barely put my empty plate on the floor when he was back again. That answered one question: he *was* able to watch me in total darkness. This cretin loved his gadgets, so he probably had night vision goggles or infrared cameras or something. Either way, I couldn't get the drop on him using darkness.

"Slide the plate to me, then roll the thermos after it."

"Can't I just walk over and hand it to you like a civilized person?"

"You're not a civilized person."

That sort of shook me. "What do you mean?"

"I saw your behaviour in Venice with that Hudson man you were using as your security guard. You wanted him, didn't you?"

"I did not!" When he didn't answer further, I added, "Is *that* what this is about?"

"You were given a great gift," he began after a long wait, "many people helped you, and you have been squandering it. Your performance in Rome last month was a disgrace. It was entirely your fault you sang so poorly."

"So you're trying to teach me a lesson by kidnapping me?"

He went silent again, before finally saying, "Bring me your plate and thermos."

"I deserve an answer."

"You *deserve* nothing! Bring me your plate and thermos."

That dangerous tone was in his voice again. It was too risky to continue.

"You mean hand them to you?"

He sighed. "If you must."

Score one for my side. About time.

Under the relentless glare of the spotlights, it was difficult not to shield my eyes with my forearm, but I needed both hands — or at least I hoped he thought I did so I squeezed my eyes as tightly shut as I could.

Shuffling toward him, I knew roughly where the limit of the chain was, so it was no problem to pretend the end of it surprised me, causing a stumble right in front of him. I fell down convincingly, hurting my knees in the process. The things I was carrying skittered away.

A strong hand under my left armpit dragged me to my feet again.

"Clumsy woman!"

I feigned subservience again. "I'm so sorry. I'm so sorry."

He quickly backed away, picked up the plate and thermos, and left the room without a word. He was back a moment later. I was still sitting on the floor, rubbing my bruised knees.

"Hold out your hand!"

I had no idea what this was about, so I just did what he asked.

I knew at once what had been put into my hand: one of his damned roses.

"Why did you give me this?" I asked.

No answer as he turned and walked out. The lights went off and this time I heard the bolts securing the door.

I sat on the bed, rather pleased with myself. He hadn't been quick enough to back away when I'd fallen, so I'd been able to see to the top of his chest fairly clearly. He'd been dressed in expensive slacks and shoes. He was slender and I thought I detected facial hair.

That information is worth two sore knees, I thought as I rubbed them.

More importantly, by startling him, he'd dropped his guard a bit. His voice sounded different when he'd called me a "clumsy woman."

I felt up the stem of the rose. I tried to imagine its colour. As I touched it to my face to smell its faint perfume, I realized something had been done to it. A quarter section of the blossom had been very neatly cut away.

What did it mean?

Chapter Thirty

Lili was at the desk in her sitting room working on the abductor's profile when she became aware she was not alone. It wasn't due to any sound the intruder made. He'd been utterly silent getting into her house. It was as if the atmosphere around her subtly changed, or perhaps it was that particular bond that has always existed between the hunter and the hunted.

"I have a gun," he said in a surprisingly gentle voice. "Please don't turn around."

"So you have come," Lili calmly replied. "It is not unexpected."

"For you, probably not. What are you working on?"

"You already know or you would not be here."

"And that's what has made you dangerous to me."

"You took a chance waiting this long."

"Originally, you were of no concern, but lately you've been growing more important in my mind."

Lili sighed. "I suppose I always knew you had a troubled soul. I should have helped when I was asked. But I was being selfish, and I suppose a little unsure of myself, and now …" Her shoulders rose and fell once as she sighed again.

"How long have you known it was me?"

"If I had thought about it from the correct perspective, I might have known right from the beginning."

"I guess I *am* fortunate, then. I should have ended it when I first had the chance."

"But when? Ah … But of course: the streetcar."

"I wasn't sure I could do it, so I hesitated for a moment. I suppose it's because I liked you at one time."

"And now with more experience, it is even easier to kill."

"Yes."

"Please do not hurt Marta."

"How can you be so certain she's still alive?"

"It is obvious, or you would not be here."

"It is not up to you to beg for her. In fact, it is beneath you."

"She is my friend."

"Regardless, it is not up to you, nor, in a way, is it up to me. You shouldn't have involved yourself so deeply in her problems."

"As I have said, I had been selfish the first time. I would not make that mistake again — so I helped Marta.

Is it too late to apologize, to tell you how sorry I am?"

"Oh please, Lili. There is no need to try to grovel. It won't do any good."

Again she shrugged. "One has to try."

His voice betrayed his rising impatience. "Hand me those papers."

Lili calmly picked them up, but instead of handing them over her shoulder, keeping her eyes on the wall in front of her, she spun her chair around.

A clear flash of anger crossed his face as he snatched them out of her hand.

Lili smiled sadly. "You are not as I would have expected from the last time I saw you."

"Just shut up, woman!"

She watched as he quickly scanned the four sheets of handwritten notes, nearly complete. If he had not arrived when he did, it indeed might have been too late. As she'd been working, the man who had been pursuing Marta so doggedly (and effectively) had been stepping farther out of the shadows for her. Lili knew she was getting closer to finally whisking off his mask. She'd known him well enough at one time; her profile would have pointed to him most strongly.

Now he was about to win yet another round. She knew she had nothing to protect her but her hands. If she hadn't been so stubborn to move without her cane, it might have been hanging from the edge of her desk as it had many times over the past few weeks. There was no evidence that he actually had a gun, unless it was in one of the pockets of his ski jacket. There certainly wasn't one in the waistband of his pants.

Finished, he looked up. "You must have been thinking you were so smart as you wrote this."

Lili shook her head. "No. Just observant. It has always been my forte."

"You conceited cow. If you were so fucking observant, why didn't you see what was right in front of you, how desperately you were needed?"

"You are correct. I should have helped you, too."

"And why is that? So you could have avoided dying today? That says a lot about the person you are, Lili."

The end, when it came, was swift, but not painless. The man merely sprang forward, plucked Lili from her chair. After throwing her to the floor, he sat astride her body, pinning her arms beneath his legs. Of course, she struggled as hard as she could, but it was futile. Lili's killer outweighed her by nearly a hundred pounds. It seemed as if she was about to say something as he almost leisurely wrapped his gloved hands around her throat, smiled down at her in satisfaction, and strangled the life out of her.

In her mind, Shannon was giving her group until the end of the day to come up with anything that looked solid. She'd call all her operatives off whatever cases they had, and damn the consequences. She needed tails on every person of interest. This situation had long ago gotten up her nose, and she was out to win.

Dan had spent the morning installing new security equipment in her office and Michael's condo (except for the one bug they'd decided to leave in the living room). Then he'd checked everything again at Tony and Marta's condo, everyone's phones, cars. You name it, he'd checked it.

Tony and Karen had been manning the computers, gathering background information on each of the people on the list. Shannon was searching databases to which she had paid access, to see if she could come up with any records that might help them in their quest. For the records that needed official access, she was calling in favours from every cop she'd ever helped. Dan was doing the same with his contacts in Ottawa. All they needed was a little whiff, something upon which they might build a case to take to Dobbin.

So far, they'd turned up sweet bugger all and it was nearly two. And where the hell was Lili with her damned profile?

"Tony, give Lili a call. Ask her when she'll be finished. We need what she's working on."

Across the room, Tony picked up his mobile. "Sure thing."

Shannon turned back to her monitor and began reading an interview Karen had found with one of the subjects.

"Shannon!" Dan said.

She looked up at him and he immediately pointed at Tony. The expression on his face was of complete shock.

"She is a very good friend of mine, and my vocal coach…. Yes, I can. It's spelled L-U-S-A-R-D-I…. I don't know what to say…. Yes. Last night, sometime after one. I dropped her off at her house…. Yes. Two other people. As a matter of fact, I'm with them now…."

Shannon waved her arm to get his attention. "What's going on?"

"Just a moment, constable." He pulled the mobile away from his ear. His eyes were huge and unfocused. "It's the police. They're at Lili's. Oh my God…. She's been murdered."

In a flash, Shannon was across the room and took the phone out of Tony's hand. "Who are you speaking to?" she asked him.

"I, I don't remember his name. Constable something…."

"Constable, this is Shannon O'Brien. I'm a private investigator working for Mr. Lusardi. I used to be a detective with the Toronto police. Tony's wife, Marta Hendriks, was abducted two evenings ago…. Yes, that one. Is Les Dobbin there…? Well, I'd suggest you let him know about this right away. Unless I'm very wrong, the abduction and this murder are connected. We're currently up in Unionville at my office. Please tell him we'll all be down there ASAP."

For simplicity's sake, they decided to use Shannon's SUV. Karen was told to go home. It was too dangerous for her to be working alone in the office.

On the way out, Dan punched in the activation code on the new control panel behind Karen's desk. "If our boy tries to come in here, your smartphone will tell you immediately."

The traffic on the Don Valley Parkway was surprisingly light for that time of day, but it seemed to take forever. Shannon had to keep reminding herself to not strangle the steering wheel.

Her mind was in overdrive. This latest development was beyond the pale, but it told them something. Obviously, *somehow* this bastard knew what they were up to. He also felt Lili was specifically a threat to him. Why was that? She knew better than to hope he'd left anything behind that would help them.

Once on Lili's street, they were let through the police roadblock immediately. A mobile command centre had been brought in since Lili's whole house was a crime scene. Dobbin was just coming out the front door as Shannon, Dan, and Tony walked up. Les's greeting was warmer than past days. Obviously, he knew he needed their help.

"Shannon, glad you got here so quickly. Tony, thanks for coming. And you're …" he said, looking at Dan.

"Dan Hudson. I work for Shannon. I was supplying security for Marta in Italy."

"Well, it looks as if we're all in the same boat. This guy has made monkeys of all of us."

"Yes, sir, he has."

Dobbin seemed satisfied Dan knew his place. "Come inside, everyone. We can all bring each other up to speed."

There was a large table at one end of the long trailer. They sat down and coffee was offered. "Or whatever else you want, I'll send someone out for it," Dobbin said.

Shannon thought she should handle asking the questions. Tony still looked completely zoned out.

"Can you tell us what happened?"

"Someone showed up for a vocal coaching around one. When Ms. Doubek didn't answer the door, he waited, then eventually tried the door. He found her lying in her front room, obviously dead."

"Cause of death?"

"Not official yet, but I know strangulation when I see it."

Tony put his head down.

"Any of the neighbours see anything?"

"We've got constables knocking on doors, but so far no. Immediate neighbours who were home didn't see a thing."

"The front door was unlocked?" Tony asked. "Lili never left it unlocked, not in this neighbourhood."

Dan said, "He couldn't have risked picking the lock, not here: too much traffic, too many prying eyes. I suppose he could have gotten a key somehow. This guy is *that* good."

"Lili kept a key under one of the flowerpots to the left of the door," Tony told them.

Dobbin looked at him. "Do you know which one?"

"Sure."

"Mike!" Dobbin shouted over his shoulder. "Go with Mr. Lusardi. We're looking for a key." As Tony got up, he added, "How many people would have known about this?"

Tony shrugged. "No idea. Marta and I knew, but we were really good friends. I don't think she told most people."

Dobbin looked closely at Shannon. "Why today?"

"Lili was working up a suspect profile for me. You know the drill. Were any papers found near the body? Is Lili's laptop in the house?"

He picked up his walkie-talkie. "Easily found out. Samotowka? When you're done with Lusardi, send him back in here, then I want you to look in the house for papers, handwritten. They most likely would be in the room where we found the body. If not, there is that room with the piano. Also, look for a laptop. Let me know ASAP what you find. Okay?" Dobbin turned back to Shannon. "If they're around, my men will find them."

Dan said, "Trust me. You won't find either thing."

"But the effort has to be made. Sooner or later this guy will slip up. They all do."

"Not this guy."

"If we don't find Lili's profile," Shannon said, "then we'll know for certain it was this bastard we're after — not that I have any doubts."

Tony returned. "No key," he said.

"So was there anything else you were working on, Shannon, that might have got up our boy's nose?"

It took her ten minutes to run down their latest theory, finishing with, "Thing is, we haven't come up with much."

"Why didn't you come to me with this?"

She shrugged. "I felt we needed something solid to get you to listen."

"Shannon, you know me better than that. You were always too much of a lone wolf for your own good. That's why we're so leery of you. I know you were a good cop, but after that cock-up with the jazz singer a few years ago … Well, what can I say?"

"Precisely."

"What have you come up with?"

"I'm fairly certain it isn't Tallevi. It's fairly easy to get his itinerary. He could have been in some of the cities where Marta received those roses, but definitely not all of them. Ditto with Odynski, the director of the COC's board. He's too old, anyway."

"So what are we looking for?"

"That would have come primarily from Lili's profile. The abductor has money and isn't afraid to spend it. He's familiar with the backstage of opera houses. He may or may not have someone working with him in that regard, but Lili had already told us she didn't think so. He would want to do it all."

Dan added, "He's a dab hand with surveillance, and he's got access to cutting edge technology."

Dobbin blew out some air. "In short, you're saying this guy is a bloody genius."

Tony finally looked up. "He knew Lili." Everyone around the table turned to him. "I've just been thinking. I don't ever remember her needing to use that spare key. I know she only told certain people where it was. The person who murdered her has to either be a good friend, or someone who saw her use the key. Either way, it *has* to be someone who knew her, someone who came over here before, probably multiple times."

Dobbin asked, "And you're certain?"

"Lili was a very careful person. She lived alone and there are a lot of people around here who wouldn't hesitate to take advantage of that. She was pretty security conscious. If she were to need to use that spare key, she would be very careful to make sure she wasn't seen."

Shannon had pulled out her flip notebook and been scribbling notes. She looked up. "Our boy may have made a tactical error. This is something pretty solid to go on. We need to find a suspect such as I outlined earlier *and* who had more of a passing relationship with our late friend."

"May she rest in peace," Tony said as he crossed himself.

Shannon reached over to put her hand on his arm. "Tony, I didn't know her anywhere near as well as you, but I can safely say she will rest a lot better if we catch this bastard."

"He's probably already done the same to Marta."

"Don't say that! We've got to believe we can do this. I *know* we can."

Tony nodded. "I just don't dare to hope sometimes, but you are right."

Dobbin smiled. "Forget what I said before. Shannon O'Brien, you never should have left the force. We need cops like you."

She shook her head. "Thanks. But you wouldn't be saying that if you knew the number of stumbles and the amount of bad judgment we've had on this case. Our quarry has made us look foolish at every turn."

"Mr. Lusardi, we'll start with you. The murderer knew Lili Doubek, you say? I need a list of everyone who saw her on even a casual basis, and you can help me get that list started."

Tony nodded. "Sure. Anything I can do to help."

"And Shannon, I'm bringing you onboard for this fully. We need every sharp mind we can get. I'll just have to make them understand downtown. I'm going to call a meeting of everyone who's working on this case and we're going to shift our focus. I need all three of you to tell us everything you've got — and I mean everything. We're going to get this bastard before he does any more harm."

"Then we're going to have to move fast," Dan said under his breath.

Chapter Thirty-One

Blackness flowed within and without me.

I knew now why solitary confinement could be such a harsh punishment — especially when it was *this* solitary. Time had ceased to have meaning. I drifted from waking to sleeping and back again with virtually no seam. I could have been locked in this room for a week, or a month with no clear idea how much time had passed. The only way I could reliably gauge at least the general passing of time was when he brought food. I certainly wasn't being served three squares a day, but based on my hunger, I was probably being fed twice a day.

As my feeling of detachment increased, my dreams became luridly vivid and intense. I dreamt of my dead mother and father, of Tony, and my first husband, Marc. Then came ones of being buried alive. I couldn't stop them and they were just too horrible to contemplate.

My captor didn't seem to care if I sang, so I did that. But with so little sonic feedback due to the soundproofing, it didn't feel right. Music needs resonance, but the impenetrable darkness swallowed up the notes I sang as soon as they left my mouth. I forced myself to keep on, but with decreasing enthusiasm.

I measured the chain as best I could and guessed it was seven feet. I walked back and forth at its length to get some exercise until the clamp around my ankle began to chafe. Sit-ups, push-ups, and the like have never been something I enjoy, but I did them until my whole body ached.

All of this at least made me feel marginally alive. Somewhere in the blackness I still existed.

There was a longer gap between my fourth and fifth meals. I had the horrifying thought that something might have happened to my enemy. It was shattering to realize anything that happened to him happened to me, too.

With thoughts like these running through my head, it was a struggle not to completely freak out. What would it be like to be trapped here, gradually starving to death? My brain couldn't really process the horror of something like that. I needed to change the tune.

I got off the cot, stood up straight and tall as my teachers had taught me, and began vocalizing. I did it thoroughly and I concentrated as hard as I could in order to block out bad thoughts.

It was either that or risk going mad.

⁓

I must have been deeply asleep, because I didn't hear him open the door. I stirred as the lights suddenly came on, blinding me because I didn't react quickly enough and opened my eyes. That much light when you've spent hours in utter darkness was completely overwhelming.

"Can't you just turn the damned lights off?" I asked. "I can't see you anyway." They clicked off, and I took my arm from my eyes. "Thank you."

A moment later he said, "I brought you this."

Something made of cloth landed on my stomach. Lord be praised! It was a T-shirt, and while it wasn't all that long, it was something.

"Thank you," I said as I got off the cot and slipped it over my head.

I thought it was part of his plan to keep me naked in the darkness and silence, just to make my misery complete. Why the change? What had happened?

"I brought you something to eat. Do you want it?"

"Absolutely. I'm famished."

"Slide me the chamber pot and I'll empty it for you."

Even though the soundproofing made it seem as if the room was stuffed full of cotton, I could pinpoint his position exactly. Moving carefully because I didn't want to risk dropping it, I went unerringly to where he stood. It became clear that he must have been wearing night vision goggles or something, because his hands reached out and took the pot from me when I reached the limit of the chain.

Light from the outside world flooded in as the door opened and shut. Though nothing like full sun, it still seemed overwhelmingly bright. At least we weren't underground. That was something — a big something.

I counted off just short of five minutes before he came back. This time he turned on his bloody lights. I squeezed my eyes shut as tightly as I could, but it still seared my eyeballs.

"Hold out your hands."

A plate and thermos were thrust into them. "Don't dawdle," was all he said before leaving again.

This time it was pasta with chopped sausage in a tomato sauce. Again it tasted very familiar. I'd eaten this before. That gave me something to think about while I wolfed it down, once again using my fingers. The thermos was filled with some sort of cola.

He came back in immediately after I'd eaten the last mouthful. He definitely had a way to watch me when the room was dark.

At the chain's limit, I exchanged the plate and thermos for the rinsed out chamber pot.

Something was different about him and I decided to push my luck.

"So, how is your day going?"

"*What?*"

"I'm just trying to make conversation. It's lonely in here, as you can imagine. And you seem preoccupied."

"I am *not* having a good day."

"Anything I could help with?"

I seemed to have struck him totally speechless with my attempt to draw him into conversation.

Eventually he said, "Hold out your hand."

I was suddenly very frightened, but I didn't want to show it. "Why?"

"Because I told you to!" he shouted. "Hold out your hand."

I did as requested and he again placed one of his damned roses in my hand.

"Are you going to release me?"

"Yes."

I was shocked. "When?"

"Soon. Very soon."

"Why not now?"

"Because there are still things I must do."

"Will you tell me why you're doing this to me?"

"Yes. Just before I release you."

"Thank you."

"You owe me no thanks, Marta. None at all."

He left the room hurriedly. The lights went off and I again heard the bolts sliding into place. Surely that was for effect. He used the bolts for their aural impact, wanting me to know it was hopeless to think I could ever escape.

He'd sounded different this time, almost distracted. Something had happened. It was as if my enemy was unnerved by something. What was it? And did it have anything to do with me? I didn't dare to hope that maybe the police or Tony and Shannon were getting closer, that he was in danger.

I ran my right hand up the stem of the rose to the large blossom. This time a vertical half-section had been removed, almost as if it had never been there. A chill ran down my spine.

I got the feeling if someone was going to come and save me, they'd better do it soon.

Chapter Thirty-Two

Tony felt completely lost back in the apartment.

Even when Marta was away — far too often, but then he knew that going into their relationship — something of her, maybe just her scent, remained behind. Now it felt like she'd never been there. It was hard to bear. He walked through every room, as if he might find her presence hiding in a closet or behind a door. There was nothing.

It's just the end of a long, depressing day, he told himself. *What else do you expect?*

The apartment phone rang. He answered it in the living room, but not before checking the number. This was a local one, but he didn't recognize it. Having memorized most of the media numbers by this point, he still felt reluctant about answering and picked up only at the last minute.

"Yes?"

"Tony Lusardi?"

"Yes."

"This is Peter Grant speaking."

Why would the main sponsor of the new opera be calling him?

"I'm just calling to say how appalled I am by what has happened and also to inquire if there's anything I can do by way of assistance."

"Other than bringing my wife back? It's very kind of you to call, though, ah, Peter."

"Has anything new come to light?"

"Not really."

"Nothing from the kidnapper? A ransom demand, something like that?"

"No. The police have instructed me not to say anything about the status of the investigation — although I suppose I just have with my previous comment. I hope you understand."

"Quite, quite. How are you holding up?"

"As well as can be expected, I guess."

"If there's anything you need, or any news, please don't hesitate to get in touch. Needless to say, I'm a huge fan of Marta. My late wife also spoke glowingly of her many times. I was really looking forward to her performance in the new opera's premiere."

"You make it sound as if Marta not being able to sing is a foregone conclusion."

"No, no, you misunderstand. Nothing would please us more than to see her grace the stage at the Four Seasons Centre on opening night, nothing."

"My faith has to be in the police. I also have other resources being brought to bear."

"Ah. The blond detective I saw in your wife's entourage."

Tony didn't know what to say, so he didn't answer.

After an awkward pause, Grant added, "As for my offer, anytime, day or night, call. Do not hesitate."

"I'll remember that. Very generous of you."

"Nice speaking with you, Lusardi. Bye for now."

Perplexed by the call, Tony stood for several minutes wondering what it was all about. He'd hardly spoken a dozen words to Peter Grant before this.

Of course, he could have been trying to show his support, but Grant didn't strike him as the warm and fuzzy type. He certainly didn't have that reputation in the business world. There had to be another meaning.

He picked up the phone again.

"Leonardo?" Tony said, switching to Italian. "Tony Lusardi. Listen, I just had an unexpected phone call from Peter Grant. What's up at your end? Have there been any discussions about replacing Marta in the production?"

A very awkward silence followed before the general manager of the COC answered. "Tony, my friend, I am sure you understand that we are all appalled and devastated by what has happened. But I also have the good of my company to look after. That is my job, after all. A great deal of money has been spent, many tickets have been sold, publicity put into place.

"Yeah, yeah, and the show must go on. You forgot that one."

"Tony, we would like nothing more than to have Marta performing on opening night, but we have to be realistic, as well. Every hour that goes by with no news of her brings the company closer to an inevitable and sad decision. It is far too late now to bring in someone else and it would be unfair of me to keep our understudy waiting until the very last minute to be told that she has the responsibility of carrying the entire opera — because that's what the role of Naomi involves."

"The understudy? It's part of an understudy's job to never know when they are going to have to step in and perform. We both know that. You're ready to write Marta off, damn you."

"Nothing of the kind! But if, God forbid, Marta doesn't come home in time, do you expect us to cancel the run? That would be a disaster for the COC."

Tony knew what Tallevi was saying made sense. The small company Tony was singing for had no compunctions going elsewhere for someone to replace him, almost before he had told them he'd have to bow out of their production. Still, it filled him with both sadness and anger that everyone was willing to write off Marta after she'd been missing for not even forty-eight hours.

"Tony, I assure you we will wait until the last possible second, but I would not be honest if I didn't tell you that a decision will have to be made soon."

After hanging up, Tony went to his computer to see what the media's take was on Marta's kidnapping. Was he being a fool for believing they could find her?

Of course, it was the top story, and the horrible incident in Paris was a large part of their lurid coverage. Everything he read and watched seemed to reinforce that the world was breathlessly waiting for his wife to be found dead. No wonder Tallevi and Grant were thinking of covering their asses.

Tony opened his mail program. Over three hundred new emails stuffed his inbox, many from the media asking for interviews. But there were also a surprising number from friends and colleagues offering support and best wishes for a speedy and happy end to the ordeal. As he idly read them over, he felt a bit better.

As he was reading the last few, his mail alert sound pinged. Another one had come in. Looking at the subject line almost caused his heart to stop.

Marta's kidnapper had contacted him.

⟳

Tony was in Dan's face the moment he walked in the door.

"What the *fuck* is this all about? What did you do with Marta when you were in Italy? I swear to God I'll pound you to a pulp!"

Shannon quickly got between the two men. "What the hell are you talking about, Tony?"

"He sent me a video. It was shot in Venice. This, this bastard was holding Marta's hand and then they went into a doorway, and I swear to God they were kissing. You bastard! *I trusted you!*"

"Tony," Dan said calmly. "It's not what it looks like. I can explain."

Shannon put her hands on Tony's shoulders and forced him to look at her. "Dan and I have already discussed this. He's right: it's not what it looks like."

"But they were walking arm in arm. You can clearly see that on the video."

"Marta had too much champagne at the post-performance party," Dan told him. "I was concerned she might fall, so I was holding her arm. That is the sum total of what happened — the whole time we were gone. She was just feeling a little too good that night, that's all. It was stupid for me not to insist that we take a water taxi back to the hotel, but I'd kept such a tight rein on her all week, I felt she deserved the night out. It was stupid, but there you have it. Nothing, Tony, *nothing* more happened! If Marta were here right now, she'd tell you the same thing. He's playing with your head, man. He's playing with all our heads."

Shannon said, "And that's exactly what Dan told me the day after he got back. Now, would it be possible for me to view the clip? We're going to have to let the cops know about this, but that doesn't mean we have to do it immediately. I want to study it. Do you have headphones? I'm hoping we might get some clues from background noises."

As soon as Tony disappeared into the extra room, Shannon gave Dan "the look," so he'd be absolutely certain how unhappy she was. He sighed heavily and shrugged, acknowledging he'd completely blown this one.

Tony handed the headphones to Shannon. He looked and sounded calmer. "It came in while I was reading emails. It's as if he knew I was doing it."

Dan asked, "And the security camera didn't show him in the apartment?"

Tony shook his head.

"Shit! How the hell does he do it?"

Shannon was watching the video clip, earphones held tightly against her ears, brow furrowed in concentration. She sighed as she removed them.

"There's nothing on the soundtrack of any use."

Eventually, Shannon called the cops. Dobbin appeared at the door with two tech guys in tow and Dan took them through the apartment yet again. They eventually left, taking Tony's computer with them.

Shannon flopped onto the sofa. "It has been a horrible day."

Dan agreed, but Tony, surprisingly, was upbeat.

"I take this as a sign that Marta is still alive. Why else would he send me a video like that? If she was dead, he either would've dumped her body where it would be quickly found, or he would've sent us a video of her body. She's alive. I *know* it."

Shannon and Dan looked at each other, but kept their faces carefully blank.

"But we're missing something," he added. "That's the reason we keep running into walls. C'mon, the bastard *can't* be that smart. I refuse to believe that three of us can't out-think him."

Dan was resting his chin on his palm. "Do you think we're not trying?"

"No, Dan," Shannon said. "Tony's right. He's trying to make us feel whipped. We're a danger to him, more so than the police — just as Lili was." A look of amazement came over her face. "Of course …"

Dan still wasn't buying into the new mood in the room. "What's that supposed to mean?"

"Why kill Lili *this morning*? Obviously he could have done it anytime. Why today? It was because of what she was working on. I'll bet there was something in her profile that pointed directly at him. That's why she had to die."

"The thing I'm wondering is why did he snatch Marta when he did? If he was out to punish her, as Lili said, then why not wait until the last minute? She called him out, and he felt he had to react. But if he'd waited … who would have won, who would have lost?"

Tony added, "I feel more and more that our guy has something directly to do with *The Passage of Time*."

Shannon nodded. "We've struck out everywhere else. We should concentrate there."

"Give me your notebook, Shannon," Dan said. "We need to make our own profile."

"Dobbin said they have one of their people working on that."

"Not a psych profile — a *suspect* profile. We need to find the people who fit every one of our search criteria."

Tony looked around. "Let's go somewhere else, okay? I don't want to take the slightest chance he'll get wind of this."

Shannon nodded. "Good idea."

Chapter Thirty-Three

My mind was beginning to drift quite badly. I had zero concentration. One moment I'd be singing to myself, then seemingly the next minute I'd be waking up. At least, I thought I was waking up. How do you know? I might have just been in some sort of trance.

My nose told me I could really use a shower. I could sing and make other noise, touch myself and the things around me, but it was as if life was slowly being sucked out of me by my jailor and his prison.

Singing, talking out loud, moving around in some form of limited exercise, all held no interest any longer. Memories of my life outside this dark box were becoming grey and lifeless.

The food my captor sporadically brought was always things I'd eat for dinner, uncannily so, but hardly surprising. Point is, I couldn't get any clue from the food what time of day it might be. With no light, no information, the passage of time had become completely meaningless. I had no idea how long I'd been chained in the dark.

Sleep was my only escape. Dreams seemed more real than waking thought. Every time I woke up, I was filled with profound regret. If part of his agenda was to unhinge me, it was working.

Those mutilated roses were his way of counting down — but to what? My release? I doubted that. The end of my life? Probably. My growing fear was that he would keep me captive, stuck by his whim in this awful purgatory. I was beginning to accept that I would die in this room. My greatest fear was that I would be alone.

Those horrible spotlights came on again, presage of another visit by my heartless captor.

What meal would I get this time? Chinese takeout? A bowl of mediocre pasta? A burger and fries? I longed for a bowl of Nonna Lusardi's wonderful *pasta e fagioli* soup, but couldn't clearly remember what it tasted like. I mentally shrugged. All I wanted was something that would fill my achingly empty stomach.

This time, the door opened but he didn't enter. Except for the manacle around my right ankle, I would have tried to make a break for it — damn the consequences.

Getting off the cot, I walked out to the limit of my chain. I raised my forearm above my eyes, attempting to see through the crippling glare of his lights.

"Are you there?" I called out.

No answer.

"What's going on?"

Silence.

"Talk to me!"

"Get back on the bed."

His voice once again sounded completely devoid of emotion. I did what he asked, sitting primly erect with my hands clasped in my lap, waiting for the next move.

Nothing happened for over five minutes — I was counting — until the tension was absolutely unbearable, all part of his game, I felt sure.

"Your friend Lili is dead."

I'd been toyed with so much, I couldn't accept anything he might say. "You're lying."

"Suit yourself, but it's true, I assure you. I had to kill her."

"You *had* to kill her? No one *has* to kill somebody unless they're attacked. Lili was half your size, old, and had a broken ankle, for Christ's sake. How can you stand there and say she *had* to die?"

"You know absolutely nothing about it! Your great friend did a horrible thing once. She herself acknowledged that before I ended her wretched life."

"You inhuman bastard!"

I leapt up and walked to the limit of the chain again, straining to break the bond that held me in place. If it had snapped I would have attacked him with my bare hands, trying to do to him what he said he had done to Lili.

Of course, it didn't happen. I fell to my knees. Helpless and hopeless in my rage, I began to cry even though I couldn't bear to have him see me being so weak. She *was* dead. I instinctively knew he was telling me the truth.

Eventually shuffling back to the cot, I laid down on my side and curled into a ball. At least *now* I could feel. I continued weeping for the passing of the woman who had meant so much to me. It was not stretching the truth to say that Lili had saved my life and was responsible for me being able to resurrect my career.

I had no idea whether he was still standing in the doorway, observing the latest handiwork of his obsession with me, nor did I care. If I was depressed before, it was nothing to what I felt now. Eventually, the lights went off. I didn't hear the door shut.

Several minutes passed, then from the darkness, he asked, "Are you hungry?"

It sounded a bit more, I don't know … human.

"Of course I'm hungry! How can you even ask?"

The anger had just burst out of me, and I immediately feared I had done something very unwise. Surprisingly, though, I got no blowback. He simply left.

On his return, his entry was more normal: the lights came back on and his voice held its usual arrogance.

"Slide me the chamber pot. I'll hand you your meal."

I wearily got off the bed and did as he asked. Even through the despair that gripped me, I had an overwhelming hunger.

My meal was two mediocre ham and cheese sandwiches. I wolfed them down as if they were the best thing ever. The thermos was again filled with cola. Out of the ordinary was the fact that he stayed in the room to watch me eat. Having lived in complete silence for so long, I could hear his breathing quite easily whenever I wasn't chewing. It seemed rather rapid. Was he anxious about something?

"Bring me your plate and thermos now!"

"But I'm not done eating."

"I said *now*!"

When I didn't do this fast enough, he screamed at me to hurry. As soon as I'd shuffled over, he snatched them from me, flinging them to clatter in the darkness behind him. "Hold out your hand."

"No."

"I said hold out your hand, and if you don't do it now, I'll wring your bloody neck just like I did your friend's this morning."

An icy shudder of fear ran up my spine and I meekly did as he asked. No sooner was the rose in my hand than he bolted from the room and the lights snapped off. The bolts on the door were slammed into place.

Something was wrong. I prayed to God in heaven that help was on the way, because when I slid my hand to the top of the rose stem only a one quarter section of the blossom remained.

Chapter Thirty-Four

"How about picking up one of those rent-by-the hour cars?" Tony asked. "I sometimes use them when we're taking my nonna out for a ride. We should be able to find one within a couple of blocks from here. I'll book it online while we walk."

"Sounds good."

After snagging a car, Tony drove up to the Eaton Centre where he ran inside to get something from the store where he worked. He quickly returned carrying a brand new iPad.

"I want to be absolutely sure that bastard can't track what we're doing," he said.

Shannon was astonished. "You bought an iPad just for that?"

"I'd buy five if I thought it would help." Then Tony grinned. "Besides, as assistant manager, I get a fantastic discount."

He drove them down Yonge Street to Adelaide and was soon swinging around the looping northbound ramp from Eastern Avenue onto the Don Valley Parkway.

"Whenever I need to relax and do some heavy thinking," Tony told his passengers, "I drive around the city on the big highways: up the Don Valley Parkway, across on the 401, down the 427, and then along the lake front on the Gardiner. It calms me down and helps me to focus on whatever my problem is."

From the back seat, Dan snorted. "Driving in Toronto traffic helps you relax? Amazing. It makes me either want to chew the steering wheel in frustration or pull over, get out of the car, and just walk away."

Shannon laughed. "Dan, I think Tony's talking about doing it late at night."

Traffic on the DVP was light and moving well.

"Perfect," Tony sighed.

Dan said, "As long as an idiot driver doesn't do something stupid and bring the whole thing to a halt."

"Have faith."

Tony stayed in the slow lane and the faster traffic was indeed zooming by at breakneck speed.

Shannon fired up the iPad. "Okay, troops. Time to get to work. Dan, got my notebook ready?"

"What do you have in mind?" Dan asked.

"Lay out the parameters for our suspect, and I'll use the iPad to do research while we're talking. Tony, you start us off. You understand Marta's world far better than we ever will. What should be top of our list?"

"Besides the fact that our man had to know Lili and had been to her house, I'd say the fact that he knows his way around backstage so well. Those things sort of go hand in hand, though, don't they? Not only that, he blends in and raises no questions. So say he's comfortable in the opera world."

"Do you think our adversary is a singer?"

Tony laughed. "No. He has to be wealthy, remember? Most singers only have the kind of money we're talking about in their dreams. I feel certain our man hangs *around* with singers, but isn't one himself."

"Good points. We don't need to worry about how he delivered the roses. That's what the cops are working on. All right, our suspect is someone who's wealthy, knew Lili well, and is comfortable backstage. Next?"

Dan said, "The gadgets being used are difficult to source. You have to personally know the top guys to get hold of some of the things I've seen. Money talks in this business, but he'd have to make contact with the right people and they can be pretty skittish. And don't forget, he has to be very conversant with electronics. You don't just plug and play with a lot of these devices. You have to know what you're doing."

"Electrical engineer?"

"Possibly."

Shannon nodded. "Check. Now to my mind, it's his intelligence that really frightens me, and that slides in with what you just told us, Dan. There's a saying in my world: the only criminals who get caught are the dumb ones or the unlucky ones. Our guy is neither. Anything else?"

Tony said, "He speaks rather good Italian."

"A small point, but a good one. Right. To be included on our list, a suspect has to fit every one of these points. Agreed?" When Tony and Dan didn't raise any objections, she added, "Tony, you know this crowd better than either Dan or me. Any ideas who might fit the bill?"

They drove as far as the exit junction for the southbound 427 before he spoke.

"Only two."

"And all our points can be applied to them?"

He nodded. "Leonardo Tallevi or Peter Grant, but I don't know about all the points with either of them."

"You're kidding."

"I can't say how much money Tallevi has for sure, but I know he gets paid well by the opera company. Previous to becoming the GM in Venice, he was a successful production and lighting designer for many years. He's the inventor of a very compact and reliable computerized lighting console. It's used all over the world. I don't know how well he knew Lili, but he was at her Christmas party the past two years."

"I'm looking him up now. You're right, Tony." She turned around and handed the iPad back to Dan. "Look at this. He sold the rights to his lighting console a year ago for ten million. I'd say he has enough money to be our man. And he certainly fits our other criteria. Okay, Tony, what about Grant?"

"Peter Grant made a pile of money early and has been adding to it ever since."

"Isn't Grant too old?" Dan asked. "I think we're looking for someone young and energetic."

Shannon had been staring down at the iPad again. "Listen to this: 'Peter Augustus Grant remains an avid tennis player, and even at sixty-eight, he is one of the top-ranked amateur doubles tennis players in Canada.' That's from a corporate profile for a board he sits on, dated last fall."

"Okay, he's still in. Tony, does Grant speak Italian?"

"Yes. His wife was Italian. They had a villa in Tuscany. I've heard him speaking Italian to Tallevi."

"Are you getting all this down, Dan?" Shannon asked. "I'll search for more information on both of them while you two talk. I'll see if I can find out whether Grant has an electronics background."

The two men continued the discussion as the car reached the Gardiner Expressway eastbound. Being after ten on a weekday night, traffic was really zipping along.

Near the bridge over the Humber River, it happened.

Since traffic was light, Tony didn't need to concentrate on the cars around him very much, so he didn't notice the black car that had been very close behind them for several minutes. Some emergency road work was being done on the right just past the bridge where something had gone into the guardrail. Like everyone else in Toronto, Tony wasn't paying any attention to the lowered speed limit.

Just before he came to the bridge, the car behind him sped up and began to pull out. As it came level with

Tony, the driver turned hard to the right and slammed broadside into Tony's rental car. Taken completely by surprise, he didn't stand a chance.

The car shot off the road into the emergency pylons at twenty kilometres above the posted limit and slid along the partially repaired guardrail. Ricocheting off, it shot across all three lanes, narrowly missing a transport truck and into the opposite guardrail where it came to rest, miraculously still on its wheels. For good measure, a skidding car clipped the rear end and spun them around.

Tony was aware of screeching brakes and people running toward them. Looking to his right, Shannon was out cold, leaning heavily against the still-intact side window.

He heard Dan curse from the back seat and then his head appeared in the rear view mirror.

"What the hell happened?"

"I think our friend just tried to kill us," Tony said, surprisingly calmly.

"Shannon?"

Tony undid his seat belt and felt her throat for a pulse. "Alive. She must have hit her head. Can you see if there's any blood?"

By this time, people were trying to wrench open the damaged doors and it got through to both men that the interior of the car reeked of gas.

"We've got to get her out of here," Dan said.

Someone appeared with a crowbar and started working on Tony's door, which was the least damaged. It popped open fairly easily. Helping hands gently extracted Shannon and two people carried her a safe distance from the car. As they were setting her down by the side of the road, the car burst into flames.

Shannon's eyelids fluttered and she groaned. "What happened?"

Dan knelt down. "He may not have been able to listen in on what we were talking about, but our adversary certainly seems to have known where we were."

As the sound of approaching sirens came from the distance, Shannon swore.

Police, fire department, and an EMS van arrived in a bunch. Shannon wouldn't be kept down despite protestations from the medics and cops. She had a huge knot on the right side of her forehead. Caution would dictate an x-ray at the very least, but she wouldn't hear of it.

Wandering off to the side, she had her mobile out and was speaking angrily to someone.

Dan, looking at the fiery mess from which they'd barely escaped, said to Tony, "It could've been a whole lot worse."

"Yeah, but the rental company is going to be pissed."

"I never thought for a moment we'd be the ones to screw up Toronto's traffic tonight."

They burst out laughing, a bit too enthusiastically. Both realized just how close a thing it had been.

"I don't care where he is," Shannon shouted into her phone. "Let him know what's just happened. Got that?" A sour expression on her face, she jammed her phone into a front pocket of her jeans as she walked over to Tony and Dan. "Luckily my phone wasn't in my shoulder bag. Shit! Replacing all the I.D. is going to be such a pain in the ass."

Dan raised his eyebrows. "Somebody came out of that in a feisty mood."

The accident site secured, a senior officer came over to them. "You three were in the car?" After they answered in the positive, he asked, "Who was driving?"

Tony answered, "I was."

"Have you had anything to drink this evening, sir?"

Before Tony could sputter an indignant answer, Shannon peeled the cop off and spoke intensely to him for a few minutes while he nodded and scribbled into his notebook as quickly as he could.

A half hour later, they were leaving. Shannon had finally been convinced to take a ride in the ambulance. Tony and Dan were in the back of a police cruiser, being driven downtown for further questioning. With the arrival of two of Dobbin's detectives, the matter had taken on a more urgent air.

By the time the police were satisfied, it was nearly four in the morning. Out on the sidewalk in front of Toronto's police headquarters at College and Bay, though it was still dark, it felt to the two men as if the new day had already begun.

Dan turned to Tony. "What are you thinking?"

Tony seemed taken aback by the question and didn't answer immediately. "What do you mean?"

"Are you up for continuing this, I mean, like right now? That bastard almost killed us a few hours ago. Four murders in one day? He's obviously getting desperate. I think we need to take him out now."

"You're saying you don't trust the police to handle things?"

Dan put his hand on Tony's shoulder. "Tony, Marta's life could be on the line right now. The cops will take it slow and easy. We're not ratting out some gangbangers here. These men we've told them about are movers and shakers in this city. The cops will certainly go slow and easy, not break down doors and rush in. Do you think it's wise to wait for that?"

"You're saying we should take this on ourselves?"

"I don't want to alarm you, but if you were this guy and the heat was being turned up under you, what would be the logical thing to do?"

Tony's eyes opened wide. "Get rid of the evidence."

"Exactly."

"Tell me what we need to do."

"First, we need to find out if either man was in Italy when Marta and I were there — and I know just the person who can help us. She works in the Canadian embassy in London. She owes me a big favour." He made the call, spoke quickly about what was needed, nodding as he listened. "Okay, Pamela, it's really important. Seriously, it's a matter of life and death…. I will, and I will be forever in your debt…. I just bet you will…. Yes, right away. Speak to you soon." After putting his phone back in his pocket, Dan clapped Tony on the shoulder. "We're good to go. I wish we'd hear from Shannon. She knows her way around this sort of thing far better than we do."

"What do we do if she's not available?"

Dan walked into the street to hail a cab. "I don't know. I'm making this up as I go along."

They took a cab uptown to Dan's apartment in the tall high rise at Yonge and Eglinton. His apartment was a maze of cardboard boxes, but the coffee brewer was hooked up, the kitchen table was mostly clear, and they'd stopped at a Tim Horton's on the way to pick up some breakfast sandwiches.

As they filled their empty stomachs, Dan said, "I was just thinking about how our guy was able to get on our tail so quickly last night."

"And?"

"Somehow this bastard can still listen to us. I have no idea how, especially this time, and it's driving me nuts. This sort of thing only happens in movies."

"Or bad detective novels."

A few minutes later, Dan's smartphone rang. "Yeah…? My place…. He's with me…. Sure." He passed his phone across the table. "Shannon."

"Shannon?" Tony asked after switching on the speakerphone function. "Are you all right? Where are you?"

"Just leaving St. Joes. They wanted to hold me for observation, but that ain't gonna fly. Not today."

"Are you sure that's wise?"

"Like I told them, I was born with a good, hard head. I'll be fine. What are you guys up to?"

"We're going to choose the most likely subject of the two and go after him."

"I may be able to help you there. I had my boyfriend Michael bring down his iPad, so I could do something useful while I sat around in Emerg."

"And you found something useful."

"You could say that. First of all, Tallevi isn't even in the country. He was at the Metropolitan Opera last night, sitting in the general manager's box."

Tony asked, "What about Peter Grant?"

"About an hour ago the cops told me he was at home, supposedly asleep when someone was trying to kill us. He has a corroborating witness."

"I don't see how that's useful — except running us up another dead end."

"There's more. His late wife was an opera singer —"

"I already knew that."

"Give me a minute! I looked up her obituary and a posthumous profile in a magazine. Both of them quoted her long-time vocal coach: Lili Doubek."

"I never knew that!"

"We have to assume Lili knew Peter Grant in more than a passing sort of way."

Tony whistled. "Holy shit."

"There's more. The obit said Rosa Latini 'died unexpectedly after a short illness.' That's newspaper-speak for suicide when the family doesn't want the true story to get out. One of Lili's quotes also makes an oblique reference to it. I don't know how yet, but I'm willing to bet this is all tied in to what's happened to Marta."

Tony couldn't sit still. "When can you get here?"

"I should go to the police with this."

"There's not time."

Shannon's voice suddenly became muffled as she spoke to someone else, then, "Michael is threatening to take me to police headquarters instead of up to you guys. I'll call you back, okay?"

Tony looked at Dan. "Is your computer hooked up? I want to read up on Grant and I don't want to search the Internet from my smartphone. Too slow."

"It's in the living room."

"Lead on."

"Grab the coffee pot, will you?"

Dan handed Shannon a mug of coffee as soon as she was in the door.

"Thank the Lord," she said after a sip. "I couldn't bear to drink the hospital coffee."

Tony helped her off with her jacket. "Shannon, you should be in the hospital."

"It looks worse than it is. My mom wouldn't even bat an eye at this tiny mark on my head."

"The whole right side of your face is swollen and bruised."

"Believe me, I've looked worse." She took another sip from her mug. "So what have you boys found out since I called?"

Dan handed her a sheaf of printouts. "Want just the highlights?"

Tony spoke. "I knew Rosa Latini a bit. She played some minor roles at the COC back when I was starting out in the chorus. She had a nice voice, but somewhat small and limited. Reading her obituary, though, jogged something loose in my memory. My cousin, who was also in the chorus and knew Rosa better, once told me Grant was always on the GM of the opera at that time to hire his wife for a major role. He intimated he would make a big donation if they did. Funny thing was, *she* knew she didn't have what it takes to carry an opera. She enjoyed her small roles."

"And she committed suicide," Dan added. "I wonder if there's a connection."

"I sure wish Lili was here," Tony said. "She would know about the dynamic between Grant and his wife. If you want my opinion, after the death of his wife, Grant latched on to Marta — who is everything in the opera world that his wife wasn't."

"Look, we could sit here and psychologize all day. It's after six. We've wasted enough time. Grant must be edgy that he didn't manage to kill us last night."

Shannon grinned. "I've bought us a bit of breathing room. I talked the cops into telling the media that the three of us were taken to hospital with very serious injuries. If we get over to his house soon, I think we may catch Mr. Peter Grant in bed, sleeping without a care in the world."

Both men kissed her on the cheek.

"Let's boogie," Dan said as he threw Tony his coat, "and give him a personalized wakeup call."

The trip didn't take long, but Dan was on the phone nearly the entire ride. His contact in London had done her work well. Peter Grant had indeed been out of the country the entire time Marta and he had been. The fact that he'd supposedly been in the UK was of little consequence. They all knew how easy it was to cross borders once inside the European Union.

The Grant house was located in Hoggs' Hollow where Yonge Street, Toronto's main drag, descends into a large bowl-shaped depression. At the bottom was a secluded enclave of homes, most rather grand, and Peter Grant's turned out to be the grandest.

"Likes to show off," Shannon observed.

"Guy has a real edifice complex," Dan added.

Tony rang the doorbell while Shannon used the brass door knocker vigorously. After a minute's wait, they were about to try again when the door was jerked open.

A strikingly pretty woman stood there in a rather revealing robe. "You people again? Wasn't it enough to bother us last night?"

Shannon took the lead. "We need to speak to Mr. Grant."

"What do you want now?"

"And you are?"

"Jennifer Glendon, Mr. Grant's executive assistant."

So that's what they're calling it now, Shannon thought. "It's rather urgent that we speak to your employer."

"He's still asleep. As I already told you, his evening was interrupted by you people."

"May we come in?"

"No, you may —"

Shannon, followed by Dan, pushed right on by. Tony hustled to catch up. The foyer was large, two storeys tall, and impressively lined with carved wood panelling.

"You cannot just come barging in like that!" the woman spluttered. "You need a warrant."

"They don't need a warrant, Jennifer, because this bedraggled group is not the police." Clad in an elegant dressing gown, the master of the house was partway down the staircase. "What is the meaning of this intrusion, Lusardi?" he asked, staring daggers.

Tony stared right back. "Where is my wife?"

"How the hell should I know?"

Shannon stepped forward. "We'd like to ask you some questions."

Grant's face grew red. "I'm not answering any of your damned questions," he said, continuing down the stairs. "What I am going to do is phone the police and have you arrested for trespassing!"

Pulling out her cell phone, Shannon said in an icy cold voice, "No need. I'm perfectly willing to call them for you. I'm certain they'll want to ask you the same questions we would."

Not waiting for an answer, Shannon made the call.

Tony stepped right in front of Grant who was now at the bottom of the stairs. "Why don't you just come clean, Grant? We know you're involved in Marta's kidnapping, a murder in Rome, and now one in Toronto. All we want is Marta back, safe and sound."

Peter Grant's eyes literally bugged out. "Are you insane? Is that what you honestly think?"

Tony's body was rigid with anger, his arms at his side, fists balled and ready. "And if you've harmed her in any way, I swear to almighty God, I'll kill you with my bare hands."

Chapter Thirty-Five

Inspector Leslie Dobbin, preceded by two police cruisers that sealed off the house from the curious, showed up in record time. Shannon brought him up to speed outside the house, after which he entered and spoke quietly to Peter Grant for a couple of minutes. Grant was silent except for nodding a few times. After that, Grant led Dobbin and Shannon into his study, followed by a notebook wielding constable. The door shut and the entry hall became silent, except for the ticking of an ornate clock at the bottom of the grand staircase.

Dan found a seat on a padded bench near the front door. "I guess we're expected to wait while the important people have their confab. Wonder if we could get Grant's live-in executive assistant to make us some coffee?"

Tony sat down next to him. "I don't think I'd trust her after what was said, mostly by me, I'm afraid. I always was a hothead."

"You've a perfect right to be in this case, old man," Dan replied clapping him on the back.

"How long do you think we'll have to wait for a search of the house to be started?"

"If Grant involves his lawyer it might be hours, or even days."

"He seemed genuinely surprised when I accused him of two murders and an abduction."

"Would you expect anything less from the guy we've been chasing?"

⌣

Inside the elegant study, things were tense.

"For the third time, I would like nothing more than for the Hendriks woman to be found. I even called Lusardi yesterday to tell him that. Ask him. I've waived my right to have a lawyer present in order to clear this up without delay. I am not involved in her disappearance."

Dobbin ignored the comment. "We appreciate that, sir. But I do need to ask where you were yesterday morning between nine thirty and eleven.

"At my health club, for heaven's sake."

"Do you have any witnesses who can corroborate that?"

"Of course I do! Why is this so important?"

Shannon cut in, her eyes fixed on Grant. "Because somewhere in that time span Lili Doubek was murdered."

"Lili is dead?" Grant looked genuinely shocked. "I hadn't heard."

Dobbin asked, "Then you knew her?"

"Well, I wouldn't quite put it that way. Lili was my late wife's vocal coach. I met her in passing because of that, but never really had anything much to do with her personally."

Shannon was over by a side wall covered with framed photos. "You look pretty chummy with her in this photo," she said, pointing to one.

The photo showed four smiling people, arms around shoulders. Grant was on the left side, Lili and Rosa Latini-Grant in the middle, and on the right end was a handsome lad of about eighteen.

"Let me see that." Grant moved from behind his desk with surprising speed. "This photo was taken after a recital my wife gave. Lili Doubek accompanied her."

"And the young man?" Dobbin asked.

"My son Alan. He never missed one of his mother's performances."

"What was the date?"

"Nine years ago this month."

Shannon felt they were getting bogged down in details.

"Wasn't that shortly before she took her own life?" she asked, not taking pleasure in blindsiding Grant that way, but he needed to be shaken up. So she took the chance her earlier hunch was correct.

He blanched. "Where did you come up with such a preposterous idea?"

"Are you saying she did not commit suicide? And before you answer that, let me warn you we can verify the truthfulness of your statement by checking the medical records, regardless of what the newspapers said about it at the time."

Grant went back behind his desk and sat heavily, squeezing his eyes shut for a moment. "Surely you can see why we kept that from the media." He looked down at the blotter. "In her final months, Rosa was growing more and more despondent. I urged her to seek professional help, but she refused, said she could cope. My son, who was very close to his mother, also tried to help. Unfortunately, neither of us knew how much my wife was covering up. Alan was the one who found her. She'd hung herself at our weekend home in Caledon. It was a horrible day."

Dobbin glared at Shannon as he said to Grant, "I'm very sorry such a painful subject was brought up. Shannon, can you get to the point of all this?"

She went to her shoulder bag and pulled out a folded piece of paper. Smoothing it out as she crossed the room, she handed it to Grant. It was time to play her trump card.

"Mr. Grant, this is a list of dates that Marta Hendriks received bouquets of roses from the person we believe not only kidnapped her, but who is also responsible for the death of Arturo De Vicenzo in Rome and Lili Doubek here in Toronto. With my limited resources and time, I haven't been able to corroborate all the dates, but the ones with check marks are times when we know you were also in the same country as Marta."

Dobbin looked amazed. "How did you get that kind of information?"

"Ask me no questions and I'll tell you no lies, Les. Just ask Grant how he explains those coincidences."

Turning to Grant, he asked, "Well?"

Still with his eyes on the list, Grant looked flustered. "Some of these dates are fairly old. I travel a lot for business, you see. I would have to check on these with my executive assistant."

"And how about the most recent one?" Shannon asked. "Surely you can remember where you were a week ago."

Grant squinted down at the paper again. "I was here. In Toronto. I haven't been out of the country since the first week of January when I was skiing in France."

Dobbin pulled Shannon to the far end of the room. In a low voice, he asked, "How reliable is your information?"

"Are you beginning to come around?" she asked in return.

"Just answer my question, O'Brien, goddamn you."

"Very reliable. My source says records show Peter Grant was in England at the time that opera singer was murdered in Rome, and Marta Hendriks and my employee were attacked in Venice. Grant returned to Toronto a day after Marta did. You and I both know it's not difficult to move undetected once you're within the E.U. these days, especially if you have money."

"Okay. I'll go with you on this for now." He walked back to Grant. "Well, Grant, you've had a few minutes to collect your thoughts. Has your memory improved?"

"My memory is fine. I was not out of the country at any time since early January."

"You did not travel to the United Kingdom two and a half weeks ago?"

"Absolutely not. And I can prove it."

Shannon stepped right to the edge of the desk and looked across it. "Then how do you explain that Peter Grant entered the UK at Heathrow Airport on February 8th?"

"I explain it by saying that your information must be incor —" His voice trailed off and an expression of anxiety flitted across his face. "I think I would like to call my lawyer now."

Dobbin, sensing blood, also moved in. "First you said you could prove you were in town, and now you want to call your lawyer? What gives?"

Grant had his face covered by one hand. "Oh my God," he said, "Oh my God."

Shannon asked, "Mr. Grant, could you tell us what is bothering you so much?"

It was as if he hadn't heard her question. "Why would he do such a thing? Hasn't he caused me enough grief?"

Shannon put her hands on the desk and leaned across. "Grant! Who are you talking about?"

He looked up, startled. "I suppose I have to tell you. My son, of course, my damned son."

She shook her head. "You don't have a son named Peter."

"My son's name is Peter Alan Grant. He doesn't use Peter anymore. His initials are the same as mine, too. Both our passports say Peter A. Grant. My middle name is Augustus, after my grandfather."

"And was your son out of the country at that time?"

"I have no idea. He hasn't lived here for at least six years and I haven't seen or talked to him since last October."

"You're estranged from him?"

"No. He's estranged from me. Alan and I have always had a difficult relationship. From birth, he's been an odd boy — brilliant but odd. His mother was the only one who could deal with him. Our relationship deteriorated further after Rosa's death. They were very close. He blames me for … what happened."

Dobbin was suddenly all business. "Do you think your son is capable of murder and kidnapping?"

Grant looked up, a totally lost expression on his face. "I gave him everything and now he does this. Oh God. What am I going to do?"

Shannon raised her voice in order to get through to the distraught man. "Do you know where Alan is?"

"I … I have no idea. I tell you, I have no contact with him. That's what our argument was about last fall. I wanted to know why I should keep giving him a generous allowance when I have no idea what's going on in his life. I told him he needed to act like a grown man, get a job, and stand on his own two feet. Heaven knows he has ability. One of the big computer companies in California practically begged him to work for them."

Dobbin looked frustrated. "Surely you have a phone number?"

Grant shook his head. "Since he moved out, Alan has always called me — and not very often, I might add. It's only when he wants money."

"Are any family members on friendly terms with him?"

"No. He dislikes them as much as I do."

Shannon cursed under her breath. Once Alan knew they were on to him, he could do anything. They needed to move in on him quickly.

Dobbin persisted. "Does Alan have any friends we might —"

Grant's hand sliced the air angrily. "Alan never had any friends — except for his mother. He followed her everywhere."

Dobbin said to Shannon. "We need to get this information to our boys on the street, pronto, without the media getting wind of it. Mr. Grant, do you have a recent photo of Alan?"

"There's one from the last family gathering we attended two years ago."

Shannon asked, "How old is your son?"

"He turned twenty-nine last week."

"And there was no contact at that time?"

Peter Grant sighed heavily. "None whatsoever."

The photo was soon retrieved by Grant's executive assistant, now properly dressed.

Dobbin went to the study door and yelled, "Somebody find Samotowka for me — pronto!"

When Shannon emerged from the study, she found Tony and Dan side by side on a padded bench by the door, boredom and not a little irritation plainly on their faces.

"Sorry that took so long."

"That's all right," Dan said. "We had nothing better to do. So what's up?"

"It's not Peter Grant. It's his son Alan."

"But that's impossible. The passport clearly said Peter Grant. My contact couldn't have gotten it wrong."

"His son's full name is *Peter* Alan Grant."

Tony stood up, clearly agitated. "So the cops are going to reel this punk in?"

Shannon sighed. "As soon as they find him. Dad doesn't know where he lives and has no way to contact him."

"But we're running out of time!"

"I know that, you know that, and the cops know that. I'm going to go to police headquarters with Dobbin and see what help I can be. I'll call you as soon as we learn anything."

"So we're supposed to just sit around and wait?" Dan asked. "That totally sucks."

Shannon threw up her hands. "What can I say? I know it sucks, but our hands are tied. Right now the cops are the best people to move this forward."

From the front door, Dobbin shouted, "O'Brien! The bus is leaving. If you're coming, you better shake a leg."

Turning to go, she said to Dan and Tony. "I promise I will call you the moment I know anything, okay? And Tony, try not to worry. The police are going to move heaven and earth to find Alan and get to Marta."

The two men followed her out of the house, stopping on the doorstep to watch the police cars race off.

"So what do we do now?" Tony asked.

"I guess we wait — unless you happen to know where Alan Grant lives."

While they'd been talking to Shannon, Tony's phone had pinged its alert that he received an email. Tony took out his phone and began reading.

Hudson had continued walking toward his car. When he realized his companion was still back on the doorstep, he turned around and shouted, "Come on, Lusardi!"

It was meant in jest, but Tony looked up, his expression deadly serious. "He just sent me another email."

Dan sprinted back. "Here, let me see that."

Tony handed over the phone. The subject line of the email was blank, the return address was Tony's own, so obviously the email was spoofed and they'd likely never trace it back to its source.

It read simply: "Don't think you clever people are ever going to find her. I have Marta in a place you'll never think of looking. I can keep her until she dies and you can't do a thing about it. Learn to accept your complete and utter failure."

Dan shook his head as he handed Tony the phone. "The guy sure has balls."

Tony's face was hard. "He's spitting in our faces." He looked as if he was about to hurl his phone to the ground. "I could kill this bastard with my bare hands! *Figlio di puttana!*"

"Whatever that means, I'm with you."

"I'm so filled with rage I can barely think. I know he's trying to do that, and still I can't stop it. We're dancing like puppets on his strings."

"You know, Tony, I'm thinking that maybe this time his massive ego has made him step in it."

"How?"

"Take his taunt literally: where *would* we never think of looking?"

"You mean for real?"

"Yup."

Tony shrugged. "I don't know. A police station? The opera house? My condo? City Hall? The top of the CN Tower?"

He listed a few more outrageous locations, not noticing Dan had held up his hand.

"Just a second. You mentioned one place that is a distinct possibility."

"Where?"

"Your condo."

"Huh?"

"Well, not your condo exactly — but the building where it is. Think about it. It's brilliant, just the sort of thing that would appeal to Alan Grant's warped sensibilities. I'll bet he's been enjoying watching the cops and us struggle to figure out where he's taken her, and all the time, he's got her right under our noses. Make sense?"

"I don't know. He'd be taking a huge chance."

"No, he wouldn't be. Your building really *is* the last place anyone would look.

"I guess it's worth checking out."

"You've got that right. Let's go."

"Shouldn't we tell Shannon?"

"We just got blown off, remember? I know when I've

been patted on the head and told to stand in the corner. I vote we check this out on our own."

"I don't know …"

"C'mon, Tony. We'll just go down there and take a quick look around. If we find even a whiff of Grant, we'll call in the cavalry, pronto. Can you imagine the looks on their faces when we tell them we've found Marta?"

Tony nodded. "Okay. Let's do it." As they got into Dan's car, he added, "You know, we're probably going to end up looking like the two biggest jackasses on the planet if we got this all wrong."

"Another reason not to tell anyone. But I prefer to look at it positively. We might be the heroes of the day. But most important, if we do nothing and it turns out we were right, how would we feel then — especially if he does his worst."

"What's the plan?"

"How well do you know your building's doorman?"

"Sam? Pretty well. He's a nice little guy, always helpful. We can count on him. Marta's one of his favourites."

"Good. If I've learned one thing about doormen, it's that they know everything going on in their building: all the gossip, who's blissfully happy, whose relationship is on the rocks, who just got a new job, and who just got fired. Let's hope your Sam is cut from that cloth."

"Oh, I think you can count on that."

They both knew this was a Hail Mary pass, but it sure beat sitting around waiting for someone else to do something.

Chapter Thirty-Six

I was deep inside myself, trying to find a place without darkness and fear where I could remember my dear friend who was now dead — and whom I would probably soon join.

So far, I'd only managed to replace fear with a slow-burning anger directed at my captor, who seemed to feel it was his God-given right to end her life so cruelly. It would be my turn next, whenever he decided my time was up. He was going to "release" me. Yeah, right. The ultimate release.

I didn't believe any longer I would be saved. Hollywood endings don't happen in real life, as much as we'd like them to. Someone would find my body, probably Tony.

The monster who'd taken the outside world away from me would see to that. What was going on was not about me, Lili, or De Vicenzo back in Rome. Everything that had happened or would happen was at its heart all about him.

When the end came, I would fight if I could. I wouldn't cry or beg for mercy. My end would be faced with dignity — if there was even a shred of dignity to be found in being strangled. This monster had stripped me of liberty, light, sound, freedom of movement, even clothes and human contact. But he would not strip me of dignity.

How ironic it was that my last hours would be so lonely, much the same as Naomi's in *The Passage of Time*. Maybe that was part of my enemy's plan. The new opera was certainly a factor. Naomi was a captive, too, although the dark world she inhabited was partially of her own making.

Her long third act aria, "Once I roamed in a place of light," began in my head, the tragic meaning of its lyrics driven like spikes into my brain because of my own desperate plight. In it Naomi sings that she had given everything to those around her, family, friends, even strangers. She had not harmed a soul, had lived a good life, and yet, this grace didn't save her from the end that she saw coming to her. It is a desperate and desolate piece of music that to me was the high point of the opera I would now never perform.

I began to sing — the only refuge I had left. I sang for Naomi, an imaginary person whose plight I now understood completely. I sang for Lili. I sang for myself.

Sadly, no one would ever hear it. I hadn't discovered the core of my role in the opera until it was too late.

Chapter Thirty-Seven

Tony directed Dan down Mount Pleasant Road and onto Jarvis Street. The morning rush was beginning to ease up and they were making good time.

"I don't think we should park out front of the building," Dan said. "Where else would you suggest?"

"There's a small parking lot right behind the St. Lawrence Farmer's Market. Since there's nothing going on there today, it should be empty. Hopefully, you won't get towed."

Dan laughed. "Hell, they can have the damn car if it gets us Marta back."

"We'll buy you one, okay?" Tony was only half kidding.

Luck was with them. The lot was deserted. After getting out of the car, they retraced back up Jarvis to King, and then down the open space between the market building and the building where Tony and Marta lived. Partway down, a colonnade began and they used that to further avoid detection from above. The winter wind was blisteringly cold so there weren't many people about.

At Front Street, they ducked into the lobby of the bank at the corner of the building.

"I think we should assume our friend has a direct feed into the building's closed circuit system," Dan said. "Do you know if there's a security camera at your building's entrance?"

Tony shrugged.

Dan stuck his head out and looked up. "We're in luck. There's nothing. I want you to go to the door. Hopefully, your doorman will be behind his desk. Motion him outside and bring him here. Okay?"

In less than a minute, Tony returned with Sam.

"Yes, sir. Mr. Tony has told me that you need my help. You have got it. What do you need from Sam?"

During the trip downtown, Tony had used his phone to search online for a photo of P. Alan Grant to show to Sam. He finally found one, but it was taken at his mother's funeral so it was nearly ten years old.

"This is who we're looking for. Does he live in the building? Have you ever seen him?"

Sam stared at the small screen for several seconds. "I cannot be sure, Mr. Tony, but it could be Mr. Rache. He has a beard, so I cannot be sure. His eyes look the same, however."

Dan smiled grimly. "*Rache* is German for revenge. I'll bet it's our boy. Like I said, too clever for his own good."

Tony said, "Tell us about him, Sam."

"He moved in perhaps two years ago. He is not in town much, I do not think. He seldom talks with me. Airport cars come to pick him up many times. He is a musician, I believe."

"What does he play?"

"That I do not know. When he moved here he remodelled his apartment completely and builded a soundproof room so that he may practise."

"I don't remember that coming before the condo board."

"When the materials were coming in, he most assured me he had permission. There have been no complaints."

"Is he in town now?" Dan asked.

"I do believe so, but I cannot be certain."

Dan nodded. "Do you have access to the security videos for Wednesday night?"

"Oh, yessir. We store everything. I can show you anything you want to see, right at my station in the lobby."

"Next question: do any of the lobby cameras show your station?"

"There is one behind it that faces outwardly. It will show my head if I stand up."

"Is there space behind your station where Tony and I can crouch while we look at your computer screen?"

"Oh, yessir. It is most spacious back there. No one coming through the lobby will be seeing you."

Dan thought for a moment. "Here's what we'll do. Tony, you and I will enter the building as quickly as possible, get behind the doorman's station, and stay crouched. The less time we're on camera, the better. And you, Sam, will follow us in a minute later. Act just as you normally would."

"Sam will do anything that you ask, sir."

"Okay. Let's get this show on the road. Sam, you saunter in after us." Dan flashed a grin. "Just don't make us wait too long."

In the end, it went off beautifully. Tony and Dan barely had time to get behind the chest-high wooden doorman's station when a taxi pulled up, disgorging one of Tony's neighbours, a large elderly woman with a yappy little dog and several shopping bags. It took two trips for Sam to carry it all in, and, of course, she wanted him to help her get it upstairs.

When Sam finally sat down behind his station, Dan whispered, "All right, gentlemen, show time. Sam, can you cue up the video for us? We're interested in seeing three nights ago from ten at night to maybe four in the morning. If our man indeed brought Marta down here, he would have done it in the dead hours."

"You want all cameras, sir?"

"Yes, all cameras."

"I am able to split up the screen and show you all cameras at once."

"Sure. Do that."

"I play with this all the time when I not have work to do, so I can be ready when the policemen come."

Sam stabbed at the computer keyboard with two fingers. The monitor changed to twenty-five small squares, all of them filled with various views of the inside of the building and the basement parking area.

Hitting a few more keys brought up a splash panel for choosing a date, time, and review speed.

He punched it in, then asked, "Please, sir, is this correct?"

Dan rose to his knees. "Yes and set the speed to 8X. Tony get up here. We need as many eyes as possible."

Sam clicked on "Start" and the video began rolling.

"Sam, you watch the lobby monitor, Tony, take the elevators, and I'll watch the parking garage. If anyone spots something, let us know."

The time stamp read 12:37 a.m. when a large black car came down the garage ramp.

"Slow it to normal speed, Sam. This looks promising."

An older man got out of the car, obviously not their quarry.

Two more smaller cars came in, both with couples getting out.

At 2:09, a black van rolled in.

Dan said, "Slow it down again, please."

The van parked in a dark corner so they couldn't see what was going on, but it was taking some time. Then a tall figure wearing a baseball cap under a pulled-up hoodie came into view, pushing a low flight case in front of him.

"Think Marta could fit in that?" Tony asked.

"It would be damned uncomfortable, but yes."

From the camera inside the elevator, it seemed the case was fairly heavy from the way the man worked to muscle it inside. He never looked up at the camera but they saw he had a full beard.

"I believe that is Mr. Rache," Sam said.

"What apartment does he have?"

"It is on the floor above yours, Mr. Tony, and it overlaps your floor space at one end."

Dan shook his head and swore. "This just keeps getting better and better. He's played us for chumps right from the beginning. All that broadcast equipment I found on the roof was a blind to throw us off. He could have put contact mics on his floor and heard everything in your apartment, the clever bastard. He's been right above our heads the entire time."

When the man reached out to press a floor button, Tony said, "Yup. That's the floor above mine. Should we call the cops now?"

Dan never got a chance to answer. The chime sounded and the doors slid open on one of the elevators.

"It is Mr. Rache," Sam whispered. "Good morning, sir," he said loudly. "You are going out early today."

There was no answer as the man exited. He waited several seconds for a break in traffic before crossing Front Street and disappearing through a side door of the south building of the St. Lawrence Market.

"What should we do?" Tony repeated.

"It doesn't look like he's leaving town. Sam, by any chance do you have keys to the apartments?"

"We do, sir. I will get his for you." Sam unlocked a drawer in his desk and rummaged around in a rack of keys. "This is most odd. There doesn't appear to be one for Mr. Rache's apartment."

"Why doesn't that surprise me," Tony said.

"It's not a big deal, Tony," Dan answered. C'mon. He's gone out. This is a golden opportunity. We have to grab it."

"But the cops …"

"Marta is up there. We have to move *now*." He started for the elevators. "Coming?"

Tony followed but stopped the elevator door from closing. "Sam, you have my mobile number?"

"Yes, Mr. Tony."

"Call me when he comes back."

"Sam will not fail you. You can count on me."

On the ride up, Dan said, "We won't have much time and we have no tools, so getting into that apartment is not going to be a finesse job. If the door is metal, we're screwed."

"Mine isn't."

"Dan nodded. "Since last night, luck has been on our side. We only need a few more minutes of it and we'll be home free."

When the elevator door opened again, they were out of it at a run. The apartment was not far away.

"Hallelujah," Tony said. "It's wood."

Dan looked at the metal frame around the door. "It's going to take both of us hitting the door hard — together. Ready? On the count of three, we go."

They crashed against the door four times before it gave way. Unable to stop their momentum, they tumbled clumsily onto the floor.

Unlike his father's meticulously neat house, Alan Grant's apartment was a pigsty: dirty, smelly, take-out food and pizza boxes strewn about. The furniture consisted of a cheap single bed, a table, two chairs, and a small TV. Contrasting with the chaos were two metal clothes racks against one wall, full of crisply pressed suits, shirts, and pants. Clearly, Grant had priorities.

"Marta?" Tony called out. "Are you here?"

When there was no answer, his shoulders slumped.

The apartment was larger than Tony and Marta's. They began their search. Behind the large living room was a small dining area and kitchen. A corridor between led to the rest of the living space.

Dan led the way. The kitchen was also a mess while the dining area was stacked floor to ceiling with boxes. Next was a bathroom, disgustingly dirty, followed by two bedrooms that were empty for the most part. They also passed a room clearly meant to be a study, and like the clothes in the living room, this space was spotless and tidy — and bristling with electronic equipment. One wall was covered with monitor screens. Several of them showed news feeds. Disturbingly, though, some showed feeds from the building's security system, including the lobby. Sam was nowhere to be seen.

"We're living on borrowed time," Tony said. "Let's get going."

At the end of the corridor was an ornate wooden door — the last room. If Marta wasn't in there, then they'd run out of luck.

Dan again stepped forward and swung the door open. The large room had been nearly filled with another room, clearly the source of the construction about which Sam had spoken. All they could see of this inner room were thick sheets of dusty foam insulation and electrical cables. Directly in front of them was another door, metal and invincible-looking. Bars were locked across it, as well as six large deadbolts going into the floor, sides, and top of the frame. Without keys, they'd need a cutting saw to gain entry.

"This is overkill, Tony," Dan said. "I don't need Lili's training to know the way this door has been fastened is more symbolic than practical. One big lock would have been sufficient."

Tony pounded on the door. "Marta! Are you in there? It's me. Tony. Dan's with me. We've come to rescue you."

No response.

Dan put his ear to the door and listened, then looked at Tony. "It's super faint, but I swear I can hear singing."

Tony, too, pressed his ear to the metal and listened for several seconds. Pulling back, his face had a huge smile. "That *is* her. She's singing an aria from the new opera. We've got to get her out of there, Dan."

"How very observant of you, Lusardi," came a soft, almost gentle voice from behind them. "Turn around slowly, gentlemen, with your fingers laced together behind your heads."

Alan Grant stood halfway down the hall, too far away for any hope of an attack before the gun comfortably gripped in his right hand could do its deadly work.

Dan's face was grim. "It's no good, Grant. The police know where we are."

"I think not, Mr. Hudson. You see, that distinctive little metal compass that's dangling from the zipper of your ski jacket — a memento of your Special Forces days, I suspect — is not exactly what you think it is. While it looks just like your cherished heirloom, I replaced that with one that has a sub-miniature microphone and transmitter. As long as I stayed within 400 metres of you, I could hear everything you and your companions said. I've been following you ever since you left the police station this morning. So drop the bullshit. Help is not on the way."

Tony and Dan looked at each other.

Grant continued, "And if you're thinking your little friend in the lobby will call the cops for you, let's just say he won't be opening any more doors for the residents of this building. My going out was simply a ruse to split you up. Two I can handle. Three I wasn't sure about."

"You sick bastard," Dan said through gritted teeth.

"Undoubtedly you'd think that. But a sick bastard *way* smarter than you idiots — although you did figure out my little clue to get you down here in the nick of time. I was worried I'd made it too difficult. It's unfortunate you didn't bring the O'Brien bitch along. That would have given me the trifecta of people who have been really annoying me lately."

Tony's expression was grim. "What are you going to do to Marta?"

"Now that's just the sort of inane question I would expect from a person of your limited intelligence, Lusardi. And before you ask, she's still alive."

"I know. We could hear her singing."

"I hope she knows it's her swan song. I've kept her around long enough."

Dan said, "You won't get away. Your father told the police —"

"I know all about that. You don't think I have my dear old dad's house and office bugged? This is all planned for. First, you can watch me strangle your wife,

Lusardi, then I'll set fire to this apartment with all of you inside to get gently toasted. After that, I will deal with *pater familias* and his concubine before leaving the country for places unknown, using my second identity. You see, I'm one step ahead of you all every single time."

Reaching into his overcoat pocket, Grant pulled out two long cable ties. "Time to get this show on the road, gentlemen. Put these around your wrists, behind your backs, and pull them tight, if you please."

Grant forced Tony and Dan to the living room where he had them sit on the two chairs there. He'd lined them up facing down the apartment's central hallway. With a few more cable ties, they were securely fastened down. Each man then had a ball gag forced into his mouth.

Grant leaned down next to Tony's ear. "Now you can enjoy the beginning of the tragic third act of our opera. Pardon the gag, but I don't want to risk you interrupting the performance."

He walked down the hallway to unlock the heavily barred door.

Chapter Thirty-Eight

The faint sounds of someone outside the door finally interrupted my singing. It had taken several minutes to realize it wasn't the normal sounds of my enemy opening the door. This was a pounding sound, distant and unmistakable. He had no reason to do that.

My heart soared. Someone had finally come to release me! Soon, I would be unfastened from the horrid chain, I would be taken out into the light and sound of the real world. My time in this dark purgatory was finally over. Getting up, I walked to the extreme limit of my chain and craned forward, hoping to hear more.

"I'm here! It's me!" I called out as loudly as I could, then turned my head, hoping to catch some words from my rescuer.

There was nothing.

That's all right, I told myself, *they probably need to get something to cut away the locks and bars so that the door can finally be opened. It won't be long now.*

I sat back on the bed to wait as patiently as I could.

When nothing continued to happen, I began to question whether I'd really heard what I thought I'd heard. I wanted so desperately to be rescued that my mind had tricked me.

Crashing disappointment hit, and hit hard.

More time passed, it could have been minutes. It might have been hours. But then, I did hear, louder and more clearly, sounds that meant the door was being opened. Only it wasn't someone breaking in. This was like every other time the door was opened by my enemy.

Those horrendous lights came on and the door opened as it always did. Nothing had changed.

It had been many hours since I'd last been fed. "I'm hungry," I called out.

I could see his form outlined against the door. It took me a few seconds to realize that there was again light coming in from outside the room. I lowered my head in an attempt to defeat the brightness of the room lights.

I could definitely make out a dim corridor behind him. The doorway, too, was different than I expected. There were two of them with about a foot of space separating them. Of course, my prison was built like a recording studio with inner and outer doors to defeat the transmission of sound.

"What's going on? I said, trying to keep both fear and hope out of my voice.

"Lie on the bed face up," was all he said. "Put your hands on top of the bar on the end of it and do not move. Do you understand me?"

"Yes," I said, and did exactly what he asked.

"Good. If you move, it will go very badly for you. Do you understand?

I nodded my head.

He came swiftly to me then and before I realized what his intent was, my wrists were tightly fastened by cable ties to the bar they rested on.

"Stretch out your legs and do not move."

He went to the end of the bed, grabbed my ankles and pulled me down so my arms were extended above me to their limit. My ankles were then tightly fastened to the bar at the bottom end of the bed. He unlocked the manacle on my right ankle. It clanging loudly as it hit the floor. I was finally free of the blasted chain but now I couldn't move.

While he'd been bent over me, I'd gotten my best glimpse of him yet, tall and thin as I already knew, I was surprised he had a full beard, and one not neatly trimmed, either. He looked like a wild man.

"What are you going to do to me?" I asked.

He walked out of the room and down the corridor, not bothering with the doors or lights. Something was definitely up, but I had no idea what.

Chapter Thirty-Nine

It was pretty clear to Shannon that she wasn't needed by Dobbin and his crew. Other than stressing to them that they should not underestimate the person they were after, she hadn't done much good at police headquarters.

She was also feeling a bit ashamed of the way she'd left things with Dan. Leaving Grant's house with "the big boys" was an unfair way to treat a fellow professional who'd already done so much.

She went over to Dobbin. "Les, I'm going to head out. I've got some things that need doing."

"What you should do is go home, Shan. Quite honestly, you look like hell. I know you're a tough broad and all, but —"

"Yeah, I know. You don't have to tell me I nearly bought the farm last night. Anyway, I need a favour. My wheels are down on Front near Jarvis — if my SUV hasn't already been towed. Can someone give me a lift down there?"

"I will. I've got some questions for you about our boy, and since you know the dossier better than anyone, you're the person who can help me out."

"You've got a deal. I'll even buy the coffee, and not the burnt swill you serve in this dump. It's as bad as I remember."

Dobbin laughed. "Don't I know it. Damn stuff is eating a hole in my stomach."

He drove across town to Jarvis, then south, peppering Shannon with questions, many of which had embarrassing answers when she admitted just how Alan Grant had always been one step ahead of them.

"We just can't figure out how he does it. Everywhere Dan looked, he found surveillance devices; really expensive, hard-to-get ones, too. Even so, it was as if he was always standing just behind us, listening in. Take what happened last night as an example. We thought we were in the clear. Do not underestimate this man, Les, do not."

Waiting for the light at King and Jarvis, Dobbin wrapped up the conversation. "Shannon, if you come across anything, think of anything, give me a call pronto. We're all in the soup together and it's going to need a team effort to bring this to a satisfactory close."

"Do you think we're going to find Marta Hendriks alive?"

Dobbin looked across the car at her. "I'd put the odds at no more than 50/50. How about you?"

Shannon suddenly felt weary. "I'd put it less than that."

The light changed and the car continued south. If the despair flooding her brain hadn't made her turn her head to look out the side window, she would have missed it. Even then, it was a close thing. A lot of trucks used this road and her view could easily have been blocked.

"Pull over, Les. Stop the car!"

He hit the emergency lights and chirped the siren and stopped, blocking the curb lane traffic.

"What is it?" Dobbin asked.

"I think that's Hudson's vehicle in that lot." She flung the car door open. "I'll be right back." A few seconds later she was back. "It's his, all right."

"So he's down here."

"Yes. But why would he park there? Something is wrong."

"I'm calling for backup."

Shannon put her hand on his arm. "Tell them no sirens. Have them park here where they'll be hidden by the market building. We can't take any chances on this."

Dobbin nodded, then got on the radio to call it in.

"We can't wait, Les. We've got to move now."

"We should wait."

Opening the door again, Shannon said, "I'm not willing to do that."

Grabbing a mobile radio, Dobbin answered, "Always the hothead, O'Brien. Well, you're not going in there alone."

As they ran along the colonnade of the market building, the detective was speaking rapidly into the radio, giving instructions on what should be done. "Cover all exits from the building. I want the block surrounded, but no sirens and nobody is to enter until I tell you. Everyone got that? We're on our way to scope out the front lobby. Dobbin out."

They stayed close to the front of the market building on Front Street to minimize the chance of being seen from above and ran across the open space between that and Tony's building. The few people on the sidewalk stopped to stare. As they passed by the bank at the corner of the building, Dobbin drew his gun.

Moving forward the twenty feet to the first window of the lobby, Shannon peered through the corner of the glass for a few seconds.

Over her shoulder, she said to Dobbin, "Lobby's empty."

"Let's chance it."

They moved into the building quickly. Shannon's bloodstream was flooded with adrenalin, and it felt good. This was the one aspect of her former occupation that she really missed.

A familiar smell hit them first.

"Someone's fired a gun," Dobbin said unnecessarily.

"There's usually a doorman."

"He's here, Shannon, behind the desk, with a bullet in the brain." Immediately back on his radio, Dobbin asked for more backup. "And I want people in the bank and supermarket to either side of the lobby. Lock those places down. Cut off the street and sidewalk traffic. If there's gunfire, I don't want anyone in the way. I want coverage on both sides of every exit to this building. Our suspect is armed and dangerous. I repeat, armed and dangerous. I'm in the lobby of the building now with Shannon O'Brien. Look for me there."

Shannon was behind the desk looking at the monitor screen. "It's showing the buildings cameras live. I'm not seeing anything."

Dobbin joined her, but keeping a sharp eye out. His gun was now up and ready. "Can you make this thing play back the last hour?"

"I can try." Shannon leaned over the keyboard and typed in some things. It took a few tries but a splash panel finally overlaid the screen. "I'm in. Last hour?"

The monitor began playing back the multiple camera views.

"Stop there," Dobbin said. "Isn't that Hudson?"

Shannon got the system to show the lobby feed in real time. First Dan got on the left-hand elevator, then Tony, who turned to say something to a person standing about where they were, presumably the murdered doorman. Staying in real time, they now focused on the elevator camera.

"Stop there. What button is Hudson pushing?"

"Sixth floor. That's the one above Marta Hendriks's. Son of a bitch! That's how he's done his magic tricks. I'll bet the bastard has the apartment right above Tony and Marta."

Dobbin looked incredulous. "You mean he brought her back here?"

"That's obviously what Tony and Dan thought."

They continued watching the video until the elevator door opened and the two men got out. She stopped the playback as there was a metallic tap on the window to their left. The cavalry had arrived, and they'd all followed Dobbin's instructions to arrive silently, Shannon noted.

He went outside to talk with two uniforms, but returned quickly. Even so, Shannon had enough time to do some fast thinking of her own. If Alan Grant had shot the little doorman, then he must have known Dan and Tony were upstairs. Following that line of thought, he must be tapped into the building's CC cameras. It followed that he might well know the police had the building surrounded.

Dobbin was followed by one of the detectives from his crew. Shannon quickly outlined her thoughts.

"Jesus!" he replied. "I didn't think we'd be getting into a full-scale assault here. What about the people currently in the building? We can't risk them."

"We also can't flood the building with cops. If he's watching, he'll freak for sure."

"Are you suggesting what I think you are?"

"What other choice is there? We have to get this done quickly. Bring in Tactical and it's going to be an hour before anything happens. Admit it."

"Point taken. Give me a workable alternative that won't get one of us shot."

"Les, we don't even know who's up there — and we don't have time to scope out the all the videos. My best suggestion? Get someone in here to check video while we're upstairs. Call Tactical in so they're here if we need them. You, me, and one or two others can handle a recce of the sixth floor and keep anyone in their apartment."

"If you weren't Dave O'Brien's little girl and a darn good cop in your own right, I'd tell you to take a flying you-know-what." He turned to the detective he'd brought in. "Howie, you heard the lady. Find me someone to run this computer and grab a few uniforms to come upstairs with Shannon and me. You're in charge down here." As Howie nodded and turned for the door, his boss added, "And get me two vests."

Shannon was back at the monitors.

Dobbin asked, "Are you carrying?"

"In the current climate in this country? Are you kidding?"

"License up to date?"

"Of course."

"Here, take mine. I'll borrow one."

Three minutes later, four people got into one of the elevators. As Dobbin pressed six, he said, "Everyone ready? When these doors open again, Shannon and I will be back on each side. You two will hit the deck. If we don't see anything, then we'll move forward. Clear?"

⟃

Tony began to struggle against his bonds but Dan was curiously still. They watched as Grant unlocked the inner door at the end of the long hall. He paused to flick a switch next to it then walked into the room beyond.Under the intense lighting, they could see Marta, clad only in a T-shirt that hardly covered her, standing near what looked like a metal bed. A chain was fastened to her right ankle.

Dan got Tony's attention with a long, low growl. He then began tossing his head toward his left shoulder. Tony thought he understood what his companion was getting at, so he nodded.

As Tony kept a close eye on the opposite end of the apartment, Dan began hopping, slowly rotating his chair. Another low growl and Tony realized if he were to also hop-rotate his chair, they would accomplish whatever Dan wanted in less time.

When both captive men were back to back, Dan began pulling on Tony's right coat sleeve. He had to do the same thing twice more because Tony's attention was divided as he watched Grant direct his wife to lie down on the cot.

Finally he figured out that Dan wanted him to stick his fingers up his left sleeve. The two men struggled to get closer together so Tony could get his fingers farther up. It took more seconds than they could spare but eventually Tony felt something hard and rough. He pulled on it and it came free. It didn't take long to figure out he was holding a short knife with a very sharp blade as he sliced open his thumb. The pain caused him to nearly drop it.

Carefully he pressed the blade against the cable tie holding Dan's hands together. With a slight sawing motion it cut through. Dan's hands were free. He grunted loudly and Tony handed him the knife.

That's when they ran out of time.

Both men looked down the hall as Grant was unlocking the chain on Marta's ankle. Dragging his chair to which he was still fastened, Dan got up and spun Tony's chair back to its original position, then did the same to his and sat down again. The last thing he did was shake his head in warning. If they were left alone again for even a brief period, Dan would have them both free.

Alan Grant was striding down the hall toward them. Tony hoped his face looked suitably blank as Grant stopped in front of him.

"This is a once-in-a-lifetime performance, Lusardi, your wife's lifetime, that is. She was given a great gift, a gift that was denied my mother. It was something that cost her life eventually, because nothing my mother did was good enough for my father. Oh, it was never in public. He hid his abuse of us away. She and I became united by the way he treated us. I tried to get your dear friend Lili to help my mother as she sank further and further into depression, but Lili refused. Eventually, my mother couldn't take the abuse any longer and ended her life. Do you know why? Because she found out my father was about to throw her onto the scrap heap. It was the final straw. She left me a note apologizing for leaving me alone with him, but urged me to be strong. I would triumph in the end.

"As for your wife, I cheered as she rose from the ashes of her life, unlike my mother. But then I've watched in dismay as she squandered her gifts over the past few months: bad performances because of drinking, arguments with fellow cast members. It filled me with disgust. Venice was the last straw, and I knew I had to remove her. I couldn't believe it when she called me out at her news conference. Who the hell does she think she is?

"Audiences have watched Marta Hendriks die in countless operas, but today you're going to see her die for real. I'm going to strangle her with my bare hands.

You're going to have to watch, helpless to save her as I squeeze the life from her body. And after that, you'll die."

Grant bent lower and smiled. "What's the matter, Tony? Cat got your tongue?" He turned to Dan. "You deserve to die, Hudson, just because you're a royal pain in the ass."

Chapter Forty

By raising my head, I could battle the lights enough to dimly see down the length of the apartment. My eyes teared up when I realized Tony was there with Dan next to him, but from the way they were sitting and by the things jammed in their mouths, it wasn't hard to tell they were captives of this evil man, same as I.

My enemy stopped in front of them and a one-sided conversation ensued. A few seconds of struggle made it clear the plastic bands holding me to the bed were too strong.

It didn't take much to realize what was about to happen. He'd already threatened to strangle me as he had Lili. Now he was going to do it and force Tony to watch. It was just too monstrous. Pulling and rolling my body, I could feel the plastic bands cutting into my flesh, but I didn't care. If I could have pulled off my extremities to get free, I would have gladly done it.

Eventually, the conversation at the end of the room finished. My enemy had clearly had his say and was walking with a purpose back down the hall. I looked closely at his face but could not recognize him.

Without stopping he entered my prison, came over to the bed, and swung a leg over, straddling me. Reaching back with a knife he took from his coat pocket, he cut the ties holding my ankles to the bed.

"I've decided I want your husband to see your struggles at least a little bit, Marta. You *are* going to struggle, I hope?" He reached into an inner pocket of his jacket. "I almost forgot this."

It was the last rose stem. No blossom adorned its top. With a tiny smirk, he dropped the bare stick on my chest.

Then he leaned forward, wrapped his hands around my throat, and began slowly tightening his fingers.

I did struggle as mightily as I could, legs thrashing, pushing up and twisting to try to throw him off me, but he was too heavy.

My windpipe was closed off, and even though I'd sucked in as much air as I could when his hands moved to my neck, his weight on my lower body kept me from taking my deepest breath. What good would that have done anyway? It was only postponing the inevitable. Blackness was descending into my brain as I struggled futilely for life-giving air.

As death stood over my enemy's right shoulder, the bed under me jerked as if a great weight had been thrown on it. The hands around my throat relaxed for a moment, then tightened again. Drops of something wet spattered my face and I opened my eyes. Someone was on top of my enemy. More drops hit me as I heard voices shouting. My enemy's hands finally relaxed and I gasped to fill my empty lungs as his body slid to the side and off the bed, taking whoever else had been on him.

My addled brain heard noises I couldn't quite recognize and I wished I could see what was going on but the lights in the room were too much for me.

A shadow fell over me, and through the glare I could vaguely make out Shannon's face.

As if coming from far away, I heard her voice. "It's all right now, Marta. You're safe. You're safe."

Darkness closed in on me again.

But it was a good darkness.

Chapter Forty-One

One ambulance waited for the dead.

Another ambulance had come and gone with the living.

Marta had obviously needed medical help and Tony had been allowed to accompany her to hospital, but with one of Dobbin's men in tow. Shannon didn't think Tony would be charged with anything, but there you were. The big man had always been known as a careful cop.

"I couldn't believe it," Dan was telling a detective who had been assigned to take his statement. "Our situation was dire, but once Tony got my knife free and I could cut my bonds, I knew we had that bastard Grant."

"And once you were free, you handed Mr. Lusardi the knife?"

"Not exactly. Grant came back to taunt us some more. He told us what he was going to do to Marta. Fortunately, he didn't check to see if I was still secured. Once Grant went down the hall to carry out his threat to strangle Marta, I cut the cable ties on my legs, and then handed the knife to Lusardi. My intent was for him to cut himself loose while I was going down that hall the way I was trained in Special Forces: swiftly and silently. I had everything under control, or so I thought. But I'd hardly gotten three steps when Tony blew by me."

"And that's when Lusardi attacked Alan Grant?"

"No. He tried to pull him off. When that didn't work, he used my knife and stabbed Grant in the back."

"How many times?"

"I'm not sure. Obviously enough to kill him. I would have stopped him if I could, but it all happened so fast. My boss and your boss burst into the apartment and that caused me to hesitate for a moment. Don't think it would have done any good, though, except to stop Tony from cutting Grant into a thousand tiny pieces."

"Was anything said?"

Hudson shook his head. "I don't remember it. Tony just went batshit. You would have, too, if you'd seen and heard what we had."

"So you felt Lusardi was out of control?"

Dan shook his head in disgust. "It was his wife, man. And Grant had a gun. Don't you have a drop of humanity in your veins?"

"I have to ask these questions."

Dobbin stuck his head into the living room. "You got what you need, Mike? I need you down here to help go through these cartons with us. You won't believe the stuff this bastard had stockpiled."

"Sure. I'm done here."

Shannon sat down next to Hudson. "This was just a preliminary chat, Dan. When you have to give your official statement, the one you'll have to sign, make sure you say you think Tony feared for his life as well as Marta's. That's important. We have to make sure Tony's not charged for manslaughter."

"Is that really a concern?"

"I don't think so because Dobbin and I saw what happened. It was clear that Tony tried to pull Grant off Marta, but you never know." She clapped him on the back. "I'm sure glad I brought you onboard, Dan. Even though it didn't quite end as we would have wanted it to, the bad guy got stopped. You did good."

He smiled tightly. "And you used to work like this every day? No wonder you got out. I thought I was a tough guy when I was in Special Forces, but this was up front and personal today. If old habits didn't die hard and I'd stopped carrying that old blade, Marta would have died a horrible death, even though you and the cavalry got there in the nick of time. You didn't see. She'd stopped struggling. It would have been over in seconds."

"Put that thought out of your head."

"How can I? What about Sam downstairs? I keep thinking of his family. He's not going to come home from work tonight. Alan Grant left a huge trail of destruction behind him."

Shannon put her hand on Dan's shoulder and looked in his eyes. "He was stopped. It would have been even worse if you hadn't come through. Dobbin's men found enough jugs of liquid paraffin in the kitchen to light up this place like a Canada Day bonfire. It's pretty obvious that after killing the three of you, he would have doused the entire apartment. There was also an incendiary timer. Everything was ready to go. The resulting fire would probably have taken the entire building with it. You don't easily stop something that's burning that hot. By the time the fire marshal sorted through the ashes, Grant would have been long gone."

Dan Hudson could only shake his head. "I can't wrap my brain around any of this."

"It's still too close. While you were talking to Dobbin's man, I took a look around the apartment. You would not believe all the makeup stuff Grant had in the bathroom. The beard he was wearing today was a fake, for instance. It would not surprise me to find out he stood right next to us a few times. Dobbin found the passport for that second identity he told you about. You would not recognize him from the photo in it." She sighed heavily. "When you run up against a psycho, bad things happen. When you run up against someone who's as screwed up and as *brilliant* as Alan Grant, truly horrible things can happen."

Hudson nodded at that. "Please don't tell me again what a bloody genius this guy was, okay?

"You've got a promise on that."

"Do I look as bad as you do?"

Shannon snorted. "We all look and feel horrible. Nothing a good night's sleep won't fix."

"What about Marta?"

"They had her pretty drugged up when they wheeled her out of here. She's not going to be able to sing for awhile, if that's what you're asking."

"Tony?"

"He was given a shot, too, to calm him down. I don't know how he's going to react when it completely sinks in that he killed somebody — even if it was completely justified. I know from experience that everyone reacts differently. When I next get a chance to talk to Tony, I'm going to tell him he did the only thing he could. He stopped a madman."

Dan chuckled. It was low and carried absolutely no humour.

"When I found out I was going to Italy and would be hanging out with the opera crowd, I figured I better read up. The only things I knew about opera were from Bugs Bunny cartoons. I read about one opera called *Pagliacci*. That mean 'clowns' in Italian. It's about a seriously evil man inciting another man into killing his wife because she rejected the first guy. I downloaded a video so I could see it. The story is very sordid, very powerful, even if I didn't understand a lot of it. The final words in the opera are spoken: '*La Commedia è finita!* — The comedy is ended!' That's what happened here today."

Finale

The sound of crashing waves came from the rocks seventy feet below us. Tony and I were out on the deck built right above the edge of the cliff, seemingly floating in space, and enjoying yet another glorious Bruce Peninsula sunset. Since early April we'd been blessed with many of them and that was unusual for this time of year.

He reached over and took my hand. "A bit windy tonight."

Even though I was chilly, I answered, "It's perfect. I adore the feeling of wind on my face."

We'd jumped at the chance when one of the COC board members offered us his beautiful modern cottage perched high on the cliffs at the end of the Bruce Peninsula.

Tony had wanted to go to Italy for the nearly eight weeks I had off since I'd been forced to withdraw from singing in *The Passage of Time*. The idea of Italy did have merit, but I didn't think I could face being there. The Italian press and paparazzi don't know the meaning of backing off.

No lasting damage had been done to my throat. After a pretty bad seven days, it began to feel better, but it was far too late for me to be involved in the production of the new opera. The young woman who moved from understudy to star did a decent enough job according to the reviews. The notoriety my problems brought to the opera provided over-the-top tickets sales. The opera itself was the star, though, and if the cast didn't commend itself all that well to the critics, McCutcheon's composition sure did. The reviews for the music, libretto, and Simon Stone's staging were absolute raves.

I was heartbroken I hadn't been able to take part in it.

"You're thinking about it again, aren't you?" Tony asked. "I can see it in your face every time you do. It's like a black cloud crossing over the sun."

My sigh was a heavy one, the direct descendant of many others over the past weeks. "I'm sorry. It just washes over me sometimes. I wish I could stop it happening, but so far …" I couldn't hold another sigh back. "No luck."

"I'll say it one more time, Marta, you really should consider professional help."

"And I'll answer right back again, so should you."

"I'm at ease with what I did — was forced to do." He gave my hand a hard squeeze. "For instance, if I hadn't ended the life of that animal, I couldn't have squeezed your hand just now. I would be alone and missing you more than you can imagine."

"I wish I had your ability to just step back from it all."

"You will, given time and some help."

"Lili is still all the help I need, Tony. She's still living up here, you see." I tapped the side of my head. "I can hear her talking to me, giving advice in her no-nonsense manner." I started to tear up yet again. "God, I miss her so much."

"I do, too." He hesitated for a moment, then added, "I talked to Shannon while you were napping. She told me Peter Grant has been more forthcoming lately with the police about his son. She thinks she finally understands the deep connection between Grant's son and Lili — and why he did what he did."

Both of us found it difficult to use my stalker's first name. It seemed to humanize him somehow, made him seem less of the monster he was, and neither of us wanted that.

Tony didn't continue and I turned to watch him staring north at Flowerpot Island six miles away. Ever since that awful day he occasionally zoned out like this, but would never reveal where his thoughts took him. I didn't want to break into his reverie, but I needed to know everything Shannon had told him.

"Earth to Tony. Come in, please."

"What? Oh sorry … Yes, dear?"

"What else did Shannon say?"

"Right." He gathered his thoughts. "Peter Grant told the police that his son always accompanied his mother to her coachings with Lili — even well into his teens. He said the boy liked her very much. It seems there was a request from him to help his mother with her depression. Lili refused. Like he did with his father, the boy never forgave her when his mother took his life."

"I'm sure Lili didn't forgive herself, either. Perhaps that's why she came to my assistance."

"It wouldn't surprise me."

"I keep asking myself why this happened in the first place."

"Do you mean all of it, or Lili, or just the part that involved you?"

"All of it, certainly, but also: why me? Why did this creature pick on me?"

"Apparently Grant senior often compared his wife's abilities and talents to yours — in very disparaging terms."

"Surely he didn't admit that to the police."

"No. Shannon heard that from a COC director who knew the Grants socially. He really is an odious human being. He had a whole string of barely concealed affairs over the years, brutalized his wife and son verbally, and treated many of those around him with utter contempt."

I shook my head. "He sure covered it up well. I always found him so charming and genteel."

"Sociopaths are often like that. And if Lili were here, I bet she would call him just that."

"Yes, if Lili were here…."

Inside the cottage, the phone rang. Tony jumped up to answer it.

I turned to look at the whitecaps disappearing into the watery distance. One of the local tour boats was making its way from Tobermory's Little Tub Harbour on my left to travel down the coastline on one of those nightly cruises.

It struck me that my life right now was very much like that boat, fighting its way over the waves to an unknown future off in the hazy distance. I would begin performing again very soon with renewed energy. The one positive I had taken from my dark ordeal was that I would never again take anything in my life for granted.

Tony opened the sliding screen door, holding the phone. "It's Alex. He wants to talk to you."

On the subject of not taking my life for granted, I put my ear to the phone, even though I really didn't want to speak to anyone at the moment — not even my manager in New York.

"Are you sitting down, Marta?" Alex asked.

"Yes, Alex. I'm sitting down."

He always said that when he had something exciting to tell me.

"I finally got everything nailed down, contracts in hand."

"What *are* you talking about?"

"Didn't Tony tell you my big surprise?"

"It would hardly be a surprise if he'd told me, would it?"

"I didn't want to jinx it by mentioning it to you early in the process, but how would you feel about singing Naomi in the first recording of *The Passage of Time?*"

I was flabbergasted. "Who? What?"

"They're using the London Symphony and McCutcheon will be conducting. The rest of the cast is outstanding, too. This is going to be a big deal."

"And they want me?"

"McCutcheon insisted, apparently."

"Probably feels bad because of what happened."

"Perhaps, but who cares? I can *just* fit it into your winter schedule. Know that gap you had after Christmas until the second week of January? Well, that's now filled up!" When I didn't respond right away, he added, "You *are* willing to do it, aren't you?"

"Of course, Alex. It's just that I'm completely taken aback, that's all. I thought that boat had sailed without me."

"Well, it didn't. And if you want to know something else, I think you'll be asked to do the role in Sydney in two year's time. McCutcheon's also conducting the Australian premiere. And Toronto will be staging it again, of course. Tallevi's promised me you'll get it."

"I thought McCutcheon didn't like me."

"Everybody loves you, Marta. When are you going to believe that?"

I knew where the truth lay, but good managers always talked that way to their clients and Alex was one of the best.

"That's really lovely news, Alex. Thank you so much for all your hard work. Just send anything that needs my signature up here. Tony will give you the address before he hangs up."

My husband took the phone and disappeared back into the cottage. Now I knew the reason for those secretive phone calls over the past two weeks. Alex was probably trying to find out if I could face up to the challenge.

It was now pretty dark, the sun well past the horizon. The few clouds were dissolving in the coolness of the

night air. A couple of stars were already twinkling overhead and low in the east I could see many more joining them. The heavens tonight would be spectacular. Perhaps Tony and I could sit out here again after supper.

I began humming Naomi's opening aria from act 1 of *The Passage of Time*. I'd finally found her in the darkness of that awful prison. Now I'd have the chance to share her with the world.

But to my mind, she seemed most at home, comfortable, in the darkness.

Perhaps she always would be.

Acknowledgements

While books always have only the author's name on the cover, they are the result of a great deal of work by many people. As always, I have relied on my "mighty three" the most: my wife Vicki, Cheryl Freedman, and Andre Leduc, whose photographic skills always come through for me and for to whom I'm very grateful. I also want to thank my agent, Robert Lecker, for his steady hand on the tiller; my editor, Jennifer McKnight, who so diligently worked with me on "getting it all right"; and everyone at Dundurn who helped in getting this book into your hands. Also once again lending his vocal knowledge and operatic experience most generously was Robert Künzli. Thank you everyone!

Also by Rick Blechta

The Fallen One

When renowned opera singer Marta Hendriks sees her dead husband in a Paris street, she fears she's losing her mind — or did she actually see him? Back home in Toronto, she decides she must find out exactly where the truth lies.

Available at your favourite bookseller

Visit us at
Dundurn.com
@dundurnpress
Facebook.com/dundurnpress
Pinterest.com/dundurnpress